WORDS OF PASSION

"Why is it we cannot exchange more than a half a dozen words on any topic before you begin to patronize me? I am not some silly child you can scold whenever you like!"

Alicia's cheeks were flushed with a most attractive blush and the ferocity of her expression took away nothing from her charm. Rafael thought her one of the most desirable women he'd ever met. He enjoyed her fiery spirit as greatly as her fair beauty and made no attempt to apologize, since he found her anger so very exciting.

"Would you prefer this instead?" he asked in a teasing whisper as he stepped forward and wound his fingers in her tangled curls to tilt her mouth up to his. She placed her palms upon his chest and struggled to push him away, but he simply ignored her protest. He brushed her lips lightly with his to explore the sweetness of her mouth until he felt all her resistance cease. At that precise moment he released her and asked with a taunting leer, "Well, what's your choice? Do you wish to _____ woman?"

STARLIT ECSTASY

PHOEBE CONN

ZEBRA BOOKS
KENSINGTON PUBLISHING CORP.

ZEBRA BOOKS

are published by

Kensington Publishing Corp.
475 Park Avenue South
New York, NY 10016

First printing: August 1987

Printed in the United States of America

Starlit Ecstasy is enthusiastically dedicated to
the Kid Cowboy—
the fascinating man who fills my life with the
true beauty of romance.

Chapter I

Joaquin dug his heels into Diablo's ebony flanks and the magnificent stallion lunged ahead of Flame's Appaloosa, sprinting the last ten yards of the race with the ease of a frisky colt. When the horse flew by the agreed-upon finish line, the stand of oaks at the end of the valley, Joaquin ripped off his broad-brimmed hat and, waving it in the air, gave a war whoop that would have curdled the blood of all but the staunchest of Indian braves. Wheeling Diablo about in a tight circle, he flashed a dazzling grin as his wife caught up with him. "You see, I knew Diablo could beat Sultan handily if he were just inspired to do so."

"And today you finally managed to give him that inspiration?" Flame replied with a saucy toss of her golden red curls, obviously finding that possibility totally absurd. She was trying her best to appear deeply disappointed in her mount's performance, for were Joaquin to suspect she'd merely let him win the race by holding Sultan back, it would rob him of all joy in his victory. She was a clever young woman and knew that if she did not allow her husband to win their races at least occasionally, he'd begin to find excuses not to go riding with her, and she enjoyed the mornings they

7

shared too greatly to risk losing them. Joaquin was a man with enormous pride, both in himself and his accomplishments, and deservedly so. Flame understood that, and rather than finding it a flaw in his personality, she simply accepted it and did her best never to wound the pride that was so much a part of him. Sultan was the more swift of the stallions. She was positive of it, for his elegant conformation was that of a champion, and while Diablo was a fine horse, he could not equal the Appaloosa's spirited gaits, either in grace or speed. His deep red coat sparkled with gleaming traces of white, which covered his back and rump with the delicacy of a crocheted shawl. Flame loved the beautiful horse dearly, for he, like his mate, Lady, had been a gift from Joaquin, whom she adored.

"We'll just see who the better horse really is tomorrow," Flame vowed dramatically, playing her mood of embittered defeat to the hilt.

Joaquin patted Diablo's neck, thinking the gleaming black stallion the finest horse God had ever created. His mount was now nine years old, however, and since Sultan was only five, he excused his pet's usual second place finish to the unfair advantage the Appaloosa had in age. Today, however, Diablo had run his best race in weeks and Joaquin was very pleased with him. "Let's rest a moment before we start back," he suggested with a sly wink and, knowing his wife would not object to his plan, he quickly dismounted. After leading Diablo into the small forest of oaks, he tied his reins securely to a low limb and waited while Flame tethered Sultan a good distance away. Even with no mares about to incite a fight, the two high-spirited stallions despised each other and could be relied upon to show it whenever they were given the opportunity. Joaquin and his lovely wife, however, were the best of friends, lovers of extraordinary closeness, and he rushed

8

forward to take her hand and lead her to an invitingly secluded spot.

Finding the lush green grass as soft as a feather bed, Flame stretched out beside her husband and laid her head upon his shoulder. She sighed contentedly as she snuggled against him, all trace of her pretended anger at losing their race gone. Wrapped in his loving embrace, she said a silent prayer of thanksgiving for the endless joy their life together had become. They lay together enjoying the quiet splendor of the summer morning for a long while before her thoughts became troubling enough to prompt her to speak. "This has been the best of summers, Joaquin, but I fear I've been a terrible influence upon your sister rather than the good one your mother thought I would be when she sent Alicia to us." Rising up on her elbow, her deep green eyes shining with a loving sparkle, she looked down at her handsome companion. His once jet black hair was now lightly flecked with grey, but his brows and lashes were still dark, and with his warm brown eyes and deeply tanned skin, the slight silver cast to his hair only made him all the more attractive. As she leaned down to kiss him, he wound his fingers in her thick curls and extended that affectionate gesture until she began to giggle and had to draw away.

"Must we discuss my sister now?" Joaquin asked in a seductive whisper, his interest clearly in pursuing a far more entertaining pastime.

"Yes." Flame insisted emphatically. "We must, for this might be our only opportunity to speak privately. The rest of the day she is usually with us."

Joaquin knew better than to waste his breath arguing or being flippant when Flame wanted to hold a serious discussion, and so he resigned himself to taking part. "All right," he began agreeably. "Of my three half-sisters, Alicia is apparently the only one who has

9

ever given my mother a bit of trouble. She reminds me of you to a great extent, and while I have learned to accept what can be a maddening desire for independence on your part, my mother doesn't have that same patience with Alicia." Seeing his first flicker of anger deepen the clear emerald of his wife's gaze, he raised his hand in a request for silence. "Just hear me out. The girl has alienated every bachelor in San Francisco with her indifference to their charms. All the young women are jealous of her beauty, so she's understandably without either close male or female friends. You and she get along so well because you not only appreciate her independence but also encourage it as well. Indeed, you are a perfect example of the bright and resourceful woman I think she is striving to be. At eighteen, she has matured far too much for us to have any effect on her personality, but, frankly, I love her as she is since she's so like you, and I've given no effort at all to changing her outlook on life to a more passive one."

"That is the whole problem!" Flame agreed with a sparkling laugh, not in the least offended by his observations, since she considered them quite accurate. "We love her and she obviously enjoys being here, so let's just not send her back to San Francisco in September. Let's ask her to make her home here with us for as long as she'd like."

After a moment's pause, Joaquin pointed out a difficulty he was certain she had not considered. "We can do that, but I doubt that mother will allow it and I'm certain her husband won't."

Flame frowned thoughtfully. She knew Joaquin and David Caldwell were simply too different ever to get along, but that really wasn't the issue now. "Surely they must want what's best for her, and if she's content here, why wouldn't they let her stay?"

Joaquin was surprised she didn't see the reason

behind their objection, but rather than tease her, he explained politely, "Isn't it obvious that what they think best for her is marriage?"

"Yes," the pretty redhead admitted reluctantly, "but a marriage to just anyone is no answer."

"No, just anyone won't do," Joaquin observed with a sly smile. "The man has to be rich or Alicia will suspect him of being a fortune hunter, and while he'll undoubtedly be a few years older than she, he'll have to be bright and have enough life left in him to make her want to accept his proposal."

Flame considered her husband's words for a moment and then purred sweetly, "What we're looking for then is an intelligent, wealthy, older gentleman with so romantic a nature Alicia will immediately fall in love with him? Is that it?"

"Precisely, but unfortunately such an eligible bachelor does not seem to reside in San Francisco, or if he does, Alicia has not met him."

Flame lifted her hand to sift through the silver strands at Joaquin's temple. Whenever they were together they were constantly touching, for they shared their love in each expression and gesture. "As you said, Alicia is very much like me. We don't look alike, but in so many ways our thinking is the same. I'd never have fallen in love with, let alone married, any man but you. There has to be someone special for her too."

Surrounded by the lush beauty of nature, Joaquin saw only the wistful expression that graced his wife's pretty features. While her eyes were partially veiled by a thick fringe of long, dark lashes, her thoughts were easy to read in their emerald depths. They had married three years ago, when she had been only sixteen and he thirty-one. A free-spirited young woman born in California but raised in Philadelphia, she was in many ways a most unusual bride for a man raised in the strict

11

Spanish tradition of the Californios, but he considered her his perfect mate despite the many differences in their backgrounds. They had a two-year-old son and a one-year-old daughter, but in that moment he did not feel in the least bit like either a responsible parent or a concerned brother. He wanted only to be Flame's husband. "I will be happy to invite Alicia to stay with us indefinitely, but even in the unlikely event her parents do allow it, I won't take it upon myself to find her a husband and neither should you." He reached up to again lace his fingers in her glossy curls and drew her lips to his for a kiss he did not allow her to end until he was ready. "Let's make love," he whispered hoarsely, his desire kindled, as it always was, by his wife's loving response to his generous affection.

Flame did not even bother to look up, for they knew every spot on the ranch where their privacy would be undisturbed and this was most definitely one such perfect place. There was nothing she enjoyed more than making love to her husband, for his boundless affection was an endless delight. Her smile was teasing as she reached for the buttons of his soft cotton shirt, her acceptance of his invitation clear in that enticing gesture. "I would not even know where to begin to look for a husband for Alicia, and since I insisted upon a man of my own choosing for myself, I will gladly grant her that same privilege."

Considering the matter settled for the moment, Joaquin gave his full attention to removing his wife's riding clothes so he could enjoy her delectable figure to the fullest. Knowing how devious the graceful beauty's thinking could be, however, he thought it most unlikely Flame would allow his sister to continue her solitary life for long when she enjoyed the benefits of marriage so greatly herself. Perhaps sending Alicia to them had been a stroke of brilliance on his mother's part, for if

12

their loving example of a blissful happy marriage did not inspire his sister to wed, then surely nothing ever would.

Alicia played with her nephew and niece on the patio of their rambling adobe ranch house for a long while that morning. They were such a cute pair that she enjoyed their company immensely. The boy, Joaquin, was a dark-haired, dark-eyed miniature of his dashing father, while Marissa was as pretty as a princess with her mother's beautiful golden red hair, green eyes, and creamy complexion. Leaving the children in the care of their nursemaid, a sweet-tempered girl by the name of Perla, Alicia began a meandering stroll toward the cliffs that overlooked the sea. Located below Monterey, the sprawling lands of her brother's ranch were several days' ride from San Francisco, but she felt not in the least bit isolated or homesick, for here she was free to do exactly as she pleased. At home she had found the many constraints placed upon her time and behavior suffocating. It was not the fault of her parents, for they expected no more from her than they did from her younger sisters. Modesty in both thought and deed were required of all wealthy young women. There was really no one to blame but herself for the emptiness she had found in constantly having to conform to society's standard of conduct for well-bred young ladies. She was simply too restless by nature to be content to spend her days shopping when she already had more clothes than she could possibly wear in a month's time. She greatly enjoyed reading, but only at night when the house was still; otherwise she always felt as though there must be something more important to be accomplished. Her mother and sisters enjoyed making small tapestries and doing other forms of needlework, but she always lost interest before she finished anything. And so, unlike them, no one had ever praised her for the beauty of her embroidery. While her parents had spared no expense in raising her to appreciate the arts, she had displayed no talent for either art or music. An extensive series of voice lessons had failed to improve her range or to remove the husky quality that marred both her speech and her singing, so she had never dreamed of a career in theater or opera. She could not play more than a few simple chords on the piano, and while she enjoyed listening to music, her teacher had been as certain as she that she lacked even the smallest trace of musical ability. She was bright and inquisitive, and the dark, candle-scented silence of the Catholic church held no appeal; she had never once considered joining a religious order. And though she loved her little niece and nephew, she knew she lacked the patience to be a full-time governess.

Happily, all her failings went totally unnoticed in her brother's home, for Flame also had scant interest in the array of skills most young women endeavored to master. But Flame has Joaquin, Alicia mused thoughtfully to herself. Surely there were few men on earth, let alone in California, who could match her brother's tolerance when it came to allowing his wife the freedom to be her own person, but Alicia had vowed never to settle for anything less for herself. The mere thought of marriage made her slightly ill, however, for none of the men her parents and sisters admired could hold her interest in a simple conversation, much less win her heart. All came from fine families, most were handsome, well dressed, and well groomed, but so horribly dull it was all she could do not to yawn repeatedly when they came to call. Her choices seemed to be either to live as a spinster or to marry one of them and die of boredom, and neither of those options appealed to her.

When she reached the wooden bench placed near the cliff to reward anyone who had come that far with a comfortable spot from which to enjoy the spectacular view of the Pacific Ocean, she felt little need to relax but sat down to rest for a moment anyway. She thought it fortunate she did not share Flame and Joaquin's passion for riding, for surely the lively couple appreciated the time they spent alone and would not have welcomed her company. While she did ride with them occasionally, it was usually in the afternoon after the children's naps, when the babies went along too. Joaquin swore he had been raised in a saddle and seemed to think his son had every right to such an upbringing too. Not one to allow her daughter to be slighted, Flame would place Marissa in front of her as they rode so the little red-haired girl missed none of the adventure. Alicia smiled as she thought of those outings, for they were always filled with laughter and fun. The ranch was a marvelous place for a vacation, yet she knew her stay there was only a temporary one and before too many more weeks went by she'd have to return home. The wretchedness of that prospect filled her with dread. It was time she did something with her life, but other than continuing to object violently to playing the obedient role society demanded of a young woman, she didn't know what else to do.

When her head began to ache painfully, she forced her problems aside for the moment and sat dreamily contemplating the rhythmic pattern of the cresting waves until a sailing ship suddenly appeared on the horizon. As it drew nearer to shore on its way to San Francisco, she recognized it as a China clipper and wondered if the sleek vessel might be one of Joaquin's. He owned a fleet of ships to transport his hides to the markets on the East Coast, but she knew the elegant China clippers were his favorites. At that moment, the prospect of a voyage was enormously appealing, although she doubted either her brother or her parents would ever permit her to travel alone and she could think of no one she'd care to invite to go along as a companion except Flame. She knew her sister-in-law would never leave her family to take a pleasure cruise. It would be so much fun though, she thought with a lilting giggle, and she imagined herself aboard the ship. Since her destiny had yet to find her, she mused, perhaps she'd be wise to take to the seas in search of it.

Olaf Pederson handed the spy glasses to Rafael with a ready chuckle. "Well, Mr. Ramirez, I know how much you appreciate pretty things. Tell me what you think of this one."

Rafael leaned against the rail to brace himself as he brought the brass instrument to his eye. He had been in Los Angeles on business and had welcomed the chance to return to San Francisco on *La Reina del Mar* since the accommodations were such fine ones. What had caught Olaf's eye he couldn't imagine, but since he knew they were passing close by Joaquin's ranch, he expected he'd recognize it; but to his dismay he did not. There was a stunning blonde seated upon a bench near the cliff's edge, and as he watched, she rose and stepped forward as though wanting a better look at him, although he knew she couldn't possibly make out his features from so great a distance. She appeared tall for a woman, very slender, with elegant proportions that made her all the more lovely. Her hair was the pale golden color of honey, so warm and sweet in appearance he longed to reach out and touch the sun-kissed curls that blew carelessly about her shoulders in the sea breeze. Her delicate features were familiar somehow, her loveliness simply astonishing even at this distance, and while he could not discern the color of her eyes, he was certain they would be as sparkling a clear blue as the summer sky.

"Well?" Olaf prompted. "Do you know her?"

"Unfortunately, no," Rafael replied sadly, not once taking his eyes from the beauty standing upon the cliff. Without stopping to think he raised his hand and waved as if they were old friends, and to his delight, she returned the gesture and impishly blew him a kiss. He watched her until *La Reina* had passed by and he could no longer separate her from the sunlight that drenched the cliffs; like a fairy princess she vanished from sight. Handing the spy glass back to its owner, he smiled warmly. "Thank you. That was an enjoyable sight indeed."

"Who might she be?" Olaf inquired curiously. "Since he's married to a great beauty, I cannot imagine why Joaquin would have another such woman as his guest."

"If I'm not mistaken, the girl is one of his half-sisters. In coloring, she obviously remembers her father rather than her mother, but I don't know which of the three girls she is, so I can't provide her name."

"Well, when you do meet her, I'd appreciate an introduction," the husky Swede requested with a broad grin.

"I'm no fool," Rafael responded with a hearty chuckle. "You'll have to find your own women, Pederson, as I intend to find mine, but I think we'd both be wise to avoid Joaquin's sisters, for surely they are such fine ladies they'd want nothing to do with the likes of us."

"Aye, you've a point there," the fair-haired captain agreed ruefully. When Rafael turned back to look out to the sea, Olaf made no further effort to engage him in conversation; instead, they shared a comfortable silence. He liked the young man, for he knew him to be

17

both fair and honest not only in his business dealings, but in his private life as well. One of San Francisco's most successful attorneys, Rafael frequently defended clients without charging a fee when he knew their cause to be just and their resources meager. Like Joaquin Villarreal, he was of Spanish stock, dark haired and dark eyed, with a deeply tanned skin that did not grow pale even in winter. While Olaf had heard rumors that both Rafael and Joaquin had been hellions in their youth, he had met the pair after they had become enormously successful men of the most responsible sort. There was an aura of power that surrounded each of them like a tangible force, but, paradoxically, their natures were kind, not menacing. Joaquin was outgoing and warm, his charm very physical in nature. Rafael Ramirez was just as polite and pleasant to talk with, but he kept a greater distance between himself and others. That type of reserve naturally inspired respect and Olaf was glad they were friends, for he had no doubt the handsome attorney would prove as deadly an adversary out of a courtroom as he was in one. For a reason he could not even express to himself, Olaf sensed that if he had had a sister, he would not have wanted her to meet Rafael. The man was handsome and rich, but his fierce determination to pursue any cause in a quest for justice often placed him on treacherous ground and Olaf feared such a lust for danger would overrule any other considerations, even the very natural concerns of a wife. He was also positive that if anyone knew how impossible Rafael would make the life of a woman who loved him it would be Joaquin. No, neither of them would ever be introduced to that lovely blond sister of his, Olaf decided, and, giving up that desire as a hopeless fantasy, he turned his thoughts to the several women in

18

San Francisco who would be eagerly awaiting his return.

As he took his place at the head of the table, Joaquin was pleased they had no guests other than his sister that night. He knew Flame wanted him to invite Alicia to extend her stay and it was not an issue they could discuss with strangers present. His wife was dressed in a ruffled gown of bright red satin, which showed off the creamy smoothness of her shoulders to such perfection that he directed frequent, lingering glances her way. Not that he did not find Alicia attractive that night, for the soft blue of her gown accented her fair beauty well, but the young woman was, after all, his sister, and his love for her was far different from his love for Flame. When they had each been served their entrées, he winked slyly at his wife, then addressed his remarks to his sister.

"We have all enjoyed having you here, Alicia. I don't believe I've told you that nearly often enough, but I want you to know you will always be welcome here. In fact, Flame and I would both be pleased if you'd make your home here with us permanently. I'm positive our children would also love to have their favorite aunt stay far longer than you'd originally planned—forever, if you'd like." He paused then to give the attractive blonde an opportunity to respond, but he was shocked by her hasty refusal of his sincerely worded invitation.

Alicia lay her fork carefully upon the edge of her plate and, placing her hands in her lap, began to twist her napkin savagely, though the frantic gesture was unseen and her manner appeared to be one of genteel composure to her dinner companions. "That is more than generous of you, Joaquin, but I cannot accept

19

more than this one summer of your hospitality. I have been thinking of traveling, of seeing more of America or going to Europe, perhaps, or—"

"What?" Joaquin asked in an astonished gasp, his handsome features mirroring his disbelief.

After giving her husband's arm a reassuring squeeze to stay his anger, Flame smiled warmly. "I think travel is a wonderful idea, Alicia. I can still recall the excitement of coming here from the East. The world is a large one and if you wish to see it, then I think you should."

As Alicia's eyes brightened with a mist of grateful tears at her sister-in-law's encouragement, Joaquin easily thought of a dozen objections to sending the lovely young woman off to see the world. "While travel is certainly a commendable pursuit, I think that's really a decision for you to discuss with your parents, Alicia. I don't want them to think I'm encouraging something I doubt they'll allow. No, indeed, that will only create a rift between us that might take years to mend."

Inspired by Flame's remarks, Alicia refused to let the matter drop. "If you would only help me, Joaquin, I'm sure you could convince my mother and father that travel would be beneficial. If I were to sail on one of your ships, then—"

"Alicia!" Joaquin cautioned sternly, alarmed by the gleam of determination in her eyes, but before he could offer any compelling reasons to inspire her to consider the many dangers of an extended voyage, the massive front door of his home flew open with a resounding crash. The clear sounds of a struggle echoed down the hall to the dining room and he leapt to his feet, unable even to imagine who might have entered his home so rudely. He heard his foreman, José Garcia, shouting the vilest of curses but was given no time to send the ladies from the room before a disheveled young man ran through the arched doorway. José's valiant attempts to eject the unwanted visitor had obviously failed, but Joaquin never permitted such riffraff access to his home and decided that if the foreman needed help in throwing the vagrant out, he'd be happy to provide it.

His clothes worn and covered with what appeared to be the dust of a lengthy journey, the beleaguered young man made one last attempt to elude José's grasp as he shouted, "Are you Villarreal?"

Who else the ill-mannered stranger could have expected to find seated at his table Joaquin didn't bother to ask. "If you have some reason to speak to me, come back tomorrow and knock politely at my door. Now, whoever you are, get out of my house while you're still able to walk. Should you ever dare to disturb my family again, I'll not hesitate to have you shot." Joaquin never made idle threats and the clear ring of authority in his voice was enough to send most men running in fear but, to his surprise, not this one. Noting the pistol on the intruder's hip, Joaquin wished he had some weapon handy, but he had not thought it necessary to be armed in his own home. Seeing José had his Colt, he was confident that if the impudent young man did not exit quickly, he would be dragged out feet first.

Undaunted by Joaquin's order to leave, the young man grew angrier still. "You'll not toss me aside the way you did my mother!" he screamed accusingly. "I am your son and I've come to claim what's rightfully mine!"

Joaquin did no more than give an almost imperceptible nod and José brought the butt of his gun down upon the back of the young man's head, knocking him to the floor where he lay unconscious in a rapidly expanding pool of blood. "Get the fool out of here and if he is ever stupid enough to come back, shoot him dead," Joaquin ordered simply, and, returning to his place at the table, he proceeded to eat his dinner as though the interruption had been a very minor one.

While Alicia could do no more than stare in horror at the fallen man, Flame rushed to assist him. She used her napkin to stem the flow of blood from the deep gash in his scalp as she cried out to her husband, "He says he is your son! How could you be so cruel to him?"

Laying his fork aside wearily, Joaquin explained what he thought she should already see about the logic of his actions. "The only son I have is yours and he's sound asleep in his crib. That fellow is therefore a liar and I've no wish to hear anything else he might have to say, since it would undoubtedly prove to be every bit as ridiculous."

This argument failed to impress his wife, however. "He has obviously come a long way to see you. His boots as well as his clothes are completely worn out. Even if you don't want to hear what he has to say, I most certainly do!"

José stood at a respectful distance, not about to haul the stranger outdoors while Flame was protecting him so fiercely. "He just rode up, jumped off his horse, and came crashing through the front door. I came right in after him, but—"

The gaze Joaquin turned upon the foreman was black indeed. "Must I post guards on my doorstep to avoid scenes such as this?"

"No, sir," José assured him quickly. "He must have passed the men at the gate by saying he was looking for work."

"Which would be another blatant lie!" Joaquin finished the last of his wine in one gulp and again rose to his feet. Well over six feet in height, he was an impressive sight at any time, and especially so when his

22

expression was dark with rage. "Leave the bastard alone, Flame. He got exactly what he deserved."

"Is that who he really is, one of your bastards?" the vibrant redhead asked pointedly.

"Flame!"

Alicia had never in all her life witnessed such a heated argument as the one that was now taking place in front of her. If her parents had ever had any type of disagreement, she had not been aware of it and she could only stare wide-eyed as her strong-willed brother and his equally opinionated wife proceeded to trade insults now. Clearly Joaquin wanted the bedraggled stranger tossed out in the dirt, while Flame wanted to know exactly who he was and why he seemed so certain Joaquin was his father. Since those were two completely irreconcilable views, she did not see how the argument could be settled, but, fortunately, José was far wise than she and offered a sensible suggestion.

"We don't want him spreading his lies, sir. I'll take him out to the bunkhouse, post a guard on him, and you can get the truth out of him tomorrow."

Seeing his wife's obvious relief at that offer, Joaquin reluctantly agreed, knowing Flame would argue until dawn rather than allow him to turn his back on the wounded man. The stranger could scarcely be called a man, he realized then, for he didn't appear to be out of his teens. It was his height that had fooled him at first, for the lad was tall, but Joaquin had absolutely no interest in interrogating him, for he simply didn't care who he might be. "He's not my son, Flame, but if it will please you, I'll allow him to spend the night in the bunkhouse and give him breakfast before I send him on his way in the morning."

Satisfied the young man would not bleed to death, Flame rose to her feet, but she spoke to the foreman as though they were alone in the room. "Call someone to help you move him, José, and don't let him leave tomorrow before I've had a chance to speak with him. Just because my husband isn't curious about him doesn't mean that I'm not."

"Then we will speak to him together, Flame," Joaquin vowed through clenched teeth. "I don't want you prancing out to the bunkhouse on your own."

"Prancing?" Flame responded in a sarcastic imitation of his tone. Not in the least bit intimidated by the wealthy *ranchero*'s domineering attitude, she put her hands on her hips and responded confidently, "Well, no matter how I wish to walk out there in the morning, I will damn well do it!" With that bitter farewell she left the room, clearly insulted by her husband's obstinate refusal to believe a young man claiming to be his son had something to say worth hearing.

Alicia still hadn't moved. She sat watching the poor soul lying on the floor, thinking him a pitiful sight, until finally José returned with the first two *vaqueros* he had found lounging nearby. After they hastily cleaned the blood from the floor, they carried him out of the house. She looked up at Joaquin then, not really knowing whether or not she should comment upon this bizarre turn of events.

Seeing her inquisitive glance as he sank back down into his chair, the irate man asked brusquely, "Surely you have some opinion in this matter, Alicia. Don't you wish to voice it? Since my wife never fails to tell me exactly what she thinks, I don't want you to think I won't afford you the same courtesy." Yet he was obviously so furious, his manner was anything but courteous.

The slender blonde forced herself to swallow, then took a deep breath, for while Flame obviously had the courage to oppose him, she didn't want to risk harming the good relationship they all shared. Hoping to be as

24

diplomatic as possible, she spoke in the most soothing tone she could manage. "It all happened so quickly. I really don't know what to say about that young man's surprising accusation other than, like Flame, I'd like to know why he calls himself your son."

"Because he's a damn liar! What other reason could there be?" Joaquin snarled angrily, not pleased that his own sister had chosen to take sides against him.

Once she had begun to voice her thoughts, Alicia found it not nearly so difficult to continue. "I didn't say that I believed him, but would you mind if I went with you in the morning? I'd like to hear what he has to say for himself."

"Oh, of course." Joaquin dismissed her request with a sweep of his hand. "His tale is sure to be entertaining. I should have playbills printed up and charge admission to all who wish to hear his slander!"

Since she had not meant to offend her brother, Alicia rose and went to his side. She placed her hand upon his shoulder as she leaned down to kiss his cheek. "I can see you'd prefer your own company to mine so I'll bid you good night. I'm certain no matter what that young man says tomorrow, you'll tell us the truth."

Puzzled, Joaquin reached out to catch her hand before she could move away. "Wait. What do you mean?"

"Well, no matter who he thinks he is, I'm sure you know the truth," Alicia replied with a reassuring smile.

Exasperated by the tardiness of that vote of confidence, Joaquin asked pointedly, "Then why didn't you and Flame believe me tonight? That filthy drifter couldn't possibly be my son."

"Then you should easily be able to convince him of that tomorrow, shouldn't you?"

Joaquin simply stared sullenly at his sister, his dark eyes blazing with fury, until she realized he was never

25

going to respond and left the room. Dear God, he thought to himself, the boy had been no more than seventeen, half his age. Could he possibly have fathered a son at seventeen? As his thoughts retraced the years of his youth, he knew it was not only possible, but highly probable, but he'd be damned if he'd welcome every stranger who had the audacity to call him father as though he were a long-lost child.

Chapter II

Flame sat cross-legged in the middle of Joaquin's bed. Although it was still early evening, she had already changed into a sheer white linen nightgown trimmed with rows of tiny tucks and delicate lace. She was brushing out her long curls with savage strokes, but she found the longer she remained in their bedroom alone the more furious she became. "His son!" she scoffed aloud, too upset by the harshness of Joaquin's treatment of the boy to grow calm. Maybe the stranger was a lunatic, or worse, simply a scoundrel bent on blackmailing her husband with the threat of a vile scandal. The youth had certainly seemed convinced his grievance was a just one, however. She paused then, wondering how they would be able to discern if he were telling the truth. She knew Joaquin would never lie to her about anything. Her trust in her husband was absolute, but her curiosity simply would not allow her to remain silent while he threw out a young man who claimed to be his son before he had given him an opportunity to plead his cause fully.

Her eyes stung with the hot tears of anger she had refused to shed. The very last thing she had expected that evening was to have had such a bitter fight with her husband. She had not expressed herself at all well, she realized sadly, and, understanding why Joaquin had gotten so angry with her, she lay her brush aside and slid down off the high bed. Since the house had a dozen bedrooms, she feared he would undoubtedly choose to occupy another one that night. She'd not waste another minute pouting. She'd go find him and attempt to rephrase her concerns without losing her temper this time, because she didn't want him to think she preferred to take the word of a stranger over his. She knew she was far from being the first woman in his life, but since she was determined to be the last, she didn't want their disagreement to continue a moment longer if it was in her power to end it. To her dismay, as she moved toward the door, it suddenly flew open and she had to leap back to avoid colliding with her husband as he strode into their room.

Joaquin had prepared no clever speech to placate his volatile mate, but he dared not allow such enmity to continue between them. When he saw her expression brighten from surprise to a delighted smile, he was so charmed by that unexpected sweetness he pulled her into his arms and gave her a warm hug. "I'm sorry, Flame. That whole wretched scene was my fault. Your compassion was very natural and—"

Astonished that he seemed willing to be the first to apologize, Flame was far too wise to gloat. "The hostility of your reaction was only natural too, Joaquin. I'm sure if you truly had a son that age you'd know of his existence and would have provided well for him all these years. He'd not come begging at our door dressed in filthy rags."

Since he had not expected to find her in such an understanding mood, Joaquin needed several seconds to realize the advantage was his, but seizing it, he pushed it to the limit. "Don't get involved in this any further, Flame. I'll talk to the boy. Why he'd come seeking me I don't know, but I'll see he leaves here in a far better state than he arrived. I'll do that much for him."

Flame frowned slightly but did not step out of his warm embrace. "I know you will always tell me the truth, Joaquin. I know that, but it seemed to me that he believed what he said to be true too."

"But it can't be!" Joaquin insisted again, not wishing to begin another round in the same argument when he wanted her trust in him to be complete.

"I agree, he must be mistaken, but I'd still like to hear what he has to say. That does not mean I don't trust you, Joaquin, only that his story, no matter how bizarre it is, must have had some inspiration somewhere and I'd like to know what it was. Let's not argue about it anymore tonight. Let's go out on the patio. Will you bring your guitar and play for me awhile? It's far too early to go to sleep."

Her smile was inviting, her mood so unexpectedly charming, and Joaquin decided immediately that if she wanted to sit up until dawn listening to him play, he'd not repeat a single tune. "Of course I'll play for you. You are so appreciative an audience, how could I ever refuse?" He waited for her to get a warm shawl and then, fetching his guitar from the corner, he escorted her out upon the spacious patio around which the ranch house was built. Just as he'd hoped, the moonlight and his lovely melodies created a mood so romantic that Flame did not ask him to play long at all.

Alicia raised her eyes from her book as she strained to listen to the sound of a distant guitar, then, recognizing the song as one of Joaquin's favorites, she smiled and refocused her attention upon her reading.

29

She had expected their argument to rage for weeks, but it certainly sounded as though her brother were serenading his wife as if they were still on their honeymoon. They were a temperamental pair but seemed perfectly suited to each other, and ceasing to worry over them, Alicia lost herself in the excitement of her novel.

Joaquin did his best to speak in soothing tones as he addressed his wife and sister the next morning, for he needed their full cooperation. "I must insist you let me do all the talking, ladies. If you should think of a question, or a dozen of them, please wait until I am finished speaking to ask them. Will you agree to that, please?"

They had shared so blissful a night, Flame thought his request for patience quite reasonable. The joy of his loving filled her with a warm glow still and she wanted him to know she'd not embarrass him needlessly. "I realize that young man might say all manner of peculiar things, but no matter how difficult it is, I will try to hold my tongue. You'll do that too, won't you, Alicia?"

The pretty blonde hated to promise anything when the situation had the potential of growing quite exciting, but she reluctantly agreed to be quiet. "Yes. I think we should all hold our tempers if we can."

Joaquin raised a dark brow quizzically. "I was sorely provoked last night, Alicia, but I'll be in complete command of my temper today," he assured her.

"I only meant—" Alicia began apologetically.

"I know exactly what you meant." Since he knew it would be futile to deny he was hot tempered, Joaquin gestured toward the door. "Let's just get this over with quickly and send that fool on his way."

With a lovely young woman on each arm, the tall *ranchero* walked across the yard with a long, confident stride, but he paused at the steps of the bunkhouse to make certain it was occupied solely by José and his prisoner before they entered. He was pleased to find the stranger tied securely to a single bed at the far end of the long, narrow building. José had arranged chairs for them and Joaquin waited for Flame and Alicia to take their seats before he spoke, though he preferred to remain standing.

Joaquin was surprised by the improvement in the young man's appearance. José had apparently gotten him up early and allowed him to bathe and shave. He had even been provided with clean clothes, though not replacements for his badly scuffed boots. His features were pleasant, his skin deeply tanned, his coal black hair glossy if overlong. His eyes were a deep brown fringed with long lashes, which veiled his gaze for the moment. He was a handsome lad, if too thin, but other than his height and coloring, Joaquin saw nothing in the youth that reminded him of himself. Nodding toward Flame, he explained matter-of-factly, "You have my wife to thank for the courtesy of this interview, but I expect you to explain why you came here as briefly as possible, for she has as little patience as I." When the captive did not respond immediately, Joaquin prompted him again. "If you are too ashamed of yourself to repeat your lies, I'll understand and let you go, but if you've something to say to me, tell us now."

The young man's hands were tied behind his back, the rope secured to the bed so tightly he could scarcely breathe, let alone talk. "That red-haired slut is no more than your whore! My mother was your only true wife until the day she died!"

With the back of his hand, Joaquin silenced what

31

surely would have been a long string of insults, but Flame leapt to her feet and stepped between him and the bed before he could do more. "Joaquin, please!" She placed her hands upon his chest and pushed him back a step before she turned to face the bound youth. "Please. Trading insults is ridiculous. My *husband*"— she emphasized the word purposely—"is a reasonable man, but you must begin at the beginning of your tale and tell us why you believe he is your father. Where were you born and what was your mother's name?"

"He knows it all. Ask him!" His lip was cut and bleeding from Joaquin's blow, but the defiant young man had lost none of his spirit.

Joaquin would not allow what had surely been a ridiculous mistake to grow any worse. "I do not care where you were born, but you'll die right here if you don't answer my wife's questions with the courtesy she deserves!" He had taken the precaution of wearing his own Colt that morning, and drew it now. "You have five minutes and not a second more."

After a long silence, the stranger began to speak hoarsely, the effort to be civil obviously difficult for him, but clearly he knew his story well. "I am Domingo Villarreal y Muñoz. My mother's name was Carmela. You met her in Tierrasanta in the summer of 1855. Your ship, *La Reina del Mar*, was badly damaged in a storm and had to anchor in the small harbor near our village for repairs. My mother was only fifteen, very beautiful, but so innocent you seduced her easily. My grandfather discovered what you had done and made you marry her. You knew she was carrying your child before you left. You never came back for us, so by God, I've come for you!"

Flame had no idea where Joaquin might have been in the summer of 1855, but she knew he sailed on *La Reina* for several years in his youth. She could only marvel at him though, for despite his earlier outburst, her husband's expression now showed not the slightest trace of emotion, and while Domingo wouldn't realize it, she knew he was using the same iron-willed control that made him unbeatable whenever he played poker. He was a master at concealing his hand, at bluffing, but she dared not consider why he would have to resort to such a technique for deception now.

"You were born in the spring of 1856?" Joaquin inquired calmly.

"Yes. I am seventeen, exactly your age when you fathered me!" Domingo responded with another rude sneer.

"That's a very creative tale, Domingo, but I never knew a woman by the name of Carmela Muñoz, let alone married her. I am not your father, regardless of what fantasy you were raised to believe."

His denial had no visible effect upon the agitated youth. "I can prove you are my father, Villarreal. I have the marriage certificate you signed nine months before I was born!"

"That is impossible," Joaquin assured him. "I was thirty-one when I married for the first time, not seventeen."

"My mother died only last month. Marrying that little red-haired bitch only made you a bigamist, in addition to all your other crimes!"

Joaquin used his left hand this time to deliver another backhanded blow. "Must I remind you again that I allow no one to insult my wife? If I have to impress that point upon you by putting a bullet in each of your knees, I'll damn well do it. Now where is this marriage certificate? I'd like to see it right now."

Domingo's left lid twitched slightly, betraying his courageous manner for the bravado it was. He was hurting, and badly, but he couldn't afford to let his pain show. He had no doubt Joaquin Villarreal was his father, but he also knew exactly how ruthless the wealthy man was and did not doubt for a moment that he would start shooting if he did not get his way soon. "I left it where it will be safe."

"That does you little good now," Joaquin pointed out sarcastically. "You tell me an outrageous tale, swear you have proof but refuse to present it. What you hope to gain by being such a fool I can't guess. Can you even tell me where Tierrasanta is?"

"It is on the Pacific Coast of Mexico, in the state of Guerrero near the border of Michoacan," Domingo replied in the first reasonable tone they'd heard him use.

"A fishing village?" Joaquin asked with casual interest.

"You know it is!"

"That you speak any English is remarkable. That you speak it so well is absurd for the tale you've spun. Just who are you and who put you up to this? If you have partners in this scheme, they've given you an impossible task. I'll not pay you a red cent in blackmail. You're no son of mine and you know that as well as I do."

As the tall man turned to leave, Domingo shouted at him, "Wait! Everything I've said is true! My mother paid the priest of our village to tutor me so you'd not be ashamed when . . . when . . ."

Intrigued, Joaquin asked softly, "When what?"

"When you came back for us," Domingo answered in a barely audible whisper. "My mother never stopped loving you and she prayed every day that you would come back to her." As tears began to roll down the hapless youth's cheeks, he had no way to brush them away, but he quickly turned his head so that his weakness would not be seen.

Joaquin jammed his pistol back into his holster. "Your tale is pathetic, Domingo, but I doubt one shred of it is true. I plan to get to the bottom of it, however, and you'll not leave here until I do." He turned to José then. "Untie him and see he has plenty to eat. He looks half starved, and I don't want anyone to think that it's a result of my hospitality when he leaves. Keep a guard on him for the time being." Without giving either of them any opportunity to speak, he swiftly escorted Flame and Alicia out of the bunkhouse. When they were a sufficient distance away so that he was assured his remarks would not be overheard, he stopped and turned to face them. "Well, what did you make of him? Other than the fact that he's an arrogant fool, I don't know what to think."

A perceptive young woman, Alicia was eager to share her impressions. "Where were you in the summer of 1855? Won't that disprove his story right there?"

Joaquin shook his head slowly. "Hardly. I spent two of the worst months of my life in Tierrasanta. As luck would have it, it was in the summer of 1855."

His candor only made Flame feel faint and she quickly reached out for her husband's arm to steady herself. "Dear God, Joaquin, you didn't marry that boy's mother and then leave her pregnant with your child, did you?"

Her fear was obviously so devastating that he couldn't be insulted by the question. Rather than respond angrily, he drew her into his arms for a reassuring hug, then chose his words carefully. "Of course not. You know yourself how much I enjoy a woman's company, but I have never in all my life pursued the virtuous maidens of any village. That's what makes Domingo's story so absurd!"

Alicia watched her sister-in-law's expression closely, so embarrassed by her brother's words that she tried

35

frantically to think of some way to steer the conversation in another direction. She knew exactly what kind of women Joaquin had pursued before he had met Flame—the polite term was courtesan—but she fully expected him to explain his preferences in more common language. To her immense relief he did not, but it was Flame's comment that shocked her then.

"Perhaps the girl wasn't virtuous at all, Joaquin. Perhaps she worked in a cantina or—"

Joaquin looked away for a moment, his glance growing dark as though he considered that a likely possibility, but when he looked back at his wife, he was completely self-assured. "I have never been married to another woman, Flame. I won't deny that I was in Tierrasanta in 1855, or that I knew a certain class of women there, but it is absolutely impossible for Domingo to have proof I married his mother. That is simply a flat-out lie."

"He'll just go to someone else with his so-called proof if you don't get it, Joaquin," Alicia pointed out quickly. "You have enemies who would delight in embarrassing you with such a scandal. They'd say you aren't legally married to Flame and that your children are illegitimate."

Flame had not even considered that possibility. "Please, Alicia, you are only making matters worse than they already are. If we can gain Domingo's trust, then he won't even be tempted to go elsewhere."

"Gain his trust!" Joaquin was astounded by that seemingly impossible challenge. "It's obvious he hates me for what he mistakenly believes I did to his mother, and I refuse to allow you to speak with him alone, Flame."

Seeing a chance to be of some real help, Alicia volunteered quickly. "I'm only a year older than he is, so perhaps I can get him to confide in me. We didn't

36

even ask him what he expects of you, Joaquin. I could ask him that for a start. If he asks for money, then you can demand to see the marriage certificate first."

Joaquin thought his sister's enthusiasm for deceit a bit too keen. "Then what do you recommend I do, Alicia? Agree to a simple exchange, offer cash for this supposedly incriminating evidence he claims to have? Why should I bother? If I were the devious sort, I'd just shoot him now and be done with him."

If any man looked capable of murder, Alicia knew it was Joaquin. His height and powerful build alone made most men unwilling to cross him. He was one of the richest men in the state and therefore one of the most powerful, which certainly discouraged opposition. She also had not the slightest doubt he would kill if he were ever backed into a corner and had no other choice, but she also knew he was far too clever a man to ever exhaust his options and have to resort to brute force. "Don't be silly," she responded, clearly annoyed by his questions. "I know you don't wish Domingo any harm, whether he really believes he's your son or whether he's just someone else's pawn. No matter which is the truth though, it cannot hurt our cause to gain his trust. I think I am the most likely person to win his friendship too."

Without a moment's hestiation, Flame agreed. "She's right, Joaquin, but the beauty of using Alicia is that Domingo will have to insist she's his aunt. To prove the truth of his story, he'll have to treat her respectfully, for to treat her as though she were merely a very pretty girl would give away his hand. If he has come here simply to blackmail you for someone else, he might become so smitten with her he'll reveal who's behind the plot. If he is simply some poor, misguided boy whose mother lied to him all his life, then he'll need someone to trust too."

Joaquin considered the wisdom of that strategy for a long moment, then decided since the situation couldn't get much worse, he might as well allow Alicia to have a try at befriending the youth. "After he's had something to eat, you may talk with him again, Alicia, but make certain the guard is close at hand. Don't come between them so he can use you as a hostage either. He seems bright, whoever he is. Don't give him the slightest opportunity to harm you. If he is not respectful, leave. I mean that. If he starts calling any of us names, tell him you'll not talk with him until he's learned some manners."

Delighted to have her brother's permission for such a mission, Alicia promptly gave him an enthusiastic hug. "I will insist he treat me as though I were his favorite aunt. You needn't worry. There won't be the slightest bit of trouble."

Joaquin looked down at his wife. "I'd say we already have a whole mess of trouble. Let's just go for our ride as we always do. There's no use letting Domingo spoil the whole day."

Flame nodded agreeably. "Of course, a ride would take our minds off this for an hour or so at least. Do you want to come along, Alicia?" she invited politely.

"No. I'll play with the children for awhile and then see what I can get Domingo to tell me." Turning toward the house, she waved to send them on their way, her mind already filling with questions she could ask the handsome young man with the astonishing story.

"Take Lady today," Joaquin suggested softly. "I'm not in the mood to race."

"No, neither am I," Flame agreed. After saddling their own mounts, they rode at a leisurely pace for nearly half an hour, each lost in his own thoughts until she asked, "Just to squash whatever rumors Domingo might wish to spread, do you think we should ask

Father León to marry us again?"

Joaquin started to object loudly, then seeing by the confusion of his wife's expression that her question had been a sincere one she had not dreamed would give offense, he assured her such a precaution was completely unnecessary. He reached over to take her hand and gave it a warm squeeze. "We are already married, Flame. Were we to recite our vows anew, it would just cause undue curiosity."

"No one need know about it," the vibrant redhead insisted. "But for the children's sakes—"

He had tried to remain calm, but Joaquin's temper flared now. "Flame, don't you think I'd know if I married this Carmela Muñoz or not? That's hardly the sort of event a man forgets!"

Flame bit her lower lip apprehensively, determined to convince him of the wisdom of being cautious, but not certain how best to do it. "I have seen you very drunk, Joaquin. Not recently, that is true, thank God, but how can you be so certain that when you were seventeen you didn't marry some fisherman's daughter?"

That question was so absurd Joaquin was tempted to ride off and let Flame find her own way home, sorely tempted, in fact, but he retained what he feared was a fragile hold on a gentlemanly calm and made another suggestion. "I won't deny that I have been quite drunk on more than one occasion, but never that drunk, Flame! If this is going to turn into a battle of whose word you'll accept, your husband's or an imaginative drifter, then I am simply going to treat it as a legal question and summon Rafael. I'll dump the whole mess in his lap and let him straighten it out, because I simply don't want to fight with you."

"What if he determines Domingo's story is true and that he really is your legitimate son?" Flame asked pointedly. "Will you marry me again then?"

"I will marry you each and every week if it will please you, Flame, but there is no possible way Rafael can substantiate the boy's claims, because they aren't true!"

"Oh, I know that, truly I do," Flame replied sorrowfully. "It is just that Domingo's appearance was so unexpected. We have been so happy together and I can't bear to think it won't last forever."

Her words and expression were so wistful that Joaquin drew Diablo to an abrupt halt, dismounted, and quickly pulled his wife from her saddle. He set her upon her feet gently, then wrapped her in a warm embrace, pressing her lithe form so close to his own he could feel the beat of her heart throbbing steadily against his chest. "My beloved, no one will ever come between us, not Domingo, or anyone else. I promise you that. You are the only woman I have ever married or that I ever will. What must I do to convince you of that fact?"

Flame clung to Joaquin, so lost in the magical spell of his affection she was willing to believe anything he said without question. She was sorry she had not thought to suggest they rely upon Rafael's expertise. Since she hadn't, she complimented him on his plan. "Rafael is the perfect person to help us. He's settled far more difficult disputes than this one, hasn't he?" she asked shyly.

Joaquin took a step backward so he could look down at his wife. "Yes, indeed. He's an excellent attorney and this is a legal question if ever I heard one. I also know you'll believe him when he tells you Domingo is no son of mine, even if you won't believe me," he teased playfully. "Now, do you wish to continue our ride, or would you rather go up to that bluff, which has such a splendid view of the sea, and listen to me talk about the life I plan to give you?"

Flame appeared to give the matter careful consideration. "Must we talk?" she finally asked coquettishly.

"I'll certainly not insist upon it if you would prefer I simply showed you," Joaquin replied with a devilish wink, and after helping her to remount Lady, he returned to his saddle and led the way to the secluded bluff, whistling happily the whole way.

As soon as she entered the bunkhouse, Alicia had second thoughts about the wisdom of speaking with Domingo alone. Since Joaquin had failed to introduce her that morning, she would have to explain who she was first, and that was not all that simple a matter to do. Domingo was now seated at a small table at the end of the room playing cards with one man, while another holding a rifle kept watch a few feet away. He looked up from his hand briefly, then appeared to be more interested in his cards than in having a visitor.

"I'd like to speak with you a moment, Domingo," Alicia explained with an inviting smile. "Would you rather I came back later?"

Apparently greatly irritated by the interruption, the young man threw down his cards and rose to his feet. "What do you want now?" he asked with an insulting leer that swept slowly over the soft swells of her figure before rising to her face.

"I'd like to sit down first. Then I'll introduce myself and tell you why I wanted to see you again."

Domingo looked over at the heavyset *vaquero* who held a rifle trained at his back, and when the man nodded his consent, he pushed a chair toward Alicia. When she was seated, he took the one farthest away. He rocked back on it until the rear legs were raked at a precarious angle, then, apparently comfortable, he eyed her suspiciously. "Well?" he asked sullenly.

The young man's insolent stare didn't inspire her

41

imagination, but Alicia knew that now she'd begun her ruse, she couldn't simply excuse herself without at least giving it a fair try. "Joaquin's mother is also mine, but my father is her second husband. I have two sisters, but they aren't nearly as blond as my father and I." She did her best to appear too innocent to be up to mischief, but he still didn't believe a word she said.

"You can't expect me to believe you are my aunt!" Domingo responded with obvious disgust.

"Well I most certainly am!" Alicia replied, genuinely insulted that he had not believed her. She realized exactly how Joaquin felt then, and also why he was so angry. Domingo's anger was reasonable too, but only if he were telling the truth. "Look, I am really Joaquin's sister, but whether or not you believe me about that really doesn't matter. You're the one who has to prove himself here, not I. Now what did you expect from Joaquin last night? Did you think he'd welcome you with open arms and give you an honored place at his table?"

Domingo let all four legs of his chair drop to the plank floor with a thunderous crash. "I don't have to explain anything to you!"

"Of course you don't," Alicia agreed sympathetically. "I just thought that since you and my brother have taken such a thorough dislike to each other, perhaps I could serve as a neutral party and help to straighten out your disagreement. Each of you is convinced he is right, no matter how impossible that is."

Domingo's sneer grew even more pronounced then, the whiteness of his teeth contrasting sharply with his deeply tanned skin. "Your brother is the same lying son of a bitch he always was, but he's still my father and I can prove it!"

Alicia found the young man's contemptuous attitude extremely tiresome and said so as she rose to leave. "I have no more interest in listening to your insults than my brother has. Being so obnoxious is just plain stupid. Can't you understand that?"

"The bastard killed my mother!" Domingo shrieked as he leapt to his feet.

Fearing their prisoner was going to strike the pretty blonde, the two guards swiftly blocked such a move. They shoved him back down into his chair, where they promptly secured him with a length of rope as handily as if he had been a yearling they were intending to brand.

Alicia hesitated to remind the men that Joaquin had not wanted the youth bound, for clearly he deserved no better. "You said your mother died last month. Joaquin did not leave the ranch, so there's no possible way he could have been responsible for her death. That charge is as utterly ridiculous as your others."

"She died of a broken heart, a tragedy that will never befall a bitch like you!" Domingo ducked as he shouted, certain he'd be hit again for voicing that opinion. He wasn't disappointed, for had he not been tied to his chair, the hearty slap Alicia gave him would have knocked him to the floor.

Chapter III

Drawn by Flame's excited call, Alicia came out on the long porch that spanned the front of Joaquin's home, but she hung back, reluctant to join the exuberant throng surrounding the newly arrived guest. She had expected a man so respected in his profession as Rafael Ramirez to arrive in a fine carriage, not astride an immense black and white pinto. The magnificent stallion was attracting as much interest as the rider, but that the noted attorney would have chosen such a primitive means of travel from San Francisco simply amazed her. She had to admit she knew precious little about the man other than that he'd grown up on a ranch nearby and was Joaquin's closest friend. That he would choose to travel alone for several days on horseback struck her as very curious indeed, for most of the men she knew could scarcely survive for an hour without the pampering of their servants.

When the high-spirited horse tossed his head, sending his glossy black mane flying, Rafael gave his neck an affectionate pat, indicating that the animal was obviously a great source of pride to him. She feared, however, that if Rafael were as proud an individual as her brother, he would do no better with Domingo than

45

the rest of them had.

The memory of her one brief encounter with the belligerent youth brought a bright blush to Alicia's cheeks that nearly matched the magenta of the bougainvillea growing in glorious profusion and shading the whole length of the porch. She had been so confident the young man would respond to her kindness. She had hoped to learn his true purpose, to help Joaquin straighten out an impossible muddle, but her temper had swiftly betrayed her. None of them had approached Domingo since then, but it would soon be Rafael Ramirez's turn to try to put him in a reasonable mood.

Despite her many misgivings, she wished him well. It would be interesting to see just what he could do here, since Joaquin had sworn he routinely performed the impossible in San Francisco courtrooms. A bunkhouse was a far more informal setting, she mused thoughtfully, but somehow the few minutes she had observed the attorney had already given her the impression he could undoubtedly conquer challenges of any sort as easily as he handled his lively mount.

Rafael was pleased by the compliments regarding the pinto, since he had had to pay far more for the beast than he had originally intended. He had renamed him Renegade because of his obstreperous nature, but he genuinely liked the handsome stallion and had enjoyed traveling with him. While still responding to the teasing of his friends, he let his glance drift lazily toward the house, where the sight of the pretty blonde who stood alone silently observing him gave him a moment's pause. He recognized her instantly as the beauty who had blown him a kiss from the cliff, and he thought her even more lovely at close range, for her coloring, while fair, was quite vivid. The honey blond shade of her hair glowed with bright highlights in the late afternoon sun.

Her eyes were exactly the bright, clear blue he had hoped they would be and a thick fringe of dark lashes made them all the more attractive. Her delicate features were uniquely her own, yet simply perfection. It was a great pity she was Joaquin's sister, for that would make even the most innocent of flirtations unwise. He chuckled to himself then, thinking her presence might well prove to be the most diverting facet of his visit. Tired after a long day that had begun before dawn, he was glad to hand Renegade's reins over to José and follow Flame and Joaquin toward their home. When they paused to introduce him to Alicia, he quickly removed his hat and gave her a courtly bow. *"Con mucho gusto, señorita,"* he remarked with a rakish grin.

Despite being covered with a fine layer of dust from the trail, Rafael was so handsome Alicia needed a moment to find her voice. His hair was so dark a brown it was almost black. His teeth were even and very white, making his grin all the more charming, and his dark eyes shone not only with intelligence but a lively wit. Realizing she was staring quite rudely, she blurted out nervously, "I'm so terribly sorry, but my Spanish just isn't what it should be."

Rafael looked first at Joaquin and then at Flame, for he'd not meant to embarrass the girl with his greeting. When they turned away to cover their laughter, he knew he was on his own. "Fortunately I speak English as well, Miss Caldwell, so we'll have no problems communicating," he assured her with another warm smile.

The introduction complete, Joaquin gave his friend no time to chat. "I'm the one with the problems, my friend. Let me give you a drink and I'll explain them more fully than I did in my wire." As Joaquin opened the door, Rafael paused to remove a pair of wicked looking Mexican spurs from his boots. He hung them upon a nail driven into the post nearest the door, then turned back to give Alicia a sly wink, which made her blush all the more deeply, before he followed his friend into the inviting coolness of the house.

Flame had never expected to see Rafael flirting so openly with any woman. That he seemed so taken with Alicia pleased her enormously. "It's a shame he didn't have an opportunity to bathe and change his clothes before you two met," she purred innocently. "He is actually very handsome when he is well dressed."

Alicia thought that opinion ridiculous. "He'd be attractive in rags, Flame; surely you must know that," she countered absently, her eyes still focused on the now empty doorway where he had stood momentarily to bid her a teasing good-bye.

"Hmm, yes, I suppose he would," Flame agreed softly, a mischievous plan lighting her green eyes with a saucy sparkle.

It was difficult to judge the true height of a man wearing boots, but Alicia thought Rafael had appeared nearly as tall as her brother. That would make him at the very least six feet two in his bare feet. He had Joaquin's easy grace, but a far leaner build. Like Joaquin, he was naturally dark, but the warm bronze of his skin had been deeply tanned from frequent exposure to the sun. Neither of them had the pasty complexions or paunches of the city-dwelling bachelors who called at her door. They were trim and fit with the dashing good looks that would set any woman's heart aflutter. Her brother had long been described as a rogue who would never marry, but that had been before he had met Flame and had fallen so deeply in love. She could not help but wonder who had laid claim to Rafael's heart. "Why is a man as handsome as that traveling alone? Doesn't he have a wife?"

"No," Flame replied sweetly. "He claims that devotion to his profession leaves him too little time for the responsibilities of marriage, but the truth is simply that he has yet to find the woman of his dreams. Your cousin, Maria Elena, had no success in winning his heart, but I'll wager it can be done. It would be a challenge, of course, but not an impossible one for a clever woman."

Flame had such a confident manner that Alicia found her an easy person to trust, but on matters of the heart she did not really want her advice. "I don't need lessons on how to inspire a man to propose, Flame. I want only to meet a man who'll excite my interest as Joaquin does yours. If he likes me too, well, then things should proceed quite naturally, shouldn't they?"

The pretty redhead shook her head at that touching bit of naïveté. "That is the way we'd all like things to be, Alicia, but you should have learned by now that life does not always progress in so smooth a manner. Instead, it is continually fraught with difficulties of one sort or another and love has its own special kind."

Alicia certainly could not dispute that opinion, for all she knew of love was what she had seen in the lives of those she held dear. Her own mother had suffered through a miserable first marriage followed by the anguish of a bitter divorce from Joaquin's father before she had found lasting happiness with David Caldwell. The turmoil Domingo had caused Flame and Joaquin was simply the latest problem in a romance that all who knew them described as turbulent. "Is love worth the pain it causes, Flame?" she finally asked, her thoughts no longer focused upon Rafael Ramirez but on the complexities of life itself.

Taken aback by her sister-in-law's suddenly subdued mood, Flame nonetheless gave her a serious response. "You make it sound as though a person has a choice.

49

That just isn't true."

"Well, it isn't mandatory that we all fall in love," Alicia argued. "Some of us probably never will."

"You are far too young and pretty to be so cynical," Flame cautioned sternly. "Now come and help me with the final preparations for supper. Since Rafael has arrived, I want to make certain Maria has something special to serve." She was simply skirting the issue of love, she knew, but attempting to explain its magic to someone who had yet to feel its spell was far too time-consuming a task to begin that late in the afternoon.

Joaquin showed Rafael into his study, saw to his comfort, and then briefly described his predicament, concluding once again with the denial he had repeatedly given Flame. "I won't deny I was in Tierrasanta, but to say I married any woman, let alone Domingo's mother, is preposterous because it simply didn't happen."

Rafael nodded thoughtfully, convinced his old friend was sincere. He tipped his chair back, stretched out his legs, and crossed his ankles, his pose relaxed but his keen mind alert to the complexities of Joaquin's dilemma. Withdrawing his knife from its sheath at his belt, he nonchalantly began to clean the grime of the trail from beneath his nails with a casual disregard for both the seriousness of their discussion and the deadly edge on the gleaming blade. "What is it you really want me to do, Joaquin, investigate the boy's claims thoroughly and discredit them, or see that he meets with a fatal accident?"

Joaquin was silent for a long moment, his choice already made but not easily voiced. "Domingo is an obnoxious pest who has delighted in insulting us all, but he's no more than a headstrong young man with a gigantic chip on his shoulder and I wish him no harm."

50

"Especially since he might well be your son after all?" Rafael inquired perceptively.

Determined to make his point understood, Joaquin leaned back against his desk and folded his arms across his chest before he replied. "I'll not deny that I was acquainted with several women in Tierrasanta, so it's possible I fathered a child there, but since there is no way Domingo can prove I was married to his mother, there will also be no way he can prove he is my son. I intend to steadfastly deny that any relationship exists between us. I'll not offer him a job, or give him any hope that someday I'll acknowledge him and make him one of my heirs."

After a moment's reflection, Rafael agreed and advised calmly, "That's your only choice, my friend, for to do otherwise would only put Flame's son at grave risk."

That was a possibility Joaquin refused to accept. "Domingo is bitter. That will be obvious to you at first glance, but he's so outraged at what he sees as the injustice he and his mother suffered, I doubt he'd consider murdering my child the proper way to put things right."

"He has a sense of honor then?" the seemingly preoccupied attorney asked casually.

"Yes, I'm sure he does."

Rafael looked up then, his glance puzzled. "You know nothing of this young man except for his astonishing claim that he is your son and you do not see the threat he poses to your other children?"

"Of course I see it!" Joaquin exclaimed heatedly. "That's why he's been kept under guard since the hour he arrived. I've not given him free run of the ranch or made him feel in the least bit welcome. It's precisely because I am so damn suspicious of his motives that I sent for you so quickly. I'm not without enemies. If this

51

fantasy that I was married years ago is not just some mistaken belief of Domingo's, then one of them could easily be behind this. Now do you think you can help me out of this mess, or not?"

Rafael rose, slid his knife back into place at his belt, and reached out to give his old friend's shoulder a reassuring grasp. "I don't like the sound of this either, Joaquin, but I'm too tired to question Domingo now. I'll speak with him in the morning and give you my impression of him then. Once I discredit whatever evidence he has of your supposed marriage to his mother, it should be a simple matter to send him away in disgrace."

"Good. The sooner we're rid of his disruptive influence the better. I don't care whose son he is, I just want him gone."

"He'll not have the slightest desire to stay once I finish with him," Rafael assured his friend confidently. "I assume you still dress for supper?"

"Of course we do. Your things have been taken to your usual room. If there is anything you don't find, simply let Maria know and you'll have it immediately."

"Your hospitality is unmatched, Joaquin. I know I'll want for nothing."

As he watched his best friend leave the room, Joaquin realized sadly that he felt no less troubled than he had before Rafael's arrival. He could not shake the nagging feeling that something was seriously wrong. Rafael had readily agreed he had no choice but to send Domingo away, so why did that decision still bother him so greatly? When he thought of the happiness he had found with Flame, of his pride in their two small children, he knew he was right to protect his family at all costs, and Rafael was just the man to help him do that. He was not only methodical but relentless as well. Joaquin shuddered then, fearing he had just loosed a tiger on an innocent lamb. "I had no choice!" he argued with his anguished conscience, but that excuse sounded pitiful even in his own ears.

Rafael was seated by her side during supper so Alicia found it difficult, if not impossible, to study his expressions as he spoke. She was surprised to find him a far more serious individual than he had impressed her as being at their initial meeting. Now immaculately groomed, dressed in a well-tailored suit, his speech refined, his manners those of a perfect gentleman, she unfortunately found his personality far too reserved for her taste. He seemed reluctant to discuss his recent cases and answered Joaquin and Flame's questions with only the briefest replies. He appeared to be far too modest to accept congratulations on his unbroken string of courtroom victories, as though his successes were simply a source of embarrassment to him rather than pride. He was very bright, his comments interesting despite the soberness of his mood, but somehow she had liked the dashing fellow who had arrived that afternoon astride the handsome pinto ever so much better.

The conversation grew more relaxed as they moved into the parlor for brandy, but Alicia found she still had little of any value to contribute. She and Rafael had seen many of the same theatrical productions in San Francisco that spring, but since Flame and Joaquin had not, she considered it impolite to discuss the plays in depth. She found herself wondering why they were making such an effort to discuss mutual friends and family or simply meaningless trivia when surely they were all more concerned about Domingo than anyone else. At her first opportunity she smiled warmly at Rafael, who was now seated opposite her. "I cannot help but be curious; if you have some clever plan for dealing with the rascal who insists he is my nephew, I'd certainly like to hear it."

Seeing Joaquin's startled glance, Rafael raised his right hand in a plea for understanding. "Please, Miss Caldwell, I've only just arrived here. Allow me to talk with the young man before I offer any opinion on how I'll proceed."

Disappointed that he had given her no clue to his plans, Alicia frowned pensively. When it became obvious no one cared to break the awkward silence her request had created, she asked to be excused. "I'm sorry, but I'm really rather tired and I think I'll just go on to my room. I hope you have a pleasant stay here, Mr. Ramirez, and I'll look forward to hearing your report as soon as you're ready to make it."

The two men rose as Alicia did, and knowing they would appreciate another opportunity to speak together alone, Flame also bid them good night. When Joaquin finally came to the bedroom they shared, he was surprised to find her pacing the floor with an agitated stride. He caught her hand and pulled her into his arms, where he attempted to soothe her obviously troubled spirit. "Please do not worry so, Flame. Rafael will undoubtedly settle everything before the week is out."

"Well, why didn't he just tell Alicia he was confident he could take care of the matter promptly then? She hardly said a word all evening and then, when she expressed an interest in the reason for his being here, Rafael very nearly told her to mind her own business!"

Puzzled by the unexpected focus of her anger, Joaquin slipped his arms around his wife's narrow waist to hold her more tightly. "He is not used to plotting his strategy aloud to provide an evening's diversion, Flame. I don't think he was deliberately rude though."

"That's only because he wasn't speaking to you! Alicia was crushed!" the hot-tempered redhead pointed out with piercing logic. When she realized from her husband's befuddled expression that she had only succeeded in confusing him, she took a deep breath and tried to explain more calmly why she had become so upset. "It was only that Rafael was so friendly this afternoon and then, tonight, instead of being just as charming, he paid Alicia no attention at all. When she tried to draw him out, he was so curt she didn't even want to remain in the same room with him, and I didn't blame her. I'm sure he hurt her feelings, and badly."

Joaquin leaned down to give his wife's earlobe a playful nibble before he whispered, "I warned you not to play matchmaker, but how could you possibly imagine Rafael and Alicia would be interested in each other?"

"But they obviously are!" Flame argued as she tried unsuccessfully to elude his confining grasp. "Didn't you see the way they looked at each other when you introduced them? Why, the excitement that flowed between them was so thick you could have reached out and touched it. Then tonight that magic was completely gone. Did you tell him to stay away from her? Is that what you did?"

"Of course not," Joaquin denied emphatically. "But I'd certainly not encourage whatever interest he might have in her either. He'd only break her heart, Flame. You of all people should know that."

"What makes you think that? Because he tends to be cynical, or because he's too set in his ways? Or is it because he's so busy being a successful attorney? None of those reasons would have any merit if he fell in love with Alicia."

Joaquin sighed wearily as he let his hands drop to his

sides. "How plain do I have to make this, Flame? If you encouraged Alicia's interest in Rafael, you've been very thoughtless and needlessly cruel. He enjoys the company of lovely young women as much as any man, but he only proposed to one and you turned him down to marry me."

Stunned by his calmly worded rebuke, Flame clenched her fists at her sides, determined not to lose her temper or cry. "That's a decision I've never regretted making, but I don't want Rafael's heart as a trophy. I want him to have someone to love too! Alicia is beautiful, very bright, and she seems so lost without someone to love."

Joaquin had to agree with her description of his sister. "That's true enough, but Rafael most certainly isn't the one to give her life the direction it needs. He'd undoubtedly enjoy seeing her a few times. He'd treat her with the utmost respect and be very charming, but then he'd move on to the next girl who caught his eye and she wouldn't even understand why. I wouldn't wish that heartache on any young woman, most especially not Alicia when she's so very dear to me."

Exasperated by her lack of success, Flame nevertheless continued her attempts to sway her husband to her point of view. "You can't be certain he'd lose interest in her. They could just as easily fall in love and be as happy as we are. It could happen, Joaquin, it really could."

Joaquin could not help but chuckle at the futility of that hope. "Are we happy, Flame?"

"Yes! Deliriously so!" She slipped her arms around his waist and laid her head upon his chest as she snuggled close. "At least I am happy. Aren't you?"

Joaquin had never been able to decide which of his wife's many remarkable assets was his favorite. Her beauty was an endless delight, her affection one of his greatest pleasures, and her lively charm had captivated him from the start. She was a high-spirited creature, untamed still, despite the years they had spent as husband and wife. He knew no matter how diplomatically he worded his request, she would simply disregard it and do exactly as she pleased where Alicia and Rafael were concerned. He would not waste his breath in arguing when she was wrapped around him so tightly she would know precisely what he was thinking regardless of what he said. "I love you," he whispered instead and, lifting her into his arms, he carried her to his bed where he swiftly proved just how happy she had truly made him.

Alicia lay stretched out across her bed, trying to get comfortable enough to concentrate on her book, but she was far too restless for so passive an activity as reading. When she heard a light tapping at her door, she leapt off the bed and rushed to answer, ready to welcome any distraction. She was amazed to find Rafael Ramirez standing in the hall.

"I must speak with you a moment. May I come in, please?" the handsome attorney requested politely.

"Surely you don't expect me to invite you into my room at this hour!" the startled blonde exclaimed in a hushed whisper. Though he was still fully clothed, she was wearing a filmy silk nightgown and she feared he would quickly discover that the lace at the bodice was transparent.

"Would you prefer to talk in my room?" Rafael inquired with a sly smile.

Exasperated with him for being so bold, Alicia didn't know what to say. She was enormously intrigued, but still this was her brother's house and she dared not disregard convention so completely as to invite the man into her room. Being a resourceful young woman, she quickly offered another alternative. "The night is warm. Would the patio suit you?"

"The patio would be fine. I'll meet you there in five minutes," Rafael agreed, and hurriedly turning away, he disappeared down the hall.

Alicia closed her door, then leaned back against it to collect her thoughts. She could not imagine why the man would wish to speak with her now, since he had had no interest in doing so earlier. She was too curious not to meet him, however, and after wrapping herself tightly in a light woolen shawl, she crossed her bedroom and opened the door that led out into the large central courtyard around which the house had been built. Filled with fragrant fruit trees and flowering shrubs, its inviting scent teased her senses with a promise of pleasure she could only dimly imagine. While the night wasn't cold, it was quite dark, and she was sorry she had not thought to give Rafael specific directions about where to meet her. When he spoke her name as he stepped from the shadows, she jumped in fright, then felt very foolish and apologized. "I'm sorry, but you startled me."

"Then I should be the one to ask your forgiveness," Rafael assured her, and taking her arm, he led her to the bench just outside her door. He waited for her to be seated, then took the place at her left. "I did not mean to insult you earlier this evening, but if you had seen Joaquin's face, you would have known why I couldn't discuss my plans. The less said about Domingo in Flame's presence, the better."

That explanation only puzzled Alicia all the more. "I'm afraid I don't understand what you mean. Joaquin hasn't tried to hide anything from her. Indeed, he swears he had nothing to hide. Isn't that why you've come? To expose Domingo's tale for the outrageous lie it so obviously is?"

"Yes," Rafael agreed hesitantly, "but that might well prove to be far more complicated than it sounds."

"From the conversation at dinner, I gathered that difficult cases were your forte, Mr. Ramirez."

"Oh, yes, indeed they are, but my approach is somewhat different than many attorneys. You see, a clever man can manipulate the evidence, play upon the jury's sympathy, so cloud their minds that he can get a verdict of not guilty for the most villainous of murderers. I simply refuse to stoop to using theatrics of that sort. My only criterion for accepting a case is that I be convinced of my client's innocence so that when he receives a verdict of not guilty I know justice has been served. I have never used my talents to set a guilty man free."

In the darkness, the brightness of his smile was but a taunting glimmer and she wished now that they were seated closer so that she could see him better. He seemed to be trying to tell her something important and she was dreadfully afraid she simply didn't understand what it was. "May I call you Rafael?" she asked shyly. "You are treated like one of the family and for me to call you Mr. Ramirez sounds so terribly formal."

"I insist you call me Rafael, but only if I may call you Alicia."

"Please do," the young woman invited warmly, and hoping he would tell her more, she continued to encourage him to confide in her. "My brother is very protective of his wife, but she is a strong woman, so I doubt any of Domingo's absurd claims have hurt her. Is that what's worrying you?"

Rafael tried to recall the last time he had had the opportunity to sit in a darkened garden with so perceptive and charming a young woman. The setting was perfect for a romantic interlude, but unfortunately this was the wrong time and most definitely the wrong woman with whom to sample such delights. The subtle fragrance of her perfume was as enticing as the honey-scented air, but he had no choice other than to ignore that teasing reminder of her femininity. Forcing himself to think only of business, he continued, "Joaquin has immense holdings, which he plans for Flame's children to inherit. The problem is, he thinks there is a chance he is Domingo's father and—"

"You can't believe that!" Alicia challenged instantly. "You simply can't!"

"What I believe doesn't matter. Joaquin thinks its a possibility and not merely a remote one, but he will never acknowledge an illegitimate child, since that would only diminish what his legitimate children will one day own. He's fought too long and hard to hold onto this ranch to see it divided among warring factions. Now do you see why he dares not discuss the case in front of Flame? She'd never allow him to turn his back on his own child, but that is precisely what he is determined to do. It is what he must do."

Alicia was silent for a long moment, then chose her words carefully. "I can scarcely imagine what sort of man my brother was eighteen years ago, but I am positive he would not have left a pregnant wife in Tierrasanta."

"So am I, Alicia, and the first thing I plan to disprove is Domingo's claim that Joaquin was married to his mother. Once that's out of the way, all I need to do is show that your brother is but one of several men who might have been his father. I can humiliate the young man so thoroughly he'll not show his face in California again, let alone claim he belongs here."

Alicia drew her shawl more tightly around herself, chilled clear through by Rafael's detached tone. Now she understood, and her voice was filled with horror as she spoke. "I see. Joaquin thinks Domingo might be his son, but he's asked you not only to disprove his claims but to completely destroy him as a person as well."

"Precisely, but truly he has no other choice. It's the only way he can protect Flame and their children. I think you'll understand now why such a plan would have made an extremely poor topic of conversation for the four of us. Joaquin is a wealthy man. If he acknowledges one bastard, there is sure to be a parade of others waiting to be welcomed into the family. That would bring chaos that would never end."

"And what of your passion for justice?" Alicia asked pointedly. "If Domingo truly is Joaquin's son, will his fate be just?"

"You needn't worry about him. I'll see he returns to his home with enough money to give him a start in whatever endeavor he wishes to attempt. His trip here won't have been for nothing."

Alicia found such generosity astonishing. "You would do that for my brother's child, when he won't?"

"As you said, I have a passion for justice," Rafael admitted with a sly chuckle.

"Is that your only passion, Mr. Ramirez?" Alicia wondered aloud, not realizing so bold a question was in fact an invitation.

"Rafael," he reminded her, pronouncing each of the three syllables of his name distinctly. While they had been together only briefly that day, he could not help but like Alicia very much. She was not only extraordinarily pretty, but bright and sensitive as well. Her manner was open and sincere rather than coy and flirtatious, and he found such honesty quite appealing. He had not forgotten whose sister she was, however. He raised his hand to her cheek, but his caress was sweet rather than possessive. "Unfortunately, this is neither the time nor the place to arouse my passions,

61

Alicia. I must ask you not even to try."

His warning carried surprisingly little weight compared to the delightful warmth of his touch, and the graceful blonde disregarded it completely as she leaned forward to brush his lips with a tender good-night kiss. He surprised her then by lacing his fingers in her flowing curls to hold her mouth pressed to his. His tongue parted her lips, then lazily explored the warm, moist sweetness of her mouth until he felt her whole body tremble with desire. He knew what he was doing was lunacy, but he had to tell himself that several times before he found the resolve to release her and draw away.

Alicia could only stare at him then, wishing the shadows did not hide his expression so completely, for the fiery intensity of his kiss had simply stunned her and she wondered if he had enjoyed it as greatly as she. He was easily the most fascinating man she had ever met. One moment he had the ready charm of a rake, the next he was the most proper of gentlemen with a dignified reserve that inspired the greatest respect. It was obvious, however, that he had a most passionate nature, which he had to endeavor mightily to conceal. "Just who are you?" she whispered breathlessly, her heart pounding so wildly within her breast she feared he might actually be able to hear it and discern how deeply his kiss had affected her.

Rafael found her question highly amusing and extended his hand as he rose. "I am Rafael Ramirez, your servant, my dear. Who else could I possibly be?"

Alicia placed her hand in his and he pulled her gently to her feet, but she hated to see their brief conversation end. "You wished only to tell me about Domingo? Was that all?" she asked softly, hoping he had at least another hour's worth of conversation planned.

"Yes," Rafael replied matter-of-factly. "I want you

to trust me to do what's right for both Domingo and your brother. Can you do that?"

"I'll try," Alicia promised hesitantly, still uncertain just what his plan was but so confused by the lavish affection of his kiss she could think of little else.

"Good." Rafael had meant to walk away, to simply leave the striking blonde by her door and pretend they had not kissed, but he could tell she was as reluctant as he to see them part. When she took a step closer, he did not back away but instead drew her into another warm embrace and lowered his mouth to hers. She knew what to expect this time. Her lips opened invitingly and her tongue began to tease his. His hands slid down her back with a languid caress, hugged her narrow waist, then moved to tease the soft, pink tips of her breasts to firm peaks. Her lithe body seemed to melt into his, and he savored that moment of complete surrender while he searched his mind for a way to continue the romance they would have scant opportunity to begin in the few days he would be at the ranch. Satisfied he had the perfect solution, he brought their lengthy kiss to an end and explained in a hoarse whisper, "My purpose here is a very serious one, Alicia, and I'll have no time for a distraction as compelling as the one you present. When you return to San Francisco, however, we'll be able to see each other as often as we like."

"Won't I distract you from your work there too?" the lively blonde asked curiously, thinking that possibility very likely.

"Probably, but not all my cases are as serious as this, and it will not matter so much."

The thought of being considered a distracting nuisance was not at all flattering to Alicia; neither was the fact that he wished to simply ignore her for the time being when it was so obvious he enjoyed her affection as greatly as she enjoyed his. Perhaps he was used to manipulating other women's feelings so casually, but she was deeply insulted and reached for her door. "I'm sorry, but I've made plans to travel and it might be years before I return to San Francisco. Good night."

"Alicia!" Rafael reached out to catch her wrist, but she slipped from his grasp and slammed her door shut, leaving him with only the aching need she had created within his heart as proof that despite his usual cool reserve, she had ignited his passions with shocking ease.

Chapter IV

Alarmed, Domingo sat up straight as a tall man clothed entirely in black entered the bunkhouse. His attention was instantly riveted upon the man's pearl-handled Colt revolver worn in a low-slung holster tied securely to his thigh. The stranger's spurs scraped the floor as he walked toward him, giving each step the menacing ring of a death knell. The brim of his hat cast a shadow across his face, concealing his expression, but the youth knew instinctively it could only be the menacing frown of doom. For the first time since his arrival, Domingo was truly afraid, for the approaching man had the unmistakable bearing of an executioner. He had known all along that Joaquin Villarreal was a lying swine, but he had not imagined he would sink so low as to hire a gunman to kill his own son. He swallowed hard to force back the urge to leap to his feet, for surely there was no escape now. The guard standing behind him held a shotgun trained on his back and he feared he would be shot dead no matter in which direction he tried to flee.

Rafael glanced only briefly at the thin young man who seemed so determined to establish himself as a Villarreal before silently signaling to the *vaqueros* who had been standing guard. The two men left immediately without questioning his command and he grabbed a chair, spun it around backward, sat down, and rested his arms on the back. "You must be very bored by now," he remarked with an inviting grin, his expression pleasant despite his somber attire.

Domingo coughed nervously, then shrugged, not understanding why this man would care about his mood if he had come to kill him. Was he only trying to lure him outside so his blood would be spilled in the dirt and disappear as swiftly as his body surely would? "Does Villarreal care?" he finally found the courage to ask, determined not to die without fighting until he no longer had the breath to do so.

After studying the young man's features intently, Rafael, like Joaquin, recognized nothing in them that would lead him to suspect a kinship. Domingo was undeniably handsome but resembled no one the attorney knew. Ignoring the sarcastic question he had been asked, he apologized. "I should have introduced myself. I am Rafael Ramirez, an attorney. I've been hired to investigate your claims."

Domingo had never met an attorney, but he doubted this man could possibly be one. His skin was too deeply tanned, his body too well muscled, far too lean and hard for one who made his living by intellectual effort alone. He was certain his first impression had been correct: this was his father' paid assassin. Stalling for time, he asked another impudent question. "What is there to investigate? My father knows the story as well as I do."

"I'm sure he does, but since Joaquin denies he is that man, it is up to you to prove that he is. You've told him you have proof of some sort. I'll have to see it before I can make any decision one way or the other about you," Rafael explained matter-of-factly, again using

66

another of his most charming grins in an effort to win the youth's confidence.

"I won't take money to go away!" Domingo announced proudly, forgetting for the moment his fears that he would be alive for no more than a few minutes longer. "I want to live here with my father, to take my rightful place as his son."

Rafael nodded thoughtfully, impressed by the vigor of Domingo's insistence that he belonged there on the ranch. He had caught enough people in lies on the witness stand to recognize an honest man when he met one. He had assured Alicia that the harsh treatment Domingo would receive would be tempered with compassion, but now he began to wonder at the wisdom of attempting to send the youth away in disgrace. He knew he had shocked the bewitching blonde by disclosing what he planned to do, but she had certainly repaid that surprise with several of her own. When he realized Domingo was simply staring rudely at him, he forced the image of the delightful young woman from his mind, cursing his own weakness where she was concerned. "I can make no promises of any kind. My only task is to examine whatever proof you have and determine whether or not it substantiates your claims. I think I know where you left it. If you won't come with me now, then I'll go and fetch it myself. Joaquin wants this matter settled as promptly as possible."

Domingo sat rooted to his chair, unwilling to agree to anything. "Is that how my father refers to me, as a matter that must be settled?"

Rafael's dark eyes narrowed slightly, no more pleased by Domingo's belligerent attitude than the others had been. "Joaquin refers to you as an obnoxious pest, which you most certainly are." He rose to his feet then and gestured toward the door at the far

67

end of the long, narrow structure. "You are wasting my time, and mine is far more valuable than yours. Let's go."

Although startled by that command, Domingo did not obey it, for he was still reluctant to leave the safety of the bunkhouse. "Where are we going?" he asked suspiciously, not about to walk calmly to his own execution.

Exasperated, Rafael raised his voice slightly. "You left your evidence with Father León at his church, didn't you?" The priest had seemed the most likely person for the young man to have trusted, and as Domingo's deep tan faded noticeably, the clever attorney knew his guess had been correct. "I know the *padre* well. He'll give me whatever you left with him for safekeeping. Had I wished to cheat you out of what you swear is your birthright, I would have already done so. I have our horses saddled and waiting, now let's go!" He turned and left the bunkhouse with a long, fluid stride, knowing without having to look back that Domingo would be right behind him.

Domingo tripped over his chair as he scrambled to his feet, then had to run to catch up with Rafael. He had been a fool, he realized suddenly, terrified he would lose the only tangible link he had to prove Joaquin was his father. He should never have trusted the priest when surely the wealthy *ranchero's* influence would extend to him, too. "Wait!" he cried out, hoping to catch up with the attorney, but he had already mounted his pinto stallion with an agile leap.

Rafael was a born teacher, and he planned to teach Domingo how to behave before the day was over. "No, I'll leave you if you don't hurry up. Your own horse can scarcely stand, let alone make the trip into town, so I've provided another mount for you. I hope you can handle him."

Domingo warily eyed the black gelding standing at the hitching post, certain he had been given a wild horse who would swiftly buck him off into the dust. He untied the reins but still hesitated to mount the beast.

"Do you want a sidesaddle?" Rafael asked with a taunting leer.

Having no tolerance for ridicule, Domingo was outraged by the insulting jest. He quickly put his left boot in the stirrup and swung himself upon the gelding's back, praying as he did so that the earth beneath them was not nearly as hard as it looked. To his delighted surprise, the black horse made not the slightest objection to carrying his weight.

"His name is Sampson," Rafael offered with a satisfied chuckle. "He's not fast, but he is reliable. Just try to keep me in sight." With that challenge he touched the tips of his spurs to Renegade's gleaming flanks and the stallion responded with a powerful burst of speed that left Domingo as well as his docile mount coughing in a cloud of dust.

Rafael laughed out loud when he knew he was too far ahead for Domingo to overhear. He drew Renegade to a halt when he reached the gate marking the entrance to the Villarreal Ranch, but he had to wait several minutes for Domingo to appear. He was pleased to see the young man could ride well, for his fine horsemanship showed clearly despite the fact that Sampson wasn't swift. Rather than leave him behind again, Rafael held Renegade's pace to one the gelding could match.

"What makes you so certain I'd trust the priest?" Domingo called out suddenly.

The handsome attorney merely shook his head, dismayed by the youth's naïveté. "He is the most obvious choice, a trustworthy man, but also a close friend of Joaquin's. You would have to go a long way

69

to find an honorable man who isn't." When Domingo responded with his oft-stated, profanely worded opinion of the man, Rafael touched the brim of his hat in a silent farewell and sped off, demonstrating quite effectively that he would not listen to anyone malign his best friend. He arrived at the small Catholic church a full ten minutes ahead of the loudmouthed youth and put his time to good use.

Father León was at work in the cemetery beside his church, lamenting the dullness of his hoe as he hacked away at the weeds that grew in never-ending abundance, ceaselessly trying to obscure the names inscribed in the flat stone grave markers. When he saw Rafael, he quickly cast the rusty implement aside and lifting his long robe above his sandals came running to greet him. "Señor Ramirez, it has been far too many months since you've been this way." Out of breath from his exertion, he paused then for the attorney to respond with what he hoped would be a lengthy reply.

"There is little to call me home now," Rafael responded regretfully, thinking it odd he still thought of the valley as his home. It was the home of his ancestors, but no longer his. Ignoring the stocky priest's flushed cheeks and breathless greeting, he remarked first on his health. "I am glad to see you looking so well, for I need your help. I've come on a matter of great importance to Joaquin." He explained his mission quickly but did not ask the priest to violate his promise to Domingo. "I wish only for you to speak for the goodness of my character to the young man, to put him at ease."

The chubby cleric spread his hands in a gesture of dismay. "But of course, it will be my pleasure, señor. He seemed like such an earnest lad, I am sorry to hear he has caused so much trouble. He did not tell me what he planned to do, merely asked me to keep a small wooden box for him. I have not opened it."

"I know you are a man of your word, *padre*. I did not expect that you would have betrayed the boy's trust." Rafael offered the compliment sincerely. "All I ask is that you tell Domingo I am an honorable man as well." Hearing the sound of hoofbeats, he turned to watch the young man approach.

Thoroughly humiliated, Domingo was certain he had been purposely given a mount that could never match the magnificent pinto's speed. Furious with Joaquin, Rafael, and himself, he leapt off Sampson's back and greeted the priest with a hostile insult. "You are a disgrace to all that is holy!" he screamed accusingly.

Rafael stepped forward to block what he feared would become a physical as well as verbal assault upon his pious friend. "Domingo, your greatest enemy is your own temper, not Father León. He's done you no harm."

Had he run head on into a stone wall, Domingo could not have been stopped more effectively. Rafael did not even lift his hand; the fierceness of his glance was enough to stop the youth cold.

"If you will consider your thoughts more fully before you voice them, you will save us all a great deal of aggravation."

The dark-eyed youth took a step backward, his expression still murderous as he tried to decide what to do. Surely the priest had already given the box to Ramirez, so why was the man still there? Why hadn't he just returned to the ranch?

Domingo's confusion was understandable, but Rafael had not intended to add to it. "We interrupted your gardening, *padre*," he apologized with a warm smile, clearly dismissing the man. "Come into the church with me for a moment, Domingo." He reached for the

71

wrought-iron ring attached to one of the heavy oak doors and gestured invitingly. "Come inside where we can talk privately for a few minutes."

When the priest excused himself and started back toward the cemetery to resume his work, Domingo yanked off his hat and followed Rafael into the small adobe chapel. The interior was cool and dark, the air still scented with the exotic fragrance of incense from the morning Mass. When the attorney walked clear to the front pew, genuflected, and then crossed himself before taking a seat, Domingo decided he had better follow his example. He knelt as he crossed himself hastily, then slid into a place at the attorney's side. There was a large painting of the Crucifixion above the altar, a dark and forbidding image that made him shiver with dread, for he had not shaken the fear that his own death was near.

"Are you a religious man?" Rafael asked in the hushed tone the sacred setting required. He had noted the young man's self-consciousness and was glad he had insisted upon coming into the church, since it appeared to be working to his own advantage. They could just as easily have talked outside, but he was determined to put the youth in a reasonable mood before they continued their discussion of his claims. Domingo had a man's height and the beginnings of what would one day be a powerful build, but he had the emotional instability of a spoiled child. Temper tantrums were dangerous in one old enough to wear a gun, and he meant to put a stop to them now.

Domingo considered the question irrelevant but gave his opinion anyway. "No. Since God ignored my mother's prayers, I knew he would never honor mine."

Rafael folded his arms across his chest as he considered that response silently for a long moment. "So you despise not only your father, but God as well?"

72

he finally asked in a pleasant tone he frequently used to inspire a witness to confide in him in the courtroom.

Domingo raked his fingers through his hair, certain his companion was still trying to trick him into admitting something he shouldn't. "I have a good reason to hate them both."

"For their obvious neglect?"

"Yes!" the young man responded immediately.

Rafael nodded thoughtfully, gathering his thoughts before he began to spin his tale. "I knew my father very well, perhaps too well."

His curiosity piqued, Domingo could not let that statement go unchallenged, and when Rafael did not continue, he prompted him, "How could that be?"

Knowing he had the young man's full attention at last, Rafael told his story with the spellbinding finesse he used to such stunning advantage in his law practice. His voice, while low, had an almost hypnotic rhythm. "My grandfather and Joaquin's were boyhood friends who came to the New World together. Each had received a land grant amounting to a million acres of the finest land in all of Alta California in payment for their service to the crown. They were an ambitious pair, brave men with a clear vision of a world that was theirs to create. You have seen but a minute portion of Joaquin's vast holdings, so you must take my word that my grandfather's empire was every bit as grand. By the time California became a state, my father and Joaquin's were the heads of their families. When all the *rancheros* were required by law to submit proof of their land titles held from either Spanish or Mexican grants, Miguel Villarreal was able to substantiate his claim. Unfortunately, my father's records were not nearly so complete. That meant a legal battle that lasted several years, incurring expenses of almost unbelievable proportions. In the end, we were left with little more than the house in which we lived. Everything else either went to the government or had to be sold to pay our attorneys' fees. My father was a gentleman in every sense of the word. That the government of the United States had deliberately cheated him out of the land he had inherited, land he knew had been entrusted to him, land that should have remained in our family for generations, was more than he could endure. A broken man, he sought refuse in drink, gambled away what little money we still had, then mercifully suffered a fatal heart attack. My mother, who was a very beautiful but delicate woman, was so devastated by her grief she soon followed him to the grave." He paused then, the sorrow of his memories obviously still deep. "I was about your age when I buried my parents. I had been raised to lead a life that no longer existed. Nothing was as it had been, or in my mind should have been still. It was a blessing my parents had had no other children, but at the time it seemed to me my loneliness was simply an additional curse. It was Miguel Villarreal who convinced me to go to San Francisco and channel my rage into the study of law so that the travesty that had befallen my father would not be repeated. I took his advice simply because I could think of no other alternatives, but to my amazement, I found the legal profession fascinating and the fortune I have made from my practice is entirely my own. That is an accomplishment that gives me a great deal of pleasure as well as pride. In the face of adversity my father was unequal to the challenge, but I was not. I not only survived, I prospered." He turned then to look at his youthful companion, his dark glance curious. "What sort of man are you, Domingo, one whom fate can destroy, or one who can survive any defeat?"

Ignoring the question, Domingo blurted out his own. "You really are an attorney then?"

74

"Of course," Rafael assured him. "What did you think?"

Domingo shrugged sheepishly. "I thought you'd been hired to kill me."

Forgetting the solemnity of their surroundings, Rafael laughed out loud. "Had Joaquin wanted you dead, he'd have slit your throat himself the night you arrived at his ranch. You needn't fear for your life, regardless of the outcome of my investigations. Now, do you have any other questions? I want to put your mind at ease."

The young man shook his head, not about to voice any other fears, when surely they would bring another outburst of laughter. He trusted no one and reminded himself that Rafael Ramirez worked for his father, so surely his kindness was some sort of trick.

When Domingo remained silent, Rafael rose to his feet. "Let's ask Father León for the box you left with him so I may have the rest of the day to study its contents."

"It won't take you nearly that long," Domingo boasted proudly. Then he thought of a question he was too curious not to ask. "If you are wealthy now, why haven't you bought back your land?"

Glancing toward the painting above the altar, Rafael again crossed himself before he replied. "No amount of money can restore the past, Domingo. Flame's father bought most of our land and it is hers now. She and Joaquin are welcome to it, for I prefer living in San Francisco and have no wish to return to the pastoral life of a *ranchero.*"

As he moved out into the aisle, Domingo snorted derisively. "My mother was Joaquin's wife, not that red-haired bitch."

Rafael struck so quickly the youth had no chance to escape the attorney's grasp before he was lifted clear off his feet. He held Domingo firmly with one hand while he drew his knife with the other. "If you ever dare to insult that dear woman again within my hearing, I will make you extremely sorry," he vowed in an evil whisper, the power of his threat as deadly a force as his blade. "You may have been taught no manners, but it's about time you learned some, and fast!"

Terrified, Domingo could do no more than bob his head up and down as he dangled in midair. The razor-sharp tip of Rafael's blade pressing against his throat was inspiration enough for him to agree to learn anything.

Satisfied the young man understood his demand, Rafael lowered him gently to his feet. "You need friends desperately now, Domingo, not enemies. Try to remember that the next time you are tempted to insult one of us." Rafael slipped his knife back into its sheath and turned away without waiting for a reply. He went outside and waved to the priest, anxious to begin what he was certain would be merely a brief examination of documents that had to be crude forgeries.

Stepping out into the sunshine, Domingo used his shirt sleeve to wipe the sweat from his brow before jamming his hat down upon his head. He was still shaking and thoroughly disgusted with his own cowardice, but Rafael had taken him by surprise. He had moved with the speed of a rattler and Domingo had no desire ever to feel the man's blade touch his flesh again. His father might be a liar who had abandoned his wife and unborn son, but his smooth-talking attorney was the devil himself and not even thinly disguised. He made a point of staying out of the man's reach as they followed the priest through the side door of the small church.

Father León hastily brushed the dirt from his hands as he hurried into the sacristy. He had hidden the box

Domingo had given him at the bottom of the carved chest that held his vestments. He withdrew it reverently, as though it contained a priceless treasure, and handed it to the young man. "You will find the contents undisturbed. I did not examine them."

Domingo held the old box awkwardly, still so shaken he feared the priest would see the tremor in his hands. "Thank you," he said breathlessly before turning to Rafael. "My mother had little other than her dream that Joaquin Villarreal would one day bring us here to California. This should provide all the proof you'll need that I am truly his son."

Rafael frowned slightly as he accepted the small box, again struck by the sincerity of Domingo's manner, but he knew what the boy believed to be the truth surely could not be proven. He opened the box, which had no lock, and withdrew two neatly folded certificates. The age of the paper was the first surprise, for the parchment was obviously old, stained with age along the creases. The first was a marriage certificate and he carried it over to the open doorway and unfolded it carefully. He noted the date: August 2, 1855, and then the signatures. He barely glanced at the names of the witnesses, since it was the others that were suspect. Carmela's name was written in a childish scrawl, while her new husband's had been penned with bold confidence. The ink was faded, a few letters slightly blurred, but the signature was the distinctive one he knew as well as his own and it was unmistakably Joaquin's. While that discovery was a severe jolt, his expression remained merely curious. He refolded that certificate and opened the next. It proclaimed that the son of Carmela Villarreal y Muñoz and Joaquin Villarreal had been baptized on the tenth of May in 1856 in the church of San Esteban, El Martir, in Tierrasanta. The sacrament of baptism had been performed by a Father Adolfo Casteñeda and attended by the same couple who had witnessed the marriage of the babe's parents. He handed that document to the priest. "What do you think of this, *padre?*" he asked nonchalantly.

The perspiring cleric wiped his hands on his robe before taking the parchment certificate. He read it slowly, pronouncing each word softly to himself. He turned it over, held the paper up to the sunlight where it became transparent, and then with a puzzled frown handed it back to Rafael. "Forgive me, I am no expert in such matters, but this baptismal certificate is like dozens I have seen from Mexico and it appears to be genuine to me."

"Thank you, Father." Rafael refolded both certificates, then replaced them in their carved container. He withdrew from his pocket what he considered to be a fair price for the priest's help, added a bit more, and placed it in the man's hand. "Your assistance has been invaluable. Please accept this small donation for your time."

Beaming from ear to ear, Father León was already thinking of how he could put such a generous sum to good use. "It is always a pleasure to see you, Señor Ramirez." Turning to Domingo, he offered what he hoped would be taken as a worthwhile suggestion. "You are fortunate to have met Señor Ramirez, my son. Pay strict attention to his advice, for he is not only clever but honest, and there are many who would pay a fortune for the privilege of calling him their friend."

Certain he and Rafael Ramirez would never be friends, Domingo could no longer hold his tongue. "Well, isn't that all you needed? I am Joaquin Villarreal's son just as I swore I was and these documents in your hand prove it."

Rather than debate that issue, Rafael bid the priest

farewell and ushered the young man out the door. As they made their way toward the horses, he gave the only explanation he could. "My investigations are still far from complete, Domingo. This was merely the beginning."

"But what more do you need?" the youth cried out in frustration, knowing he had no more to offer.

Swinging himself up into the saddle, Rafael was in too great a hurry to confront Joaquin with what he had found to give Domingo's fears much thought. "Let's go back to the ranch. If you'll give me your word you'll stop behaving like an impudent ass, I'll see you're given more freedom."

Fearing he would again be left behind, Domingo grabbed Sampson's reins and leapt into his saddle. "It is my father who has behaved badly, not me," he argued sullenly.

Rafael eyed the youth with renewed curiosity but still saw nothing in his appearance that proclaimed Joaquin was his sire. He could have been any man's son, including his own. "Think whatever you like, Domingo, but keep the blackness of your thoughts to yourself or they will be the last you have." He did not look back once on the return ride to the ranch, then had to wait impatiently at the gate for the youth to arrive.

"I will speak to Joaquin and then we'll talk with you. Sit down on the porch and do not move until I invite you to do so. It will not help your cause if you infuriate Joaquin again. His temper is even worse than mine and I am certain you'll be wise enough not to provoke me again."

Domingo had no choice but to agree to whatever demands the man made. "If I have to sit there all night I'll do it," he promised sincerely, but the darkness of his scowl did not lessen.

Even knowing such a wait was highly unlikely,

Rafael merely nodded. "Good. I knew you'd learn fast once you had the right teacher." The gate was located a good distance from the house and he did not speak again as they rode there. He left Renegade tied to the porch rail and entered the house without bothering to knock. Flame and Alicia were seated in the parlor, but he did no more than wave as he passed by on his way to the study. Finding his friend seated at his desk, he took the precaution of closing the door before he approached him. *"Dígame la verdad,"* he demanded in the same threatening whisper that had terrified Domingo.

Mystified if not frightened by that greeting, Joaquin rose to respond. Since they were nearly equal in height, the move was scarcely hostile. "The truth about what?" he asked with a perplexed frown. "If you're going to accuse me of lying about something, you should at least let me know what it is."

"You know damn well what I'm talking about!" Rafael replied angrily, his temper uncharacteristically short. "Give me something with your signature, or better yet, just sign your name on any scrap of paper you have there."

"You walk in, demand the truth about Lord knows what, and now you want a handwriting sample?" Joaquin asked in dismay.

Undaunted, Rafael repeated his request in a menacing snarl. "I want your signature now, Joaquin. If you are insulted, you can try to thrash me later, but I want that signature now!"

The two men eyed each other warily, Rafael's gaze filled with fury while Joaquin's mirrored only his confusion. Finally he leaned across his desk to grab his pen, and after signing his name with a dramatic flourish, he gave the sheet of stationery to his friend. "There. Now what does that prove?"

Rafael waved the cream-colored paper to dry the

ink, then opened Domingo's small wooden box and withdrew the marriage certificate. Carrying them both over to the window, he placed the faded parchment against the newly signed sheet of stationery and, pressing them against the glass, aligned the two signatures to make a perfect match. "This one is faded, the V smeared slightly, but you can see for yourself the name is clearly your own."

Joaquin stepped up behind the attorney and after studying the worn certificate for a long moment spoke emphatically. "The signature might look like mine, but I didn't sign that, Rafael. I haven't lied to you. I'm not merely trying to cover up a youthful indiscretion. Carmela Muñoz is a complete stranger to me and I was never her husband."

Before Rafael could contain his temper sufficiently to argue that the evidence clearly declared otherwise, Flame entered the room. Her voice was breathless with excitement as she greeted him. "Well, what did you learn, Rafael? Can you expose Domingo's claim for the vicious hoax it is?"

When Joaquin's gaze held his for a moment too long, the attorney made the most noncommittal reply he could summon to mind as he turned to face the inquisitive redhead. He held behind his back the papers he had been examining, hoping she had not had time to see what they had been doing. "I have nothing conclusive as yet, Flame." As Joaquin stepped in front of him, Rafael quickly replaced the marriage certificate in the old wooden box and dropped the sheet of stationery Joaquin had given him among the papers on his desk.

"I was hoping you'd have all our problems solved." Flame sighed regretfully.

"He will, my love. Rafael merely needs a few days to tie up the loose ends, that's all." Joaquin pulled his

81

lovely wife into his arms and gave her an enthusiastic hug.

When Flame caught sight of Rafael's worried frown, she was not fooled by her husband's soothing words. "I won't become hysterical if you tell me the truth, Joaquin, so I wish you'd just do it."

Keeping his wife's fingers laced in his, Joaquin turned back to face his friend. "Everyone seems to be calling me a liar today, an insult that is totally undeserved. Since the marriage certificate Domingo brought has what appears to be my signature, how can we prove that it isn't?"

Rafael's expression filled with amazement at his question, for he had not expected Joaquin to be so frank in his wife's presence. "That is your story then? It is a forgery is all you'll say?"

"Well, the damn thing is a forgery! What do you expect me to say?" Joaquin countered immediately.

Shocked by the passion of the two men's exchange, Flame interrupted quickly. "You were arguing when I came in, weren't you? Not about this surely, for if Joaquin says his name was forged you'd believe him, wouldn't you, Rafael?"

"I want to believe him, of course," Rafael admitted with no real enthusiasm.

"But for some reason you do not?" the redhead challenged in an incredulous gasp.

"Stop it, Flame. If he prefers to believe a trick played upon his eyes rather than my word, don't badger him about it. He'll get to the truth eventually," Joaquin promised reassuringly.

Disregarding this request for silence, Flame continued to ask questions. "Is that true? Do you really think Joaquin married some innocent Mexican girl and then deserted her?" She was as insulted as her husband by such a shocking lack of faith.

Had they not been interrupted, Rafael was not certain what Joaquin might have been inclined to admit, but clearly he would stick by his denials now. "After my first look at the documents Domingo brought with him, I don't know what to think. If Joaquin's name was forged on the marriage certificate, then it must have been done eighteen years ago. We'll find no answers here, but at this late date I doubt we can unearth the truth in Tierrasanta either."

"What choice do we have?" Joaquin asked sharply. "I'll not allow this slander to continue. If I have to go to Tierrasanta to locate the witnesses of this mythical wedding and shake the truth out of them, then I'll damn well do it."

Alicia had waited impatiently in the parlor for Flame to return with some sort of a report. When the young woman had not reappeared, she had gone to Joaquin's study. Flame had left the door ajar, and hearing what was clearly an argument, she had stepped into the room unnoticed. It took her but a moment to realize how desperate the situation truly was. "Is that what we should do, Mr. Ramirez, go to Tierrasanta and search for witnesses?"

Another opinion was all they needed, but Rafael couldn't tell the pretty blonde to stay out of her brother's business when Joaquin failed to speak up to send her on her way. "I had not expected this case to become so involved, Miss Caldwell, but unfortunately it certainly has." He looked over at Joaquin then, exasperated he had not had more time to discuss the matter alone with him. This was not the coolly logical manner in which he preferred to make decisions. "There are chemists in San Francisco who could provide an analysis of the ink and date on the parchment more accurately than I can merely by eye, but frankly I think it would be an expensive waste of time. Domingo

83

hasn't been hired to repeat a carefully rehearsed tale. He truly believes he is your son. I think you and I should take him back to Tierrasanta. The answer to this riddle has to be there."

"Joaquin?" Flame tugged on her husband's hand to gain his attention, but he anticipated her complaint and silenced it.

"I've not forgotten my promise never to leave you. If we go to Tierrasanta, you'll not be left behind." Seeing his wife's delighted smile, he turned to his sister. "I vowed we'd never be separated again, and since Flame will need a companion, I'd be happy to have you come along too, Alicia. I know Tierrasanta isn't what you had in mind when you said you wished to travel, but give it some thought. If you want to come along, I'll gladly take you. We'll be back before your parents can learn of the trip and forbid it."

"Joaquin," Rafael cautioned firmly, "what I had in mind was a brief trip to investigate Domingo's claims, not an extended pleasure cruise."

"Flame and I won't get in your way," Alicia promised quickly. "We won't distract you from completing your investigations."

Rafael winced inwardly, sorry he had ever tried to explain to the spirited young woman why he refused to combine business and romance. "You'd not bother us intentionally, Miss Caldwell, but your beauty alone would set the entire town to gossiping. We'd find witnesses willing to swear to anything simply to gain your notice. That's something we must avoid at all costs."

Seeing the fierce light in Rafael's dark eyes grow amazingly similar to the bright gleam in Alicia's, Joaquin made what he thought was the perfect suggestion. "The women needn't ride into Tierrasanta with us. We can stop by Eduardo Lopez's home first.

He might have another Appaloosa or two I'd be interested in buying, and he's sure to invite Flame and Alicia to stay with him while you and I go on up the coast. Doesn't that sound like a better way to plan this trip?" Joaquin asked with a good-natured grin, certain there was no way Rafael could refuse to agree.

"Infinitely," Rafael replied hoarsely, feeling as though he had been backed into a very uncomfortable corner. He leaned against the massive desk as the others began to leave the room. Joaquin intended to send a wire to San Francisco to summon his ship, *La Reina del Mar,* and Flame clung to his arm, excitedly asking questions about the trip. Neither of them noticed that Alicia remained behind.

She approached Rafael slowly, thinking him far more handsome in his riding clothes than he had been the night before at dinner. There was a recklessness about him now, a daring that she found fascinating. Since she could not compliment him upon his appearance, she remained with the subject at hand. "I can understand your reluctance to take such a large group to Mexico, but what do you really hope to find there?"

"I really have no idea," the perplexed attorney admitted with a helpless shrug.

"Oh, I see. You still don't wish to discuss the case with me. I'm sorry I bothered you about it then."

As she turned to go, her cheeks now flushed with a bright blush at what she clearly considered a sarcastic rejection, Rafael reached out to catch her arm. "Please don't think me so rude as that. It's just that I don't know what we'll find in Mexico or how we'll handle what we do discover." It was clear to him, however, that Joaquin wasn't going to let Flame anywhere near Tierrasanta and that intrigued him all the more.

Puzzled by his obvious confusion, Alicia stood still,

making no effort to elude his touch, which was surprisingly tender. "Domingo doesn't look anything like Joaquin, but that's not enough proof for you, is it?"

"No, appearances can be misleading. Just take your own fair coloring, for example. It would be difficult to convince a stranger you and Joaquin are even distantly related, let alone brother and sister. Besides, Domingo resembles Joaquin in many ways you probably haven't considered. He certainly has his obstinate pride. He has his height and dark coloring even if he doesn't have his features. Perhaps he resembles his mother; many men do."

Alicia knew that was true enough, but she saw something more in the attorney's glance. "You think Domingo really is Joaquin's son, don't you?" she asked in a hushed whisper.

"I'll not speculate on the matter," Rafael stated simply, but he could see that his noncommittal response disappointed Alicia again and he tried to explain his comment more convincingly than he had. "Joaquin has a great deal at stake, Alicia, but if he knows more than he's told me, he's keeping it to himself."

The pretty blonde considered that possibility thoughtfully before she spoke to defend her half-brother. "I think he's already told us everything there is to tell. My brother simply couldn't have deserted a pregnant bride. He just wouldn't have done it. Even if he had despised the woman, he would have brought her home and raised their child."

Rafael thought such an eventuality doubtful but didn't admit it. "I'm certain he appreciates your confidence in him, but it's still my responsibility to provide the proof to justify it."

Alicia thought Rafael Ramirez the most maddeningly aloof man she had ever encountered. That he would not trust the word of his best friend without tangible proof irritated her immensely. "Don't worry, Mr. Ramirez, I'm sure you'll do just that and I'll be certain to stay out of your way while you do it."

Her blue eyes glowed again with a defiant sparkle as she bid him that bitter farewell, but as Rafael watched her leave the study with a seductive sway, he mouthed a long string of bitter oaths again, cursing not only his folly in being so frank with her, but also his complete inability to resist her charms. He doubted he could even think, let alone accomplish anything worthwhile in Tierrasanta, knowing she was anywhere nearby.

Chapter V

Domingo had been sitting on the porch for more than an hour before Rafael came out the front door and joined him. The attorney had the marriage certificate in his hand and pointed to the signatures of the witnesses. "This appears to be Juan Carlos Muñoz y Romero and Amparo Muñoz y Silva. Who might they be?"

"My mother's parents," Domingo explained hesitantly. "They're the ones who demanded that the marriage take place."

Rafael nodded impatiently, unwilling to listen to that tale again. "Are they living still?"

"My grandmother is."

"What about Father Casteñeda? Is he still the parish priest in Tierrasanta, the one who acted as your tutor?"

"No." Domingo swallowed nervously, suspicious as always of where Rafael's questions were leading. "Casteñeda died years ago. The priest who taught me to speak English is a man named Ortega."

Rafael began mentally checking off the list of witnesses he'd drawn up. If there was only the grandmother left alive, it was possible she would not be able to pick Joaquin out of a group of men of similar height and appearance. He and his friend were often mistaken for brothers, and if there were several more men on *La Reina* who were tall enough to add to the confusion, such a ploy just might work. It would add credence to the forger theory if the woman could not recognize her own son-in-law. It was resorting to the theatrics he abhorred, but he feared in this case he might have no other choice of tactics. "We're all leaving for Tierrasanta as soon as the ship arrives to take us."

"What?" Domingo cried out in dismay. Tears stung his eyes as he began to argue furiously. "But I've just come from there and there's no reason to go back!"

Rafael eyed the young man's horrified expression with a curious glance. "What frightens you so much? Won't anyone know you there? Is that your fear, that the villagers won't recognize you and the fact that your story's a lie will be painfully obvious to all?"

Domingo leapt to his feet and took several paces away before jamming his hands in his hip pockets and wheeling around to face the attorney. "Everyone knows me. They will all tell you I am the son of Joaquin Villarreal. Why can't you accept it when you have the proof in your own hand?"

Rafael gave the old certificate a brief glance, then shook his head. "This isn't enough in itself, Domingo." Not nearly enough when Joaquin swore it was a forgery, he didn't bother to add, for the less the youth knew the better. "The trip by sea is far less arduous than the one you made overland on horseback, but I'll see you're not stranded in Mexico if that's your real worry."

"I am the son of Joaquin Villarreal!" Domingo shouted again. "Why should I have any worries when my father is such a wealthy and respected man?"

How he had allowed himself to become responsible for the obnoxious youth Rafael didn't quite understand, but someone obviously had to be when clearly he was incapable of looking out for himself. Rather than argue, Rafael pointed to Domingo's worn boots. "You'll need new boots for one thing. Let's take care of the horses and then go over to the tannery and see how quickly the cobbler can make you a pair." Since he knew Domingo would probably object to that plan, he didn't wait to listen but untied Renegade's reins and began leading him toward the barn.

Domingo thought the attorney daft. He wasn't going anywhere so he certainly didn't need new boots. He looked down at the pair that had been worn out long before he had left Mexico and cursed his rotten luck that he had not been able to provide his own. Since he seemed to have little choice in the matter, he grabbed Sampson's reins and started after Rafael. "I've come to California to stay!" he shouted emphatically, his heart too heavy with the thought of returning to Tierrasanta to yell they'd have to take him back in chains when he knew the domineering attorney wouldn't hesitate to do just that.

Alicia stepped back from the window once Rafael and Domingo were out of sight. They had been arguing, but she had not been able to understand their words clearly enough to know what had upset the young man. She was so thoroughly confused by the day's strange turn of events that she still didn't quite know what to make of them. Joaquin had convinced both Flame and her that once Rafael arrived Domingo would be dispatched with all possible haste, but that prediction bore no relation to what had actually happened. Domingo was obviously distressed; that had been easy to discern from his sullen scowl as he had walked away, and she felt a sudden sympathy for the headstrong young man.

"He's as confused as I am," she whispered softly to herself. Surely he would not be eager to return to Mexico, and she was undecided as to whether or not she should make the trip. The prospect of returning home to San Francisco was scarcely attractive, but could a voyage where she'd have no way to avoid seeing Rafael Ramirez at every turn possibly be pleasant? What had she expected from him, the same eager fawning she found so offensive in other men? Surely that wasn't what she'd hoped for, but it pained her greatly that he had no desire to enjoy the attraction he plainly felt as deeply as she. To at last meet a man who was both intelligent and attractive and be turned away as a nuisance was more than a young woman with her pride could bear. Perhaps making the trip to Mexico would be a grave mistake, for wouldn't she simply be torturing herself with the feelings Rafael had no intention of returning?

Flame interrupted Alicia's gloomy reverie as she entered the parlor. She was carrying Marissa on her right hip while her son skipped along happily by her side. "I just realized Joaquin gave you no time to respond to his invitation. We don't want you to feel you must come to Mexico with us if you'd really rather remain here or return to San Francisco."

Alicia scooped up the boisterous little boy and gave him a loving hug, which he enthusiastically returned, being far too young to have any reason to refuse a beautiful woman's affection. She combed his dark curls away from his forehead and kissed his chubby cheek as he snuggled contentedly in her arms. The thought that Rafael would also father such handsome, dark-eyed sons brought a frown to her brow she made no attempt to hide. "I'm not certain what I should do, Flame. I'd love to visit Mexico. I'm certain that would be wonderful fun, but the purpose of this trip is so, well, serious in nature that—"

"Nonsense!" Flame interrupted with a sparkling laugh. "Joaquin promised me a trip to Mexico more than a year ago and I know he'll never allow Domingo's fanciful claims to ruin it. We'll have a marvelous time despite the reason for the trip. Please say you'll come along. I don't want to have to stay at Eduardo Lopez's ranch all alone. Joaquin told me he's a bachelor and a very charming one, but why should he waste his efforts amusing me when I'm certain he'd much rather entertain a young woman as pretty as you."

Since she knew very well how charming Latin men could be, Alicia could not help but smile. "Is this some sort of trick? Is Lopez a bachelor in his eighties, is that it?"

"Good heavens, no!" Flame giggled, amused by that thought. "He's near Joaquin's age, or just a few years older; certainly not too old to be interested in romance."

Alicia's blue eyes lit with a mischievous sparkle as she considered the fascinating complication the unexpected presence of Eduardo Lopez might add to the trip. Surely Rafael would conclude his investigations swiftly, and with the matter of Domingo no longer occupying his thoughts, he would have plenty of time to notice her. If Lopez proved to be handsome and charming, so much the better. Maybe a little lively competition would rekindle the flame of desire she had tasted so clearly in the attorney's delicious kiss. "A trip to Mexico and the promise of romance? What could be more enticing? Tell Joaquin I've already begun to pack."

"Good! I've not seen Mexico either, but as much as I'll hate to leave my babies here, I'd miss Joaquin even more if he went off alone. I'm so glad you want to go along; it would undoubtedly be awkward for me to travel alone with the three men, and Domingo's company couldn't possibly be enjoyable. You and I can leave Joaquin and Rafael to deal with that rascal while we find our own amusement."

"Yes, let's plan on making it a splendid trip in every way," Alicia agreed brightly as she placed little Joaquin on his feet. Taking his hand, she followed Flame out to the kitchen where Perla had prepared the children's lunches. Her nephew and niece were a precious pair, but somehow she simply could not imagine herself ever being any child's mother.

La Reina del Mar was as magnificent a China clipper as had ever been christened. While the days of sailing ships were acknowledged as over by the advocates of steam-powered vessels, Joaquin had no plans ever to retire this graceful ship. Fortunately, a man of his wealth could afford to indulge his passions no matter how impractical they were. He stood at the rail as the last of Flame's trunks was carried on board. He had placed no restrictions on her luggage and she had packed far more gowns than she could ever wear, but he had not murmured the first word of criticism. Had she wanted to bring every stitch she owned he would not have complained. Despite the distasteful purpose of the trip, the chance to have his dear wife all to himself was so exceedingly pleasant he was really looking forward to it. The size of her travel wardrobe was of absolutely no consequence. Lost in erotic daydreams, he didn't realize Rafael had spoken to him until he repeated his question.

"I'll need to speak with you privately quite often. Can you arrange it?" The attorney leaned back against the rail, his pose relaxed even though he was deeply troubled by the purpose of their journey and couldn't help but be tense.

"Yes, of course. Flame will expect me to devote part of each day to the running of the ship so there will be plenty of opportunities for us to talk. I told her Olaf needed a vacation and I felt like taking command of the ship for this voyage myself, but, truly, the few people who know about this trip the better. Is there anything we can settle now, since it seems everyone is occupied but us?"

"Not everyone," Rafael pointed out with a sly smile. "I'd like Domingo to be kept busy. Despite the fact that Tierrasanta is a fishing village, he's never been on board a sailing ship. He lacks all knowledge of the skills required of a merchant seaman, but he's certainly got the intelligence to learn them."

Joaquin rubbed his hand over his chin slowly, thinking the ship's makeshift brig a far better place for the surly youth. "Do you think he'd have the sense to follow Arturo Duran's orders without question? We might as well put him in the brig to begin with if that's where he'll soon land."

Duran was the first mate, a stern-faced man who was not above wringing the last ounce of energy from each member of the crew, and then some. "Whether or not he ends up in the brig isn't the point. If he does find himself there, at least he'll know why he is being punished. If we put him there to begin with, he'll just think you all the more a villain."

"I doubt his opinion of me could get any worse," Joaquin replied with bitter sarcasm. "Not that I care."

"The situation is more than merely difficult, but mistreating Domingo won't make things easier for any of us," Rafael pointed out with his usual passion for fairness.

"All right," Joaquin agreed reluctantly, "but be sure to tell Arturo that he's not to whip the lad. If he won't follow orders, won't work as hard as the rest of the crew, he's just to be sent to the brig where he'll have no one to curse but himself until we've visited Lopez's ranch and are ready to leave for Tierrasanta."

Rafael had to laugh then, for Joaquin obviously understood the young man's temperament very well. "Fortunately this isn't a long trip."

"No, it isn't, and tell Domingo he's not to make it seem long either."

"I'll give it my best." Actually, Rafael had found the youth's violent temper amazingly easy to control since he had drawn his knife on him in the church. That wasn't something he'd suggest to Joaquin, however, since he knew his friend wouldn't merely be bluffing for dramatic effect if he should ever pull his knife. No, were Joaquin to be angry enough to have a knife in one hand and Domingo's throat clutched firmly in the other, it would most certainly be the end of the tiresome youth. "You don't seem terribly worried about what we'll find in Tierrasanta, or is your show of confidence merely a front to fool Flame?"

Annoyed by that question, Joaquin shot his best friend a warning glance. "You seem to think I'm hiding something from you as well as from her and that's just not true. I know that marriage certificate is a phony and that gives me all the confidence I need. I've tried to recall the women I met in Tierrasanta and while none stands out in my memory, I'm positive none was the innocent child Domingo describes his mother as being. Hell, you know me well enough to know none of the women I enjoyed romancing was in the least bit innocent before Flame entered my life. There was only one reason I was interested in feminine companionship before then, and I didn't waste my time seducing children to get it either."

Rafael knew his friend wasn't ashamed of his past

nor bragging about it, but merely stating the truth. It was an extremely confusing situation all the way around, but he knew he'd get nowhere as long as he kept questioning Joaquin's word. They had been friends for so long, he knew Joaquin wouldn't jeopardize that friendship by lying when surely he knew any confidence he revealed would be kept. "All right, I've repeatedly asked you for the truth and you swear you've told all of it. I'll work under the assumption the marriage certificate is a forgery, an old and good one, but a forgery all the same. That leaves us with several possible scenarios for the summer of 1855. Carmela might have been a pretty girl you met, slept with once, and promptly forgot. When she found herself pregnant, she somehow managed to stage a wedding in which she had the groom use your name in a desperate bid for respectability for herself and her child." When he saw Joaquin was about to object, he raised his hand. "Hear me out before you argue with me, because that's only one of my theories. Tierrasanta is a small village; surely if she'd used such a ruse, someone must know about it. A secret like that would be difficult to keep. I'll wager if that's what happened, then we can find one of her friends willing to tell us now, since Carmela is no longer alive to get even with anyone who reveals the truth about her wedding."

Intrigued by that possibility, Joaquin quickly agreed. "Yes, every town has its gossip and someone who delights in spreading it. Tierrasanta will be no exception, but I think you're overlooking a far more likely prospect."

"Just a minute. Let me finish, then you can have all the time you need for rebuttal," Rafael insisted confidently. "There's also the possibility Carmela never met you. Since the town must have been swarming with men from your ship, she could have slept with any one of the others or perhaps all of them. Who knows? It must have been no secret the ship belonged to your father, so you would have been the best one to claim as the father of her child. To cover her indiscretion she might actually have told her parents you'd seduced her, but perhaps that was merely a convenient lie she fed her son."

"Well, regardless of how convenient those lies were for her, they've proven damn inconvenient for me," Joaquin observed bitterly.

"That's certainly an understatement," Rafael agreed readily, certain his friend hadn't meant such ironic humor. "I think a lot depends upon what sort of young woman Carmela actually was. If she was the tramp I've just described, Domingo may or may not be your son. Although the odds are slim of this being true, she might also have been an innocent young girl who was seduced by one of your men. She might actually have thought she was marrying Joaquin Villarreal, when all along the scoundrel was deceiving her."

"Then the man obviously had no respect either for her virtue or for my reputation if he had the audacity to use my name, but how could he have hoped to get away with it?" Joaquin interjected sharply.

"Well, someone sure as hell had the audacity to use your name at the wedding; whether or not it was used before then we may never learn, but the fact is, they did get away with it for eighteen years."

Joaquin shook his head. "That's all imaginative speculation; you're forgetting the most obvious eventuality. If any woman even remotely suspected that I was the father of her child, she'd have come straight to me to demand money. Neither she nor her parents would have arranged a sham wedding. That just wouldn't have made any sense. The wealthiest family in Tierrasanta was poor by any standard. None would have missed the chance to ask me for money, and they'd have known they could ask for a great deal as recompense for what they would have mistakenly thought I'd done to their virtuous little daughter."

"I am merely proposing possibilities, *amigo,* speculating on what might have occurred so we don't overlook the obvious when it presents itself," Rafael explained in his usual, dispassionately logical manner, but he had to admit Joaquin's point was well taken.

"Well then," Joaquin responded with more than a slight edge of anger deepening his voice, "I am simply telling you why the possibilities you've presented so far are absurd! Tramp or not, any woman carrying my babe would have come straight to me to ask for enough money to provide a secure future for herself and our child."

Rafael gasped in surprise, astonished he had not considered the matter of money more thoughtfully. "From what Domingo says, his grandparents forced you to marry Carmela, whom you promptly deserted. Why didn't they come after you, or at the very least demand money to support their grandson?"

"Because they knew damn well I wouldn't know what the hell they were talking about!" Joaquin blurted out loudly. "None of that kid's story makes a bit of sense."

"You'd be surprised just how much in this life doesn't," Rafael mused regretfully. Every idea he had posed had some merit, some element of the possible, which could have been woven by a clever woman into the web of lies Domingo mistakenly believed to be the truth. He had barely begun to work on the case and at the blistering pace Joaquin planned to set it would take them less than a week to reach the Lopez Ranch, which lay just north of Acapulco. He had sailed with Joaquin once years ago and knew the man didn't merely sail the ship competently as Olaf Pederson did; he used every inch of canvas to capture the wind in a nearly successful attempt to make the graceful vessel take flight. A passionate man, he faced every challenge with the same unrelenting zest, but Rafael knew logic was often more valuable than raw emotion. "Every riddle has an answer and we'll find the solution to this one. I'm sure of it."

Joaquin straightened up proudly. "That's something I've never doubted, but I can't help wondering what Domingo expected me to do about him. He couldn't have imagined I'd be pleased to meet him after so many years of what he assumes was deliberate neglect."

"I don't think he gave any thought to anything other than claiming what he insists is rightfully his," Rafael offered calmly.

"Well, nothing is going to be rightfully his but the wages he'll earn on this voyage. See if you can't help him stay out of the brig so he'll not leave as penniless as he came."

As his friend left to make the last preparations for their departure, Rafael tried unsuccessfully to stifle a wicked grin. That Joaquin liked to keep hidden the fact he was a very generous man was something he found greatly amusing. It was also a trait that made it highly unlikely he would send away empty-handed any pregnant woman who came to him, regardless of her tale. He would need more answers from Domingo, and since he had no desire to interview him in the brig, he decided this was as good a time as any to tell him how he would pass the voyage. He headed back to the stern where the young man was standing by himself, sullenly trying to ignore his guard.

"I have convinced Joaquin to allow you to work as one of the crew, but I'll warn you now, the first mate is a man named Arturo Duran and he expects a full day's work from every hand."

Glancing toward his guard, Domingo asked sarcastically, "Will he be working too?"

"Yes, but his job is different from yours and doesn't concern you. I will expect you to keep your opinion about your identity strictly to yourself. You'll find nothing but ridicule if you start telling the men you're Joaquin's son, because it will be more than plain that he doesn't recognize any such relationship. Spare yourself that embarrassment and keep your thoughts to yourself."

That order angered Domingo so greatly he could barely see, and he spit out his reply in a fierce staccato rhythm. "I am good enough to be part of his crew—is that it?—but not good enough to be his son?"

"No," Rafael assured him warmly, and although he knew what he was about to say was unlikely, he said it anyway. "It is plain to him you are a young man with both intelligence and courage, traits he'd welcome in a son. Do not think for a minute his objection is to you personally, because it's not. His only objection is that your claim isn't a valid one, which is why we're going to Tierrasanta to investigate it more thoroughly."

"You won't find a damn thing there you don't already know," Domingo protested bitterly.

"You're wrong, because we won't leave the town before we find exactly who signed that marriage certificate and why."

Astonished by that promise, Domingo responded with a furious challenge. "Joaquin Villarreal signed it because he knew he was responsible for my mother's condition! Is he too great a coward to admit that

101

fact now?"

Rafael gestured to the guard, indicating he wanted him to accompany them. "I want to show you something, Domingo, then I'll give you a choice in your accommodations." With that brief explanation, he led the young man and his guard below deck to the small storeroom Joaquin jokingly referred to as the brig. It had seldom been used as such because the cramped quarters were so uncomfortable the members of the crew would obey any command rather than suffer through being confined there.

"The word of a ship's captain is the law at sea, Domingo. Thanks to Joaquin's generosity you have a choice. You may work as one of the crew, live in the crew's quarters, and share their rations, or you may take up residence in this small, dark closet. Here you'll be given no more than a bucket to take care of your personal needs and if the cook can remember to send you a crust of bread and a cup of water once a day he'll do it. It is as close to being confined in a coffin as you can come before your death and I suggest you avoid it at all costs. Above deck the fresh air and sunshine are invigorating. You'll work up a hearty appetite and the cook provides plenty of good food to satisfy it. Down here in the bowels of the ship, you'll soon notice the rolling motion is far more pronounced than up on deck and you'll probably be so dreadfully seasick the entire voyage that the peace of a coffin will seem quite attractive. It's not a pleasant prospect, but if your pride will not allow you to work and keep your thoughts to yourself, then I'll lock you in here right now."

Domingo's mouth was so dry he could barely free his tongue to form the words he wished to speak. He couldn't stand any sort of confinement; the prospect of being locked up in a miserable cell like a common criminal when he'd done no wrong terrified him. What if he were forgotten, left alone for days at a time and went mad? Tears filled his eyes before he finally forced himself to volunteer to work at whatever task Joaquin cared to give him.

"Good. I knew you'd see reason," Rafael complimented him sincerely. "I'll introduce you to Arturo now. He'll assign you the most menial duties, of course, but I'm sure you'll not disappoint him by failing to carry them out." When Domingo's only reply was a sullen stare, Rafael again motioned toward the guard to follow them. A tall man in his thirties with piercing brown eyes and thick black hair, Tomás Valdez had been selected by the attorney to make the voyage, although the *vaquero* had not been given the slightest clue as to why a man of his age, size, and coloring had been chosen.

Although Alicia had been understandably apprehensive about sharing dinner with Rafael in the close confines of Flame and Joaquin's cabin, the evening proved to be not only relaxing but highly enjoyable. They had all taken the trouble to be well dressed for the first night of the voyage and in their party clothes the handsomely appointed cabin took on the cozy atmosphere of a private dining room in one of San Francisco's exclusive clubs. Flame's gown was fashioned of black lace while Alicia's was midnight blue, not quite so daringly low cut as her sister-in-law's but every bit as flattering to her slender figure. The men wore handsome black dress suits, their formal attire as fashionable and well tailored as the ladies' gowns.

Joaquin made a point of refilling their wine glasses often to put everyone in a mood as mellow as his own.

He and Rafael kept up a steady stream of amusing tales, recounting some of the more hilarious misadventures from their youth until both Flame and Alicia were in tears from laughter and begged them to stop.

"It is remarkable you both survived to adulthood!" the lovely redhead exclaimed as she brushed the sparkling beads of moisture from her long lashes.

"We did a lot better than merely survive, my dear," Rafael responded with unmistakable pride. As he glanced over at Alicia, his smile grew wider still. He was well on his way to becoming quite drunk, and while he was usually far more cautious, he was so comfortable in the company of his good friends that he had relaxed his usual restraint, something he was swiftly beginning to regret.

Priding herself on being even more reserved than he, Alicia returned Rafael's bright smile with no more than a friendly nod before she spoke to her half-brother. "Was there nothing your father forbade you to do?" she asked with real curiosity brightening her smile. She thought the evening had gone rather well, but she had expected nothing from Rafael in the way of special attention and had not offered him any.

Joaquin gave that query what serious thought he could, considering he was far from sober; then he burst out laughing, "Nothing that I can recall!"

"Well, I shall expect you to be a far more proper father than your father was," Flame insisted as she gave her husband's arm a loving pat. "I'll not allow either of our children to run wild and I'll certainly never encourage our son to go to sea at sixteen as you did."

Joaquin's dark eyes danced with amusement as he responded with a rakish grin, "Need I remind you that you considered yourself mature enough to come to California alone and to marry me at that tender age?

Surely your son wil be adult enough at sixteen to take a cruise or two if he wishes to do so."

"He has an excellent point there, Flame. You've already set a precedent for independence your children will probably find most inspiring," Rafael pointed out with a deep chuckle.

"You stay out of this!" Flame scolded, then unable to stifle her giggles, she reached over to give his hand a playful squeeze. "I can't fight both of you, so let's just change the subject to something less controversial than how I wish to raise my children."

"Our children," Joaquin corrected her with another booming laugh.

Rafael could not help but laugh too, then had to raise his hand quickly to cover a wide yawn. "Forgive me. Perhaps it's the sea breeze, but I'm so sleepy I'm afraid I'm going to have to call it a night."

Since she was as tipsy as the rest of them, Alicia thought Rafael's excuse an exceptionally good one. "Yes, it is late and I'd like to return to my cabin too. Thank you all for a wonderful evening."

Rafael struggled to his feet so he could assist the slender blonde from her chair. "Allow me to escort you to your door, Miss Caldwell," he offered graciously.

Alicia laughed as she turned to face him. "I shan't get lost on so short a walk."

"Probably not, but let's not take that risk." As he took Alicia's arm, he turned back to wink at Flame. "You were adorable at sixteen. Don't let Joaquin tease you about it."

"You needn't worry. I'm not in the mood to fight with him tonight," Flame responded with a smile so sweet, the seductive nature of her thoughts was easily read.

When Joaquin leaned over to whisper an enticing

invitation in his wife's ear, Rafael drew Alicia through the cabin door, but he found the fragrance of her perfume so distracting he couldn't recall just where he had promised to take her. "I think I'll feel far better in the morning if I get some fresh air before going to bed. Would you like to go up on deck for a moment?"

Alicia hesitated slightly, wanting no repeat of the ridiculous scene they had played on the patio, but he had been so polite all evening she had no reason to suspect he would behave any differently now and agreed. "Why yes, the stars must be lovely."

They found the sky overcast, however, and the midnight air heavy with a fine mist. When she shivered slightly at the unexpected chill, Rafael quickly put his arm around her shoulders and drew her close. His warmth was so comforting she did not object, but that she longed for far more was a secret she had sworn to keep to herself for the time being. Before the silence between them could grow awkward, she asked the first question that came to her mind. "Did you know Joaquin's father well? Naturally my mother never mentioned the man she divorced and I'm very curious about him."

Since he had been savoring the soft swells of her figure that were pressed so delightfully close to his side, Rafael was so surprised by her unexpected question that he needed a moment to form a coherent reply. He provided the most flattering response he could, since he had always been grateful to Miguel for giving him good advice at a time when he had desperately needed it. "He was a fine man in many ways, but, like everyone, he also had his failings. Joaquin resembled him in both appearance and manner at one time, but Flame's love has tamed the wildness of his nature considerably and apparently your mother wasn't nearly as successful with Miguel."

"No, I suppose not, but if he was as bright and handsome as Joaquin, it's strange he never remarried," Alicia mused thoughtfully, totally unaware of the torment her nearness was causing Rafael. "He must have been very lonely."

While he knew it was a common assumption that a man with no wife was unbearably lonely, Rafael heartily disagreed. He grew defensive but did not relax his hold upon her, since he found the closeness of her supple form so very enjoyable despite their difference of opinion. "Maybe not. Many men never marry once, let alone twice, so it's not so strange he didn't take another wife. Perhaps he was perfectly content without one," he replied brusquely, displeased he had not foreseen the direction their conversation might take since marriage was the last topic he cared to discuss with Alicia or any other young woman for that matter. He decided the best way to end their conversation was with a deeply satisfying kiss, but as he bent his head, she suddenly shifted in his arms, turning away slightly, and he had to straighten up quickly rather than allow his kiss to slide clumsily off her ear. She was irresistibly lovely, but he could not recall ever meeting a more impossibly difficult female, and that he could not have her on his own terms infuriated him so greatly he could barely conceal his frustration. She might be standing in his arms, but there was a wide gulf separating them still.

Startled by the sudden bitterness of her companion's mood, Alicia had instantly stiffened. She didn't know what else to do but attempt to end the evening as gracefully as possible, so she asked him one last question about Miguel. "Do you suppose he still loved my mother? I know he was quite a few years older than

107

she, so he might have been in love with her even after their divorce, mightn't he?"

"What has the man's age got to do with it?" Rafael wondered aloud, angry with himself for not kissing her the moment she had stepped into his arms. He had loved the way she had snuggled against him to get warm when they had first come up on deck, but now her body felt totally unyielding, as though she had simply turned to stone in his arms. It seemed it was impossible for them to speak without one or both of them growing too hostile for the conversation to continue. That was a tragedy for which he was certain he was not to blame, for she simply misinterpreted every word he spoke and he was positive she did it on purpose just to spite him. He didn't realize how argumentative his tone had become. "He wasn't all that old when the divorce took place; probably not that much older than I am now."

"No, I suppose not," Alicia agreed. "It's only that I think older men are more serious in nature and therefore capable of a deeper love than many young men seem to be. My brother is a good example, isn't he? He didn't fall in love until he reached his thirties." She was grateful the deck was cloaked in darkness, for she was dreadfully afraid Rafael would think she was deliberately trying to provoke him when she had never dreamed he would react to her questions about Miguel Villarreal in such a hostile manner.

"Regardless of his age, were your brother not such a romantic individual, he'd not be in the horrible mess he's in now!" Rafael responded sarcastically.

Afraid they would be overheard, Alicia lifted her fingertips to his lips to prevent another such intemperate outburst. "Please, I'm certain the men on watch needn't know that."

108

Her cool caress jarred him sufficiently that he remained silent for a moment, but Rafael then took her hand in his and forced her back a step. "Miguel Villarreal was like a father to me when I lost my own, but, quite naturally, he did not confide the secrets of his heart to me. Since your mother is very happily married now, it's pointless for you to brood over her past sorrows and I'd advise you to forget them."

Disappointed as well as insulted by the coldness of his tone, Alicia yanked her hand from his. "I'm most certainly not brooding over it. I merely thought that since you'd enjoyed reminiscing so much tonight, you might tell me a little about my mother's past. Forgive me if it seemed as though I was prying into matters about which I have no business knowing, for that wasn't my purpose at all."

Rafael could think of no comment that would not only make matters worse, but as Alicia turned away, he again took her arm and silently escorted her to her cabin, where she did not bother to wish him a good night before she slammed the door far too soundly. He heard her ram the bolt into the lock and the hollowness of that sound echoed as a further rejection. What had possessed him to invite the volatile young woman up on deck when they had never been able to speak more than a few words together without nearly coming to blows? He raked his fingers through his hair and was surprised to find his hand damp from the mist. The way his luck was running he would probably catch pneumonia. Vowing never to be so foolish as to speak with Alicia Caldwell alone ever again, he entered his cabin, tore off his clothes, and after wrapping the blankets snugly around himself, fell upon the bunk where his conscience prodded him sharply. Why was Alicia so concerned about whether or not Miguel

Villarreal had been lonely when she didn't give a damn about him?

"Women!" he complained bitterly as though that one word explained the complexity of the female mind. As he tried to get comfortable, he caught the faintest strains of Flame's sparkling laughter, but being reminded how dearly she and his best friend loved each other only underscored the emptiness of his own life. Why had he taken Alicia up on deck? Had he hoped to kiss her again, to enfold her in his arms and taste the sweetness of her kiss instead of the perpetual sting of her anger? Despite his earlier claims, he was now wide awake and lay in the narrow bunk forcing himself to concentrate again upon the difficulties of Domingo's case rather than the disastrous way an enjoyable evening had ended, since there had not been a damn thing he could have done to prevent that sorry outcome.

Alicia tried pacing her cabin but soon found the gentle rocking motion of the ship made her far too dizzy to continue. She had just learned something she already knew: Rafael Ramirez was insufferably arrogant and impossibly conceited! He was also almost painfully handsome and so complex a man she didn't think she'd ever tire of his company—what little she could take of his company before they began to argue, she reminded herself. Maybe he was right. Maybe this wasn't a convenient time or place to pursue their friendship, but at least they had managed to share dinner together in good humor. Why hadn't the pleasure of that interlude affected him as it had her with a desire for further closeness? She flopped down upon her bunk and began to yank the pins from her hair. Joaquin always seemed to enjoy being with

Flame, but it was more than plain she wasn't Flame, and Rafael most certainly wasn't Joaquin. "I think it's Rafael who needs to be tamed now," she announced aloud to the empty cabin. The blue of her eyes grew as bright as sapphires as she vowed she would one day be the one not only to attempt that feat, but to accomplish it as well.

Chapter VI

While Flame enjoyed Joaquin's generous affection and lavish attention, she had an annoying suspicion his motive wasn't simply the enjoyment of their love. She was a clever young woman and time and again the true purpose of their trip occupied her thoughts. She had enjoyed spending most of her time the first two days of their voyage on deck with Alicia, but it seemed no matter where they sat or stood Domingo could be seen working nearby. He was constantly in motion and always engaged in what appeared to be backbreaking toil. Arturo Duran never overlooked him when he had a particularly tedious or dirty chore, but she had not heard the young man utter a single word of complaint, no matter how hard he was made to work. That simply amazed her, for she had never expected such a display of ambition or restraint from him. That he would be so willing a worker puzzled her, for what possible motivation could he have for exhausting himself on a voyage he had announced to anyone who would listen he had no desire to take? He preferred to work shirtless, and while his body was not nearly as muscular as her husband's, there was something all too familiar about his build. His hair was the glossy black Joaquin's had

113

once been, and his skin tanned to the same shade of golden bronze. Despite his long hours, he still exhibited a confidence that set him apart from the rest of the crew as surely as her husband's proud bearing made him unique among any group of men. The more she saw of the handsome youth, the more uncomfortable she became, for clearly he was no peasant despite the humble setting of his birth. He was obviously convinced he was destined for something far better than the hardships he had known, but she could not look at him without being chilled by the threat he represented to the comfortable life she and Joaquin shared with their children.

"Joaquin?" she called softly as they prepared for bed.

"Yes, my love?" Joaquin took her silver-handled hairbrush in his hand and, sitting down behind her on the bunk, began to brush out her golden red curls with surprising tenderness, curling each strand over his fingers before moving on to the next.

Flame enjoyed her husband's attentions so much that a long moment passed before she turned slightly to glance over her shoulder and spoke. "There is something about Domingo that disturbs me."

Joaquin frowned slightly, and laying the brush aside he leaned down to kiss the creamy expanse of shoulder that peeked invitingly through her lace nightgown. "He is of no consequence, Flame, but if he bothers you in any way I'll not allow him to come up on deck tomorrow."

"No, it is not Domingo himself who is the problem, for he's been careful to keep his distance. It is his manner, the way he carries himself, his pride, even though you insist he has no reason for it."

Joaquin's gaze did not falter from his wife's as he replied with a seriousness he seldom had reason to use with her, "I want no secrets between us, Flame; no

114

questions or doubts. Were the boy mine, I would say so gladly, but he is not."

Flame turned toward her husband then so she could face him squarely, her emerald gaze now sweeping his expression with rapt interest. She knew wanting to believe him was not the same as believing him, but that he needed her to have faith in his word was something she knew even better. Rather than say anything that might give offense, she focused her attention solely upon Domingo. "I think he wants to be your son very badly."

"While that's flattering, it doesn't make it so," Joaquin reminded her.

Flame placed her fingertips upon his shoulders and leaned forward to trace with her lips the thin scar that crossed his right cheekbone. "Perhaps it is only that since I never knew my own father, I know what it is like to love someone who is no more than a dream."

Joaquin wrapped the lovely redhead in his arms, eagerly returning her gesture of love. "You are the dearest creature ever born, Flame, but Domingo despises me and I can't blame him for it. If I'd really deserted his mother and neglected him all these years as he insists I did, I'd deserve no better."

Flame was positive her husband could not be charged with the crime of neglecting a child he swore wasn't his, but the circumstances of Domingo's birth simply baffled her. "I don't understand why Domingo was raised to believe he was your son."

Joaquin did not repeat any of Rafael's theories, for he considered it most likely that Carmela Muñoz had merely chosen his name to embellish her tale when she had had no idea who her baby's father might be. "We'll find out all we can and do our best to put everything right. You know Rafael has the tenacity of a bulldog. If there's any way to discover who Domingo's father really is and why I was selected instead of him for that

115

honor on the marriage and baptismal certificates, then I'm certain he'll do it."

While Flame hoped that was true, she could not help wondering aloud about their friend. "I know your confidence in Rafael is justified, for he's very hard-working and determined, but it's unfortunate that he's become so preoccupied with refuting Domingo's claims. Perhaps if you and he can settle things quickly in Tierrasanta, he'll be able to relax and enjoy himself on the voyage home. He can be such marvelous company and I'd like Alicia to see him at his best."

Dismayed by both the persistence and the absurdity of her hopes, Joaquin sighed deeply. "How many times must I ask you not to meddle in their affairs?"

"But that's just the problem, Joaquin—they're not having an affair!" Flame giggled at her own joke, then snuggled back into his arms. "They don't even seem to be speaking to each other and I can't imagine why not since they got along so well last night. They were laughing together as they left our cabin, but I didn't hear Rafael say a single word to Alicia all day and she didn't even glance his way during dinner. Do you suppose they had some sort of argument after they left us?"

"They must have, but let's not concern ourselves with them tonight. Can't we find something far better to do with our time?"

As Joaquin's lips moved slowly down her throat with teasing nibbles, Flame lifted her arms to encircle his neck. Certain she could do little to help Alicia that night, and much to please her husband, she quickly made her choice. "I want only to spend my time with you, my love, for it is your happiness that means the most to me." The lithe redhead then moved with the elegant grace of a ballerina, while her passions were, as always, unrestrained. As her fingertips peeled away his

116

shirt and her lips moved slowly over her husband's deeply bronzed shoulder, she whispered tantalizing promises of the delights she wished them to share, loving promises Joaquin insisted she keep.

Like Flame, Alicia found Domingo's constant presence on deck disquieting, for the glances he gave her were so threatening they were positively evil. She knew he had absolutely no reason to hate her so, but clearly he considered her beneath contempt. The only time they had ever spoken together she had slapped him for speaking rudely to her, but he had deserved that and she would never apologize to him for it. Clearly he despised her simply because she was Joaquin's sister, but she thought such hatred very foolish, since it had no cause other than the betrayal he imagined his mother had suffered.

She swept her wind-tossed curls away from her eyes and tried to focus her attention upon the horizon. It was another glorious day. The sunshine sparkled upon the calm waters of the Pacific Ocean with a near blinding brilliance. Joaquin and Flame were standing nearby, so lost in each other she doubted they had even noticed what a splendid day it was. At the opposite rail, Rafael had drawn Domingo aside for another lengthy chat. They seemed to have a great deal to discuss, but since she knew how reluctant the attorney was to talk about the case, she had not bothered to ask him what information he had hoped to get from Domingo. Apparently he was interested in every detail the young man could supply, but he had shared nothing with the rest of them. The handsome youth appeared to be listening to the attorney, but his eyes never left her face, and, repelled by his insolent glance, she turned away. She would not hide in her

117

cabin like some frightened rabbit, but other than pretending Domingo did not exist, she did not know how else to deal with him. She tried to become interested in the activities of two men who were coiling ropes in the stern, but when she again glanced in Domingo's direction, she found his taunting gaze as unsettling as before. Dark, forbidding, she wondered what he expected from her or from any of them, for that matter, when he was always so hostile.

Unfortunately, she found it no easier to look at his companion, for Rafael's dark good looks were so compelling a sight it made her heart ache to recall how reluctant he had been to allow her to become part of his life. Reluctant was too kind a word, she mused thoughtfully, for he had simply refused to grant her that privilege. His pose was relaxed as he leaned against the rail, but she knew he was totally absorbed in his conversation with Domingo. His agile mind would be dissecting each tidbit of information he gleaned in a relentless search for the truth. She no longer hoped, as she had on the first two days of the voyage, that he might have a few minutes to spend with her, for she knew by now that when he finished speaking with Domingo he would simply return to his cabin to study his notes and refine his deductions before returning with another round of questions. She was certain that by the time the men reached Tierrasanta, Rafael would know Domingo better than the boy knew himself. There were other men on board who wasted no opportunity to stop their work for a moment to speak with her, but Rafael Ramirez was not even remotely interested in her company. She would probably not see him until supper, when he would be excruciatingly polite and, as always, maddeningly aloof.

After having had three days at sea in which to suffer the sharp sting of his neglect, Alicia was so filled with

118

resentment she was truly beginning to look forward to meeting Eduardo Lopez. That prospect was positively exhilarating compared to her present situation. Joaquin and Flame were, as always, devoted to each other, and Rafael was so deeply engrossed in his work she felt hopelessly left out and alone, as though she were the only girl at some wonderful dance without the attentions of a partner. She was really looking forward to Eduardo's hospitality, since her stay at his ranch was bound to be far more enjoyable than she had found her days on *La Reina* to be. Perhaps he would be interested in more than merely breeding Appaloosa horses, but even if he wasn't, she would appreciate hearing him talk about the unusually beautiful horses. The thought that she might even deliberately invite his advances made her blush, but it was a pleasant diversion so she allowed her mind to fill with amusing fantasies of an Eduardo Lopez who would be not only incredibly handsome, intelligent and witty, but wonderfully amorous as well. The tension eased from the taut muscles of her neck and shoulders as she began to relax, and in another few moments the deep disappointment that had been mirrored in her expression had become a blissful smile.

As Rafael left his young charge, he found Alicia's wistful expression as taunting as Domingo's evasive replies. Whatever could the pretty blonde be daydreaming about so intently that she could not even be bothered to return his wave? She seemed to have a great deal of time to return the greetings of the sailors on board but not even one second to offer him a smile. Why did she take such delight in torturing him with her indifference? While that was an even more fascinating mystery than the one he was being paid to solve, Rafael

119

knew he dared not devote any time to it now, for he wanted to have his plans fully made before he and Joaquin set out for Tierrasanta rather than be forced to hope they would merely stumble upon the right leads once they had arrived in the small coastal village. He swore softly to himself as he returned to his cabin, for he feared there were too few hours until the journey's end for him to get any sort of glimpse of the truth when Domingo seemed to know as little about his past as the rest of them did. As for the radiantly beautiful Miss Caldwell, regretfully, she would simply have to wait. Resting his chin upon his palm as he thumbed through his notes, he prayed the wait would not seem as dreadfully long to her as it would to him.

Flame made an extra effort to involve both Rafael and Alicia in the dinner conversation that night and each seemed genuinely pleased by her attentions. They smiled warmly and gave witty responses to her questions, but she failed miserably in her attempt to generate a lively exchange between the two of them as she had hoped to do. When Joaquin began to nudge her knee with his, and not at all gently, she realized she couldn't possibly inspire a romance between the attractive pair if they weren't interested in beginning one themselves. She smiled coquettishly at her husband then and concentrated her charms solely upon pleasing him. When their guests left together as they did each evening, she didn't bother to remark upon her lack of success with them when she knew how easily her seductive ploys worked upon her husband.

All too conscious of his gentlemanly reserve, Alicia bid Rafael a cool good night but soon regretted returning to her quarters, since she was far too restless to sleep. The cabin was cleverly designed, the wood paneling beautifully carved by master craftsmen, but she felt confined rather than comfortable. Knowing she had been perfectly safe up on deck in the daytime, she was certain all the men on board would give her the proper respect now and saw no reason to deny herself the pleasure of a few minutes in the moonlight. She promptly wrapped her shawl around her shoulders and went up on deck, not in the least bit concerned about having no escort, since she had never grown used to having one. She moved to a spot in the stern where she would be protected from the chill of the wind and tried to concentrate solely upon the beauty of the sparkling sea in an attempt to relax in order to enjoy a good night's rest. She was taken completely by surprise when a man suddenly leapt from behind, gripping her so tightly around the waist she could not draw a breath to scream before he covered her mouth with his hand. She struggled frantically to get free, but he was as strong as he was quick and swiftly dashed her hopes of escaping his grasp. When he whispered in her ear, she froze, totally unnerved by his unexpected demand.

"You needn't fear me, *tía.* I will let you go as soon as you promise to be quiet."

Alicia recognized Domingo's voice instantly and not wishing to ignite the fires of his temper when she feared he might then hurt her seriously, she forced herself to stand calmly in his arms. When he released her, she turned to face him, but he was completely hidden by deep shadows and seemed to have simply vanished into the night. "I am not your aunt!" the disheveled blonde hissed emphatically, hoping to lure him out of the darkness.

"You are my father's sister," Domingo insisted in a threatening whisper, unwittingly revealing his position.

"That's why you will help me."

"Why would I wish to help you when you do not even have the decency to ask?" Alicia inquired suspiciously, wondering if she shouldn't just scream hysterically now that she had the chance.

"I've seen the way you look at me. You know I am your brother's son. Joaquin knows who I am too; so does that bastard of an attorney. They'll find nothing in Tierrasanta but the truth they've refused to accept. Their only choice then will be to kill me. You must not let them murder me for speaking the truth!"

Shocked not only by his words but also by the sheer terror in his voice, Alicia took a step backward, then quickly looked around for the man she knew had been assigned as Domingo's guard, but there was no one standing nearby. She could see little and hear nothing except the whine of the wind whipping the sails overhead and the constant creaks and groans of the wooden ship. Knowing it would be a waste of breath to call for help, she drew her shawl more closely around her shoulders and began to argue with the belligerent young man. She could not deny she had been watching him, for he was constantly underfoot, so she dismissed that accusation from her mind and took up the most important of his points.

"You are completely mistaken. Joaquin means you no harm." She had learned from Rafael that under no circumstances would her brother admit to being Domingo's father, but she was certain he would never stoop to murder for any reason. "He is a fine man despite your misguided opinion of him, and he'll not hurt you."

When Domingo stepped out of the shadows, the anguish etched upon his handsome features was clearly illuminated by the soft rays of the moon. "He's already hurt me deeply by denying I am his son, and his neglect caused my mother's death! How many times must I repeat my story before I am believed?"

While he was obviously sincere, Alicia was just as positive he was wrong. Since she was certain Joaquin would make no attempt to kill him, she quickly offered the only solution she could. "How may I help you? If you wish me to speak with my brother about you, I will gladly do so."

"No!" Domingo warned sharply. "He must not even suspect I know what he plans to do with me. He threatened to lock me up for this voyage, to put me in a cage like an animal, then decided instead to have the first mate torture me with more work than any other three men could do. I haven't complained because I'm no coward. All I ask is that when he decides to kill me, you'll warn me so I can get away before he succeeds."

Alicia was shaking with fear as well as the coldness of the night. She could not believe Domingo was really in danger, and yet he seemed so convinced his fate was close at hand that she was becoming frightened too. "What are you talking about? There are no cages on board this ship."

"A cell then; it's the same as a cage. Ramirez gave me a choice: to be locked up or work. That is how bad my father treats me when he is the criminal, not I! Why must I beg for your help when you know I deserve it?"

After a long pause, Alicia agreed to give Domingo whatever assistance she could, all the while praying no help would be necessary. "I will find out whatever I can. If there is even the vaguest mention of dealing with you harshly, I will let you know immediately. How you wish to act upon that information will be your own decision, but I do wish you'd believe me when I say your life truly isn't at risk."

Domingo knew he had taken a big gamble in assuming she could be trusted, but he had seen her frequently alone rather than with the others and hoped that meant she was independent of them in her thinking too. There was one way she could ease his torment now though, and he bent down to kiss her cheek sweetly. "You are very pretty. Were you not my aunt, I would not stop with a kiss."

Startled by his insolent boast, Alicia raised her hand, but he caught her slim wrist before she could slap him. "Let me go!" she ordered firmly.

"Do not forget your promise of help," Domingo responded before he stole another kiss, this time possessively bruising her lips. "Until tomorrow, *tía,* sweet dreams." He dropped her hand then and sauntered off nonchalantly whistling a sea chantey popular among Joaquin's crew.

Thoroughly disgusted with him, Alicia wiped her mouth to remove the horrible memory of his kiss, then remained on deck until she was so chilled she had no choice other than to return to her cabin. But as she reached it, she turned instead to knock upon Rafael's door. When he answered, she did not bother to wait for an invitation to enter but swept past him as she began to explain the reason for such a late visit. "You've just got to speak with Domingo. He thinks he's about to be murdered!"

The rakish grin that had crossed the attorney's face when he had found the lovely blonde at his door disappeared before he turned around to face her. It was very late, and after several brandies, he was in no mood to talk about Domingo's ridiculous fears. He had been stretched out across his bunk, in his shirt sleeves and so comfortable he soon would have fallen asleep had she not knocked upon his door. She had not been out of his thoughts since they had parted so quickly after supper, for he had been taunting himself with a succession of fantasies so erotic her sudden appearance had seemed like a dream come true. She was, however, as usual, totally uninterested in him. "Why didn't you speak to me about this at supper?" he demanded crossly, his handsomeness undiminished by his sullen frown.

"Because I didn't know how he felt then. We've just been talking though and—"

"What?" Astonished by that surprising revelation, Rafael stepped forward to confront her. His cabin was slightly larger than hers, but still there was little room to stand and walk about. "How could you possibly have been talking with him at this hour?"

Alicia shivered, as much from the chill of his dark glance as from that of the night air. His eyes were a deep, rich brown, but they seldom appeared black as they did now, and she realized she had made a serious mistake in disturbing him. Since she could not simply excuse herself, she continued with all the confidence she could summon forth. "I went up on deck for a moment and he, well, he happened to walk by and stopped to talk with me." That was an outright lie and she knew it, but she could not bring herself to reveal how badly Domingo had behaved when she knew it would bring him even more trouble than he already had. "Arturo is working him awfully hard, and he's certain he'll be murdered when you all reach Tierrasanta and Joaquin is forced to admit the story of his marriage to Carmela is true."

Having no sympathy for the subject of their discussion, Rafael frowned more deeply as he looked down at her. "It really doesn't matter what Domingo thinks. No one is going to kill him, and if he's tired of working, I'll simply remind him he still has a choice in the matter."

Now it was Alicia who was taken aback. "Did you really threaten to lock him up?" she asked accusingly.

Rafael shook his head slyly. "It was no idle threat,

merely a very unpleasant alternative."

Alicia bit her lip nervously as she recalled how terrified Domingo had been. "I don't know what to think now," she admitted hesitantly. "Perhaps Domingo really is in danger and I'm just too naïve to see it."

"You are in far more danger at this very minute than he will ever be," Rafael teased with a trace of the grin her unexpected arrival had brought. "Are you really too naïve to know you should not be in my cabin at any hour, let alone this one?"

"Must you always be so tiresome?" Alicia responded sarcastically. "Why is it we cannot exchange more than half a dozen words on any topic before you begin to patronize me? I am not some silly child you can scold whenever you like!"

Her long curls had been tossed wildly about by the wind and now provided the perfect frame for the vivid blue of her hostile glance. Her cheeks were flushed with a most attractive blush and the ferocity of her expression took away nothing from her charm. Rafael thought her one of the most desirable women he'd ever met. He enjoyed her fiery spirit as greatly as her fair beauty and made no attempt to apologize, since he found her anger so very exciting. "Would you prefer this instead?" he asked in a teasing whisper as he stepped forward and wound his fingers in her tangled curls to tilt her mouth up to his. She placed her palms upon his chest and struggled to push him away, but he simply ignored her protest. He brushed her lips lightly with his before sliding his tongue between her pink-tinged lips to explore the moist sweetness of her mouth until he felt all her resistance cease. At that precise moment he released her and asked with a taunting leer, "Well, what's your choice? Do you wish to be treated as a child or a grown woman?"

The question was clearly a dare and Alicia despised

him for it, but rather than slap the smirk from his face she paid him back with a challenge of her own. She raised her arms to encircle his neck and stood on tiptoe to trace the outline of his lips with the tip of her tongue before giving him a kiss filled with such passionate abandon he was completely fooled as to her purpose. He wrapped her in a warm embrace and responded eagerly, returning her enticing affection with a more than generous amount of his own. She had meant to draw away, to laugh in his face and leave him cursing his own folly for ridiculing her, but she found it impossible to play such a foolish trick when the emotion in his kisses was so overwhelmingly real. She clung to him as that powerful realization swept through her, her seductive surrender more compellingly erotic than the wildest of his fantasies.

The fine brandy Rafael had sipped so generously in the last hour had filled his lean body with a comforting glow, but it was Alicia's lavish kisses that had set his blood aflame with desire. He felt her fingertips at his nape, lightly sifting his hair with a fluttering caress. That was what he craved, the tenderness of her touch, the magical spell of true affection. He had fought the attraction between them with such little enthusiasm it was no wonder he had confused her so, but his intentions were shockingly clear now. He wanted her with a desperation that stunned him. He refused to acknowledge the constraints his rational mind had invented to keep them apart and instead released the full force of his passion. There was no turning back now, for he was determined to claim what he knew had been meant to be his all along. He began then with a calculated expertise to lure her gradually toward the ultimate bliss. His touch was light, teasing, for he thought of her as fragile, as delicate as her blond beauty made her appear. He moved very gently, seemingly in no rush, when the force of his desire made such a relaxed pace a nearly impossible feat.

The slow, rocking motion of the ship as it sped through the night forced Alicia to cling to Rafael for balance, but her thinking was now so far from lucid she wanted only to enjoy the pleasure she had found in his arms. She let her shawl slip to the floor and made not the slightest protest when he began to undress her. In return, she slipped her hands beneath his shirt to caress his bare skin. His flesh was very warm, alive beneath her fingertips, the muscles of his broad back rippling as he cast away first her gown and then the seemingly endless layers of her lavender-scented lingerie. When he began to carress her bare breast, her breathing quickened to match his, catching in the back of her throat with a low moan that was nearly a sob of pain. His touch was very soft, yet so knowing he swiftly drew her emotions to the surface where his caress was the most exquisite of tortures. She wanted to help him remove his clothes, to feel the heat of his body along the whole length of hers, and, sensing her impatience was as great as his own, he stepped back, pulled his shirt off over his head, and flung it aside.

Surprisingly, for a modest young woman, she felt no shame in being nude. She expected him to speak pretty compliments if not make a declaration of love, but he remained silent. His lashes were as long and thick as her own, shadowing the gaze she hoped was at least appreciative if not openly adoring, but she had no further interest in attempting to read his thoughts when he drew her back into his arms. His kisses were filled with a hunger she had never before understood but now shared in full measure. When he led her the short distance to his bunk, she had no doubt what they were doing was right, for the tenderness of his touch and the devotion in his kisses spoke of love far more eloquently than any of the flattering words she had longed to hear.

The creamy smoothness of Alicia's fair skin invited his touch and Rafael let his fingertips drift down her ribs, over her hip, and along the length of her slender thigh to her dimpled knee before returning to the pale pink tip of her ample breast. He thought her elegant proportions perfection and drew away only long enough to douse the lamp and remove the last of his clothing before he joined her upon the narrow bunk. No man enjoyed making love more than he, but Alicia was precious to him, and so different from his usual partners he was sorry the setting was no better. "I wish we could make love under the stars, or—"

Alicia silenced his apology with the sweetness of her kiss. "Hush, we need no more than each other."

Amazed by the truth of her words, Rafael kissed each of her fingertips tenderly and made no further excuses for the spartan furnishings of his cabin. He pressed her slender body close to his, meaning to teach her all of love's mysteries in a single night. He wanted to lead her slowly to the brink of rapture so that when he took her she would feel only the greatest pleasure and not the slightest twinge of pain, but when her hands moved restlessly through the dark curls covering his chest, then slid down the taut muscles of his stomach, he could think of nothing but how desperately he longed to possess her. Her touch was not the shy, hesitant caress of a virgin but the tantalizing invitation of a woman who was in every way his equal. He did not brush her hand away as her fingers encircled his now throbbing manhood, but instead he lowered his mouth to her breast where he matched the rhythm of his tongue to her exotic touch. He knew the secrets of a woman's body so well his hand slid easily over the flatness of her stomach and through the soft triangle of curls below to sample the warm, moist sweetness hidden between her slender thighs. She lay so gracefully in his embrace, her manner open and inviting as she thrust her hips closer when he pretended to draw his hand away. Knowing precisely what she craved, he pressed closer still, the warmth of his fingertips now slight compared to the fire he had ignited within her lissome body. With an abandon he had never before experienced, he let the heat of that passion lead him until he knew the moment of complete surrender could no longer be delayed and he moved upon her to end the torment she had created within his heart.

He covered her mouth quickly with his, his tongue capturing hers to muffle any cry of pain he might cause her, but only joy flavored her kiss and not the slightest taste of fear. He had never felt so alive, as if each particle of his being were seeking release, and as that tidal wave of pleasure crested within him, he felt it shudder through her as well, stunning them both with the power of the blossoming love he knew it had been insanity to deny. In his mind he saw her blow him a kiss from the cliff, an enchanted princess who had then vanished in the sparkle of the sunlight, and he held her all the more tightly, the prospect of losing her again so painful he never wanted to let her go.

Alicia clung to Rafael, so filled with the wonder of what they had shared she had no need to speak. The searing pain that had torn through her loins at his first deep thrust had been swiftly diffused by a pleasure so intense she was astonished the knowledge of that beauty had been kept secret from her. Naïve did not begin to describe what she had been before that night and now that she understood the depth of the joy God had intended a man and woman to share, she sensed she would never be the same. She felt at peace for the first time in her life and knew it was only because she had given herself so completely to the fascinating man in her arms. Her hands moved over his broad shoulders, then back to ruffle his dark, shiny hair. She wanted both to laugh and cry, she was so delighted to have found such heady enchantment with him. When he began to kiss her again, his passion now filled with a wonderfully familiar sweetness, she realized instantly that they had found a pleasure in each other's arms that could be recaptured again and again. The warmth of her response left no doubt in his mind that her desire was still as intense as his, an endless longing only he could satisfy, and the night passed all too swiftly for them both. She did not sleep a moment until she returned to her cabin just before dawn, and then her dreams were so filled with him it seemed as though their bodies were still entwined as tightly as their hearts.

Chapter VII

It was nearly noon before Alicia appeared on deck. She had just washed her hair and shook it out as she joined Flame, apparently completely absorbed in combing her long curls through her fingers.

"I'm glad to see you," the petite redhead greeted her warmly. "Another minute or two and I'd have gone looking for you."

Alicia repeated the excuse she had carefully rehearsed; since it was logical, she prayed it would not be questioned. "I made the mistake of staying up late last night to finish a book. I wasn't sleepy at all then, but I certainly was this morning." She had spent a full fifteen minutes at her mirror trying to tame the width of her smile while she had practiced that explanation. However, she was still afraid the delight that lit her expression would give away the joy overflowing her heart no matter how hard she tried to suppress it.

"I'll have to get that book from you if it's so exciting. Not that I've found any time to read," Flame admitted readily. "I love sailing, don't you? The days are too pretty to spend anywhere but up here on deck. As for the nights, well, Joaquin usually commands my undivided attention then," she confided with a saucy grin.

"Yes, I imagine he does," Alicia agreed with a newfound appreciation for the love Flame and her handsome half-brother shared. She was relieved when her companion kept the conversation light, as she had been terribly afraid her late arrival would cause a curiosity that could not be satisfied so easily. She would have to choose one of the books she had brought along and give it to Flame before she forgot what she had used as an excuse. Greatly relieved the redhead had not been in the least bit suspicious, she glanced down the rail and noticed Domingo's guard lounging nearby, though his young charge was nowhere in sight. That was such an unusual occurrence that she waited a few minutes to be certain he wouldn't appear before she turned to Flame. "Where do you suppose Domingo is? Is it possible Arturo finally ran out of work for him?"

Flame frowned slightly, obviously not eager to discuss the young man who had caused her so much worry. "He got himself tossed in the brig. Apparently he violated some rule of Rafael's last night, so he was locked up first thing this morning."

That announcement came as such a dreadful shock that Alicia was instantly overcome by the same paralyzing fear that had filled her late-night meeting with Domingo. She could barely summon the breath to speak. "Just what did he do? Do you know?"

Flame shrugged nonchalantly. "No, I didn't bother to ask since I really didn't care. I'm sure he deserved to be punished though."

While Alicia readily understood the reason for Flame's detachment, she had a terrible suspicion she should have kept Domingo's fears to herself, for if her conversation with Rafael had caused the youth to suffer, she would never forgive herself. "Just where is the brig?" she asked anxiously.

"Why? Do you want to visit him?" Flame teased with

a lilting giggle.

"Yes!" Alicia replied immediately. "Just take me there, please. You needn't stay."

"You can't possibly be serious!" Flame scoffed in disbelief, her long, dark lashes nearly sweeping her brows in her surprise.

"I most certainly am. I have to speak wtih Domingo about something quite urgent. Now let's go!" Alicia reached out to take her sister-in-law's arm, determined to see for herself how the young man had fared.

Flame looked toward the stern where Joaquin was engaged in an animated conversation with Arturo Duran. Thinking they had better hurry before he discovered where Alicia wanted to go and forbid it, she agreed. "Well, I suppose there's no harm in my taking you to the brig, but you really mustn't stay longer than a minute."

"Fine, I won't," Alicia assured her. "Let's just hurry and go."

Flame was far too clever a young woman to risk visiting Domingo alone and went quickly to summon the man who had been assigned to guard him. He was one of the *vaqueros* she knew by name and she spoke to him with a honey-smooth command. "Tomás, come with us, please." She walked straight to the companion-way and hurried down the steps, but rather than turning toward the stern where their cabins were located, she went toward the bow. When she reached the next ladder, she led them down to the deck below.

"The brig is no more than a closet near the forward hold. Bring that lantern, Tomás, or we shan't be able to find it."

"Sí, señora." Tomás took the lantern hanging upon a nearby peg, lit it quickly, and held it aloft to light their way. When they came to a small door secured with a brass padlock, he stood aside as Flame reached up to

135

remove the key from a hook just above the door.

"Joaquin leaves the key right here so no prisoner would ever be left to perish should the ship meet with an unforeseen disaster."

"How considerate of him," Alicia remarked absently, musing that if the sleek vessel were to encounter some grave peril, she doubted any of the crew would remember to free a poor soul imprisoned in the brig. She found the close quarters below deck so objectionable she couldn't imagine how anyone penned up down there could possibly keep his sanity for more than an hour or two. Knowing Domingo wasn't all that reasonable at the best of times, she was truly worried about him. When Flame unlocked the door, Tomás stepped forward to block the prisoner's exit, but he need not have taken such a precaution, for the youth was in no condition to flee. He was seated at the rear of the small cell with his arms propped across his knees to cradle his head. As he looked up to see who had opened the door, his bruised and battered face caused even the tough *vaquero* to cry out in surprise.

Horrified, Alicia pushed past Tomás, knelt at Domingo's side, and put her arm around him. "Why did Rafael do this to you?" she asked in a voice choked with tears.

Domingo's right eye was swollen shut and he had to squint with his left to see her clearly. *"Puta!"* he swore angrily as he recognized her from her flowing blond hair.

Alicia was so accustomed to his foul temper that she did not even flinch at that insult but instead gripped Domingo's shoulders more tightly. "We've no time for your temper tantrums. Just tell me why he did this!"

Domingo shrank from her touch, ashamed he had not been able to defend himself better. "Because I trusted you, *tía.*" He was so miserable he was near tears but would not permit himself to display that weakness in front of her. "It seems they mean to kill me slowly."

Her worst suspicions confirmed, Alicia turned to look up at Flame. "Did you know he had been beaten so badly?"

Transfixed by the bloody mess that had been Domingo's face, the redhead shook her head emphatically. "I had no idea, but Rafael does nothing without a reason, so he must have had a very good one for doing something as awful as this."

Alicia was so thoroughly sickened by what the attorney had done to the handsome boy, she was positive he could have no possible justification for such brutality. "I don't want him left here alone when he's so badly hurt. There's got to be somewhere else he can stay." She patted his hair lightly, meaning to offer comfort, but Domingo pulled away, obviously repelled by her touch, and she rose to her feet rather than upset him further.

Tomás was touched by the pretty blonde's compassion and yet he was certain the miserable youth had been more than deserving of the punishment he had received. "If Señor Ramirez wants him kept in there, then there is where he must stay, *señ*orita."

Afraid he was right, Alicia asked Tomás to stay with Domingo for a moment. She grabbed Flame's hand to bring her along and ran back to the ladder. She climbed it hurriedly, then dashed to the next one, and when she reached the deck she had to stop to catch her breath before she approached Joaquin. She kept telling herself that Rafael worked for him and that she would be a fool to blame him for being so brutal if by some remote chance he had merely been carrying out her brother's orders.

Joaquin needed only one glance at Alicia's anxious frown to know something was troubling her and he

137

came forward to meet her. "What's happened?" He pushed her still damp curls away from her forehead and leaned down to give her a comforting kiss.

"Did you tell Rafael to give Domingo a beating?" she asked breathlessly. "Was that your idea or his?"

Joaquin looked over her head to see his wife running toward him. Her mood appeared to be no better than Alicia's and he chose his words carefully so as not to offend either of them. "Rafael makes his own decisions in all things, but I did not tell him not to do it. If you are looking for someone to blame, then look no further, for I am captain of *La Reina* and responsible for everything that happens on board."

Alicia bit her lower lip fiercely to force back her tears. She was devastated to think she knew so little about the man with whom she had spent the most incredible night of her life. She had thought him a gentleman, a man of honor, but clearly he was nothing of the kind. "You needn't accept the blame for Rafael's brutality, but you mustn't leave Domingo shut up like that. You just can't!"

Joaquin raised a brow quizzically. "I give the orders here, Alicia, not you. Must I remind you of that?"

"No, but—" The blonde had just begun to argue that Domingo did not deserve to be so badly mistreated when Joaquin interrupted her.

"I am certain Domingo has suffered no permanent injury and I'll not keep him confined once we reach Eduardo's ranch. A few days to contemplate the folly of his actions will do him more good than harm, but just to reassure you, I will take him his rations myself. Now I suggest you find something more worthwhile to occupy your thoughts rather than worrying about Domingo's comfort, since he'd give scant consideration to yours."

Alicia turned to Flame hoping for support, but as the

redhead slipped her arm around her husband's waist, she saw clearly where her sister-in-law's sympathies lay. "Is that a promise?" she finally asked.

"Yes," Joaquin assured her with a ready grin. "You needn't give the state of Domingo's health another thought. I will see to him myself."

"Thank you," Alicia responded dejectedly, sorry she had not been able to plead Domingo's cause more eloquently. She had wanted him released, not merely well tended. Totally dissatisfied with her efforts on Domingo's behalf, she was filled with fury as she turned away. She left her brother and Flame to enjoy the sunshine alone while she walked straight to Rafael's cabin, meaning to get their inevitable confrontation over with as quickly as possible, since there was no reason to delay it. She knew she would be lucky not to become violently ill the minute she saw him, but that was a risk she was willing to take. Her anger supplied a generous amount of courage, and when she reached his door, she pounded on it with a furious beat.

Thinking some sort of dire emergency must necessitate his immediate presence on deck, Rafael leapt up from the chair at the small desk and rushed to open the door. Relieved to find Alicia, he looked quickly to make certain no one was lurking about who might observe them together, then drew her inside. "We need to talk, but my cabin certainly isn't the place," he cautioned in a stern whisper. He was so excited to see her he wanted to pull her into his arms and smother her pretty face with kisses, but sincere in his request for discretion, he made no such foolhardy move.

"More lectures?" Alicia responded sarcastically, making no effort to speak softly as she wheeled around to face him. "Somehow I'd hoped we'd gotten beyond that." Her eyes narrowed to menacing slits as her glance moved over him in a disdainful sweep. She folded her arms over her bosom and tapped her foot impatiently. "I'm sorry to disappoint you, but I didn't come here to repeat what happened between us last night. When I told you about my conversation with Domingo, I expected you to respect my confidence, not to use the information I gave you against him. I thought attorneys knew how to keep secrets!"

Rafael pursed his lips thoughtfully, not pleased to again find the lovely blonde nearly hysterical. "Conversations between an attorney and his client are considered privileged, that is correct, but I am working for Joaquin, not you."

"That fact didn't give you the right to beat Domingo so unmercifully!" Alicia insisted sharply, disgusted he would try to justify his actions with so pitiful an excuse. Surely he felt some sense of loyalty to her after the night they had shared, and that bond should have received every bit as much consideration as his responsibility to Joaquin.

Rafael sighed impatiently, sorry she was again behaving like an idealistic child when he wanted to consider her a woman, his woman. "I made only two demands of Domingo. One, that he follow Arturo's orders, and two, that he keep his opinions to himself. By going to you, he clearly violated our agreement and he was fully aware of the consequences."

"You mean he expected a savage beating? He took that risk when he came to me?" Alicia asked with a renewed sense of guilt, for he had told her not to go to her brother with his fears and she should have been wise enough to realize speaking with Rafael had carried exactly the same peril.

"No, of course not," Rafael assured her. "I wouldn't have touched him, but he made the mistake of throwing a punch at me. Since I'd not take that abuse from any man, he was no exception."

140

"There's not a mark on you!" Alicia responded accusingly, certain he was lying. He looked remarkably refreshed considering they had gotten so little sleep, and his handsome features were unblemished by any bruise or scrape. If he had actually been in a fight with Domingo, it had plainly been completely one-sided.

"That's because I blocked his blows, while I had no trouble landing my own," Rafael explained smugly.

He was obviously proud of himself for such prowess, but that only infuriated Alicia all the more. "So Domingo made the first mistake by trusting me, and I made the second one by trusting you. I know he is difficult to handle, but he didn't deserve to be beaten within an inch of his life for confiding his fears in me!"

Rafael smiled as he shook his head. "You mustn't be so melodramatic. His life was never at risk. I taught him a valuable lesson and someday he'll thank me for it."

Astonished by such twisted logic, Alicia lashed out at him again. "What lesson was that? Not to trust a woman?"

That question struck Rafael as wildly amusing, but he knew better than to answer it in the affirmative when it would surely send Alicia into a black rage. "I am doing my best to teach that loudmouthed brat to control his temper, because the next man he crosses might simply shoot him dead rather than try to teach him a lesson with his fists. He brought his current predicament upon himself and I'll not apologize for it."

Alicia stared coldly at the man she had so recently thought she loved, appalled to find him so calculating and cruel, so totally devoid of conscience. "You're disgusting, that's what you are, and I doubt you could teach anyone anything worth learning!" With that bitter farewell she left his cabin and went to her own, where she quickly bolted the door. She had never been so terribly confused and simply didn't know what to do about it. She crawled up on her bunk and hugged her knees tightly, trying not to give in to the angry tears of frustration that threatened to spill over her lashes in an endless stream. Rafael Ramirez was a scoundrel of the very worst sort. He had used her body for his own pleasure, all the while plotting to use her confidence as an excuse to give Domingo a savage beating. She had never met a more despicable human being and she never wanted to see him again, ever. To sit at the same table with him was unthinkable and she vowed to take the rest of her meals in the privacy of her cabin.

When Alicia did not soon reappear on deck, Flame went to find her. She knocked lightly at her door and waited to be invited to enter, hoping she had not disturbed her sister-in-law if she had decided to take a nap.

"Who is it?" Alicia called out apprehensively, in no mood to speak with Rafael again.

"It's Flame. May I see you a minute?"

Alicia hesitated a long while before sliding off the bunk and going to the door. "I'd really rather be alone if you don't mind," she explained without a trace of a smile.

Flame disagreed and gracefully swept past her. "I can understand how severely you were shocked to discover what had happened to Domingo, but he really isn't your concern. Rafael knows exactly what he's doing every minute of the day. He would not have abused Domingo simply for the fun of it. He's not like that at all. He'd be angry with me for telling you this, but truly he has a very sensitive nature, which he's usually too proud to reveal. I'd hoped the two of you would like each other and I don't want someone as spoiled and spiteful as Domingo to come between you when he's just not worth it."

142

Since Flame seemed firmly planted in the middle of her cabin, Alicia closed her door and leaned back against it. "I happen to think he is," she argued forcefully. "I'd rather take my meals here than suffer through another evening in Rafael's company when I couldn't look at him without seeing the bloody mess he made of Domingo's face. That would leave me with no appetite at all, to say nothing of what I'd be tempted to say to him as dinner conversation."

Flame couldn't understand what had come over the usually cool, self-contained Alicia. "You can't mean that. I can't believe you are so shocked by the way Domingo was treated when he has taken such delight in insulting us all. In fact, he just called you a whore. Didn't you realize that's what *puta* is? I can just imagine what he said to Rafael this morning and it's no wonder he got the worst of it." When Alicia's defiant expression did not soften, Flame tried another tactic. "Surely you must know your own father is as ruthless a man as Rafael or Joaquin will ever be. All of the railroad barons are!"

"My father has nothing to do with this!" Alicia insisted tearfully, suddenly overwhelmed with a desperate longing for the tranquillity of her home. She had longed for adventure. Well, she had certainly found it, but if her life had been too placid in San Francisco, at least she had felt safe there. Now she only felt betrayed, thoroughly and completely betrayed. "I'm sorry, Flame, but what you don't understand is that Domingo came to me because he was frightened for his life. I told Rafael, hoping he'd reassure him that he had nothing to fear, but instead he beat him for confiding in me. He never should have done that, not to Domingo nor to me."

"What?" Flame needed only a second to study Alicia's pained expression to realize how deeply she had been hurt. "I won't try to apologize for Rafael other than to say he does nothing capriciously. He would not have violated your confidence unless he had a very good reason to do so, and apparently he thought he did. I can readily understand why you're so hurt and angry with him. If it will truly make you feel better, I'll see that your meals are served here for as long as you like."

"Thank you," Alicia responded gratefully, not up to another argument that day. "I'm sorry. I know this will make things awkward for you and Joaquin." She stepped forward to give her sister-in-law an appreciative hug, then opened the door for her. "Just say I'm seasick or something."

Flame laughed at such a transparent ruse. "I'll do no such thing. I'll simply say you prefer to have your supper in your cabin and let Rafael make up his own mind as to the reason. I think you're probably just overtired since you stayed up so late. Why don't you take a nap, or go to sleep early tonight, or better yet, do both."

"Yes, I think I will." Alicia remembered the book that had supposedly kept her awake and quickly grabbed one she hoped would seem exciting to Flame. "Here, I'll give you this novel now so I'm not tempted to read it again and lose another night's sleep."

Flame glanced at the title and shrugged. "I'd better not risk beginning this until after we reach Eduardo's ranch. With Joaquin gone for a few days I'll welcome some amusement to brighten my evenings."

Alicia smiled with relief as the redhead went on her way, praying Flame would never discover what she had really been doing the previous night.

Rafael knew without asking why Alicia had not

joined them for supper, but that made the pain of her insult no less acute. They had to talk, calmly and rationally, about what had happened between them, and if she planned to avoid him for the rest of the voyage, they could come to no decisions at all. He barely tasted his food, took little part in the conversation, and left without accepting a brandy. It had been the brandy that had been his downfall the previous night and he wanted no repetition of that folly. Doubting Flame and Joaquin would leave their cabin, he nevertheless waited for a long while in his own to be certain they wouldn't decide to go up on deck before he felt reasonably safe in going to see Alicia. He knocked politely on her door, and when he heard her reply, he spoke in what he hoped would be an encouraging tone. "It's Rafael. We can go up on deck if you like, but we've got to talk."

Alicia wasn't really surprised that he had come to see her, only that he had come so soon. She had not touched her supper or been able to concentrate on the book she had wanted to read. She just felt numb and did not want anything further to do with him when she feared it would only bring more pain. "I'd rather not," she replied icily.

"Well, we must!" Rafael insisted, hoping Flame and Joaquin would by that time be so fascinated with each other they would not overhear him. God, that was all he'd need, to have those two teasing him about his lack of success with Alicia. On the other hand, if they discovered how extremely successful he had been, they'd surely have his hide. "Damn it, either you come out here or I'm coming in!"

"Don't bother!" Alicia responded caustically. She held her breath then, expecting him to simply come crashing through the louvered door, but to her amazement she heard him walk away. So that was all he thought of her! If she'd not bow to his wishes immediately, he'd simply refuse to pursue whatever effort he'd planned to try to please her. She put her head in her hands and tried to understand how she had gotten herself into such an awful mess. She had simply been seduced by the first real man she had ever met, a man who cared so little for her he would use her confidences to hurt a mere boy. She was only a year older than Domingo, she reminded herself, but he seemed so very young still, while she had considered herself a woman. "Some woman you are!" she whispered accusingly, sorry she had agreed to come on the voyage since it was turning out so badly. When she heard a key in the lock, she scrambled off the bed, but before she could reach the door, Rafael had opened it.

"Arturo had extra keys," he explained with a rakish grin, and scooping her up in to his arms, he carried her up on deck while she was still too shocked by his unexpected entrance to make her protests effectively. He was grateful she didn't start screaming for her brother and hoped she realized that the need for discretion was imperative. When he placed her upon her feet, she turned away ready to run, but he grabbed her wrist and swung her back around to face him. "I know you're furious with me for the way I handled Domingo. I know that and we needn't waste any time going over that disagreement again when we have something far more important to discuss."

"I don't care what the topic is, I've nothing to say to you!" Alicia responded with a spirited toss of her long curls. Since she had dined alone in her room, she had not bothered to arrange her hair and it fell to her waist in a soft profusion of dancing waves.

"All right, just keep still then and I will do all the talking." Rafael drew her alongside an overturned barrel, sat down on it, and with a quick tug pulled her down upon his lap. "Put your arms around my neck and you'll be more comfortable," he invited with his most charming grin.

"I'd rather not." Alicia sat perched stiffly upon his knee, certain she had no wish to hear anything he might have to say. Being in his arms again was pure torture now that she knew how superficial his abundant affection had been, and she wanted only to be left alone, for she was so ashamed of how easily he had fooled her.

"Whatever," Rafael agreed politely. "Regardless of your low opinion of me, I am very fond of you, Alicia. I have no excuses to offer for my lack of restraint last night; perhaps that encounter was simply inevitable between us because I'd wanted it to happen so badly. I know you're not the type of woman to engage in casual affairs, and believe me that's not what I had in mind. When this regrettable business with Domingo is over, I'd like to accompany you home to San Francisco. I'll speak to your parents and ask for your hand properly. I always meant to do the right thing, truly I did. There just wasn't time to talk about it last night."

Alicia sat in stunned silence, her eyes stinging with the tears she could no longer contain. She had not even suspected he had wanted to see her in order to propose, but what disappointed her most was that his motive seemed to be one of guilt rather than love. He hadn't even mentioned the word *love*. He was fond of her, that's what he had said—fond. He had wanted her, that much had been plain in his very first kiss, but obviously only because she was pretty, not out of any deep regard for her as a person. Clearly he could have no regard for her at all and do what he had done that morning. "I'd like to go back to my cabin now," she requested calmly. "I haven't the slightest wish to marry a man who would undoubtedly betray my every confidence as swiftly as you did the first. That is completely out of the question, for no marriage can ever exist between a man and woman who don't trust each other and I will never trust you again."

That coolly worded rejection infuriated Rafael so greatly he could barely see as he released her hand and helped her rise. "Should a man dare to insult me as you just have by questioning the value of my word, he'd be fortunate to escape with his life. You don't know how lucky you are that I'm willing to forgive you. You've simply twisted what happened, distorted Domingo's ravings so completely you think I am the troublemaker here instead of him." When she merely stared at him coldly, clearly not swayed by that argument, he quickly took another tack. "I could go to Joaquin right now and tell him what happened between us last night and we'd be married within the hour."

"You wouldn't!" Alicia cried out in dismay, horrified by so humiliating a prospect.

"No, I wouldn't because I am a gentleman, regardless of how low, and how wrong, your opinion of me is. I have done you the courtesy of offering marriage and you have refused very rudely. If you find a marriage between us to be necessary, you will have to propose to me and pray that I have far better manners than you!"

Her cheeks burning with a bright blush, Alicia watched in stunned silence as Rafael strode off down the deck. She had been so thrilled by his affection she had shoved the thought of becoming pregnant to the very back of her mind, but now she knew just what a stupid fool she had really been. She had given herself to the most heartless man alive and the thought of bearing his child absolutely terrified her. She knew there were potions a woman could take to avoid having a child, and at the risk of her own life she'd gladly take one before she'd marry him. She sagged back against the rail, so thoroughly distraught she didn't return to her cabin until she had become so chilled her teeth were chattering. When she awakened the next morning with a blinding headache and upset stomach, she was glad she had gotten sick, for it gave her the perfect excuse to remain in her cabin where Rafael Ramirez could not torment her anew. She had completely forgotten that he now had a key to her door.

Flame sat with Alicia for a good part of the morning before the blonde could convince her her presence was not really needed. "Are you certain I can't bring you more tea or perhaps some soup? I'd be happy to do it. When the weather has been so warm I simply don't understand how you could have fallen ill, but I'll do whatever I can to make you feel better."

Although she appreciated her kindness, Alicia smiled wanly. "You are so sweet to offer, but really I don't feel like eating and you've already forced me to drink so much tea I couldn't possibly take another sip. I think I'll just try to take a nap. Maybe I'll feel better when I wake up. You needn't stay here to watch me sleep."

Flame held the back of her hand to Alicia's forehead and frowned pensively. "You're still feverish and I certainly don't want to keep you awake if you'd rather sleep. I'll come back later though. Maybe then you'll want something to eat or I could read to you. I do read very well, despite the fact I seldom have the time to do it," she teased playfully.

"Yes, that would be nice. Until later then." Alicia raised her hand to cover a wide yawn as she snuggled down into her pillow. "I'm already falling asleep and I'm sure I'll be fine here by myself." She truly did want to be left alone but was too polite to state that request any more emphatically than she had. As soon as Flame had gone, she drew the covers up to her chin and closed her eyes, hoping that she really could fall asleep. She was certain morning sickness couldn't possibly begin so soon, but that was scant consolation when she felt so wretched. She was never sick, simply never, but she had to admit she certainly was now. She had been so chilled by Rafael's unemotional proposal that she hadn't noticed the chill of the wind and that had obviously been a serious mistake. She could not blame him though; it was her own fault she had been so careless and no one else's.

She turned her thoughts then to how pleasant a place Eduardo Lopez's ranch must be. He was a wealthy man, probably not nearly as rich as Joaquin, but still he would have a gracious home; she was certain of that. It would be nice to have somewhere new to ride and someone new to fill her hours with happiness instead of the bitter disappointment Rafael Ramirez had provided. Damn the man! She punched her pillow angrily then, wishing it were his handsome face, and unable to force his taunting image from her mind, she drifted off to sleep and again dreamed of him.

When Rafael reached the brig, he was surprised to find Joaquin seated by the open door chatting easily with Domingo as the young man ate what was clearly an ample meal rather than the bread and water with which he had been threatened. Embarrassed to have been caught disregarding his own orders, Joaquin scrambled to his feet and dusted off the seat of his pants. "I've been trying to reassure our prisoner that while his accommodations are more than merely spartan I'll see that his rations aren't. I've spent too many days trying to put some meat on his bones to let him waste away now."

Rafael tried not to laugh, but it amused him to think Joaquin had become so compassionate. He had told Alicia that Flame had tamed his friend and this was clearly evidence of how agreeable the once-arrogant man had become. He glanced into the small cell and was glad to see that Domingo looked so much better. His face was not nearly as swollen as it had been the day before, and what few cuts he had inflicted had begun to heal. "Flame mentioned to me that she planned to read to Alicia this afternoon, but I thought perhaps Domingo would rather do it. You can read, can't you?"

It was Joaquin who had to hide his smile then, for he thought his friend had chosen a truly remarkable way to try to win his sister's forgiveness. "Well, Domingo, can you read? It's not a question of whether or not you wish to perform this small service, just a question of whether you can."

Domingo needed a moment to swallow a mouthful of stew before he could reply. He had been desperately hungry and was thoroughly disgusted to think he had to depend upon Joaquin Villarreal's generosity for his very survival. It had to be some trick, of that he was certain, but he had chosen to eat the food he had been brought and worry about his captor's motives later. "I can read," he finally announced proudly, then thought to ask, "Why can't Alicia read to herself?"

"Miss Caldwell, to you. Unfortunately she's made herself ill worrying about you," Rafael remarked matter-of-factly. "So it seems only right that you should be the one to keep her entertained for an hour or two."

Domingo looked down at his sweat-stained clothes, then ran his fingers through his hair, which had become no more than an unruly thatch. "I do not think I am fit company for a young lady."

151

"No, you're not, but after you bathe and dress you will be," Rafael assured him. He turned then to Joaquin. "I'll stay with him and see that this time when he's given an order he follows it to the letter."

"I'm sure you will." Joaquin winked slyly at his friend and as he left him he began to wonder if perhaps his remarkably perceptive wife hadn't been correct and that Rafael and his sister were attracted to each other. They would make a handsome pair, but he would keep such thoughts to himself rather than ever admit to Flame that she had seen something he hadn't.

Chapter VIII

Rafael had the copper bathtub taken to his cabin, but he made Domingo fetch his own hot water. "Just strip off all your clothes. Maybe if they're boiled, they'll come clean."

Domingo looked around the cabin, his glance as always apprehensive. There was a bar of soap and a towel lying at the foot of the bunk, but he knew he did not want to spend a good portion of the day half naked while he waited for his clothes to dry. "I'll need more clothes," he finally pointed out grudgingly.

"You have others. Better go and get them before the water cools." Rafael gestured toward the door. "Well, go on, get moving."

Domingo had a change or two of clothing, but he knew none of it was clean. "It all needs to be washed," he admitted reluctantly.

"Fine. You can spend part of the afternoon doing your laundry. Just get into the tub and get yourself clean first." When the youth didn't move, Rafael gave him a helpful nudge. "Go on, don't be shy. I'll lend you a pair of pants and a shirt so you'll be presentable for Miss Caldwell, but I'll expect them to be returned to me spotlessly clean."

Rafael had no intention of leaving the young man alone in his cabin, but he could see how reluctant Domingo was to strip and bathe in front of him. Such an unexpected display of modesty was surprising in so independent a boy and he began to wonder if much of his manner wasn't simply false bravado. He got out an old pair of woolen pants he wore for riding, a cotton shirt he would not miss, clean underwear, and socks. He had brought plenty of clothes and knew he would not need these things for the next few days. Tossing them upon the bed in a careless heap, he sat down at the desk and began to sift through the notes he had made. Hoping Domingo would feel more comfortable with his back turned toward him, he was nevertheless still alert to a possible assault from behind and was confident he had reflexes sufficiently quick to block it successfully. After a few tense seconds, he heard the young man finally take off his badly soiled clothes and step into the tub. Rafael hid his smile as he heard him scrubbing away with the soap. He could hardly wait to see Alicia's face when he brought Domingo to see her.

Dressed in Rafael's clothes, freshly shaven, and with his hair still damp but combed neatly back from his forehead, Domingo had no more than a black and swollen eye and a few superficial cuts to show for his ordeal. Rafael stood back to give him a final glance, then obviously pleased with what he saw, he nodded approvingly. "I'm going to leave my door open as well as hers. If I hear one single word of complaint from Miss Caldwell, you'll go right back into the brig. Is that clear? She must be delighted with your visit or it will swiftly end."

Domingo straightened up proudly, again certain the wily attorney was up to no good. He had been greatly confused by Alicia's show of concern for him the previous day since she had to know the beating he had received had been her fault. He had no idea what to say to her now. It was difficult to know what to do to stay ahead of the man whose clothes he wore, but having to read aloud for an hour or two was certainly preferable to being shut up again in that dark, cramped cell. "Do not worry, I have good manners," he announced confidently.

"You could have fooled me." Rafael laughed at the unintended joke. "Let's see if she's ready for you."

Rafael had seen Flame walk by carrying a tray bearing a bowl of soup, which was no small accomplishment on board a sailing vessel where the angle of the deck beneath their feet was constantly shifting. He knew Alicia had now had time to finish her lunch and when he knocked at her door Flame opened it. Since Joaquin had already told her what he planned to do, she winked at him and slipped out the door to make room for him to enter.

Alicia stared venomously at Rafael, but before she could tell him to get out of her cabin with the string of biting insults she thought he deserved, he ushered Domingo through the door. That the young man was not only neatly groomed but apparently fit was such a surprise, she waited a moment too long to speak.

"I can see how pleased you are to see us," Rafael remarked with a broad grin. "I hope you'll forgive me for not staying to talk with you myself, but Domingo has volunteered to read to you for awhile." Completing this brief explanation, he promptly turned on his heel and left the two of them to manage their visit by themselves, but just as he had promised, he left her door slightly ajar and his wide open.

Alicia was horribly embarrassed, for she had given no attention to combing her hair after her nap and knew she must look a fright. She hurriedly tried to smooth out her tangled curls and pulled the sheet up

155

closer to her chin, afraid she had done little to improve her appearance. "Please sit down," she invited with a nervous smile.

Domingo looked back to make certain Rafael was really gone before he sat down on the edge of the chair Flame had drawn up beside the bunk. He was certain he should not be seated so close to the pretty blonde, but the cabin was a small one and he had little room to slide back and put more space between them. "I am sorry you are sick," he finally remembered to say.

"Yes, so am I," Alicia replied softly. "You look quite well though." Truly he did look far better than she had feared he ever would again. Had his wounds merely begun to heal rapidly or had he not been nearly as badly hurt as she had first imagined? "How do you feel?"

"Fine, thank you." Domingo wiped his perspiring palms on his thighs, then suddenly remembered he had been told to read to her. "I have not read a book in English in a long while, but I can do it. Would you like me to read to you?"

Moved to say something far more important, Alicia lowered her voice to a barely audible whisper. "I didn't realize Rafael would be so infuriated to find you'd spoken with me. I asked him to put you at ease, not in the brig!"

Domingo frowned sullenly, sorry he had been so foolish as to mistakenly believe she could help him. There was no one to help him but himself. Surely this was another trick, perhaps a diabolical one, since they were using her again. She was pretending to be his friend when she had betrayed his confidence with amazing speed. Clearly she was not to be trusted; none of them were. "I came here only to read," he reminded her with a sullen frown.

Alicia felt totally defeated, for it was plain Domingo

did not believe her. She would not bother with another apology since it would probably also be rejected. He was still angry with her, that much was readily apparent in the set of his jaw, and she really couldn't blame him. She should have known better than to speak to Rafael on his behalf, but truly she had not known how devoid of character the man was then. "I know you'd rather be doing something else. Why don't you just go," she offered graciously.

"But I can't!" Domingo insisted, lowering his voice to a frantic whisper.

"Why not?" Alicia asked curiously. "I've dismissed you. You may go."

Domingo glanced over his shoulder, certain the attorney would be standing nearby even though he couldn't see him. "If you don't want me to read, Ramirez will lock me up again."

Exasperated to find Domingo was still at Rafael's mercy, Alicia grabbed a book from the shelf by the bed and tossed it to him. "Here then, go ahead and read."

Domingo straightened up, cleared his throat noisily, and then opened the leather-bound volume she had chosen. *"The Three . . ."* He paused then, embarrassed he might not pronounce the next word correctly.

Alicia leaned forward to peek over the top of the book *"Musketeers,"* she offered helpfully. "Have you read this book in Spanish?"

Domingo shook his head. "There were few books in Tierrasanta."

"Well, you'll love this one. It's a very exciting story, written by a Frenchman about the king's soldiers." Certain he would be intrigued enough to begin, she leaned back upon her pillow and, getting comfortable, closed her eyes to enjoy the adventurous tale.

Domingo stared at the pale blonde for a long moment. He had never seen a woman as fair as she, but

157

he reminded himself again that she was Joaquin's sister and undoubtedly in on any plot to rid the family of his presence. He had grown up with pitifully few relatives, so there was no reason for him to need an aunt now, but he still had the nagging suspicion that he did need her. He needed help desperately and she was the only one who seemed inclined to give it He would not make the mistake of telling her any more of his secrets, but, he vowed, should she share any with him, he would put them to good use.

When Rafael looked in on them an hour later, he found Domingo so engrossed in the story he was reading aloud he had not looked up to note that Alicia was sound asleep. The attorney raised his fingertip to his lips, then reached out to take the book and replace it upon the shelf. "Go see about your laundry. The book can wait until she's awake to hear it."

Grateful to have been freed from his tiny prison regardless of the reason, Domingo rushed off to take care of his chores before the attorney could change his mind.

Alicia was sleeping peacefully, but her cheeks were flushed, her color as high as when he had carried her up on deck to propose. Had that only been last night? he wondered. The morning had been interminable and the afternoon was passing no more quickly, much to his despair. He reached out to touch her forehead lightly and found her skin far too warm. She wasn't merely angry with him then, but truly ill. Somehow he had not expected that and it made him feel all the worse. He had heard the sweetness in her voice as she had spoken to Domingo, and even though he had not tried to overhear her words, her consideration for the hot-tempered young man had annoyed him greatly, for she had never been half as understanding with him. Well, at least she had been able to see for herself that the pounding he had given Domingo had not been all that severe. If only that reassurance would work to his advantage, he hoped silently, certain that this was too much to expect just yet. His heart was heavy with his inability to convince her of his sincerity. Was he so great a stranger to love that he could not make even the slightest impression upon her? He hesitated at the door, then giving in to an impulse he could not suppress, he returned to the bunk, leaned down, and kissed the sleeping blonde. As his lips touched hers, her eyelids fluttered slightly, then opened. Alicia looked up at him, and then still half lost in the land of her fevered dreams, she smiled prettily before falling back to sleep.

Not wanting that magical moment to ever end, Rafael straightened up slowly. Had she even seen him? Had she recognized his kiss and awakened simply to give him that lovely gift of a smile? He feared he was only fooling himself with that hope. No, she had been asleep the whole time, but he knew the sight of that smile would be as impossible to forget as all his other memories of her.

Rafael had no sooner closed Alicia's door than he began to miss her. That feeling of emptiness wasn't completely unknown to him, but it had been a long while since he had cared enough about a woman to truly miss her company. Perhaps if he came back later she would be in a reasonable mood. The odds of that occurring were slim, he knew, but he was determined to try.

Despite Rafael's hopes for a late afternoon visit with the ailing blonde, Joaquin had a more urgent need for him. He had questions of his own and hoped his friend could supply the answers. As they strolled around the deck, apparently doing no more than enjoying the sunshine, he began a series of perceptive inquiries, again going over every piece of information the attorney had uncovered. "What has Domingo told you of his childhood? Anything that might provide us with some clues?"

Rafael turned back to make certain the subject of their conversation was still engrossed in the task of laundering his clothes. Unfortunately, the boy seemed to have no more idea how to handle that chore than he did anything else. "He does not seem to have had any childhood. He was born in the spring of '56. Benito Juarez became president of Mexico in '58 and the country was soon plunged into civil war. The fury of that fighting left not even a village as remote as Tierrasanta unscathed. By the time Domingo was eight, the French had placed Maximilian of Austria on the thrown, a ruler who was scarcely loved by the common people. By the time they were able to overthrow the empire and return Juarez to power, Domingo was eleven. His mother then took the first opportunity she had had to provide schooling for the lad and placed him with the priest for tutoring, but as you already know, her purpose never was to see him enter the priesthood. So, except for the first two years of his life, which must have been relatively tranquil, he can remember nothing of his early years but bloodshed and the constant battles that raged between the warring factions. Father Ortega is apparently a stern man who believed as devoutly in education as he does in God. If Domingo did not master a lesson quickly, he was severely punished. At least that's the way he tells the story. I know the civil strife occurred, but the priest could be a saintly man who spoiled him as greatly as his mother, for all I know."

"Do you think this Father Ortega may be of some help?"

"I certainly hope so. He's got to know something about Carmela's character and I'm certain we can provide a generous enough contribution to convince him to share his wisdom with us."

Joaquin nodded impatiently. "Of course, even a modest sum would seem generous to him. While I am not nearly as keen a student of history as you, the more I thought of the bloodshed that Mexico suffered during Domingo's early years, the more I have wondered if he is even the same child who was baptized as my son."

Shocked by such a startling supposition, Rafael stopped walking abruptly, then had to shift his stance to compensate for the constant rolling motion of the deck. "God help me, Joaquin, but I would believe almost anything possible in a case as puzzling as this."

Joaquin turned back to face his befuddled friend. "I did not mean to confuse you, but merely to offer another avenue of escape. If we cannot prove the marriage certificate a hoax and the child baptized some other man's son, then let's prove Domingo isn't that child."

Rafael was amazed to learn Joaquin had seized upon such a desperate plan when he had at first appeared to be unconcerned by Domingo's charges. "Have you remembered something you've not told me? Another woman perhaps, or—"

"No!" Joaquin interrupted with a hoarse shout that was swiftly lost in the wind. They were too far from Domingo for the young man to overhear their conversation, but he still took the precaution of stepping close before he continued in a savage whisper, "Every day Flame grows more curious and more sympathetic to Domingo's plight. I know she wants to believe me, but I can give her damn little to believe while Domingo is constantly underfoot to remind her that the way I lived my life before we met was anything but moral. She knows me so well she knows anything is possible, even if I admit nothing. The fact is, I can't help but admire Domingo's spirit myself, but if the only way I can fight his lies is with some of my own, then that's what I'll have to do!"

"Well, since you have hired me to manage this 'fight,' I would prefer to use the truth, if it can be found," Rafael insisted sharply. "At least allow me to try that approach first. If that fails, then I will do whatever is necessary to protect you, you already know that."

"Of course!" Joaquin agreed readily. "We're only going to Tierrasanta in hopes of finding the truth, but if it eludes us, then—"

"Then we will face that problem then, and not before!" Rafael's dark gaze became a menacing glare as he attempted to reassure his best friend. "You know I would fight to the death by your side, but do not ask me to lie for you unless we have no other choice!"

Joaquin clenched his fists tightly at his sides, the fury of his temper nearly impossible to control. His anger was not directed at Rafael, but toward the Fates that had sent Domingo into his life simply to punish him for the wildness of his youth when he had thought he had left it far behind him. "There is no man I trust more than you. I did not mean to insult you. I obviously have and I beg your forgiveness."

Rafael hesitated no more than an instant before embracing his friend with an enthusiastic hug. "I am not offended, only as angry as you with the impossibility of our task. I have done nothing since we left the ranch but try to find some way to turn back the clock of eternity to the summer you spent in Tierrasanta so the truth might be observed as plainly as we see each other. It would have been far wiser to wait until we arrived there, for we've done little but confuse ourselves even more than we already were."

Encouraged by his friend's understanding, Joaquin slapped Rafael soundly upon the back before they continued their walk. "I know you have more than enough ideas without my contributing any, but I do think since many children are lost in any civil war my idea is a good one."

Rafael shook his head as he returned Joaquin's admiring glance. "It is positively brilliant, but I hope we do not become so desperate we have no choice but to use it."

Domingo watched the two tall men as they whispered together, cursing them soundly under his breath as he worked to scrub the collar of his shirt clean. He twisted the wet cloth so savagely he was surprised to find it unripped when he pulled it from the rinse water. They hated him. He had known that all along, and now they were undoubtedly laughing at him. His father was an arrogant swine, while his snake of an attorney had no morals either. They were as villainous a pair as had ever walked the earth and he had fallen right into their clutches. How could he have been so great a fool as to think he could demand from Joaquin Villarreal what was rightfully his when the man had scorned the woman he had promised God to love and protect? The minute the ship reached shore he would steal the first horse he saw and flee with the only treasure he would ever own: his life!

Rafael had difficulty sitting still during dinner he was so restless. He kept glancing over at the empty chair where Alicia should have been and feared his despair would show in his expression despite his best effort to be good company. He left Joaquin and Flame as soon as he could politely ask to be excused and went up on deck where he walked until he grew too chilled to continue. One thought had plagued his mind all day: what a great fool he had been to become so immersed in Joaquin's troubles he had lost Alicia's respect. There had been no time to visit her before dinner, and now, well, now he knew it was far too late to pay a proper call. When he went below to his cabin he hesitated as he passed her door, wishing he had some excuse to open it, and when he heard what seemed to be a low moan, he tried the handle before using the key he still had in his pocket. The door had not been locked, however, and peering inside, he saw Alicia had tossed the covers aside in her sleep. She was lying upon her stomach. Her gown was pulled up nearly to her hip and the creamy flesh of her slender thigh beckoned so invitingly he slipped through the door and closed it quietly behind him. He meant to do no more than see she was covered so she would not grow chilled and become even more ill, but once he had restored her gown to a more modest level and tucked her blanket in neatly around her, he could not force himself to leave. Sitting down beside her, he told himself he would remain for only a minute or two. She was still feverish, her lovely skin far too warm to his touch, and he did not want her to awaken and find no one to help her should she need something. Just watching her sleep was so pleasant a diversion he lost all track of time. He moved his chair close so he could lay his hand upon her back and patted her gently as he would a sleeping babe.

"I've been trying to do too much," he confessed softly, even though he knew she wouldn't hear. "Joaquin is my best friend and I cannot fail him. Domingo believes his cause to be a righteous one when clearly that's impossible, and that gives me no peace. Then here you are, the most beautiful young woman, who wants only the attention any man would be a fool not to give gladly, but—"

Alicia stirred slightly then, stretching with a feline grace before turning over to face him and opening her pretty blue eyes. "May I have some water?" she asked softly, her voice barely a whisper.

Startled that he had awakened her, Rafael quickly poured her a cup from the carafe at her bedside. When she struggled to sit up, he sat down on the edge of the bunk to cradle her head upon his arm and held the cup to her lips. She drank so thirstily he quickly poured her a second cup. She raised her hand then to cover his as he brought the cup to her lips and the warmth of her touch sent a jolt of desire clear through him that nearly tore a moan of anguish from his throat. When she finished that, he offered her more, but she shook her head sleepily and, closing her eyes, seemed content simply to rest in his arms. He set the cup aside, and happy for the excuse to hold her, he made no move to leave. He caressed her tangled curls and hoped she would be as receptive to his attentions when she had regained her health. When she caught his hand and brought it to her lips, he simply stared in disbelief. She kissed each of his fingertips lightly, then his palm, her gesture of affection so unexpected and so enticing he leaned down to kiss her forehead sweetly before he spoke her name. "Alicia." Was it possible she had forgiven him after all? "Alicia, I—"

Alicia looked up at him, the blue of her eyes as vivid as the summer sky, and he was lost in the wonder of her dreamy gaze. She reached up to weave her fingers in his dark, shiny hair and pulled his face close to give him a playful kiss that was so alluring he did not even think of refusing her unspoken invitation. He turned down the lamp, swiftly removed his clothes, then helped her peel away her soft linen gown before joining her in the narrow bunk. When she snuggled against him, the warmth of her breasts seared his chest with a heat he prayed was more desire than fever, for he needed her to want him as desperately as he wanted her. He pressed her supple body close, caressed the smoothness of her back, the curve of her hip, then leaned down to tease the firm tip of her breast with his tongue. He loved the sweet taste of her flesh and moved lower still, sampling the softness of her stomach as his fingertips traced lazy circles upon the tender skin of her inner thighs. Driven to know the last of the exquisite beauty's secrets, he shifted his position again to place himself between her legs and tenderly nuzzled the soft triangle of blond curls that hid his true goal.

Alicia made no attempt to end his tantalizing intimacy but laid her hands upon his shoulders to gently guide him lower still. She had found only pleasure in his arms and wanted more; whatever he wished to teach her she was more than willing to learn. His kisses were slow, his tongue teasing, then moving deeper to stir feelings so intense she gasped with wonder. His hands cupping her hips, he lifted her slightly to savor her warm, moist sweetness until he felt the tremors of pleasure spread through her with a surge he had to share. He moved over her then, his lips seeking hers hungrily as he thrust to the depths of her velvet-smooth center, exulting in the knowledge he alone had had that indescribable thrill. She was the woman God had created solely for him and he wanted her rapture to equal his own. He held his power in check, his rhythm steady as he lured her to the brink of ecstasy, then hesitated before letting the delicious tension build to ever greater heights. She clung to him, her body gracefully following his lead, taking all he could give and demanding still more until, awash with the sheer pleasure of her, he buried his face in her golden curls. He surrendered to her magic then, letting it pour through him in endless ripples, carrying them

166

aloft to the very gates of paradise where, basking in that golden radiance, they longed to stay forever.

Several hours passed before Rafael could bear to think of returning to his own cabin. He was grinning like a fool and while he could not recall ever being so blissfully happy, he was glad Alicia had fallen asleep in his arms because he knew no compliment he could pay would adequately express the joy that overflowed his heart. In so many ways they were truly one. She was his equal in every respect, bright, inquisitive, and so delightfully loving he would never tire of seeing her lovely smile at the end of the day. He was completely relaxed, more content than he had ever been, although she still had given him no answer to his proposal. Even if she had not spoken the words aloud, he felt the acceptance in her kiss and hugged her closer still. She was his woman and he wanted to make her his wife. It now seemed ridiculous to wait until he could ask for her father's permission to marry her though. The time for such a gentlemanly approach was long past. No, when they returned to San Francisco, she would already be his wife, and if her father had any objections, it would be far too late to voice them.

He knew it would soon be dawn, but still he had to force himself to leave her bed. He eased away, covered Alicia so she would continue to sleep comfortably, then hurriedly pulled on his clothes. He kissed her cheek one last time and was pleased to find her skin cool as well as soft. That their lovemaking had been so beneficial to her as well as him pleased him greatly. He held his boots in his hand as he closed her door, but as he turned toward his cabin he stopped abruptly, for Domingo was standing not three feet away.

"You bastard," the young man hissed. "You—"

Rafael wasted no time listening to insults, and throwing open his door, he grabbed Domingo's arm and pulled him inside. "Where's Tomás? He knows as well as you do that you're not to be roaming the ship alone." The young man merely stared at him, his hatred so deep it was beyond words. Rather than smash his fist into the boy's face again, which had been his first impulse, Rafael repeated his question. "Where is Tomás?"

"Asleep," Domingo finally replied with a careless shrug. "He's come to no harm."

"Well, you soon will if you don't get back where you belong. We'll reach the Lopez ranch today or I'd march you right back down to the brig. You have no business being here."

Domingo straightened up proudly. "The cook sent me to fetch a tray he'd left in my father's cabin. It is lying outside his door, but I had no time to pick it up before I saw you." Seeing a chance to finally gain the upper hand, he pushed what he was certain was a newfound advantage to the limit. "I do not think Joaquin would be pleased to know you spend the nights with his sister."

Rafael did no more than laugh, for while he knew Joaquin wouldn't be in the least bit pleased, he was certain he could counter his anger. "Not all men have to be forced into marriage, Domingo. Miss Caldwell is my fiancée and we'll be married as soon as it is convenient for both of us. We are not the first engaged couple to sample the delights of marriage and I'll wager we won't be the last. I expect you to value her reputation as highly as I do, however. Is that clear? You breathe a word of this to anyone and you will be profoundly sorry."

Domingo reached for the doorknob, certain the attorney was up to no good as usual. "She deserved far better than the likes of you!" he responded angrily.

"I agree, but nevertheless I am her choice and I'll not

argue with it. Now take the cook his tray and be quick about it." Rafael stood at his door until he saw Domingo pick up the tray and start up the ladder. Then he returned to his room and sank down upon his bunk. He had not slept more than a couple of hours, but he certainly wasn't sleepy now. "What a rotten piece of luck!" he exclaimed to himself. He was fairly confident Domingo would not go to Joaquin with a report of what he had seen, but just to be safe he would have to speak with his friend first. Joaquin would readily understand his passion for Alicia, and at least he had proposed to her and he thought she had accepted. He raked his fingers through his hair, realizing only then what a mess it was. He shook his head, certain he would be wise to speak with Alicia first and then Joaquin, since she delighted in being so contrary. At least she hadn't been in a contrary mood when she had awakened to find him in her room and he would be eternally grateful for that. Chuckling softly to himself, he stretched out on his bunk and, deciding he did feel like taking a brief nap after all, he fell sound asleep.

Chapter IX

Alicia awakened slowly, languidly enjoying the last precious memory of an incredibly enjoyable dream before she reluctantly opened her eyes. As she yawned and stretched her arms lazily above her head, she was shocked first to find she was nude and then by the sight of her nightgown, which lay carelessly tossed over the back of the cabin's single chair. She sat up straight then, trying to recall just exactly what had happened during the night. She had gone to sleep shortly after supper, tired still even though she had rested all day, but she was positive she had bathed and put on a fresh nightgown before turning her lamp down low. She never slept in the nude, so what possibly could have inspired her to remove her nightgown? Feeling slightly dizzy, she lay back down and covered her eyes with her arm.

Now fully awake, she realized the scent that clung to every inch of her silken skin was not the faint lavender fragrance of her soap and sachet but the distinctively masculine essence of Rafael Ramirez. With a low moan she rolled over on her stomach, but burying her face in the pillow only served to drown her senses in his presence, for it was more than obvious he had shared that pillow too. She began to shake then, more frightened than she had ever been, for she had not even suspected that Rafael could be so utterly ruthless that he would take advantage of her as he had.

She tried to hold back the tide of her memories but failed miserably. They simply overwhelmed her, washing over her with a crushing force. It had seemed as though she and Rafael were floating together on a dreamlike cloud, his image blurred by the darkness, the light in his eyes brighter than any stars. His touch had been as tender as a butterfly's wing and her blush deepened as she recalled how easily she had abandoned herself to that dream of love. She remembered it all with shockingly vivid clarity now. "Dear God in heaven," she cried softly, "what have I done?"

Realizing she had no time to indulge in self-pity when she would be unable to explain the cause of her tears to Flame, she pushed back the covers and rose unsteadily to her feet. Finding the door unlocked, she wondered if she had merely forgotten to lock it or if Rafael had used the key he had gotten from Arturo. Would he allow her no privacy at all? Infuriated by that prospect, she turned the bolt with a savage twist, then shoved the chair under the knob to prevent another unwanted visit. She dampened her washcloth with the drinking water still in the carafe and after adding a bit of her perfume did her best to remove all traces of his possession before hastily donning the discarded gown, which she was grateful to find bore no evidence of his touch. She brushed out her long curls, unmindful of the pain caused by the tangles, but when she glanced in her mirror she looked no less distraught than she felt. How could Rafael have used her so cruelly? How could he? Had he not the slightest respect for her or regard for her feelings? "Obviously not!" she answered herself bitterly. He had only proved it again.

While her mood continued to be one of frustrated rage, she had done all she could to make herself presentable, if without success, but she did not know what to do about the bed, for it positively reeked of him. It was a spicy-sweet smell, a combination of the pungent soap Joaquin favored and Rafael's own scent. She had thought it delicious during the night, but now it sickened her thoroughly and she wanted to be rid of all such blatant evidence of his late-night visit. She pulled the pillow from its slip, yanked the sheets from the bed, then stuffed them into the empty pillowcase and tossed them into the corner. She then took fresh linens from the drawer beneath the bunk and shakily remade her bed. What little energy she had had, had been sapped by her efforts to hide all traces of Rafael's presence in her cabin, but she dared not let anyone suspect she had not spent the night alone. She moved the chair aside, unlocked the door, and hoping she was ready to meet whomever should bring her breakfast, she climbed back into bed. It was all she could do not to weep pathetically, but she knew she could not give in to her emotions, for no one must ever learn what Rafael had done. She would take the secret to her grave rather than reveal it. Joaquin would make her marry his friend rather than allow her to silently suffer the disgrace of being raped. She was so confused she did not even know if she should consider it rape since she had been so very willing. Her body had betrayed her with shocking ease, but truly she knew it had been the fever, not passion, that had caused her ruin. She clasped her hands together tightly, terrified he would come into her cabin again and again while she was too ill to fight him. When she heard a knock at the door, she wiped away her tears and tried to smile, all the while praying it would not be he.

Domingo carried in the breakfast tray and set it

gently across Alicia's lap. "I hope you are feeling better," he mumbled self-consciously, sorry he now knew what he did about her. "You fell asleep while I was reading yesterday. Would you like me to continue?"

"No," Alicia responded too quickly, then realizing if he were with her the others might stay away, she changed her mind. "Yes, I mean yes, please do. You needn't go back, just start where you left off." She tried to take a sip of the steaming tea but was shaking so badly she could barely hold the cup to her lips.

"Are you sure you want me to stay?" Domingo asked hesitantly. "You are so pale and—"

"No, I'm much better, truly I am. Now just read a chapter for me and cease your worry over my health." She took a tiny bite of biscuit, then another, hoping to reassure him she was well. If she could not fool him, she would never be able to fool a woman as clever as Flame. She could not bear the thought that her sister-in-law might discover what had happened, since she knew the young woman thought so highly of Rafael she would be terribly hurt and disappointed to learn the truth about him.

Not wanting to repeat his error of the previous afternoon, Domingo glanced up frequently to be certain Alicia hadn't fallen asleep. She seemed so distracted despite her insistence that she felt well that finally he could not bear to watch her nibble on the same biscuit another minute and closed the book. "Miss Caldwell, would you rather I called Flame?"

"No, please don't disturb her. Just keep reading. You're doing a wonderful job." She tried again to take a sip of tea and had as little success as before, for the tremor in her hands had not subsided.

Domingo thought her lovely still, despite her agitated mood, but he did not believe she had heard a word he had read. "I'm glad you are enjoying the tale.

174

That last page was quite exciting, wasn't it?"

"Exciting? Oh yes, the whole book is exciting," Alicia agreed readily.

Since he had been reading a paragraph describing the royal gardens, Domingo had all the proof he needed that she had not heard a word of it. "Look, I know all about you and Ramirez. Since I know that much about you, I think you should trust me to help you with whatever is bothering you so much."

"How could you know?" Alicia asked in a startled gasp, nearly upsetting her tray. She was terrified that if he knew how scandalously close she and Rafael had unfortunately become, others would soon learn of it too.

Domingo leaned back to get more comfortable, savoring the heady taste of power he had gained from what he had discovered about the pretty blonde and the strong-willed attorney in the early morning hours. "I saw him leaving your cabin and he told me not to be concerned because you are engaged to him."

Appalled by that outright lie, Alicia felt her cheeks grow bright with a deep blush. Was that what Rafael meant to do? Miss no opportunity to sleep with her so she would soon get pregnant and have no choice but to marry him? The man was beneath contempt. "I think you'd better go, Domingo. Take the tray. I can't eat another bite."

"I don't think you've swallowed the first one," Domingo remarked with growing confidence. "Why are you so embarrassed? Ramirez seemed very proud that you're his woman."

"He would be!" Alicia agreed sarcastically, and shoving the tray at her visitor, she lay down and closed her eyes, clearly dismissing him. "Please go."

The young man gripped the edge of the tray with one hand while he leaned forward to replace the book upon the shelf. He was puzzled, for Alicia certainly did not seem to be anticipating marriage nearly as eagerly as Rafael Ramirez was. "Don't you want to marry him?" he asked softly. When a single tear escaped the blonde's lashes and rolled slowly down her cheek, he reached out to brush it away.

"Please go!" Alicia ordered curtly, not caring if he thought her rude. "Just go."

She was obviously so thoroughly miserable Domingo did not press her to confide in him. He decided instead simply to bide his time a while longer. "We will reach the Lopez ranch this afternoon. Perhaps you will feel better when you can rest in a real bed."

Her prayers seemingly answered, Alicia's eyes flew open. "Are you positive we'll arrive at the ranch today?" she asked hopefully.

"Yes. That's what I was told."

"Good." Greatly relieved, Alicia began to smile, certain she would be far safer in Eduardo Lopez's home than she had been on board *La Reina*. Rafael would probably leave right away for Tierrasanta, which was an even more encouraging thought. "Thank you for reading to me again."

Domingo moved toward the door, still trying to weigh Rafael's confident announcement of their forthcoming marriage against Alicia's apprehension. Something was clearly wrong and he suspected it was with the man's claims. "Are you really engaged to Ramirez?" he finally had the presence of mind to ask.

"No!" Alicia exclaimed emphatically. "He's the last man I'd ever marry."

"Oh, I see," Domingo mumbled as he went out the door, uncertain of just what he had discovered but delighted to find that the arrogant attorney did not always get his way.

*　　*　　*

Rafael wanted to take Alicia's lunch to her himself, but Flame would not allow it. "She's sleeping so peacefully, I don't think she should be disturbed. I hope if she spends the day resting she'll be able to go to Eduardo's with us tonight. I'd hate for all of us to have to remain on board after Joaquin has described the man's hospitality as being so wonderfully warm."

The dark-eyed attorney found her argument difficult to counter, but still he made an attempt. "I want her to get well quickly too, Flame. It's only that, well, I—"

Flame interrupted him with an impish laugh before reaching up to give him a light kiss upon the cheek. "You needn't explain how much you like her. It's been obvious to me from the beginning. Let her sleep. The opportunities for romance will be ever so much better tonight anyway, don't you think?"

She was flirting quite openly with him, her green eyes sparkling with mischief, and Rafael had never been able to resist her charm. His smile was wide as he replied, "I have already missed far too many opportunities to pursue romance, Flame, but perhaps waiting another few hours will not set me back any further."

"Of course it won't." Flame took his arm as they began to stroll around the deck. "Alicia has a very serious nature. She's like you in so many ways. Did you realize that?"

"It had occurred to me," Rafael admitted with what he hoped was an entirely innocent smile. "I would like to get to know her better even though the time isn't all that opportune."

"Why, what do you mean? It is perfect!" Flame exclaimed happily. "Fate has brought you two together. All you need do is begin to enjoy that good fortune to the fullest."

There was no way Rafael would admit he had already begun to do just that, so he pretended to take his lively companion's advice, all the while counting the minutes until he could be with Alicia again.

Alicia was dressed in a pale pink suit, her demure
costume a sharp contrast to the wild pounding of her
heart. She was still seated upon the edge of her bunk
while Flame placed the last of her belongings in her
trunk. "Thank you. I could have finished packing
myself, but I appreciate your help."

Flame brushed a stray curl away from her eyes and
then, after a final glance about the cabin to be certain
she had gathered the last of Alicia's things, she
slammed the trunk shut and secured the latch. "There,
you're all set. Joaquin went ashore some time ago. He
should be back any minute to fetch us. Perhaps
Eduardo will come with him; if not, I'm sure he'll be
waiting with a carriage to escort us to his house."

It seemed as though a thousand years had passed
since Alicia had so foolishly planned to make Rafael
jealous by flirting with Eduardo Lopez. Now she hoped
only that the man would tolerate her presence in his
home for a few days so she would have some time by
herself to sort out how greatly her life had changed.
What she really wanted to do was to return home and
forget she had ever had the misfortune to meet Rafael
Ramirez, but since that was impossible, she was
determined to surround herself with so many people he
wouldn't even be able to get close enough to speak with
her, let alone climb into her bed.

"Alicia? Are you certain you're feeling well enough
to go ashore?" Flame thought the attractive blonde still
pale and far too quiet, for she had said no more than a
word or two the whole day. She was often reserved in
her manner, but not as downcast as this. Sitting down
beside Alicia, she put her arm around her shoulders to
give her a loving hug. "We're going to have such a good

178

time, but I don't want you to push yourself if you're feeling in the least bit ill."

"I am so much better today, I'm certain I'll be completely well by tomorrow. You needn't worry about me." Alicia tried to smile then but was only partially successful. "Why don't we go up on deck. Maybe the road to Lopez's ranch is visible from the water and we can see the men coming for us."

Delighted with that prospect, Flame leapt to her feet, then turned to take Alicia's hands to help her rise. "Yes, let's do. Joaquin has been gone little more than an hour, but already I miss him terribly."

"He is a wonderful husband, isn't he?" Alicia asked wistfully, sorry Rafael was not more like him.

"The very best, but the world is filled with dashing men," Flame teased merrily. She did not reveal any of Rafael's confidences, for she wanted Alicia to be surprised by his more active interest in her. Surprised and, she hoped, delighted as well.

Although Eduardo Lopez was only thirty-six years old, his hair had begun turning gray in his twenties and was now a soft silver haze that contrasted handsomely with his dark skin. Despite the color of his hair, his sparkling smile and bright glance clearly announced his youthful outlook and zest for living. Just under six feet in height, he had been taught as a child to make good use of his muscular build and unusually quick reflexes to get the best of anyone who dared oppose him. The son of a *criollo*, a man of Spanish blood born in Mexico, and his Indian mistress, he had spent a good portion of his youth fighting for his country's independence. After Maximilian had been executed in 1867 and Benito Juarez had again assumed the presidency, Eduardo had had no further interest in serving in his

179

army. He had resigned his commission and had returned to the ranch just south of the Rio Balsas, where he had been raised. His father had left him a generous sum, which he had used to expand his formerly modest home into a magnificent estate. With careful management and selective breeding, his Appaloosa horses had soon become known for their superior strength and unique beauty. Handsome and successful, he was confident his future was secure, and while he often missed the danger he had once known, he was no more restless than many men who had served with him. While he knew his wealth would never equal Joaquin Villarreal's, he thought he hid his jealousy well as he welcomed him to his home.

"Thank you for your letter. I was pleased to hear your wife found Sultan so satisfactory a gift. I fear I made a grave mistake in selling him to you and should she ever tire of him I will be happy to buy him back. Be certain to tell her that, will you?"

"You may tell her yourself if you wish," Joaquin responded with a ready grin.

"She is traveling with you?" Eduardo asked in delighted surprise, very curious about what sort of woman she would be. "Where is she?"

"Still on board *La Reina*. I wanted to be certain you were here before she came ashore to pay a call. Since she is so fond of Sultan, I know she'd enjoy seeing your ranch if you can spare an hour or two of your time."

"But of course! You will stay here with me for awhile, won't you? I would love the opportunity to entertain your wife and whoever else may be traveling with you. Have you come to Mexico only to buy more of my horses?"

They were seated near the fountain in the courtyard and the late afternoon sun was still keeping the air uncomfortably warm. Joaquin had declined the offer of refreshments, not wanting to leave Flame alone for longer than necessary. He knew Eduardo to be not only a clever businessman but also a very charming host. He had wanted to give him the opportunity to extend an invitation, however, rather than merely arrive with everyone and assume they would all be as welcome as he had been on his last trip. "I do hope to buy a mare or two, then I have a matter of business in Tierrasanta that needs my attention. If Flame can't decide upon which mares she'd like in a day or so, perhaps I'll go on up the coast to take care of it while she makes her selection."

"If you trust your wife with me, then I will be honored to entertain her," Eduardo responded with a deep chuckle. With luck, the woman would have more beauty than brains and he would be able to sell her half a dozen of his best mares since he knew Joaquin could well afford to indulge her.

"My sister is traveling with us, as well as an old friend, Rafael Ramirez. I do not wish to impose upon you, however, if it would inconvenience you to have so many of us here for a visit."

"Impossible! I insist you all stay here as my guests. Stay as long as you please. I will be grateful for your company for it is not often I have visitors from California." He sent for his carriage then, knowing this unexpected diversion could prove profitable as well as amusing. He studied Joaquin's features more closely, thinking it possible his sister might also be attractive, but his imagination did not adequately prepare him to meet such a stunning beauty as Alicia Caldwell proved to be.

"Con mucho gusto." Alicia pronounced each word distinctly, hoping she had gotten them right, and when

181

Eduardo Lopez responded with a dazzling grin, she realized that she must have. He was as charming a man as promised, but her smile was a very shy one.

Eduardo thought the exquisitely beautiful blonde absolute perfection. He had had little experience courting such fine ladies but attempted to do his best to impress her. "I would like to practice my English with you if you do not mind, Miss Caldwell."

"And if I wish to practice my Spanish?" she inquired softly as she took his arm so he might help her into the boat that would take them ashore.

"We can do both," he offered agreeably, his sparkling brown eyes making an appreciative sweep over the soft swells of her slender figure. She moved with a delightful grace, nearly floating into his arms as he helped her to her seat.

"No, that would be selfish of me. I will be happy to help you with your English, but I think it is already very good."

"You are too kind."

Flame glanced impatiently about the deck. "Where is Rafael? Doesn't he plan to come with us?"

"You needn't worry, I'll not leave him behind," Joaquin assured her. "I know he wanted to tell Arturo to keep Domingo busy for a couple of days. I imagine he's talking with him."

The petite redhead watched Eduardo Lopez flirt with Alicia in the charming fashion she knew Rafael would not even attempt to affect and her heart sank. She was certain her sister-in-law knew the difference between superficial flattery and sincere affection, but if Rafael didn't hurry, there would be no choice for Alicia to make.

Amused by the seriousness of her expression,

Joaquin placed his fingertip beneath Flame's chin to force her gaze up to his. "If Rafael and Alicia are right for each other, they'll discover it without any help from you. Now I'll help you into the boat, then go find him."

Thinking she'd be wise to distract Alicia from Eduardo's generous attentions, Flame readily agreed to her husband's request. They'd all go over first, then the boat would return to the ship for their luggage. "I'm afraid I brought too many things."

"Nonsense. A woman can never have too many lovely clothes," Joaquin assured her with a teasing wink.

Flame knew he was simply trying to make her feel better and that in itself was so dear she did not argue with him. She took his hand and climbed down into the boat where she snuggled up beside Eduardo and gave him her most bewitching smile, deliberately distracting him from the shy blonde at his side.

It took Rafael some time to attend to everything, for he wanted to speak not only with Arturo but with Domingo as well. He dared not leave his notes in his cabin where the young man might read them at his leisure, so he put them into his briefcase and hurried up on deck. He had not realized the others were waiting for him and apologized hurriedly as he shook Eduardo Lopez's hand. He was almost afraid to look directly at Alicia, knowing his emotions would be so easy to read, but when he did glance in her direction her gaze was filled with such undisguised hatred that he could not tear his eyes away. *La Reina* had had to anchor outside the breakwater and while the journey through the waves to the shore was not a long one, there was no way he could ask her any meaningful questions. Once they reached the sand, they quickly boarded the carriage for the ride to Eduardo's home and he could scarcely ask her what was wrong when they were surrounded by others. He had not had all that many successful conversations with her anyway, so he remained as silent as she, all the while wanting to grab her and shake the truth out of her. If he had done something wrong, or forgotten something he should have remembered, all she need do would be tell him and he would correct that error immediately. There was no way for him to right any wrong when she would not even speak to him.

The minute they reached the ranch house, Eduardo summoned Veronica, a pretty maid, to show Alicia to her room so that she would have time to rest before supper. He was an enthusiastic host, especially so when he had such an enchanting guest, and once he had seen that his other visitors were comfortable in their quarters, he went to his own to dress. He did not know which was more exciting, that Alicia was so great a beauty, or that she was undoubtedly wealthy almost beyond imagining. He enjoyed raising horses. He took great pride in the fine ranch he had built from little more than a shack and fields filled with scrub brush, but a marriage to a woman like Alicia Caldwell would provide him with the means to fulfill any dream. That Ramirez was such a fine-looking man had given him something of a start, but the attorney had not said a word to her, so obviously they weren't close. That was good, for he would have little time to impress the shy blonde and he didn't want any competition. He traveled to the capital frequently, so he had a fine wardrobe and did not feel as though he kept himself so isolated from the rest of the world that she would find him backward. He knew important people, had many influential friends, for he had been clever enough to back Benito Juarez from the beginning. All he need do was communicate those facts without sounding like an arrogant fool. Instinctively he knew she would be the type of woman who would be impressed more by a man's character than his wealth and he could not recall ever meeting a woman he had been more inspired to please. He ordered the most superb meal his kitchen help were capable of preparing, took special care in dressing for the evening, then thanked God for sending him such a rare opportunity. Suddenly the most ordinary day had turned into one of the best of his life, and he meant to take advantage of each and every minute.

Alicia lay down upon the feather bed and closed her eyes. Her head was throbbing so painfully she had not even been able to see Eduardo Lopez's face that clearly, but already she knew his type. He had nearly drooled on her he had been so eager to impress her, and she knew it was not her beauty alone that he admired. No, indeed, it was the unmistakable promise of wealth her name implied. She had been surprised at Rafael, however, for after bragging to Domingo that she would soon become his wife, he had seemed anything but confident. What he had expected from her she did not know, but how could he possibly have thought she would be pleased to see him that day? Veronica had unpacked her trunk, but she had no desire to bathe and dress for what would surely be a most awkward evening. She was nearly asleep when she realized she shouldn't give Rafael the impression she was afraid of him. Far from it, she wasn't afraid of him, but merely afraid of her own weakness for his lavish affection, which she knew could not possibly be real. He was like a sorcerer and the warmth of his kisses had enchanted her, but she would not allow herself to fall prey to his magical caress ever again. Her mind made up, she rested a while longer, then ordered a bath and dressed in one of her most stunning gowns, a golden silk that shimmered seductively with reflected light as she moved. She would pretend to be pleased by Eduardo Lopez's fawning attentions, for there would be no harm in flattering him while it would serve to make her disgust at what Rafael had done to her more than plain.

Her head held high, the lovely blonde was the last to arrive as the group gathered in the parlor before supper. Just as she had expected, Eduardo rushed forward to meet her. He patted her hand possessively as he escorted her into the dining room and placed her at his side. She smiled at him frequently, asked questions to inspire his conversation, and appeared to be fascinated with all he said. She ate little, although the *arroz con pollo* was excellent, and took no more than a small sip of wine. Feeling as weak as she did, she wanted to have all her wits about her if Rafael should have the audacity to attempt to enter her room later that night. Since it had but a single door she could block with a chest, and wrought-iron *rejas* upon the windows, she knew she would be secure. She had merely to survive the evening rather than confront Rafael openly, and that would be a simple matter with Eduardo being so wonderfully attentive. She had to admit he was as attractive and charming as promised, but she swore when he smiled at her she could see the golden gleam of dollar signs in his dark-brown eyes rather than the warm glow of desire.

The very last thing he had expected was to be snubbed so rudely by Alicia, and Rafael's confusion swiftly turned to anger. He knew how to control that rage as every clever attorney did, how to channel the fire of his temper so he appeared outwardly calm, but inside he was seething. If she was flirting with Eduardo Lopez in a ridiculous attempt to make him jealous, he would simply not respond. He would not play such a foolish game and he was shocked to find her enjoying it so immensely. Had she only wished to distract Flame and Joaquin so they would be unaware of where her true affection lay, she was doing far too convincing a job of it. Perhaps he had been wrong about her all along. Perhaps she was no more than a pampered heiress who had amused herself at his expense. He would not embarrass her in front of the others by making that charge, but he vowed to get to the bottom of her sudden change of heart at the first possible opportunity. He had not risked lowering the guard of his emotions and giving his love so generously only to have it thrown back in his face.

The night was balmy, and when at the close of the meal Eduardo suggested they might enjoy sitting on his patio while they sipped their brandy, Rafael saw no reason not to go along. The conversation during most of the evening had been concerned with horses, a subject he did not find all that interesting, but he had done his best to take part. He was very proud of his own stallion, but since he did not have Renegade along on the trip, he had no way to prove his praise for the horse was justified, and rather than merely sound boastful he had kept still. Once outdoors, the mood grew more relaxed and he was relieved he would not have to make any further attempts at conversation when Eduardo asked several of his *vaqueros* to get their guitars and play for them. They, in turn, called Veronica, the attractive little maid who had served Alicia, and encouraged her to dance to add to the entertainment. She was a pretty girl who wore her thick black hair in long braids tied with bright ribbons. A born performer, she flirted openly with all the men, her manner coquettish as she moved in perfect time to the rhythms of the guitarists' melodies. She held the edge of the last tier of ruffles on her full skirt in her hands, frequently accenting the intricate patterns of her footsteps with a saucy toss of her braids. Inspired by the enthusiastic applause she received for her performance, she came forward to invite Eduardo or one of his male guests to join her. She teased them, her eyes sparkling as she dared each of them to be her partner.

Eduardo laughed and shook his head, then gestured to Joaquin, who also refused. He made it a point to dance only with his lovely wife, who he knew to be more than Veronica's equal in grace and charm. When the pretty young girl began to coax him, Rafael finished his brandy in a single gulp and, surprising even himself, accepted her invitation. They conferred briefly with the musicians, then chose a spirited number he had learned as a child. He focused his attention solely upon the steps of dance, his smile wide as he appeared to have no other thought than enjoying the lively girl's company. Tall and lean, he was as graceful as she, and they danced together so well they appeared to have had years of practice. They missed not a single step or turn and performed with a brilliance far beyond the merely competent. When the number at last came to its end with her in his arms, Rafael leaned down to kiss her with a passion that shocked not only her, but everyone else as well. Taking her hand, he spun her round so she might take a bow before he thanked her and returned to his seat still smiling broadly as though his only interest had been in having a bit of fun.

Exhausted by their performance, Veronica begged to be excused, but the musicians continued to strum their instruments softly to provide a musical background for conversation. Rafael dismissed the compliments for his dancing, saying his partner had been so enchanting a creature he could not have helped but look good. He looked directly at Alicia then, his smile wicked as he taunted her. "This trip is something of a vacation, and I have every intention of enjoying myself."

Alicia could not recall ever having seen so sensuous a performance. The dark-haired girl had been very good, light on her feet and almost infectiously charming, but she had seen only Rafael when he had danced with her. She had not been able to take her eyes from him, for she had been astonished that a man who prided himself on having such ready control of his emotions could abandon himself so completely to the rhythms of a dance. "I know your ancestors came from Spain, Mr. Ramirez. Were they perhaps gypsies?" she asked breathlessly, her tension clear in the hushed tone of her voice.

Rafael was so amused by her question that he threw back his head and laughed out loud. "Not a one, but that's such a romantic thought I'm tempted to say that they were anyway."

"Oh, yes," Alicia responded pointedly, "that's your profession, isn't it? You're paid to convince people whatever you choose to say is the truth."

She was as good as calling him a liar right to his face, and while Rafael had no idea what had inspired such a bitter attack, he wanted no part of it. "Well paid, and since I might be called upon to use my talents tomorrow, I hope you will all excuse me. It's late and I'd like to get some rest." He thanked Eduardo again for his generous hospitality and quickly took his leave.

"Remarkable man," Lopez mused aloud, sensing a tension between Alicia and the attorney he didn't dare attempt to analyze.

"In every respect," Alicia agreed, and seeing the confusion in her host's gaze, she encouraged him to tell her something more about his ranch. She could feel Flame staring at her, but she didn't care. She knew Rafael had kissed the pretty dancer for one reason alone and that was to spite her. She didn't care what he did, she despised him and she always would. He could kiss every pretty young woman in Mexico for all she cared, and she smiled so sweetly that Eduardo Lopez had no idea she had not heard a word he had said all evening.

Chapter X

When Alicia returned to her room, she quickly bolted the heavy door, then struggled to shove the carved chest that stood along the adjacent wall to block it. Not content with that barricade, she added the heavy chair from the desk, then stood back to admire her handiwork. She still did not feel safe but could not think of anything else to do to provide herself with adequate security. Tired after the long evening, she hoped her crude barrier would be effective and, satisfied she had done all she could, she removed her gown. She placed it in the wardrobe, then removed the pins from her hair and shook out her long curls.

Not wanting to confront Alicia while she had a weapon in her hand, Rafael waited until she had laid her brush aside and had turned toward the bed before he stepped from the shadows. "I can't help but be curious. Isn't that a rather unusual way to rearrange the furniture?"

Alicia stood frozen in midstride, so horrified to find the handsome man in her room she could not summon the breath to scream. Finally realizing he was merely laughing at her fright, she cursed him heatedly. "How dare you regard my room as your own! You may not come and go here as you please!"

"If you'd wanted me to leave, you shouldn't have blocked the door," Rafael pointed out with a teasing grin. His temper had had sufficient time to cool while he had waited for her, and, truly, clothed in no more than her lace-trimmed lingerie, she was too pretty a sight to cause any response save admiration. When she turned around to give the chest she had removed a savage kick that did not budge it an inch, he stepped closer. "We seem to be constantly looking for some private spot in which to argue. If you'll promise to talk with me calmly for just a minute, I'll move that cumbersome chest myself on my way out."

Believing such a gentlemanly action unlikely, Alicia wheeled around to face him, her fury barely contained. "How can you possibly expect me to speak with you calmly after what you did to me last night?"

Completely confused by her question, Rafael nevertheless continued to regard the half-clothed young woman with a bemused smile. "It's obvious my memories of last night are far different from yours. Just what is it you think happened between us?"

Alicia put her hands on her hips, wishing she knew language truly filthy enough to give him the tongue-lashing he deserved. Speaking in a taunting whisper, she exclaimed, "You used your key to enter my cabin while I was sleeping, then—"

"The door was unlocked," Rafael contradicted with a sly smile.

At that interruption, Alicia's blue eyes blazed with an even more menacing light. "Even if I had forgotten to lock my door, you never should have entered my cabin!"

"You were ill, moaning softly in your sleep. I heard you as I walked by and went in only to see if I could offer some small service," Rafael explained politely, perplexed that she seemed to recall so little of what had actually happened.

"You call what you did no more than rendering 'some small service'?" Alicia asked accusingly.

Alarmed by the belligerence of her tone, Rafael was hard-pressed to remain calm. "What would you call it?"

Infuriated that he seemed so unconcerned, Alicia responded with the most devastatingly descriptive word possible. "I'd call it rape!"

Stunned by so unwarranted an accusation, Rafael simply stared at the distraught blonde for a long moment, astonished to find she sincerely believed what she was saying. "You were obviously far more ill than I thought; perhaps you still are, because all I did last night was respond to your invitation, and it was a very seductive one at that ."

"You're lying!" Alicia lunged forward to slap him as she spoke, her outrage demonstrated clearly as her hostility turned to violence.

At the precise instant Rafael caught her wrist in midair, they were startled by a light knock at the door. It was Veronica, and the vivacious maid asked only if she was needed. When Alicia did not respond immediately, Rafael tightened his grip until he saw tears of pain come to her eyes. "Tell her no thank you and be quick about it!" he whispered hoarsely.

"*Gracias, no,*" Alicia finally replied, certain she had never been in greater need of assistance in all her life. When Veronica merely wished her good night and left, she made no effort to hide her disappointment.

Rafael dropped her hand then, his disgust plain in his expression. "Had you truly thought I'd raped you, you would have gone straight to Joaquin. Why are you making up such an outrageous tale now?"

"Are you denying that you slept with me?" Alicia

rubbed her wrist, wishing he had not been so quick, for she would have liked nothing better than to have seen the imprint of her hand upon his cheek. "Well, are you denying it?"

Without replying to her insulting question, Rafael walked around her. He returned the ornately carved chair to the desk, then replaced the heavy chest in its former place against the wall. After unbolting the door, he turned back to face her. "We made love for hours. It was one of the most enjoyable nights I've ever spent. You were so delightfully loving I thought you'd decided to become my wife. Now it seems you've lost your senses entirely and simply despise me. You needn't worry that I'll enter your room ever again, for the pleasure we've found together simply isn't worth the price you expect me to pay in scorn."

Appalled that he would be so spiteful, Alicia tried frantically to make him understand the cause of her outrage. "It was totally unfair of you to take advantage of me when I didn't even know what I was doing!"

Certain that that had not been the case, Rafael laughed, greatly amused by the foolishness of her remark. He came back to her then, slipped his arms around her waist to pull her close, and kissed her with a passionate splendor that left her thoroughly dazed when at last he drew away. "Do you have even the remotest idea what you're doing now, my love?"

Alicia swallowed nervously, for with him standing so close she could think of nothing other than how much she wanted him to kiss her again. Her heart was pounding so loudly in her ears she could barely hear her own reply. "Yes, I know."

Rafael drew her closer still, pressing her slender figure so close to his powerful frame that she could not possibly mistake the heat of his desire for anger. "Well, if you do want me, then you're going to have to say so. I don't want anymore misunderstandings between us."

The gleam in his dark eyes reflected the fire in her own and Alicia knew precisely what she wanted. She wanted the love between them to be real, not simply the burning passion of the chance encounters he seemed to arrange so easily. That she had changed things between them irrevocably by going to his cabin late one night had slipped her mind entirely. She stood on her tiptoes, letting the tip of her tongue trace the outline of his lips before plunging inside to claim the last recesses of his mouth for her own. She felt him shiver with pleasure, but to her dismay he quickly shoved her away.

That she would give him such an enticing kiss when she had not apologized for accusing him of rape simply infuriated him. "I've had enough of your teasing games, Alicia. Just continue to leave your door unlocked and I'm certain Eduardo will turn up soon. Perhaps you will be able to recall his affection in the morning, even if you swiftly forgot mine!" With that taunting farewell, he walked through the door and closed it soundly behind him.

For a long moment Alicia could not even catch her breath. He had wanted her to tell him what she wanted and she most certainly had, if not in words, then clearly in the devotion that had filled her kiss. Why had he walked out on her then? Was he only trying to teach her a lesson, to show her how deeply her confusion about the previous night had hurt him? Well, she had been hurt too! She threw herself across her bed as she began to sob, so thoroughly miserable she didn't care who else came into her room that night.

Rafael had taken no more than three paces toward his room when Veronica overtook him. She grabbed his right arm and clung to him tightly. "You dance so

195

well; are you as accomplished in all you do?" she asked with an enticing smile.

The absurdity of her question was particularly hilarious in light of the scene he had just played with Alicia. "No, unfortunately I'm not," he admitted regretfully.

The lively brunette found that difficult to believe. As they reached his door, she quickly darted in front of him to block the way. "I will come in to see you have everything you need."

"Thank you, but I'm certain I already do," Rafael replied firmly. He knew he had no one to blame but himself after the way he had danced with her, but he had no desire to take her enthusiasm for his company any further. "You're very pretty, Veronica, but I wanted no more from you than that one dance."

She was disappointed to discover that the handsome man's fiery kiss had not been the erotic invitation she had hoped it was and her pert features formed a petulant frown. "You prefer blondes perhaps?"

"Perhaps." Before she could pry into his preferences any further, Rafael put his hands up on her narrow waist and with astonishing ease picked her up and set her in the middle of the hallway where she would be well out of his way. "Good night." He slipped through his door before she could sling the curses he was certain were about to come flying from the tip of her tongue. He cared little for the flirtatious wench's feelings in his present mood. He tore off his coat with a savage tug and threw it clear across the room as he began to swear a bitter string of vile oaths, but releasing his temper in a verbal barrage brought surprisingly little relief. He had not thought Alicia to be the type of woman to taunt him needlessly. She had seemed to be a most straightforward and sensible young woman when they had first met. Then her sympathy for Domingo had created a hopeless tangle of their emotions. He yanked his shirt off over his head and threw it toward his coat. His belt followed next and then his boots, but as he unbuttoned his pants he realized it was ridiculous to blame Domingo for his current predicament. Alicia's concern for the young man was commendable since it was so totally unselfish in motivation. He had been right when he had told Flame the timing was poor for romance. "It is worse than poor, it is disastrous!" he shouted as he stripped off the last of his clothes. Nothing was as he wanted it to be, but that Alicia could not remember the ecstasy they had shared from one day to the next far exceeded the limits of his understanding. He was being torn apart by an impossible case and an equally impossible woman, but as he stretched out upon his bed, he could not deny he was completely fascinated by them both.

Nude, her long golden red curls falling about her shoulders and spilling over her breasts, Flame sat astride Joaquin's narrow hips as she rubbed his back with a slow, gentle rhythm. She loved the feel of his warm bronze skin and missed no opportunity to touch him. She frequently provided loving massages and although her hands were small, with his encouragement she had become an accomplished masseuse. While her fingertips moved slowly down his spine, her goal simply to relax him, she could not hide her own tension and her voice was breathless with excitement. "I was not at all surprised Eduardo was so taken with Alicia, but I was amazed she encouraged his interest so openly. Whatever could have gotten into her?"

Joaquin lay with his head cradled upon his crossed arms. He yawned sleepily and pointed out what he considered the obvious. "Why shouldn't she like him?

He's no pale dandy but a genuine hero, a man who's proven his bravery in countless battles. Mexico owes its present democratic form of government to the men like Eduardo who dedicated their youth to the cause of freeing their country from the yoke of foreign domination."

"My goodness, you sound like his campaign manager! Is he running for some office?" Flame leaned down to give her husband's earlobe a playful nibble and was swiftly caught in his arms.

Confining the giggling redhead in a fond embrace, Joaquin kissed her soundly before he added his own insights. "If you honestly believe my sister was so favorably impressed by Eduardo Lopez, how do you explain the hostility of that last exchange with Rafael? That certainly sounded like a lovers' quarrel to me."

"A lovers' quarrel?" Flame licked her lips thoughtfully, greatly disturbed by such a colorful description of the brief conversation Rafael had had with Alicia before he had departed for bed. "I certainly hope you're wrong."

Joaquin studied his wife's pained expression closely but was uncertain he could read her thoughts accurately. "For whom are you so concerned, Alicia or Rafael?"

Astonished by his accusing tone, Flame attempted to break free of his grasp, but Joaquin caught her wrists and held her tightly, needing to use little of his considerable strength to keep her still. She was far too feisty to be quiet, however. "Why in God's name would I be concerned about Rafael? You told me yourself he'd only break Alicia's heart. I don't want to believe that, but what if it's true? I know how much he enjoys dancing, but did he give that wonderful performance tonight simply to make her jealous?"

"Why would he wish to do that?" Joaquin asked with

more than a trace of sarcasm deepening his voice. "The fact that she did not take her eyes off Eduardo all evening shouldn't upset him, should it?"

Lying captive in his embrace, Flame could do no more than sigh unhappily. "I know, you told me not to meddle, but if Alicia is too naïve to realize she shouldn't flirt with one man just to make another angry, and most especially not when that man is Rafael, then I'll point that out to her first thing in the morning."

"You don't consider that meddling?" Joaquin asked as his lips strayed down her cheek to caress her throat.

"No, it's just good advice," Flame purred softly, certain now his mood had improved sufficiently for them to share another enjoyable night. "You've no reason to be jealous of any man, Joaquin, for you're the only one I have ever loved."

"Or ever will?" Joaquin's seductive whisper was muffled by the elegant curve of her bare shoulder as he continued to lavish kisses upon her silken skin, but he knew she had understood him.

"Or ever will," Flame vowed sweetly. He released her hands then and she drew him into her arms, too happy being his wife to give Alicia and Rafael's romance another thought for the moment, but she meant to speak to each of them privately in the morning.

Alicia was awakened in midmorning by Flame, who was already dressed for riding and anxious to begin Eduardo's promised tour of the ranch. "If you're not feeling well enough to ride yet, we'll all understand, but I'd hate to leave you here alone when the day will be such fun." She perched upon the end of her sister-in-law's bed and smiled invitingly. "Well, you do want to come along, don't you?"

Alicia sat up slowly, certain she had not slept more than ten minutes all night. "Who's going to go?" she asked through a wide yawn.

"Whom do you think?" Flame replied with a saucily raised brow. "Eduardo, of course, since it is his ranch, Joaquin, and I, and, oh yes, I do believe Rafael said he'd like to go too."

"He's not too busy?" Alicia asked pointedly.

Flame considered her words carefully, still uncertain how much she should reveal. "He is a very conscientious man, that is true, but he seems to have used his time aboard *La Reina* so well that he can afford to spend a day or two with us without neglecting his duties. You must do what you wish to do, however, without regard for the plans he's made."

Intrigued by that notion, Alicia leaned forward to hug her knees. "You mean I should just do as I please and let him think whatever he chooses?"

"Of course. Isn't that exactly what you were doing last night when you spent all your time flirting with Eduardo and completely ignored Rafael?"

Alicia was embarrassed then, for she had not thought her behavior had been so very obvious. "Was my motive all that transparent?"

Flame slid off the bed and smoothed the folds of the beige suede split skirt she wore for riding as though her costume were her greatest concern. "Eduardo seems like a nice man, but neither he nor Rafael deserves to be used for your amusement, Alicia. That's a very dangerous game as you're liable to turn them against each other, and I'm sure you don't want them fighting over you if you've already made your choice."

Stunned by this advice, Alicia's eyes narrowed with anger as she hastened to defend herself. "I've little choice, Flame, damn little, and you know it. Rafael Ramirez has his life planned down to the last second and there's no place in it for me. As for Eduardo Lopez, he's no different from any of the other men I know. I'm sure he'd inquire about the size of my dowry before he offered a marriage proposal and I'd never agree to become the wife of such a mercenary man."

Seeing she was making no impression at all upon the volatile blonde beauty, Flame moved toward the door. "The day's very pretty; just come riding with us. There's no point in your remaining here imagining dilemmas you may never face. If you find Rafael attractive, then tell him that you do, since today he has the time to listen. He's no fool, of that I'm quite certain."

"And you think I am?" Alicia's hostile expression demanded an immediate reply.

Laughing, Flame shook her head, "No, not at all, but sometimes love clouds our vision and we miss seeing the obvious. Now hurry and get dressed so you'll have time for some breakfast before we go." Flame closed the door before Alicia could give her another argument. She knew which room was Rafael's and knocked lightly at his door. When he came to open it, he wore only the tight black pants he preferred for riding. His razor was in his hand and lather still on his face, making it clear she had come at a bad time, but she disregarded that as unimportant and ducked under his arm. "Go on and finish shaving. I'll not take but a minute of your time."

Since it was difficult to argue with a woman as charming as Flame, Rafael did not even try. He was grateful to see a young woman smiling at him for a change and returned to the washstand to complete his grooming. "Well, what's so important it can't wait until I'm dressed to be discussed?"

Since Joaquin would soon miss her if she did not hurry, Flame saw no reason not to come straight to the point. "As we both know very well, you're a man of considerable experience, while Alicia quite naturally has had a very sheltered upbringing."

Rafael turned to face her then, his dark glance suddenly hostile. "I'm a bloodthirsty wolf and she's an innocent lamb, is that what you're saying?"

Laughing at this image since she knew how little it fit him, Flame drew a chair close to his side. It bothered her not at all to be in his room while he was only half clothed, since she regarded him as one of her best friends. "No, not at all. What I mean is, she is bound to make mistakes, to hurt your feelings or insult you unintentionally, but I hope you'll be wise enough to understand the men she's known have been nothing like you. I think she knows only how to discourage a man's attention but has no idea how to encourage and enjoy them."

"You can't be serious!" Rafael scoffed bitterly. "She had Lopez eating out of her hand last night. I'd say she's had plenty of practice manipulating men's feelings purely for her own amusement."

Flame frowned slightly, frustrated to find him in such an unsympathetic mood. "I see she's already hurt you, but trying to pay her back last night by using Veronica to make her jealous was just as foolish. As I said, she's naïve and can't be expected to behave in a sophisticated manner, but I expect better of you. Why are you both fighting love so fiercely when it is the most glorious of emotions?"

"And the most painful!" Rafael pointed out with bitter irony. Laying his razor aside, he wiped the last of the lather from his face and reached for his shirt before he spoke again. "You are the very last woman I'd ever want to talk with about love, Flame. You ought to know that and I'll thank you not to give me any more advice on how I should handle Alicia or any other woman either."

Cut to the quick by his coldly worded insult, Flame rose and nearly slammed her chair against the wall she flung it out of her way so quickly. Her eyes filled with tears as she told him exactly how she felt. "Yes, I know firsthand how painful love can be but it is precisely because I do love you that I want what's best for you!"

Astonished by such an unexpected confession, Rafael needed a moment to reply. "This is a damn awkward time for you to finally decide you're in love with me, Flame."

"I didn't say that I'm in love with you, you idiot. I said I love you!" Crushed he had so little understanding of her affectionate interest in him, she fled his room before he had the presence of mind to catch her and make her stay.

Dumbfounded by Flame's declaration of love, Rafael sank down upon his bed in an attempt to understand what had prompted her to make it now. He could not deny that he loved her too, but it was a warm, comforting type of love that bore little relationship to the passion he felt for Alicia. Surely that was what Flame felt for him too. There were all kinds of love, from the sweetest affections to the most passionate ardor, and he had not meant to hurt the petite redhead's feelings when he cared so very deeply for her. He was furious only with himself, not with her, but he had expressed himself so poorly it was no wonder she had been offended. "I can scarcely tell her the truth though," he admitted softly to himself, no longer certain what the truth might actually be.

Eduardo had personally selected the mounts for everyone and he was pleased when all his guests seemed satisfied, but as he showed them around his ranch he could not shake the impression that none of them was actually listening to his remarks. He tried to inject humor, but when they responded with no more than polite smiles he soon gave up his efforts to be amusing. They had planned to ride to the banks of the Rio Balsas for a barbecue and he hoped they would all be in a more agreeable mood after they had eaten and rested a while. By skillful maneuvering, he managed to stay by Alicia's side, but he was disappointed to find her as distracted as the others.

Alicia yawned repeatedly, ashamed to be so tired she couldn't concentrate well enough on Eduardo's commentary to make the appropriate replies. He was obviously very proud of his ranch and, she thought, deservedly so, but she could not seem to keep herself from glancing back at Rafael so frequently she feared her actions would soon draw comment. He had not said a word all morning as he had ridden along with the careless nonchalance of an expert horseman. She longed to know his thoughts, for she feared the darkness of his mood was entirely her fault, but she would not sacrifice her pride and apologize after the way he had walked out on her. She considered him as much to blame for their problems as she was and thought he ought to be gentleman enough to acknowledge that sorry fact himself.

As they made their way toward the river, Joaquin drew alongside his wife. "I know better than to think you kept your thoughts to yourself this morning, but it's obvious no matter how good your intentions, nothing has changed between Alicia and Rafael."

"You are right, my darling," Flame admitted reluctantly. "Love is so complex an emotion that I fear no one can provide helpful advice to another. I was a fool to try."

Joaquin could not recall ever hearing his wife make such a startlingly critical admission. "You may give me all the advice you wish, Flame, for I'm still learning how to love you."

Flame could not help but smile at the sweetness of his words. "Was it very wrong of me to try to help two people I love find each other?"

Knowing this was definitely not a good time for a lecture on the value of minding one's own business, Joaquin shook his head. "No, Flame, not when your very nature is to be loving and helpful."

Flame reached out to take his hand as they rode along, thinking again that Rafael and Alicia were fools to waste so much time ignoring each other when it was obvious to anyone with two eyes they longed to be in each other's arms. "We're very lucky, aren't we, Joaquin?"

"Yes, we most certainly are, my pet," Joaquin agreed with a teasing wink, praying his luck would hold long enough for him to find Domingo's real father and send him on his way.

Rafael let the warmth of the summer sun fill him with a sense of calm he had not experienced of late. There was a certain tranquillity to be found astride a horse when riding merely for pleasure, and wanting to enjoy that peace, he lagged far behind his companions. He found the ranch nestled between the shores of the Pacific Ocean and the foothills of the Sierra Madre Del Sur very impressive, but feared they were merely experiencing a calm before the proverbial storm. He planned to apologize to Flame that very day, but he wanted to get the business that had brought them to

Mexico over with before he devoted himself to repairing the shambles he had made of his personal life. Then he would turn his full attention to deepening his relationship with Alicia. If, of course, she proved cooperative, which unfortunately she never had.

Although he gave it his best effort, he could not get Flame's words out of his mind. Was he truly behaving like an idiot? Alicia was so attractive it was no wonder Eduardo was attempting to monopolize her company, but was he being a fool to allow it? So what if she snubbed him again? He could at least see to it Eduardo had no success with her either. Chuckling to himself at the cleverness of this plan, he swiftly overtook the others and skillfully cut in between the rancher and the pretty blonde. "Do you ride out to observe your stock every day?" he asked Eduardo with a pleasant smile.

Startled by the attorney's sudden appearance and annoyed to find he had pushed Alicia aside, Eduardo leaned forward so she would be sure to hear his reply. "Yes, I know each horse by name and want to be certain they are all doing well."

"Of course. I'm certain the amusements are very few here and you have to pass your days as best you can," Rafael remarked sympathetically, but the look he turned toward Alicia was a rakish grin.

Horrified to think Rafael's remark might make the lovely blonde consider his existence very dull, Eduardo contradicted him heatedly. "You are very wrong, Señor Ramirez. I can imagine no life more perfect than this. As you have seen, my home is more than merely comfortable; it is an estate every bit as fine as any in Mexico. We are blessed with mild weather along the coast, so the days are usually as splendid as today. Add to that the fact that my horses are not only beautiful but intelligent as well and a joy to train and you will see I lead the best of lives here and it's a richly satisfying one. I also have many friends in Mexico City, and since we enjoy each other's company enormously, they come here frequently and often I go there, so I never lack for amusement."

"May I assume these friends to whom you're referring are women?" Rafael asked with what appeared to be no more than idle curiosity.

Eduardo's dark eyes widened in surprise. "No, I am referring to men, married couples, fine families with whom I am close."

"Oh, you don't like women, is that it?" Rafael inquired politely.

Alicia turned away to hide her smile, for she knew Eduardo would be deeply insulted by such a show of amusement. She had no idea what had inspired Rafael to give him such a difficult time, but she was enjoying it thoroughly.

"Of course I like women! What are you saying?" Eduardo shouted dramatically, certain he had just been insulted very rudely.

"Why nothing," Rafael responded with a shrug, "but Veronica seemed so hungry for male companionship I thought perhaps having men around was a rare treat."

His face growing dark with fury, Eduardo could barely respond. "She is no more than a spoiled child. If she disturbed you in any way I will see that she does not make such an unfortunate error again."

Greatly amused by his host's discomfort, Rafael laughed as he shook his head, "I'm never disturbed by the attenions of pretty women. Are you?"

Having already taken more of the attorney's snide innuendos than he cared to accept, Eduardo touched the brim of his *sombrero* lightly. "Please continue on this trail. I'm going on ahead to make certain everything is ready for us." He gave Alicia a strained smile, then spurred his mount and cantered away.

With him gone, Alicia had no reason to contain her mirth and laughed out loud with genuine delight. "He is a rather pompous sort, but I'd be careful if I were you. I don't think he can take much more of your teasing."

"What makes you think I was teasing?" Rafael asked with feigned innocence.

Alicia gave him a suspicious look. "You were teasing him, all right. Don't deny it."

Rafael flashed his most charming grin. "I have very bad manners it seems, but since it's unlikely I'll ever want to visit this ranch again, it really doesn't matter if I'm not invited back."

"No, I suppose it doesn't," Alicia agreed. She was flattered he had gone so far as to insult their host in order to be able to speak with her alone, but she thought she would be wise to keep the conversation light if she could. "This is a pretty little mare, don't you think? Perhaps Joaquin should buy her?"

Rafael had paid no attention to Alicia's mount, but since he had been asked for an opinion, he eyed the horse closely. "Her coloring and conformation are good, but Sultan is a spirited beast. I'm sure he'd appreciate a mare with a far more feisty temperament than that horse displays."

Alicia's befuddled expression mirrored her confusion. "I didn't realize he'd notice anything more than the fact she is female."

"All mares, just like all women, are not alike, Alicia, and stallions as well as men have their favorites."

Her cheeks brightened with a deep blush, Alicia wondered how he had managed to turn a quite innocent remark about a mare into such an intimate discussion. "I know very little about horses except for the fact that I enjoy riding them."

"And even less about men?" Rafael asked slyly.

Alicia pulled up sharply on the reins to bring her mare to an abrupt halt. "Do you plan to tease me unmercifully too?"

Rafael also drew his mount to a halt. "No, I want only the opportunity to get to know you. The way you think is a complete mystery to me and I'd like to be able to understand you so we might get along better. I hope you won't think that's a sinister goal or that I'm being devious, because my motives are above reproach."

"Now I'm positive you are teasing me," Alicia cried out in dismay. None of the man's actions could possibly be described as honorable and suddenly she knew she would be better off in Eduardo Lopez's company than his. At least she knew he was interested in her money. She had no idea why Rafael took such delight in toying with her emotions. "I'm sure Eduardo is wondering what's keeping us." Tapping her heels lightly against the little mare's flanks, she started after him, but rather than allow her to escape, Rafael swiftly drew his horse alongside hers.

"You see, your mare hasn't a bit of speed!" he pointed out playfully. "Looks aren't nearly enough in a horse; she needs heart as well."

"Just like a woman?" Alicia responded angrily.

"Now you're learning!" Rafael gave her another wicked grin but fell back to allow her to take the lead. They reached the river in a few minutes, but before Eduardo could rush forward to help her dismount, Rafael was by her side. "If you'd rather I did not say another word to our host all afternoon, I won't," he promised with a seriousness he hoped she would believe.

Alicia had no choice but to put her hands on his shoulders as he helped her down. He left his hands around her waist while he waited for her reply, but since she had never been able to think clearly while standing in his arms, she could not decide what she really wanted to say. She saw through the thick fringe of dark lashes that shadowed the warm glow of admiration in his gaze, and mesmerized by that compelling light, she was unable to make any coherent reply. Then Eduardo appeared at her side and it was too late for a reasonable response. "That won't be necessary," she finally mumbled nervously, and taking the rancher's arm, she allowed him to escort her to the table his servants had set up in the clearing near the bank of the river.

They had come out well before dawn to barbecue a side of beef, and the succulent aroma that came wafting from the pit as they uncovered the meat made her mouth water. She had eaten little the last few days, and pushing all thought of her problems aside, she could hardly wait until Flame and Joaquin joined them to sample the flavorful beef. There were freshly made corn *tortillas,* the spicy rice dish, *sopa de arroz,* and the tiny sweet *tamales* she loved for dessert. She enjoyed the meal so much that again she heard little of Eduardo's flattering conversation, but when at last they had finished eating and he invited her to go for a walk, Rafael responded before she could.

"That's a wonderful idea," the attorney agreed enthusiastically, and leaping to his feet, he circled the table to help Alicia from her chair. "Is there a path down by the river?"

Astonished by the man's speed as well as his obstinate refusal to allow him to enjoy the pleasure of Alicia's company uninterrupted, Eduardo replied curtly, "Yes, but it's very narrow and somewhat treacherous. You'll have to watch your step very carefully, Señor Ramirez."

"I always do," Rafael assured him confidently.

Wanting no part of the triangle he found most

amusing, Joaquin covered a wide yawn. "I'd rather take a nap if there are no objections."

Flame was so pleased to see Rafael had already taken Alicia's hand, she readily agreed to stay behind. "Let's go over under the trees to rest. We'll wait for you three right here." While the servants busied themselves clearing the table and Eduardo, with a frustrated groan, led the way to the footpath, Flame sat down beneath an old, gnarled fig tree. After leaning back to get comfortable, she stretched out her legs so Joaquin could lie down and put his head in her lap. Bending to kiss him, she purred sweetly, "Maybe my meddling, as you call it, wasn't such a wasted effort after all. Rafael really seems to be trying to impress Alicia for a change."

Joaquin reached up to wind his fingers in her golden red curls, his smile a teasing grin. "Why do you think I'm pretending to be too tired to take a walk?" he whispered as he drew her lips down to his.

"To give them time to be alone!" she replied with impish delight. "What about Eduardo?"

"I'm sure Rafael will think of some way to get rid of him."

In the next instant they heard a piercing howl followed by a loud splash and they were convulsed with laughter, knowing their clever friend had already succeeded in retiring their host from the rest of the afternoon's fun.

Chapter XI

Alicia was not certain just how Rafael had managed to trip Eduardo and send him flying into the river, since it all happened so quickly. The poor man was soaked before she had realized he had missed a step, stumbled and, still scrambling to regain his balance, had gone sliding off the narrow trail, scattering an avalanche of small stones in his wake. Rafael appeared to be as surprised as she by the accident and helpfully bent down to extend his hand to pull their half-drowned host from the water.

Drenched from head to foot, Eduardo was certain it had been the toe of Rafael Ramirez's boot that had caused him to fall rather than the uneven surface of the old trail. Since there was not sufficient room to throw a punch without the risk of inadvertently hitting Alicia or again falling in the water, he was forced to do no more than issue a verbal challenge. His fists clenched tightly at his sides, he berated the wily attorney for turning to such an underhanded trick. "Only a small boy would enjoy playing such stupid pranks, Ramirez. Now that I've been warned, I'll be far more careful around you, but don't make the mistake of thinking I will allow this insult to go unrepaid!"

Rafael frowned slightly, then without the slightest trace of guilt marring his expression, he recounted the facts as he saw them. "You are completely mistaken, for I've never played practical jokes of any sort. I was more than three paces behind you when you stumbled or I'd have grabbed you to keep you from falling. Just look at the trail more closely and you'll see your accusation is completely unfounded. I will forgive you for it, however, since I can see you're far too upset to analyze the cause of your accident rationally. Didn't you find it very difficult to command troops in battles against the French when you have so little control of your temper?"

Infuriated all the more by his arrogant guest's continuous string of insulting questions, Eduardo was certain Rafael's protestation of innocence was an outright lie. Since the man was Joaquin's best friend, however, he dared not provoke him needlessly, fearing his whole party might leave, which would put the lovely Alicia out of his reach forever. He hurriedly scanned the trail, looking for evidence to prove he had been tripped but was chagrined to see a twisted root protruding from the rocky soil at the precise point he had lost his footing. He had not seen it before and clearly it was what had caught the heel of his boot with a savage jerk rather than a well-placed kick from behind. The mishap had truly been an unfortunate accident and nothing more. He was horribly embarrassed to have to admit he had been wrong and mortified to have insulted Rafael in front of the young woman he was trying without any apparent success to impress. Knowing she must surely think him a fool, and a clumsy one at that, he excused himself as quickly as possible. "Forgive me, Señor Ramirez, if my temper caused me to accuse you in error; the trail is so treacherous here it is no wonder I slipped. I think it is far too dangerous for you to walk so near the water Señorita Caldwell. Since I must return to the house for fresh clothing, may I suggest you come with me?"

Before she could respond, Rafael again took her hand and Alicia felt the increasing pressure of his fingers upon her own, silently beseeching her to remain with him. She refused Eduardo's invitation with a regretful smile. "Of course you should go back, but you needn't worry about me. The scenery is so wonderfully relaxing here I'd like to enjoy it a while longer, but I promise to be very careful of where I step."

"As you wish," Eduardo growled through clenched teeth, furious he had had no luck in at least winning her sympathy if he had failed to win her respect. "I will see you both later." Mustering all the dignity he could affect while dripping wet, he edged past them and returned to the clearing where the horses were tethered. With no more than a hasty wave to Joaquin and Flame he plunked his *sombrero* on his head, then leapt upon his horse and with a soggy, squishing echo rode away.

Alicia looked up at Rafael's amused expression and could not help but wonder aloud, "How did you manage to do that?"

"Do what?" he asked innocently.

"How did you manage to send him flying into the river before he had realized what had happened?" Alicia asked in a louder tone, annoyed he would not confide in her without being coaxed.

Rafael gestured again to the offending root. "Look, the evidence can't be disputed. The man lost his balance when he tripped over that blasted root. I had nothing to do with his falling into the river." As if to prove his point, he bent down and with a savage yank pulled the brittle root far enough out of the sandy soil to snap it off so no other hiker would come to grief because of it. Straightening up, he tossed the curling root into the river and then brushed off his hands before returning her inquisitive gaze with a righteous glare.

Alicia was still not convinced he was telling the truth and, ignoring the blackness of his glance, continued. "We are not in a courtroom, so whether or not there is evidence to support your claim doesn't matter," she pointed out sarcastically. "Why can't you just tell me the truth?"

She was dressed in a divided skirt fashioned of suede the same bright golden shade as her gleaming curls and a sheer muslin blouse embroidered with tiny blue flowers. The top two buttons were undone but revealed no more than a tantalizing glimpse of the fullness of her breasts. They rose invitingly as she breathed deeply while taunting him and Rafael needed several seconds to formulate a coherent reply. "The truth is that I planned to shove the fool into the water at the first opportunity. That he managed to trip and save me the trouble only proves I would have been right in doing so. Now does that satisfy your insatiable curiosity about my motives? Call me a scoundrel if you like and I'll readily admit to it."

The sound of the water rushing over the rocky river bed and the birds calling to one another overhead provided a welcome distraction as Alicia turned away in a futile attempt to hide her bright blush. If he hadn't known she didn't trust him, he certainly did now, but that thought did little to ease her embarrassment. "I'm sorry," she finally admitted softly, certain it was the most inadequate apology ever given.

"For what? I wanted to be alone with you and if he hadn't provided this opportunity, then I meant to do it myself. I'm not ashamed to admit I can be as devious as

216

any other man. Does that surprise you?"

Alicia looked up at him shyly, not certain where their conversation might be leading since his surprises seemed never to end. Everything about the man bothered her: his dark good looks, his incisive wit, his amazing ability to take advantage of her weakness for him while she seemed to be powerless to stop him. He was again dressed in casual clothes for riding and she recalled the tingling excitement she had felt when he had first arrived at Joaquin's ranch astride his magnificent pinto stallion. That same delicious aura of danger and desire surrounded him still. He doesn't even speak of love, she reminded herself firmly in a valiant attempt to hold on to her reason, knowing in another minute he might pull her into his arms and it would be too late to think at all. "I should go back," she announced primly, a little frightened of him still, but far more frightened of her own uncontrollable desires.

"No, not yet." Taking her hand again, Rafael gave her no chance to argue with his decision before he started up the narrow trail. "Watch your step," he called over his shoulder, his grin a sly one.

Alicia knew she should object, but at the same time she could not deny that being with him was where she truly wished to be. It had to be on her terms for once, though, she told herself repeatedly as they made their way upstream. Rafael had left his hat behind and the sun's golden glow cast bright highlights upon his hair and gave a copper sheen to his deeply tanned skin. As always, she found him so extremely attractive that, despite her promise to Eduardo, she paid scant attention to the trail since her guide was so wonderfully exciting.

Rafael took special care to point out every spot where the path might prove hazardous, his warnings given with real concern for Alicia's welfare. They had

217

been walking for nearly fifteen minutes before he found a grassy area to his liking at the side of the trail. Such a secluded spot at the river's edge would naturally invite rest and conversation and he hoped for once things would go his way. As soon as he had made certain the ground was as soft as it appeared, he sat down and pulled Alicia down by his side. Wanting to set her at ease, he smiled warmly as he explained he wanted no more than an exchange of ideas. "Let's just talk a while; you may choose whatever subject you wish and I'll be happy to discuss it with you." That he hoped such a conversation would last all afternoon was something he was far too clever too admit.

The frankness of his glance made her so self-conscious Alicia hurriedly focused her attention on the churning water of the river, and seeing a bright flash of color in the mist above it, she exclaimed excitedly, "Oh look, there's a rainbow! What are they called in Spanish? I can never recall."

"Un arco iris," Rafael replied instantly, pleased that she had at last asked a question he could answer without starting an argument. *"Son muy bonitos, verdad?"*

Alicia was ashamed to admit he had lost her already. She could understand his question but could not think of more than a one-word reply. *"Sí,"* she finally responded apologetically. "Yes, they are very pretty. I'm sorry, but I told you when we first met that my Spanish isn't what it should be."

"Why do you feel you must speak it?" Rafael pulled up a blade of grass and pulled it through his fingers as he gave her a quizzical glance.

"It's my mother's language," Alicia explained proudly. "Joaquin speaks both Spanish and English flawlessly and I'd like to be able to do the same."

"I doubt you'll ever be able to keep up with that

brother of yours in any of his pursuits. I'm surprised you'd even want to try," Rafael remarked with a deep chuckle.

"It isn't a question of keeping up with Joaquin, as you put it. Spanish is a beautiful language and it would please a great many people if I could speak it well."

"You haven't impressed me as a woman who is overly concerned with the opinions of others," Rafael pointed out with another of his devastatingly attractive grins.

Already wary, Alicia quickly took exception to his remark. "Are you saying I'm selfish?" she asked caustically.

Rafael reached out to take her hand, lacing his fingers in hers as if he sensed she was about to take flight. "No, not at all; only extremely independent. Since I share that trait, I certainly don't consider it a flaw in your character."

Alicia licked her lips nervously as she stared down at their hands. Hers was trembling slightly, and as if he could read her thoughts, he tightened his grasp so she could not pull free. Her hand imprisoned in his, she forced her mind to ask a question, any question, to distract her from the searing heat of his touch. "When will you be leaving for Tierrasanta?" she blurted out in a frantic whisper, certain taking her hand was only his first step toward luring her into the intimacy she dared not repeat.

That trip was the last subject Rafael cared to discuss. He had wanted to set business aside for an hour or two and concentrate solely upon getting to know the pretty blonde. She seemed always to jump at the worst conclusions about him and he had wanted to allay her suspicions if he could. Obviously she would give him no such opportunity, so he told her the truth. "Tomorrow, I hope."

"So soon?"

"Can't be soon enough to suit me," Rafael admitted quite frankly.

Alicia eyed him cautiously from behind the lacy curtain of her long lashes. His expression had grown so cold she felt chilled despite the warmth of the day and could not suppress a sudder of dread. "I know Domingo will never receive the recognition he craves, but I can't help but feel sorry for him that he won't."

After studying her wistful expression for a long minute, Rafael asked a question of his own. "Is sympathy your only emotion where he is concerned?"

Puzzled by the intent of his question, Alicia did not know how to reply. "I beg your pardon?" she asked instead.

Rafael rephrased his query only slightly. "He is bright as well as handsome. It wouldn't be surprising if your feelings for him were more than merely sympathetic concern. Are they?"

While she was certain such cool detachment must serve him well in a courtroom, she could not affect the same icy reserve, nor did she even wish to try. "How dare you?" she hissed accusingly. "Do you honestly believe I could have . . ." At a loss for words to describe the passion they had shared so briefly, she tried to rise, but he refused to release her hand and she could not escape him. "Let me go!" she cried, out, nearly hysterical now.

"Sit still!" Rafael commanded sharply. As always, she had stretched his patience far past its limit. "I have never had such a difficult time carrying on a simple conversation with anyone as I continually do with you. Just take a few minutes to calm down and I'll take you back to the ranch." He turned away slightly, the digust plain on his well-defined features as he watched the constant play of light and shadow upon the swiftly flowing water of the Balsas. She had upset him so severely that he had to force himself to take several deep breaths and then let them out slowly in an attempt to take his own advice.

Alicia was at a loss to explain why they could not get along, since she considered the fault entirely his, but she dared not say that out loud. "You obviously think me very fickle," she finally said more to the river than to the man at her side. "You're very wrong though."

Fickle was not nearly a strong enough word to describe the inconsistency of her emotions in his opinion, but Rafael held his tongue and remained silent. He wanted her for his own, and badly, but not if she wasn't as willing to marry him as he was to take her as his wife. She was young, that was true, but not so young she didn't know exactly what her constantly shifting affections were doing to him. Her warmth turned so frequently to ice in his arms, it was like trying to love something as intangible as the wind. When he glanced over at her, he was startled to find her staring intently at him as though he were the most fascinating of sights. "Well, are you ready to go back?"

"You see, you just did it again!" Alicia pointed out excitedly.

"Did what?" Rafael asked with a mystified shrug.

"I said I am not nearly as fickle as you seem to believe and rather than reply to that comment you ask if I am ready to go back. Now do you see why we can't converse about anything? It is as though you don't hear what I say, or perhaps you do hear me but simply don't care about what I think."

"That's not true," Rafael insisted firmly, his temper again threatening to explode in a fiery burst of anger. "That simply isn't true. I not only hear ever word you speak but also notice the inflection in your voice and the emotion in your expression. Nothing escapes me,"

221

he proclaimed proudly.

"Nothing but the obvious!" Alicia finally succeeded in yanking her hand from his and leapt to her feet. She started off back down the trail, keeping her eyes on the path even though her mind was still occupied with maddening thoughts of him. She realized Rafael was no more than a step behind her, she turned back so sharply he nearly went skidding into her before he could halt. "I think you've spent so damn much of your time in a courtroom you know nothing about life!" Certain she had at least communicated that thought quite clearly, she wheeled back around and strode off down the trail without giving him any chance to respond, but as they approached the clearing where they had had lunch, he reached out to catch her arm and spun her around.

"I can't imagine where you get your ideas, but as an attorney I've seen far more of the seamier side of life than I care to know! Theft, murder, adultery—I've handled cases with facts so shocking they'd turn your stomach if I recounted them. With the possible exception of treason, there's nothing I haven't heard or seen in my legal career, but I purposely keep that horror separate from my personal life. I am made of flesh and blood, exactly like you, but until you finally understand that simple fact, we will never get along!"

Alicia was so infuriated by his taunting insults, she did not bother to argue. Instead, she placed her hands upon his broad chest and with a mighty shove sent him toppling back into the river. She crossed her arms over her chest as she watched him struggle to find his footing, cursing her all the while with language so filthy she was amazed at how easily she understood it. "Thank you," she said with a haughty smirk. "I had no idea my Spanish has improved so greatly, but I understood every word you said and I wish the very same to you!"

Incensed by her taunt, Rafael hauled himself out of the water with a savage lunge, catching the astonished blonde around the knees and tossing her over his shoulder into the river before she had time to do more than let out a frantic wail of surprise. He held her under, soaking her thoroughly, in a futile attempt to cool her temper as well as her lovely body before he released her.

"You bastard!" Alicia shrieked in a hoarse gasp the second she had filled her lungs with air. The water was cold if not bone chilling, but that he had wanted her to suffer the same humiliating punishment she had meted out to him infuriated her completely. She had thought for an instant he meant to drown her and she still wasn't sure that wasn't exactly what he planned to do. Not about to die without a fight, she struck out at him, but he caught her wrists before her fists found their mark and pulled her close to his chest. He lowered his lips to hers, ravaging her mouth with a bruising kiss that sought to conquer all resistance, but he knew instantly such a brutal tactic would never quench the fires of her spirit so he raised his hand and dunked her again.

"I'll kill you for this!" Alicia sputtered as she came to the surface. Blinded by a mask of wet curls, she struggled violently to get free of his steel-like grip, finally sinking her teeth into the heel of his hand so savagely he released her with a loud howl of pain. Seizing the initiative, she quickly grabbed a handful of his hair and shoved his head under. Planting her boots in the middle of his chest, she then pushed away with a hearty kick, swam clumsily to the riverbank, and hurriedly scampered up the rocks. Exhausted by their battle, she gulped for air as she reached dry ground, but to her horror she found her brother and sister-in-law had apparently been observing them for several minutes. They were holding onto each other, laughing so hard tears were rolling down their cheeks. "You think this is funny?" she screamed accusingly, tempted to shove them both into the water too. She leaned against a tree growing at the river's edge while she yanked off her boots, dumped out the water trapped inside, then pulled them back on. "That bastard tried to drown me and you think it's funny!"

"That's a damn lie!" Rafael called out in protest as he pulled himself out of the water. "You started it; just like always, you started it!"

Without arguing the point, Alicia hesitated only long enough to give him a look so fierce it would have turned a lesser man to stone before she sprinted off to the horses. She quickly mounted the little mare and, gouging her heels into her sides, rode back to the ranch at the most furious gallop the small horse could manage.

Rafael flipped his hair out of his eyes, then shook himself off before acknowledging the presence of his friends. "I'm glad someone enjoyed that spectacle because I certainly didn't!"

After wiping the last of the tears from his eyes, Joaquin reached out to grab Rafael's arm before he could walk away. "No, wait, don't go after her. You'll only make things worse."

"Hell, I've no intention of going after that obnoxious little—" Rafael caught himself there, remembering at the last second that Alicia was Joaquin's sister. "I don't care if I ever see her again as long as I live!"

Since Rafael was shaking with rage, Flame did not doubt that he meant what he said, but she hoped he would not mean it for long. "I'm sorry, we shouldn't have laughed, but truly, we thought you two were playing, not fighting, so I hope you'll forgive us."

Rafael looked down at his right hand where blood dripped from the crescent-shaped wound Alicia had inflicted with her teeth. "Does this look like mere sport to you?" He yanked his handkerchief from his back pocket, wrung it out with a savage twist, then handed it to Flame so she might tie it around his hand. "If that bite had been any deeper, she'd have severed the tendons!"

Flame turned his hand over to examine the bloody wound more closely. "This is bleeding so freely you'll not get an infection. Human bites can be very nasty, you know."

"How could I not know!" Rafael exploded in a fit of temper.

Flame looked up at her husband, hoping he would have something soothing to say to his friend, but Joaquin shook his head slightly, warning her to keep still, and she did. She wrapped the handkerchief around Rafael's hand, then tied the ends in a firm knot. "There, that will do until you get to the house."

"Thank you," Rafael offered grudgingly, and lost in the bitterness of his own thoughts, he strode away toward the horses.

Flame bent down to put her fingers in the water and, finding it not terribly cold, made a teasing suggestion. "We seem to be the only ones who haven't been in the river this afternoon. Would you like to go for a swim?"

"Why not?" Joaquin agreed with a laugh. "I know you won't bite me."

Flame gave him a seductive grin as she began to unbutton her blouse. "Do love bites count?"

"No, they do not." Joaquin pulled off his boots, swiftly tossed his clothes aside, and waded out into the river until the water reached his chest. "Hurry up! I'm getting lonely out here all by myself."

Flame tossed the last of her apparel upon his and

225

swam out to meet him. The sun was warm, the water delightfully cool, and she could think of nothing more fun than going swimming with him until he pulled her into his arms and gave her a deep, lingering kiss. "Why, Joaquin, isn't swimming all you had in mind?" she asked sweetly, her green eyes aglow with love.

He was so tall that while the river presented no danger to him, she had to tred water to stay afloat. With a devilish chuckle he hugged her tight, guiding her supple body to his, showing her how easy it was to make love while standing in the water where her slight weight was suspended by the river's gentle current. Following his unspoken instructions, she wrapped her legs around his hips as her arms encircled his neck. "You can drown me in love any time," she whispered in his ear, pleased he knew how to turn a lovely afternoon into such erotic splendor even if Rafael very foolishly did not.

Without making any explanation for the state of her clothing, Alicia handed her damp garments to Veronica and closed her door. She took a leisurely bath with perfumed soap, shampooed the mossy scent of the river out of her hair, then lay down and took what she considered a well-deserved nap. When she awakened it was already dusk and she had to hurry so as not to keep the others waiting. She chose a satin gown of a deep rose hue and could not help but notice the color complimented the bright blush that had yet to leave her cheeks. Her skin felt cool to the touch so her fever had not returned, but she knew the tenuous hold she had upon her emotions would be readily apparent at first glance. She would not give Rafael Ramirez the satisfaction of beating her at any game and rather than have supper served in her room, which was her first

226

choice, she walked gracefully into the parlor and straight to Eduardo's side.

"Ah, Señorita Caldwell, that gown is stunning with your fair coloring, but you are so very pretty I think it matters little what you wear." The rancher smiled broadly, thrilled by the sight of Alicia's warm smile.

"Thank you," Alicia responded softly, now so used to his constant flattering comments she expected little else from him. He was dressed in a handsome suit of dark grey trimmed with black braid and shiny silver buttons. In the traditional Mexican style, the short jacket made his powerful build all the more impressive, but while she considered him an attractive man, she wanted no more than his friendship. When he offered his arm to escort her into the dining room, she turned to look back at Flame and Joaquin. "Isn't Rafael going to join us tonight?" she asked with what she hoped would sound like no more than idle curiosity.

Joaquin gave her a sly wink. "No, since we are leaving for Tierrasanta in the morning, he's asked to be excused and has gone back to *La Reina*. I'll tell him you asked about him if you like."

Forcing herself to smile sweetly for Eduardo's benefit, Alicia declined his offer. "No, I'm sure he is far too busy to appreciate any remarks of mine so please don't bother him." Attempting to hide her surprise as well as her disappointment, she turned her attention to their host. That Rafael would turn tail and run simply astonished her. She had expected him to stare at her all through supper, an icy glare in the dark brown eyes she had seen only that afternoon smoldering with bright sparks of passion as he had kissed her. She raised her fingertips to her lips where the pain of that assault still troubled her. Was there no end to the man's insults? He might be able to escape her on the trip to Tierrasanta, but as soon as they boarded *La Reina* for the voyage home he would be forced to share his meals with her again, so to avoid her tonight was pointless. Having no way to spite the man for his arrogance, she nodded politely at each of Eduardo's remarks, assuring him frequently that she was fascinated by his conversation if not with the man himself.

Rafael realized his mistake the moment he walked into his cabin, for he was in no mood to be confined in such a small space. He did have his notes to organize and condense—he'd not lied to Joaquin about having work to do—but he was loath to do it. He tossed his briefcase on his bunk, trying to jar the memory of Alicia's luscious form from his mind, but he could not look at the narrow bed without recalling the night she had spent in it. He should have kept the bloodstained sheets rather than tossing them overboard before dawn, for now that night seemed more fantasy than fact. Clearly the young woman had two completely separate identities: one an abandoned seductress, the other a spiteful she-wolf. Unfortunately, he had tangled with the latter once too often. His right hand throbbed painfully, reminding him their last encounter had indeed been all too real. "I should have drowned her!" he exclaimed only to himself. "I had every right!" Shoving his briefcase aside, he stretched out on the bunk and closed his eyes. Immediately his mind was flooded with the image of a smiling Alicia waving to him from the cliffs near Joaquin's home. She had looked so innocent that morning, so vulnerable, he had thought himself a totally unfit companion for her. How absurd that first impression had been, for her sweetness carried a sting far sharper than a honeybee's. She had torn his emotions to shreds, then hurled them right back in his face. She had made a dagger of his offer of

228

marriage and thrust it clear through his heart. His mind filled with grisly metaphors, he did not respond to the knocking at his door until it grew quite loud. "Yes, what is it?" he finally called out.

Domingo opened the door a few inches and peeked in. "The cook wants to know if you'd like some supper. Several of the men have been fishing so the catch is fresh."

"No, tell him I thank him, but no." Rafael felt more like retching than eating but sat up to address his visitor. "Wait a minute, Domingo. I want to assure you that our inquiries in Tierrasanta will be very discreet ones. We've no reason to embarrass you needlessly, so I don't want you to worry that we will."

Domingo frowned slightly, his hand still on the door as though he were anxious to be on his way. "You have sworn you are seeking only the truth and I'm certain you will find it. The whole town knows I am the son of Joaquin Villarreal even though he likes to pretend otherwise."

"Joaquin does not bother with pretense and neither do I. You will come with us, of course, and I hope by this time tomorrow the matter will be settled to our complete satisfaction."

"So do I," Domingo readily agreed, knowing full well it was impossible for both of them to be pleased by the results of the coming investigation. "The town is isolated even though it is on the coast. Few visitors wander through, so the summer a ship anchored in the harbor and the nights its crew spent ashore have not been forgotten. You will not have to bribe people to recall what happened. The events are still fresh in everyone's mind."

"That is my hope," Rafael announced confidently, for he wanted the matter resolved as quickly as possible so he could return to San Francisco where he planned to forget the infuriatingly unobtainable Miss Alicia Caldwell with astonishing speed. He dismissed Domingo with a curt nod, picked up his briefcase, and set it upon the small desk. He had been puzzled by the case all along, but the answers to the riddle of Domingo's past were within his grasp and he meant to use them to such stunning advantage that the trip would be well worth his while, regardless of the disastrous outcome of his attempt to win a fair lady's heart. "If she even has one!" he muttered angrily to himself, sincerely doubting that the volatile blonde even possessed something as precious as a heart to offer in the first place.

Chapter XII

In the eighteen years since Joaquin had visited Tierrasanta, the only noticeable progress had been in decay. The dusty main street was filled with deep ruts, the widely scattered adobe houses were in desperate need of fresh coats of whitewash, and it looked as though the same men who had been too drunk to wander home years before were still sound asleep in the shade of the cantina's wide veranda. It was nearly noon and the small square at the center of town was deserted. It would be several hours before cool breezes coming off the Pacific Ocean would provide a respite from the oppressive heat and encourage neighbors to gather together. Now the town was unnaturally quiet, with only the occasional whine of a hungry mosquito breaking the silence that gripped all other forms of life in a suffocating hold.

The two dozen local fishermen had already returned with the day's meager catch. As *La Reina* entered the small harbor, they looked up from their nets to cast suspicious glances at the magnificent ship, but if such an unexpected sight inspired their curiosity, they kept it well hidden. When Joaquin, Rafael, and their companions reached the shore in a lifeboat, none had either the interest or the initiative to come forward to ask what the reason for their visit might be. Little children, having no such fear of strangers, came running to meet them and, discovering Domingo in their midst, called out his name. They scampered about, tugging upon the men's hands in hopes of receiving a coin or two for their efforts at providing a friendly welcome and they were not disappointed. The older boys and girls, while no less curious, were far too shy to come forward and did no more than peek from their windows.

"Charming place," Rafael remarked absently as they climbed the steep incline to the church. "The houses are scattered about the hills like heaps of sun-bleached bones. I'm surprised they don't have a *plaza* built in the shape of a skull."

At the steps of the church, Joaquin turned to look down on the sleepy little village. "You're right. Except for the presence of a few children, Tierrasanta looks more like a ghost town than a thriving village and it looked no better eighteen years ago. It is no wonder Carmela Muñoz was so desperate for her son to leave here she swore she was married to me. I still recall the summer I spent here with a shudder. I swear the chickens scratching about in the dust lead more exciting lives than the people do."

Rafael gestured for Domingo to come forward. "You will introduce us to the priest. The rest of you may rest here." They had brought five men with them, Tomás and four others. They were a handsome group, tall, dark-haired, and well-built sailors Joaquin trusted to follow his orders without question.

As Domingo came forward, he could no longer hold his tongue and replied to Rafael's request with a stinging accusation. "Tell me again that you won't

232

stoop to pretense!"

"Is there something you wish to say to me before we interview the priest?" Rafael asked with exaggerated calm, thinking his efforts to teach the boy some manners had obviously failed.

"I know what you're doing!" the young man protested fiercely. "Do you think I have no brain at all? It is obvious why you've chosen the men you did!"

Joaquin interrupted then. "I choose whomever I damn well please to accompany me. Did you expect me to ask you for recommendations?"

Undaunted, Domingo continued to argue. "You've brought men who look more like you than I do!"

"That wasn't difficult," Joaquin remarked slyly, not about to admit that this had been their plan all along. "Regardless of why I picked them, they are here. Now let's not waste anymore time arguing out here on the steps. I wish to meet the priest."

"His name is Ortega, Daniel Ortega. Introduce yourself!"

"Fine. Remain here with the others." Joaquin strode to the door and, grabbing the wrought-iron handle, nearly yanked it from the old wood in his haste to get inside. Rafael turned away to hide his grin and followed his friend quickly. He knew Domingo had outsmarted only himself by antagonizing Joaquin, for now he would have no part in gathering the information they needed about his mother.

The priest was replacing the tall white candles in the hammered tin candlesticks on the altar and they waited at a respectful distance until he had completed that task.

"Father Ortega?" Rafael called out softly, not wanting to startle the man.

The arrival of strangers was so rare an occurrence that Daniel Ortega simply gawked at the two men, then noting their handsome appearance and fine clothes, he remembered his manners and smiled warmly. "Good afternoon. I am Father Ortega. How may I be of service?"

"We'd like to talk with you about a woman who grew up here in Tierrasanta. Is there somewhere we may speak in private?" Rafael inquired in a respectful tone.

The priest gestured toward the first pew. "There is no place more private than this." He was a young man, not yet thirty, with a boyish face and thick brown curls. He did not know what to make of his visitors. Apprehensive, he hoped their questions would not prove too difficult for him to answer. Once they were seated, he leaned forward to address them both. "Who is the woman in question?" he asked politely.

"Carmela Muñoz. We are distantly related and never having had the privilege of meeting her, we'd like to know what sort of woman she was." Rafael's Spanish flowed with such fluid rhythm that the priest did not doubt the truth of his words for an instant.

For a moment, Daniel was at a loss for words, then he began to describe the dead woman as best he could. "Carmela was all that any woman could ever hope to be. She was pious, attended Mass each day, and shared what little she had with anyone in need. I never saw her frown. She was always smiling and it was more than a smile really; it was an inner glow, a strength of character that lit her soul with beauty." Stopping then to take a breath, he could not help but see his visitor's astonished glances and thought perhaps he had said something wrong. "Was there something more you wanted to hear? Something else?"

"Why no, Father, please continue. Tell us all you can about the dear woman," Rafael encouraged warmly.

"Yes, she was very dear to us all," Ortega admitted readily. "She was no more than thirty-three when she died, the same age as our blessed Saviour." He crossed himself then, certain he had discovered an important comparison. "She was a saintly woman, gentlemen. Although her life was filled with hardship, she never once complained."

"What sort of hardships did she suffer?" Rafael prompted softly.

The priest took a deep breath, uncertain how to reveal the truth in a tasteful manner. "You say you are relatives?"

"Yes, we are," Rafael assured him.

"Well then, I suppose you have every right to know her story. She married when she was very young, long before I came here. Tragically, she was deserted by her husband and had to raise her son all alone. The boy is obstreperous but very bright. I tutored him myself for several years, which I must admit was a trial to us both. He's gone to California to find his father, although I tried my best to dissuade him from making such a foolhardy journey."

"Foolhardy?" Rafael prompted again.

"Yes. If Joaquin Villarreal cared so little for his wife and son that he abandoned them without a word in all these years, I knew he would not welcome Domingo and tried to convince him not to go. It had been his mother's fondest wish he would know his father though, and he felt he had to fulfill her dream. He saw the trip as a sacred duty."

"Of course." Rafael nodded thoughtfully. "Carmela was married to a man named Joaquin Villarreal? Are you certain of that?"

235

"Oh yes, quite certain. It was impossible to exchange more than a few words with Carmela before she mentioned his name. She prayed every day for his safe return to Tierrasanta, but alas, her prayers went unanswered."

"How did she die?" Joaquin asked with obvious concern. "Did she fall ill, or perhaps meet with some accident?"

Daniel pursed his lips thoughtfully as he smoothed the soft folds of his robe with a self-conscious touch. "Carmela had only one dream, that someday her husband would return to take her and Domingo to his ranch in California. When the boy reached seventeen, I think she finally realized that dream would never come true in time to help him lead the good life she'd always hoped he'd have. There is no way to explain what happened to her then except to say she died of a broken heart. After so many years of clinging to the hope of a bright future for her son, she lost sight of that vision and lost the will to live. The whole town mourned her loss, for we all loved her every bit as dearly as Domingo did. As I said, he's gone to California to find his father. I do not envy the man if he succeeds, for there can be no excuse for the shameful neglect he showed Carmela and the boy."

Joaquin nodded as if to agree. "Why did Carmela never go to California herself to confront him with that charge?"

"As you must know, when Domingo was small the times were very troubled, travel unsafe, especially for a woman with a small child. This is a poor village. I doubt she ever had enough money to allow her to consider undertaking such a journey. It was also a matter of pride. Villarreal had promised to return and she believed he would."

236

Not wanting to dwell on that unfulfilled promise since they had no idea who had made it, Rafael adroitly changed the subject. "I understand her mother is living still?" he inquired.

"Yes, she is. She is quite frail though, so you must not delay if you wish to visit her. You will pass her house as you head back into town. It is the third on the left. In front she has a small flower garden of which she is very proud. You cannot miss it."

"Thank you for the directions. We'd like to speak with her too." Rising to his feet, Rafael glanced up at the gruesome painting of the martyrdom of Saint Stephen above the altar and appeared to have a sudden inspiration. "I wonder if your church might have some record of Carmela's marriage?"

"Oh yes, of course. Father Casteñeda kept meticulous records. There is little else to occupy a priest's time here," he commented wearily as he rose to his feet and led the way into the sacristy. "I believe it would be in this volume." He pulled a worn leather-bound book from a crowded shelf and placed it upon the rickety table below. Mumbling softly to himself, he calculated the years in his head and then began to thumb through the stiff parchment pages. "It was in the summer of 1855, I believe. Yes, here it is." Standing aside, he pointed out the faded entry. "Carmela married Joaquin Villarreal on August 2, 1855. Father Casteñeda performed the ceremony and her parents were the witnesses."

Rafael scanned the stained page with a critical eye, looking for any sign the names or date had been altered, but the writing was the same free-flowing script of the other entries, the once glossy black ink now faded to a dull grey. Thinking the entire page could have been forged, he turned it to read the records of the previous marriages, then those occurring in the months afterward. If someone had tampered with the records of the village, they had done such a masterful job he could not detect it, and with a smile he stepped back and thanked the priest for his trouble.

Knowing they had found nothing of any value to their cause, Joaquin nevertheless pressed a generous contribution into the young priest's hand. "Please say a Mass for Carmela's soul and use the rest as you see fit."

Astonished by the man's generosity, Daniel realized he had not asked his name. "I don't know how to thank you. You said you are part of the Muñoz family?"

"Yes, we are. Thank you again for your time," Rafael replied quickly, and taking Joaquin's arm, he led him back through the dimly lit church and out into the sunshine. "Not a word of this in front of Domingo," he warned in a hoarse whisper.

Joaquin eyed his friend with a skeptical glance, more deeply moved by the priest's sad account than he cared to admit. "I've forgotten none of your suppositions, but I know well enough not to discuss them with him. Ortega is a priest, however, and would never speak ill of the dead."

"If we have to interview the entire town, then we will. Surely not everyone will have so forgiving a memory."

Pretending to have no knowledge of the location of the Muñoz home, the pair stopped at several others to ask directions. Their appearance was handsome, their manners fine, and their questions were readily accepted as sincere. At each house they heard a tale identical to the priest's: Carmela had been a dear woman who had been abandoned by the despicably cruel Joaquin Villarreal.

Returning to the church for their companions, they

238

went then to visit Domingo's grandmother. Just as described, her small yard was filled with flowering plants limply struggling to survive the summer's scorching heat. Taking great care to phrase his explanation carefully, Rafael outlined exactly what he wished the young man to do. "Knock on the door, then greet your grandmother and tell her you've brought men from California who wish to speak with her. You have my word that we wish her no harm."

"Your word!" Domingo scoffed bitterly, positive the attorney's word was totally worthless. He knocked at the door of the small dwelling, but several minutes passed before a tiny white-haired woman appeared. Although astonished by the sudden appearance of her grandson, she was delighted by the prospect of meeting his companions and smiled warmly. Even though she was now past sixty, she had the same sweet prettiness she had had as a child and her mind was still very keen.

"Señora Muñoz, this is a great pleasure," Rafael began graciously.

Raising her hands in a gesture of helplessness, the dear lady interrupted before Rafael could announce the purpose of their visit. "Please, will you speak a bit louder. My hearing, like my eyesight, is not all that good anymore."

Perplexed, Rafael glanced over at Domingo, who nodded. "That's the truth. My grandmother is quite deaf and nearly blind."

Rafael had seldom heard worse news, but he carried on as if undaunted. He moved close to the elderly woman and bent down, hoping he could be heard without having to shout. "We want to know all you can tell us about the man your daughter married. What do you remember about him?"

239

Amparo Muñoz's smile vanished instantly at his question. "He was the devil himself in disguise!" she spat out angrily.

"I agree," Rafael responded promptly. "Can you recall his appearance? Was he short, heavyset?"

"Oh, no." Amparo shook her head emphatically. "He was very tall, and quite handsome. My little girl was much too impressed by his appearance to see the blackness of his heart."

"Can you see my face, Señora Muñoz? Do I look anything like him?" Rafael moved closer still, praying her eyesight was not nearly as poor as she claimed.

The dear little lady squinted slightly, then reached out to touch his cheek. "I am sorry. I can tell you are a man, but little more."

"Did you speak with him often? Do you think you might recognize the sound of his voice?" Rafael was not about to abandon his cause while Amparo was being cooperative.

"His voice? No, it has been too many years."

On a signal from Rafael, Joaquin stepped closer. "Your garden is very colorful, Señora Muñoz."

"Thank you." Amparo actually blushed she was so pleased by the compliment. "Some of the plants are as old as I am, but as long as I tend them they still bloom."

"They are lovely," Joaquin stated simply before backing away.

"You are too kind," Amparo insisted bashfully, embarrassed by his praise.

Domingo glared defiantly, certain they were trying to trick his grandmother into saying something she should not in order to use her words against him. "Is there anything else?"

"Yes," Rafael assured him swiftly. Leaning down, he again spoke distinctly to be certain Amparo could understand his words. "We are trying to find your daughter's husband. Do you recall anything that would help us?"

"His name is Joaquin Villarreal. He was very rich. His ranch was in Alta California, near Monterey. Can you not find him there?" she asked with a puzzled frown. "Could you not find him, Domingo?"

"I found him," Domingo replied sullenly.

"Domingo, why don't you remain here with your grandmother while we look around a bit more. We will tell you when we're ready to go back to the ship," Rafael promised before the young man could tell his grandmother Joaquin Villarreal was standing no more than three feet away. He did not want her upset needlessly.

From where they stood they could see the masts of *La Reina* clearly, but Domingo did not know whether or not he wanted to go back on board. He was safe there in Tierrasanta, while he feared he would be putting himself in grave danger if he again placed himself in Joaquin's hands. Still, the man was his father and owed him the inheritance he was determined to collect. There was also the fact that he would never see Alicia again if he lacked the courage to return to the ship. Surely she deserved a man with more bravery than that.

"Domingo?" Rafael prompted impatiently, wondering what was troubling the young man. "If you'd rather not come with us, you needn't. We'll know where to find you."

Never had he had to make such a difficult decision, but Domingo knew if he let *La Reina* sail back to California without him, his whole life, as well as his mother's, would have been for naught. "No, I will go with you. Do not forget me."

241

"That would be impossible!" Joaquin scoffed loudly. Disgusted with the lack of results of their inquiries, he scuffed the toe of his right boot in the parched earth of the path and waited impatiently for Rafael to bid Amparo Muñoz good-bye.

That courtesy completed, Rafael headed toward the cantina. "If anyone will remember you, it's got to be the proprietor of this place."

"It's not me we want remembered!" Joaquin reminded him sharply.

"I know that, but he doesn't," Rafael responded with a sly grin. He followed Joaquin and the five other men inside, waited until they had been seated at a battered table, and then approached the long bar. The heavyset man drying glasses behind it tried not to appear astonished by the sudden wealth of customers so early in the day, but he did not succeed.

"How long have you worked here?" Rafael inquired with the ready confidence that always got him a reply.

"Fifteen, maybe twenty years," the bartender responded.

"Eighteen years ago there was a ship that dropped anchor in your harbor to make repairs. The ship and crew were here for two months. Were you working here then?"

"Maybe I was," the bartender replied with a shrug. "I remember the ship. It belonged to Carmela Muñoz's husband," he remarked with obvious distaste. "If you are a friend of his, you're not welcome here."

"I never met the man," Rafael assured him with a smile. "Would you remember him if you saw him?"

"Villarreal?" the man asked skeptically. "He'll never show his face here again."

Rafael laid a twenty-dollar gold piece on the bar. "If you can pick Joaquin Villarreal out of the six men who

242

came in here with me, that's yours."

"What?"

"You heard me. The citizens of Tierrasanta all seem to have the same low opinion of the man. Twenty dollars says you can't recognize him."

"I thought you just said you'd never met the man!"

"No, I said I hadn't met Carmela's husband. Now which of my companions is Villarreal?" Rafael stood back to be out of the man's line of vision. "Well, which one is he?"

Coming out from behind the bar, the thick-waisted man walked slowly toward the only occupied table. Six pairs of dark brown eyes regarded him with open curiosity as he approached, but none of the men seemed apprehensive. They were the calmest bunch he could ever recall meeting, their poses relaxed, their gazes steady. They all looked like murderers to him and he turned back to look at Rafael, noticing for the first time his coolly confident manner was no different than his companions'. "What manner of trick is this?"

"It is no trick," Rafael assured him. "One of these six is Joaquin Villarreal. Which one?"

The bartender walked around the table with a measured step, searching each face for some clue to the owner's identity. Frustrated when he could not recognize the man everyone had cursed for so many years, he threw up his hands in disgust. "I don't know which one he might be!"

Rafael nodded slightly. "Good. Now we'd like to rest here a while and see if any of your customers has a better memory than you." He flipped the gold piece into the bartender's hand, then took a chair with his friends. "That should cover the first round. Keep the rest for yourself."

Not about to reject such good fortune over a matter

of pride, the man quickly supplied a bottle of whiskey and seven shot glasses. "Would you be willing to offer the same bet to others?" he asked hopefully.

"Yes," Rafael agreed. "I'll provide something for your trouble if you find them, too."

With the bartender's frantic encouragement, the men of Tierrasanta were soon lining up to take a chance at winning a gold piece. The mood of the cantina swiftly grew boisterous as each took his turn, ordered a drink, and sat down to see if the next man had any better luck.

Since the odds were in Rafael's favor, and he had each man whisper his guess so as not to alert the others, he doubted there was any real danger to Joaquin, but just so there wouldn't be, he paid out the coins in a random fashion so that each man who thought he had won had picked a different man. Certain his deception would not be discovered until they had returned to the ship, Rafael waited until he had satisfied his curiosity that Joaquin's image had not been indelibly imprinted on anyone's memory before he ended the game. Everyone was more than a little drunk by then, but they managed to make they way back up the hill to Amparo Muñoz's home without mishap.

Raucous music from the cantina had assailed his ears all afternoon, but Domingo had ignored it while he had attempted to question his grandmother in hopes of learning something she had forgotten to tell Rafael, something he prayed would help him rather than the inquisitive attorney. "There must have been something about Villarreal that made him different from all the others. Try to think. Did he have a scar that you noted, or a birthmark?"

"I do not understand why you are suddenly so curious," Amparo protested, but after more than an

244

hour of prodding, she finally recalled something important. "He wore a ruby ring," she remarked with a slight frown, attempting to describe it in detail. "I'd forgotten it, but it was really quite pretty. It was in a delicate gold setting so it looked more like a lady's ring than a man's. He wore it on the little finger of his right hand. I'd hoped he would give it to your mother, but he said it was his good-luck token and he'd never part with it."

"Never?" Domingo asked in alarm, for he had never noticed Joaquin wearing any such ring.

"Well, that's what he said, but I think now it was a lie like everything else." Since his mother's death, she had no longer kept her opinion of his father's treachery to herself. It was one thing to pretend with a small child; quite another to try to fool a young man.

When Rafael rapped lightly at the door, Domingo ran to open it. Not wanting his grandmother to overhear their conversation, he stepped outside and pulled the door closed. Turning to Joaquin, he chose his words carefully. "You wore a good-luck charm years ago. What became of it?"

Mystified by his question, Joaquin shook his head. "I'm not the superstitious sort. Who told you I was?"

"You're denying you ever wore one?" Domingo challenged with a fierce determination to make him admit the truth.

Seeing barely controlled fury darken his young charge's expression, Rafael entered the discussion before it turned violent. "He's telling you the truth. I've known him all my life and he's never worn any kind of charm. He makes his own luck just as I do."

Exasperated, Domingo tried once again to get at the truth. "It wasn't a charm, it was a ring."

245

Joaquin held out his hands to prove his point. "I've never even owned a ring, much less worn one. Did your grandmother tell you I did?"

Not wanting to endanger the dear woman's life, Domingo refused to admit where he had learned about the ring. "Lots of people saw it," he insisted proudly.

"I won't argue that they might have seen someone wearing a ring, but it was not I!" Joaquin proclaimed just as belligerently.

Stepping between the two before they could come to blows, Rafael tried first to draw more information from Domingo. "If your grandmother described a ring, then tell us about it. It's possible Joaquin just might recognize it and remember who owned it."

"He should since it was his!"

"Domingo"—Rafael grabbed the front of his shirt and nearly lifted him off the ground before he was certain he had the young man's attention—"tell us about the ring. If it was your father's, then it may lead us to him!"

Domingo struggled to free himself from Rafael's confining hold so he could draw a breath deep enough to speak. "It was a ruby ring he wore on his little finger. Do you recognize it now?"

Frowning, Rafael shook his head. "No, I've never known Joaquin to wear a ruby ring."

But at that instant, an incredulous Joaquin began to shout. *"Madre de Dios!* Holy Mother of God! Why didn't you tell me this sooner?"

Startled by the violence of Joaquin's response, Domingo blurted out the truth. "I didn't even know about it until this afternoon!"

"Is that what your grandmother told you? That the Joaquin Villarreal she knew wore a ruby ring? A woman's ring in which he took such great pride he

246

never removed it from his hand?" Joaquin demanded hoarsely.

Still caught in the middle, Rafael gave his friend and Domingo each a shove to separate them. "Just a minute here. There's no need to come to blows over this. Do you know who wore that ring, Joaquin?"

Joaquin whipped off his hat and wiped the sweat from his brow with his shirt sleeve. "I knew him all right." His expression filled with hatred, he turned away then, clearly unwilling to say anything more.

Although the crowd at the cantina was still partying boisterously on the gold coins he had passed out, Rafael had no desire to tarry. "We've got to get back to the ship before there's any trouble," he warned. "Come on, we've been here too long already. We can discuss the ruby ring later."

Domingo hung back, for Joaquin's shock when he had mentioned the ring had actually seemed genuine. That was impossible, of course, but still, no man could be so accomplished an actor as that. "I'm coming with you! Just a minute!" He dashed back into the little house to bid his grandmother farewell, but as he came back to the door, Rafael blocked his way.

"I neglected to give your grandmother something for helping us." Dropping half a dozen gold coins into the boy's hand, he waited at the door while he gave them to the dear little lady. "Hurry, his may be the only chance we'll have!"

Although he had no idea why they were in such a desperate hurry, Domingo followed the others back down the hill and to the beach. There were several children playing near the boat, but no adults appeared either to try to stop them or to bid them farewell. As soon as they were all on board *La Reina* and the longboat secured, Joaquin gave the order to weigh anchor. Leaving the command of the ship in Arturo Duran's capable hands, he led Rafael to his cabin, and when Domingo followed right on their heels, he did not object. After pouring them each a stiff brandy, he sank down into a chair and, getting comfortable, rested his heels upon the seat of another.

"I know you've never believed me, Domingo, but I did not marry your mother. That's the only thing I have known for certain: that I did not marry her, but I could not imagine who had. That's what we hoped to learn here, but now that I know what happened, I am so thoroughly sickened I don't want to believe it."

Thinking brandy should be tossed down the throat like a shot of whiskey, Domingo quickly dispatched his, then realized his error. He was certain his throat was afire with the fiercest of poisons, but Rafael brought him a cup of water and pounded on his back until he caught his breath. "You are my father," he finally insisted in a hoarse rasp.

"No, your father called himself by my name, that's all." Joaquin took a sip of brandy and waited until its numbing warmth reached clear to his toes before he continued. "A man named Rodriguez was captain of *La Reina* that summer. I was the first mate. I had the responsibility for the port watch, keeping the log, and supervising the running of the ship. There was a second mate who was in charge of the starboard watch and took command of the ship when Rodriguez and I were below. His name was Julio Villalobos and I have never sailed with a meaner man. I took an intense dislike to him from the moment we were introduced and nothing he ever did improved that first impression. He was only a year or two older than I, almost as tall, and quite handsome, but his pleasing appearance was deceiving, for he had a cruel streak a mile wide. By the end of our

"Yes, indeed he does."

"Then we'll do it." Joaquin touched his glass to Rafael's their pact to seek revenge agreed upon and sealed. They then sat together lazily plotting just what they would do with the despicable Julio Villalobos until the rolling hills of Eduardo Lopez's ranch drew into view.

Chapter XIII

After spending one entire day in Eduardo Lopez's company, Alicia was now positive coming to Mexico had been the worst mistake of her life. She had stayed in her room until nearly noon, but rather than dimming the man's interest in her, her absence had merely served to make it all the more keen. He had insisted upon taking her on another ride, and seeing her hesitation, Flame had quickly invited herself along, but not even the vivacious redhead's company had distracted the Mexican rancher from concentrating his attention almost exclusively upon his blond guest. He was proud to have served under General Ignacio Zaragoza at Puebla on May 5, 1862 and deservedly so, for he had displayed great skill in commanding native troops who had been armed with no more than antique weapons yet had defeated France's well-disciplined and well-equipped military. He recounted that battle in the most stirring manner possible, but Alicia did little more than nod politely and smile, her display of interest a courtesy and no more. "That battle wasn't really all that decisive though, was it?" she asked quite casually, her knowledge of Mexico's history more extensive than he had thought.

Deeply hurt by what he considered an insulting question, Eduardo frowned pensively. "It served as an inspiration to the Mexican people that European soldiers were not invincible, as many had feared."

"Well, that was certainly an important lesson and I'm sure you must have been very brave," Flame interjected with an engaging smile, beginning to feel sorry for the man since Alicia was giving him so little in the way of encouragement that day.

"Thank you, but the honor still belongs to my courageous countrymen rather than me. It took us five long years to drive the French from Mexico, but that victory was our first and it is remembered still," Eduardo explained with renewed enthusiasm, relieved at least one of his pretty guests was sympathetic, even if it was the wrong one.

While Flame was a far more attentive companion than Alicia, she found Eduardo's company a poor substitute for Joaquin's. Rather than count the day as a total loss, however, she made the most of her opportunities to observe his stock and surprised him by recognizing exactly which animals were superior and therefore the best buys. "I'd rather have only two fine brood mares for a start, Eduardo, than half a dozen who'd produce inferior colts."

While he would never have tried to cheat her, Eduardo had expected her to rely upon his judgment when it came to the selection of mares and he was disappointed to find her such an excellent judge of horseflesh that she could handle the matter herself. "I see you share your husband's passion for fine horses, Señora Villarreal, and since Sultan is such a splendid stallion, I'm glad he has an owner worthy of him."

"Thank you," Flame replied graciously, wondering if the man would ever run out of compliments. "Since I value speed as highly as beauty, why don't we have a race or two?" she suggested with the bewitching smile that made her requests so extremely difficult to refuse.

"Why not indeed," Eduardo readily agreed, knowing it would be a mistake to tell more war stories and hoping that Alicia would be impressed with his fine horsemanship if not the heroic deeds of his past. She was content to watch their races without taking part herself, but he was chagrined to find no matter which horse Flame rode, she won. It was not simply her lighter weight that was the determining factor but her willingness to push a mare she had never ridden before to the limits of the animal's endurance. Her enthusiasm for their sport was so infectious he could not help but enjoy the afternoon, but as they returned to his house to rest before supper, he finally succeeded in drawing Alicia aside so he could speak with her alone.

"Forgive me, but we will have so little time together I do not want to waste a minute of it," he began as he caught her hand.

"I don't believe we have wasted any time," Alicia remarked with dismay, deftly eluding his grasp. "You've kept us entertained every waking minute."

"Thank you," Eduardo responded with a shy grin, "but I am thinking more of you and me than of the others. I find you very attractive, but I think perhaps you are not so impressed with me."

Alicia swallowed nervously, knowing she had been very poor company. She was sorry she could not offer more of herself than she already had, but she had no intention of leading him on as she had when they had first arrived. That had been a grave error she would not repeat. "I think you are very nice," she finally managed to respond, but she knew this was not what he was anxious to hear.

Eduardo was nothing if not persistent and did not give up now that he finally had the lovely blonde's full attention. "Tell me the truth, Alicia. Is there someone else? Another man you love and hope to marry? If there is simply no hope for me, I would rather know it now than always wonder why I had failed to win your heart when you have so easily stolen mine."

The last rays of the afternoon sun gave his hair the bright sheen of fine silver. His expression was sincere, the admiration in his gaze for once surprisingly honest, but she found it impossible to speak the truth in return. She could not deny the hold Rafael had upon her emotions, but their relationship was so far removed from what she believed love to be she dared not call it by so sweet a name. Her feelings for Rafael were closer to an obsession, and one she feared might swiftly destroy her if she gave in to it again. This anguish was clear in her expression even though she could not bring herself to voice it aloud.

"Alicia?" Eduardo could not understand her reticence to respond, for either she loved another man or she did not. "Perhaps I have been too forward, but I don't want you to leave without knowing how much I want you to stay."

He was only making matters worse, but Alicia had no experience in tactfully turning aside declarations of love. None of the young men who had come to call upon her had ever gotten that far. "You are so kind, but really, I must go when the others do."

"Then there is a man waiting for you in California?" Eduardo asked dejectedly.

"No." That at least was the truth, but it provided scant consolation to Alicia although Eduardo brightened considerably.

Since he feared this might be as close as she would come to offering him some glimmer of hope he might one day win her hand, Eduardo leaned down and gave her cheek a light kiss. "I am glad to know that at least.

Let us simply make the most of our time together then."

His suggestion only served to remind Alicia of what poor use she had made of the last hour she had spent with Rafael. With that painful memory adding to her confusion, she excused herself and went to her room, where she found it impossible to rest without recalling how furious they had both been when they had parted. She had called the hypnotically attractive attorney hateful names and demanded he stay away from her, and he had done exactly that. But why did she feel so miserable and lost now that he was gone?

Domingo stood at the rail as Rafael and Joaquin prepared to go ashore, but when they called to him to join them he looked over his shoulder, assuming they must be speaking to another man standing nearby. When he realized they meant him, he walked over to where they stood, uncertain what they expected of him. "What is it now?" he asked in his usual belligerent tone, thinking if they had more work for him to do he would flat out refuse to do it.

Joaquin glanced over at Rafael and when his friend nodded as he tried to hide his smile, he could not stifle his own deep chuckle. "Domingo, I have never been your enemy. I know that will be difficult for you to accept, but it is the truth. I plan to mount a search for Julio Villalobos and if he can be found, I'd like you to be with me when I give him the punishment he deserves for the lies he told your mother."

"What?" Domingo shouted in dismay, astonished the man had such a plan. "But I want to kill him myself!" he insisted dramatically. "You've no right to interfere!"

Joaquin considered his opinion absurd and said so.

"I'm the one he was trying to harm, Domingo. Every lie he told your mother was calculated to blacken my name and was spoken for that purpose alone. He might have gotten away with it for eighteen years, but not any longer. If you're going to fight me every step of the way, we might as well part company now. I have the resources to find Villalobos if he can be found, and I intend to do it. If you won't come with me, then you'd better make certain you stay out of my way."

Domingo clenched his fists at his sides, knowing he was beaten again. The only friends he had were in Tierrasanta, and none of them would join him on a quest for revenge that might well take an entire lifetime. On the other hand, just as he boasted, Joaquin Villarreal had the wealth and power to do whatever he pleased. He might simply post a large reward on Villalobos's head, then sit back and wait for someone to collect it.

Understanding the young man's dilemma, Rafael did his best to reassure him he would be treated well if he joined them. "I've seen that relic of a firearm you had with you. Provided it will fire without exploding in your hand, what kind of shot are you?"

Domingo's cheeks burned with a bright blush not even his deep tan would cover as he reluctantly revealed the truth. "I was hoping I wouldn't have to fire it."

"You'd be better off without a pistol, Domingo, if you have no intention of firing it. Now I've talked Joaquin into parting with one of his Navy Colts. It will take us a few days to decide just what it is we want to do and I'll use part of that time to teach you how to use it. I don't think we can expect Villalobos to have changed except for the worse, and I want you to be able to handle yourself well enough that you won't shoot one of us in the back by accident while we're going after him. Now I already know you've got no idea how to use your fists, so I'll teach you how to fight too. If you want to come with us, then you've got to be an asset rather than a liability. Since I'm willing to spend my time teaching you what you need to know, I want your word you'll do your damnedest to learn it."

Domingo looked from the attorney to Joaquin. They were still the meanest pair of men he had ever met, but he also knew Villalobos had to be worse. That thought alone was enough to inspire him to accept their offer. "I want to go with you, but you must let me kill him," he insisted stubbornly.

"I can offer you no more than that opportunity, Domingo. I can't guarantee it," Joaquin pointed out logically. "He may be dead, or it's possible he's used so many different names we'll not be able to track him down. All I can promise is that we are going to try." He held out his hand then. "Are you with us?"

Domingo felt a strange mixture of revulsion and pride as he shook Joaquin's hand. "I'm with you," he announced forcefully, certain if anyone could find the beast who had been his father they could. Rafael clapped him on the back so enthusiastically he had to gasp for breath, but he was glad they seemed so willing to include him in their plans. He had done little to deserve such consideration, he realized suddenly. "I am sorry," he blurted out then.

"About what?" Joaquin asked nonchalantly, as though the young man hadn't caused him a substantial amount of grief.

"For the things I said to you"—he winced then—"and to your wife."

"You did no more than believe what you were told. Now go and collect your things and we'll see if Eduardo can give us some help tracing Julio. It's just possible he has enough contacts to be of some use."

Domingo nodded, then dashed off to gather what few clothes he had. At least they were clean this time, he thought, too excited by what now lay in store to be frightened by it.

Once the young man had gone, Rafael voiced what he was certain was on his friend's mind too. "Whose plan is more diabolical, Joaquin? Villalobos sired a son he knew would despise your name, but we've just turned that hate-filled boy loose on him. Unless we can finally succeed in teaching Domingo to control his temper, he'll be as vicious as a mad dog."

"I believe, if you set your mind to it, you can teach a sidewinder to slither in a straight line. You'll make a pet out of Domingo in no time now that you and he are on the same side," Joaquin teased. Rafael leaned back against the rail, his pose as relaxed as his mood. "It's been years since we've had the chance to really raise hell. I hope we can find the bastard. I don't care which of us is the first to shoot. He's going to end up very dead."

"Very dead indeed," Joaquin agreed with a wicked grin. "This trip gets better with every new day. Let's just hope it keeps up."

"Oh, it will," Rafael assured him confidently, but he did not share the thought that he regarded the return to Eduardo's ranch as something of a test. He was certain the heated confrontation in the river had burned away the last trace of feeling he had had for the incredibly spoiled Miss Alicia Caldwell. He could flex his right hand without cringing in pain and he was certain he could face her without the slightest twinge of regret that their romance had ended as swiftly as it had begun. He was positive he could speak with her politely, as though they were no more than the acquaintances they had pretended to be.

He was very sure of himself until he strolled out onto

the patio and found her seated near the fountain with their host. The man was talking in an animated fashion, smiling widely and gesturing dramatically, but Rafael needed only one glance at Alicia to know she was paying the man little heed. Whenever he had talked with her, she had always been seated on the edge of her chair, leaning toward him, moistening her lips with the tip of her tongue as she anxiously awaited her turn to offer a comment, but there was no trace of that delicious excitement in her pose now. Had she been alone, she could not have appeared more lost in her own thoughts. Then she glanced up, and finding him watching her, she smiled with a delight so pure its warmth enveloped him in a flood of affection that simply stunned him it was so unexpected. The next instant she had taken such a firm hold on her emotions that her joy was carefully hidden, but it was too late. He had been given a glimpse of her true feelings for him and he longed to see the radiance of her smile again and again. His firm resolve to avoid all but the most casual contact with her was completely forgotten by the time he reached her side.

"We didn't expect you back so soon." Alicia attempted to hide her excitement as she greeted him but was far too curious to succeed. "What did you discover in Tierrasanta? Anything that will help us?"

Rafael smiled warmly at Eduardo, meaning to include him in his response, his attitude toward him also more forgiving than it had once been. "This is a lengthy tale. I'm sure you'll hear it all at noon, but I'd rather Joaquin told it since it's his story rather than mine."

Greatly intrigued by this promise, Eduardo forgot for the moment how much he disliked the attorney. "I must alert my staff that you've returned so they can prepare a special meal."

"I'm sure whatever they had planned will be

261

delicious," Rafael assured him graciously. "We've brought a young man back with us. Do you have room for him? If not, he can share mine." Rafael hoped that would not prove necessary and was relieved when Eduardo told him it wasn't.

"Of course I have another room." He hesitated then, obviously reluctant to leave Alicia in the attorney's company. "You must forgive me. I will return shortly."

"There's no reason to rush," Alicia remarked sweetly, hoping she would not see him until time for lunch. "I'll wait right here."

Rafael waited until the man had entered the house through a side door before he sat down on the edge of the colorful tile fountain. "It looks like you two have become good friends," he remarked with only a touch of sarcasm lifting the corner of his mouth before he broke into a wide grin.

Alicia knew he was teasing, but rather than invent a clever reply she whispered the truth. "He's doing his best to be charming, but I just don't find him attractive. Now isn't there some news you can give me before he returns? Is it Domingo you've brought back with you?"

Rafael watched the sunlight adorn her hair with a shimmering golden halo and could not resist the impulse to reach out and caress a ringlet that had escaped the knot of curls atop her head. She did not brush his hand away, but he drew back quickly, thinking she soon would. "Yes, it's Domingo who's come with us. Does that make you happy?"

Alicia's long-lashed eyes widened slightly, then narrowed as she replied, "Must you tease me about him again? There is nothing more between us than there is between Eduardo and me, and I resent the fact you take such delight in questioning me about him. His situation is pathetic and I feel sorry for him, but nothing more than that."

262

Knowing he was again treading upon dangerous ground, Rafael asked a question he hoped she would answer far more willingly. "Why don't we declare a truce between us, since I'm sure neither of us truly wishes to argue?"

Alicia considered that option thoughtfully for a moment, then shook her head emphatically. "No, a truce is only a temporary halt to hostilities. I want them completely over between us for good."

"All right," Rafael agreed amicably, then pushing what he considered a rare opportunity to take advantage of one of her few obliging moods, he continued. "Since you are being so generous, I will be too. I'd still like you to marry me, and now, today. It would be ridiculous for us to wait until we reach San Francisco, since it may be some time before we return to California."

At the mention of marriage, Alicia felt her cheeks flood with a bright blush, but again his reason to wed seemed to have nothing to do with a deepening regard for her. Rather than risk insulting him again, she seized upon his other comment. "What do you mean it might be some time before we return home? My parents don't even know where I am, so I certainly can't remain here in Mexico indefinitely."

Rafael frowned, annoyed she so obviously considered her parents' feeling paramount to his. "What is your real objection—to our marriage or to remaining here in Mexico a while longer?" he asked brusquely.

Alicia rose to her feet and took several steps away, deeply disappointed to find their conversation had again become heated since she had tried so hard to be reasonable. All she truly wanted was more time, a chance to become close friends, a chance for their passion for each other to deepen into love, but before she could even begin to try to make him understand the

263

painful complexity of her emotions, Eduardo came rushing toward them. She turned back to look at Rafael, the expression in her eyes a stange mixture of confusion and affection, but he did no more than shake his head to warn her to be still.

Eduardo was pleased he had been able to return to the captivating blonde so swiftly and did his best to keep the conversation amusing until Veronica appeared to announce the noon meal was ready. He placed his arm lightly around Alicia's waist as he escorted her into the dining room and, as always, he placed her at his right and the attorney as far away from the pretty young woman as possible. That there was now another handsome man at his table did not upset him, for he considered Domingo far too young to give him any serious competition for Alicia's affections. When they had all been served savory *chilis rellenos* smothered in a delectable cheese that had been made there on his ranch, he encouraged Joaquin to begin his tale. "Rafael told me you have news of some sort and I'm eager to hear it."

Joaquin winked at Rafael, certain his friend would back him up no matter how far he stretched the truth. He then gave Domingo a reassuring smile, hoping his comments would be accurate enough to keep the hotheaded youth from disputing his word. "I spent some time in Tierrasanta in the summer of 1855. *La Reina del Mar* had suffered heavy damage in a storm and it took us longer than we'd anticipated to make all the repairs. Unfortunately, one of the members of the crew behaved in a less than gentlemanly fashion with one of the young ladies of the town. Domingo traveled all the way from Tierrasanta to my ranch in hopes of locating the man who had married his mother and then deserted her."

"Was this man your father?" Eduardo asked sympathetically.

Domingo nodded slightly, amazed Joaquin had managed to twist the truth so skillfully, and yet he had gone to California seeking his father, he couldn't deny that.

"I haven't seen him since that summer, but since the man served on my ship when the incident occurred, I can't help but feel an obligation to assist Domingo in his search in every way I can."

"Naturally," the Mexican rancher agreed. "Do you have any idea where this scoundrel can be found?"

"He was from Veracruz, very good-looking, bright, well educated, but unfortunately extremely self-centered. If he's still alive, I'm certain he can be found, for it's unlikely anyone who ever met him would have forgotten him when his personality is so abrasive. Would you be willing to help us locate him?"

"But of course! Just tell me what you need."

Joaquin had thought it extremely unlikely Lopez would refuse his request, but he appreciated his offer all the same. "Thank you. You have gained many valuable contacts over the years. Would you be willing to make inquiries on our behalf?" Joaquin saw that Flame was about to interrupt, but he raised his hand to ask for her patience a moment longer.

"It would be my pleasure." Eduardo signaled to his servants to serve their dessert, and Veronica and another young girl appeared carrying large trays of fresh fruit. As they waited on his guests, he asked for more detail. "Give me all the information you can provide about this man and I'll see it is relayed to the capital."

"As I said, when I last saw the fellow he was very handsome, and so proud of his success with the ladies

265

it's highly possible some jealous husband put an end to his life years ago. His name is Julio Villalobos and—"

Joaquin was interrupted then by a loud wail from Veronica as the heavy tray slipped from her grasp. Certain she would be severely punished for such carelessness, she quickly dropped to her knees, frantically scrambling to gather up the widely scattered fruit. Distressed by her plight, Domingo left his chair to help her, but that only embarrassed the girl all the more.

"The dear child is a talented dancer, but no waitress," Eduardo explained apologetically. "It could be merely a coincidence of names, but let me describe a Julio Villalobos who once served with me on General Zaragoza's staff, since it's possible they are one and the same. This man was nearly your height, quite vain about his appearance, although I have to admit he was remarkably good-looking. He said little unless it was to pay himself compliments, and while no man I knew liked him, for some reason women adored him. He was always receiving expensive gifts from one admirer or another. He wore a ruby ring and missed no opportunity to describe the beauty who had given it to him as a token of her undying love."

"That's our man. I'd not dared hope you would have met him yourself," Joaquin remarked with a wide grin. "Do you have any idea where he might be now?"

"No, but I'll wager Veronica does. Come here, little one."

The pretty girl's dark eyes filled with terror as she looked first at Domingo and then at her employer. Hesitantly she rose to her feet, tightly clutching a ripe papaya to her bosom. "My uncle rides with El Lobo, but I hate him!" she exclaimed hoarsely in Spanish, her voice choked with sobs.

"*Su tío o El Lobo?*" Rafael asked calmly, hoping to

clarify her answer.

"El Lobo!" Veronica cried, huge tears spilling over her thick lashes faster than she could wipe them away.

Since she could understand only parts of the girl's conversation, Alicia leaned toward their host. "I'm sorry. Is this Julio Villalobos the girl's uncle?"

Eduardo patted her hand gently. "No, her uncle rides with the villain." Knowing his answer explained little, he continued. "You must remember my country was at war for many years. Some men found peaceful occupations difficult to assume after years of waging war. Not all fought for the cause of freedom, you see; some fought solely for the thrill of battle, loving the horror as much as the honor of serving our nation. That was only an excuse to cover their lust for blood. The brightest of that evil lot found it a simple matter to gather followers at the war's end. They became bandit chieftains, rogues whose craving for danger leads them to prey upon their innocent countrymen now that the French troops have been driven from our land. They are a scourge that must be eradicated and I will be only too happy to do whatever I can to see El Lobo, as Julio now calls himself, brought to justice."

"You need have no fear for your uncle's life, Veronica. Our quarrel is with Julio. He's the only one we want," Joaquin assured the frightened maid.

Shyly brushing away her tears, the girl shook her head. "No, I know nothing," she insisted.

Eduardo waved her away. "Leave us." He waited until she and her companion had left the dining room, then smiled knowingly. "It will be enough for me to spread the word that an old friend wishes to speak wtih El Lobo. I assume you will pay well for the information concerning his whereabouts? With luck, he will be within a few days' ride of here."

"I'll be happy to pay whatever it costs."

"Joaquin!" Unable to sit still another instant, Flame asked crossly, "You don't actually plan to meet with this hateful bandit, do you?"

Joaquin laced her fingers in his before he brought her hand to his lips. "I already know he is not to be trusted, and I won't go alone. You needn't worry that I'll come to any harm."

"I thought we came here only to learn who Domingo's father really was, not to call him out for what he did." Flame's sweet features filled with anguish as she yanked her hand from his.

"Forgive me if my remarks frightened you, Señora Villarreal. Like all bandits, El Lobo depends upon the fierceness of his reputation to intimidate his victims. The man has more arrogance than courage, however, and he's not invincible." Eduardo had hoped his remarks would be soothing, but clearly they were not. Flame leapt to her feet and fled the room, her silent terror as audible as a scream.

Amazed by her brother's thoughtlessness, Alicia quickly offered her opinion. "You should have warned Flame about what you planned to do before you began to discuss it in front of the rest of us. It's no wonder she was horrified. So am I."

Certain he alone was responsible for the distressing turn the conversation had taken, Eduardo interrupted before Joaquin could reply. "No, this is entirely my fault. I should have waited to tell you what I know until we could have spoken in private. It was thoughtless of me to have frightened your wife. I am very sorry to have done so."

"The fault is mine, not yours," Joaquin insisted. "You'll excuse me please?" he asked as he rose to his feet.

"Of course," the rancher replied, obviously embarrassed by his error.

Alicia looked first at Rafael's determined expression and then at Domingo's deep frown. "You already had this all planned, didn't you? Do you really want this Julio Villalobos so badly you don't care what he's become?"

When Rafael looked up, his glance was as honest as his words. "Yes, we want Villalobos and we intend to get him. We had no way of knowing he's turned bandit, but that changes nothing."

"How can you be so incredibly stupid?" Alicia responded angrily. "There's no man alive who's worth the risk of your lives to kill!"

Since he still felt he should be the one to take revenge, Domingo spoke up proudly. "I would gladly go after the man alone, but they insist upon coming with me."

Alicia shut her eyes tightly, as if to force away a ghastly image in a bad dream. Domingo had entered their lives like a vicious whirlwind and had swept them all up into a nightmare of revenge. That Joaquin would think plotting that revenge a suitable topic for conversation while they shared a meal revolted her completely. "I think I'm going to be ill," she mumbled by way of excuse and hastily covering her mouth she ran to her room.

With an entire afternoon stretching before him without any hope of enjoying Alicia's company, Rafael gave his remaining two companions an inquiring glance. "Well, gentlemen, what do you say to a little target practice?"

Alicia feared her brother had made the worst mistake of his life in deciding to pursue the lecherous bandit who called himself El Lobo, but she knew Flame would have a far better chance of convincing him of that than she ever would. She remained in her room until time for supper, but Eduardo explained with a self-conscious smile that Joaquin and Flame had decided against joining them that night, so she knew their argument had not been resolved. Seated at the table with three men, she made no attempt to join in their conversation, although they discussed little more than the superb taste of the freshly caught red snapper. As always, their food was prepared to perfection, but after taking only a few bites, Alicia found she simply had no appetite. She glanced frequently at Rafael, and each time he gave her an engaging grin, but she could not forget that they hadn't come close to finishing their conversation that afternoon. He should have warned her what to expect too, she thought bitterly. Here she was, stranded in Mexico with three fools who planned to go chasing bandits! "Tell me, Eduardo, do you plan to join Joaquin when he goes after El Lobo?"

Not wishing to begin another unfortunate scene, Eduardo chose his words carefully. Recalling how little she had been impressed by his tales of the war, he gave the answer he thought she would consider appropriate. "No, this seems to be a question of honor and I think it is best left to those most directly involved."

"Is it really something so noble as that?" Alicia asked Rafael.

"Of course. The man's actions were totally reprehensible. What would you call it?"

Alicia shook her head, uncertain how she wished to reply. She again excused herself at the first possible minute, but after pacing her room restlessly for more than an hour, she knew she would never be able to go to sleep without talking with Rafael, or attempting to talk to him, at least. Perhaps she could convince him to talk some sense into Joaquin, since Flame had apparently failed.

She left her room and went to the one she believed to

270

be his. When there was no response to her knock, she opened the door and peered inside. There was a leather vest she recognized as his hanging on the back of a chair, but no sign of the man. Disappointed, she debated with herself a moment, then entered his room to await his return. She could pace there as easily as in her own room, she decided, and quickly took up a restless stride. Long before she had grown weary, she heard someone at the door, and knowing she did not want anyone but Rafael to know she visited his room, she knelt behind the bed to hide until she could be certain it was he.

Rafael had been doing no more than walking himself, but he preferred open land rather than the confines of his room. He closed his door, crossed to his bed, and sat down to pull off his boots. When Alicia rose and spoke his name, he leapt to his feet and wheeled around to face her, startled to find her in his room. "What in God's name were you doing hiding behind my bed?" he asked accusingly.

Alicia smoothed out the skirt of her soft blue gown as she apologized. "I'm sorry. I didn't mean to jump out at you like that, but I didn't want anyone else to see me here in your room."

"I know I should be used to our midnight meetings by now, but somehow I'm always surprised when you turn up so unexpectedly." Rafael peeled off his coat and tossed it aside but made no move to remove the rest of his clothing. "Well, if you are going to become angry and scream at me again, go ahead and do it, but just to be on the safe side, try to whisper."

"Can you never be serious?" Alicia approached him cautiously, purposely choosing to stand an arm's length away. "We have so many problems I don't even know where to begin, and all you can do is make jokes!"

Rafael straightened his shoulders wearily, certain

they had covered this same ground before. "Let me remind you where our last conversation ended. I asked you to marry me and you responded by saying you had no desire to remain here in Mexico, which has absolutely nothing to do with my proposal, and you accuse me of telling jokes? Ha!"

Startled by this burst of hostility, Alicia finally realized how rude she had been by not giving him a considerate reply. "I am so sorry. Please forgive me, but any discussion of marriage between us seems very ill-timed."

Rafael raised a well-shaped brow. "Ill-timed?" he asked incredulously. "How so?"

"We barely know each other," Alicia began with rapidly rising alarm, for this was not at all the subject she had come to discuss. "We argue constantly, even when there's no reason." Her eyes widened as she watched him move closer, but when she took a step backward, he moved forward. "Please, we needn't pay our whole lives for a few foolish moments."

"Foolish?" Rafael uttered with a low moan, not believing her choice of words, since they caused him such pain.

Fighting to retain her composure, Alicia forced herself to speak calmly. "I appreciate your offer of marriage. It is very kind of you, but I intend to wait for a man who can give me more."

"More what?" Rafael asked as he stepped closer still.

Alicia murmured a soft protest, but it was too late, for in the next instant he pulled her into his arms. His warmth seemed to envelop her very soul with the heat of his well-muscled, masculine body, but she was determined not to give herself to him ever again and stood stiffly in his arms rather than returning his embrace. "Stop it," she heard herself say. "I want so much more than you have to give. Can't you understand that? I simply want more."

Rafael placed his hand beneath her chin to force her gaze to meet his. His eyes were dark, filled with a menacing light, as he asked again, "More what, Alicia? Just what is it you want so badly?"

The slender blonde could scarcely draw a breath to respond. "More love." She sighed softly, as though revealing that hope were heartbreaking in itself.

Rafael considered her remark so ridiculous, he didn't know whether to laugh or cry. "You little fool," he whispered hoarsely, "no man has more love than what I've already given you." He lowered his mouth to hers then, sealing his words with a searing kiss he deepened as he felt her initial resistance melt into an inviting warmth. His hands moved slowly up her back, caressed her slender throat, then went to her golden curls. He removed the hairpins and tossed them aside, sending her tresses falling about her shoulders in a glorious cascade of gleaming waves. He wound his fingers in her flowing blond hair, holding her mouth captive beneath his own until, no longer steady on her feet, she began to sway in his arms. He picked her up gently then, and carried her to his bed. "You clothes are all very beautiful, but I wish you wouldn't wear so many of them," he complained as he fumbled with the hooks at her bodice, for attempting to undress her slowly was pure torture for him.

Her doubts smothered by his generous affection, Alicia did no more than smile seductively, not able to think clearly enough to be of any real assistance. She struggled instead to unbutton his shirt so she could run her fingers through the coarse curls covering his broad chest. She let her hands slide down the taut muscles of his stomach, then reached for his belt buckle. As he bent down to kiss her now bare breasts, she peeled away his trousers, caressing him with a honey-smooth touch that brought a low moan to his lips. Teasing, playful, endlessly affectionate, she soon had him completely undressed while she still wore several layers of lacy slips and one silk stocking. "Here, let me help you," she offered breathlessly, and with hands still shaking with desire, she shed the last of her lingerie to expose her full figure to his view.

Rafael stretched out upon his bed and pulled her down beside him, as always so delighted by the grace of her surrender he was overwhelmed with desire. He had always pleased her, he was positive of that, so why hadn't she felt loved? He traced her lush curves with his fingertips, certain she was as perfectly proportioned as any goddess. "I make my living with words, yet none seem pretty enough to describe you."

Alicia's smile grew wide as she lay warmed solely by the glow of his adoring gaze. His eyes were a soft brown now, the richness of their hue brightened by the reflected love in her own. She reached up to caress his cheek tenderly, then rested her hand upon his shoulder. "I have always wanted to say I think you are very handsome, but I was afraid that is what all women say."

"I don't care about any other woman, my love, only you," Rafael vowed as he buried his face in the soft cloud of her fair curls. His lips moved with an exquisite lightness down her throat, then followed the alluring curve of her shoulder to the flushed peak of her breast. His tongue lazily circled the rosy crest as his fingertips wandered slowly up and down her spine and over her hip. Breathing deeply, he drank in the seductive scent of her own exotic perfume. Ignoring the frantic pounding of his heart, he forced himself to make love to her without the slightest hint of haste. It was only when they gave themselves up to this delicious passion that they found accord, and he wanted to prolong that bliss until dawn. He wanted to drown in her affection, not her anger, and pulled her closer still as their hearts began to beat as one.

Alicia snuggled against Rafael, marveling at how perfectly the contours of her slender body fit his powerful frame. Her fingers moved slowly through his hair as he pressed his lips to her breast. A glossy brown, his hair was dark and thick, but the strands were as fine as silk to the touch. His golden bronze skin was smooth and warm. The broad muscles of his back rippled with energy, his strength firmly restrained as his hands tormented her whole body with a feather-light touch. The caress of his lips set her blood aflame with longing, and when he began to nuzzle the soft flesh of her stomach, her breath caught in her throat. It had not been merely a dream, she recalled dimly; the last time they had been together had been as beautiful as the first. She knew she had no reason to fear his gentle loving and relaxed again in his embrace, knowing he would give the deepest pleasure in every way he could.

The bed was wide, the night long, Alicia's proud spirit and fair beauty completely enchanting. Rafael slipped his fingers around her slender ankle to separate her lovely, long legs, marveling that a female as delicate as she could have such a passionate nature. He would make no effort to tame her fiery defiance, for that would destroy her uniqueness and would surely be the worst of crimes. He loved her without any illusions that he could dominate her spirit as easily as her lithe body, but he feared she still might have many misconceptions about him.

It was her love he wanted that night, even if they failed to reach a complete understanding, and he gave himself up to that purely sensual quest. He thought her a delight from her dainty earlobes to the tips of her toes and he left not a single inch of her satin-smooth skin unkissed. At last his lips moved up the tender flesh of her inner thighs to the soft triangle of blond curls he swiftly brushed aside before invading the last recess of her being. He savored the deliciously salty taste of her then, his tongue teasing her senses until he had brought her to the brink of rapture, and finally covering her quivering body with his own, he lost himself in the throbbing ecstasy he had created for them to share. That warm, sweet rush flooded through him as he buried himself deep within her, his mouth now plundering hers with a kiss that sought to capture not only her heart but her very soul in a silken smooth grasp. The turmoil she had caused him forgiven, he held her tightly locked in a loving embrace until finally his reason returned and he realized sadly that she still had not agreed to become his bride.

Chapter XIV

The bedside lamp bathed them in a lush golden glow and Rafael shifted his position slightly so he could study each nuance of Alicia's expression while they talked. He leaned down to kiss her whisper-soft sweep of dark lashes, and when she opened her eyes, his mouth caressed her cheek before straying to tease her lips lightly as he spoke. "It's nearly dawn. I want your answer before you leave me."

"My answer?" Had he dashed her with cold water, Rafael could not have given her a more startling jolt. As she struggled to sit up, Alicia swept her tangled curls away from her eyes, but while that gesture served to improve her vision, it did little to help her clear the wildly disturbing thoughts swirling through her mind. "How can we possibly be married now?" she asked anxiously.

"Why not? There's nothing to stop us." Rafael propped his head on his hand to get more comfortable as he lay sprawled lazily by her side. "Joaquin can't marry us unless *La Reina* is at sea, but I'm sure he'd not object to making a brief voyage for such a romantic reason. If you'd prefer to be married in a church, then we can just go to the nearest village. I'll convince the priest an immediate ceremony is imperative. I'm sure he'll dispense with the formality of the reading of the banns and marry us this afternoon."

"How can you be so certain?" the troubled blonde inquired with a puzzled frown. "Not all priests are so wonderfully obliging."

Rafael took her hand and brought it to his lips, nibbling each of her fingertips playfully before he replied. "I've yet to meet a priest who was not in need of financial assistance."

"You can't mean you'd just bribe the man!" Alicia gasped in surprise, shocked he would even suggest such a thing.

"Certainly not," Rafael assured her with a sly grin. "I'd merely let him know we'd be so grateful for his understanding we'd provide a generous contribution to his church—immediately after the ceremony, of course."

"That's exactly the same thing!" she argued.

"It is not," Rafael insisted proudly, his smile growing wider still.

"I think who performs the ceremony is really beside the point," Alicia remarked perceptively, dropping the matter of a bribe since an argument over that subject was not worth the effort. "The real question is whether or not you still plan to go after Julio Villalobos, isn't it?"

Disappointed their discussion had again taken a wrong turn and was going to be far more lengthy than he had hoped, Rafael reluctantly pulled himself up into a sitting position. He gave his pillow a healthy thump, then leaned back against it. "I should have known better than to expect a simple yes or no from you, but if you were considering giving me an ultimatum, I'd advise you to think again."

Alicia waved his warning aside with a graceful sweep of her hand. "No, I'd never do that." Since their conversations never went smoothly, she thought it would be best if she could state the major obstacle to their marriage dispassionately. "I merely wanted to know if you planned to marry me, then leave me here to spend my honeymoon alone. Of course, I wouldn't really be alone. I'm sure Eduardo would do his best to keep me entertained."

"Alicia!" Outraged by this remark, Rafael reached out to grab her shoulders, ready to give her a firm shaking if that's what it would take to teach her not to taunt him with other men. "Trying to make me jealous won't work either!"

The feisty blonde would not give up her argument however. "I'm not trying to make you jealous. Don't be absurd. Few women have the opportunity to become a bride and then a widow so quickly, but isn't that all you're offering me?"

"Of course not!" Rafael shouted angrily, then realizing how easily his voice would carry in the quite of the early morning, he lowered it to a savage whisper. "Villalobos has nothing to do with you and me! I want you for my wife, and not merely for today, but forever, but I mean to help Joaquin settle the score with Villalobos no matter what you decide."

"Then my feelings mean absolutely nothing to you?" Alicia asked in a voice painfully choked with the threat of tears.

"What about my feelings? Have you no regard for them? When I take a job I finish it. I don't ever walk away just because the situation becomes difficult. How can you even ask that of me? My God, don't you understand how utterly ruthless Villalobos is? With lies more cunning than any you've ever heard, he seduced a sweet girl of no more than fifteen. He stole Carmela's innocence, but when he was forced to marry her the spineless bastard still didn't care enough about her to give their child his own name. He chose Joaquin's instead in a fiendishly twisted insult."

"While you'll happily give me your name, but nothing else?" the distraught Alicia pointed out instantly. "I am no better off than Carmela was!"

Outraged that she would compare his motives to those of a cur like El Lobo, Rafael shoved the covers aside. He rolled out of bed and, grabbing his trousers from where he had dropped them, quickly yanked them on. He then began to gather up the frothy piles of silk and lace that belonged to her. "Come on. Whether or not you consider yourself my fiancée, you can't stay in my bed any longer."

"I have absolutely no desire to stay!" the furious beauty responded in a fierce hiss. "If you'd choose a question of honor, as you call it, involving a dead woman, over me, then I'd be an idiot to marry you!" She scrambled off his bed, and after donning no more than her wrinkled chemise, she grabbed her apparel from his arms and stormed out of his room.

Rafael followed the indignant Alicia down the hall, stopping to pick up first her stockings and then a lacy slip so she would not leave an incriminating trail of lingerie from his room to hers. He opened the door for her, then stood aside. "If you cannot understand a gentleman's obligation to avenge a matter of honor as compelling as this, you'll never understand anything worth knowing about me. You've made your final choice this time. I won't ask you to be my wife again."

"Is that a threat?" Alicia asked through clenched teeth.

"No," Rafael vowed hoarsely, no longer caring who overheard him. "It is a promise!" He tossed the articles she had dropped upon the heap in her arms, then turned his back on her and walked away.

*   *   *

After a sleepless night, Rafael spent the day with Joaquin and Domingo. They rode a considerable distance from the house, then took turns working to improve their skills not only with their Colt revolvers but also with Sharps single-shot rifles. Considered the best possible weapon for use in hunting buffalo, it could be counted upon to bring down a human target. Joaquin and he were near equals in accuracy with both weapons, while Domingo was lucky even to come close to any target they chose, let alone hit it. Since the boy had had little or no training with rifles or pistols, his tutors patiently made helpful suggestions without once ridiculing him, but they soon realized they had taken on a considerable challenge when they had set out to make a marksman of him. Far from being discouraged, however, Domingo showed a determination to learn that they had to admire, but all three were weary by the time they returned to the house in the late afternoon.

As he stepped through his door, Rafael saw a neat pile of hairpins on the corner of the dresser and cursed himself for being so extraordinarily careless. He could not imagine how he had walked out of the room that morning without noticing them underfoot. Veronica or one of the other servants must have come into his room to straighten up and found them lying where they had fallen when he had yanked them from Alicia's tawny curls. Wanting to be rid of such a taunting reminder of her immediately, he scooped them up, shoved them into the pocket of his leather vest, and hoping the impossible young woman would be on the patio, he went outside to find her. He was still so angry with her that he did not stop to consider what he would do if she were not alone.

Alicia had again gone riding with Eduardo, but she had not made the slightest pretense of being interested in his conversation. When he had excused himself after the noon meal to attend to business matters concerning the ranch, she had felt relieved rather than neglected and had spent the afternoon with Flame. Since both the attractive young women regarded the men's insistence upon tracking down El Lobo as a personal insult, their moods were black indeed. They were too distressed to be good company even for each other but sat in companionable, if miserable, silence in the shade near the fountain where the cheerful bubbling of the water provided surprisingly little comfort. When Flame saw Rafael approaching, she leapt to her feet and rushed toward him. "Oh Rafael, you simply must help me convince Joaquin to return to our ranch. He's got nothing to gain by killing Villalobos after all these years!"

Rafael reached out to envelop the diminutive redhead in a brotherly hug. "I can't do that, Flame, so don't even ask it of me."

"But you must!" the tearful young woman insisted.

Rafael leaned down to silence her protest with a light kiss, hoping such a show of affection, while sincere, would make Alicia cringe. "Do not make an issue of this, Flame, for it will soon be over, but the bad feelings you're creating could linger forever," he admonished her tenderly. Before she could argue, he gave her another sweet kiss and excused himself. He walked straight to Alicia, reached for her hand, placed the hairpins in her palm, then closed her fingers over them. He was sorely tempted to accuse her of deliberately leaving them lying scattered about the floor of his room simply to embarrass him, but the depth of her blush indicated otherwise too compellingly for him to seriously suspect such an underhanded trick. He turned back to Flame then, but his words were meant for Alicia too. "I've never been more serious; you must trust Joaquin to do what is right. He can no more abandon this cause than he could abandon you."

282

Since that was not the advice she had hoped to hear, Flame lashed out at him angrily. "But he is abandoning me! Don't you see this situation just gets worse and worse! Why won't you help me stop it now before one of you gets killed?"

Rafael shook his head. "Vermin like El Lobo are dangerous, that's true, but we are well-disciplined men of good conscience and we'll not take any needless risks. We'll come to no harm."

"You can't guarantee that!" Flame cried out unhappily.

Clearly insulted, Rafael asked derisively, "Why do you have more faith in some cowardly bandit who doesn't even have the courage to use his own name than you do in us?"

Shocked that he would reduce their argument to such a ridiculous question, the redhead nearly screamed in frustration. "Is it disloyal to be terrified I might lose my husband?"

"In this case it certainly is," Rafael assured her. "Look, we won't set out after Villalobos until we have a damn good idea where we'll find him. The element of surprise will be on our side and we'll take enough men from *La Reina* along with us to make certain it will be the villain's last surprise. Either you have faith in our ability to follow through on that plan or you don't; it's as simple as that. What Joaquin needs is your love and support, not hysterical tears. Since he'll want to bathe before supper, why don't you go help him?" he suggested with a rakish grin, knowing just how passionate a couple they were and hoping she would accept that charming idea as a good one even if she would not take his other advice.

Flame continued to stare at her good friend, considering his words for a long moment before the anguish began to lift from her expression. She sighed softly then. "I have tremendous faith in Joaquin, but I'm terribly frightened I'm going to lose him."

"Well, then go tell him you are frightened, but don't forbid him to do what he must."

Enormously pleased to have a way to share her feelings with her husband at last, Flame broke into a delighted smile, gave Rafael a hasty kiss, then lifted her skirts and ran from the patio with a light, flying step.

Glad he had been of some real help to his dear friend, the conscientious attorney turned slowly to face Alicia. For some ridiculous reason he had hoped she had understood that what he had said to Flame was meant for her too, but the light in her lovely blue eyes was colder than an arctic wind. It was clear she despised him, and yet he knew he had done nothing to deserve such open hatred as she was displaying. "You were right. It's far better that we part now, rather than make each other miserable for the rest of our lives. This undoubtedly would have been only the first of many arguments, since I have never disregarded a matter of principle and have no wish to begin now."

"Especially not for something as insignificant as love?" As she rose to her feet, Alicia gripped the hairpins tightly in her fist to overcome the almost irresistible impulse to hurl them in his face. The tension his mere presence brought was nearly suffocating and his arrogant pride truly revolting. She felt she had to get away, but as she brushed by him, he reached out to catch her upper arm in a firm grasp.

"I have never said love is insignificant," he stated with a frown, puzzled by such an erroneous conclusion.

"Of course not. You never mention love at all, do you? Obviously it has no value in your life. You might talk about principles like honor and duty, but the truth is you don't give a damn about anything but yourself!"

With that bitter farewell, she wrenched free and was

gone before he could draw the breath to reply. In her haste to flee, she dropped one of the shiny gold hairpins, and without a moment's hesitation, Rafael bent down to retrieve it. He slipped it into his pocket, certain it would be all he would ever get from the volatile beauty except her hate.

Domingo tried to ignore the way Veronica avoided his glance as she served supper, but it was clear she had heard him say he was Julio Villalobos's son and wanted nothing to do with him. He had never been proud of his father. He was used to being ashamed of the way he and his mother had been treated, no matter how important a man like Joaquin Villarreal might seem to others. As soon as he had been forced to accept the fact that Joaquin was not his father, he had transferred his hatred with astonishing ease to the bandit who was. It was like focusing on a target, taking aim, and then slowly squeezing the trigger. He found El Lobo an easy man to despise, but he had not thought that everyone he met would despise him too. He knew he was handsome. Rafael had continued to lend him stylish clothes close enough to his size to compliment his build. His table manners, while lacking polish, were adequate, but he could not wring so much as a smile from a simple serving girl! For a young man as proud as he, that was a bitter defeat indeed.

As he glanced down the long table, he could not help but notice he was not the only one in a downcast mood, for while their host was engaged in lively conversation with Joaquin and Flame, neither Alicia nor Rafael had spoken a single word. It was not until that exact instant that he realized that since Joaquin was not his father, then Alicia Caldwell was not his aunt. He knew her to be as sympathetic as she was pretty. Clearly she had no

285

interest in Rafael, but did that mean she might fall in love with a young man who had not a penny to his name? Why not? he asked himself with a rakish grin. He'd be rich someday and all he'd need do was convince her to wait for him. As they finished supper and left the table, he hung back, hoping to be able to escort her out onto the patio, but he was disappointed when she whispered something to Flame and then turned toward her brother.

Alicia had made up her mind. She was leaving Mexico, and the sooner the better. "Just a moment, Joaquin." She slipped her arm through his and diverted him toward the parlor rather than the patio where the others planned to go. "This was supposed to be a brief trip. Do you recall telling me I'd be home before my parents knew I'd been gone? Well, it doesn't seem to be turning out that way."

"What do you expect me to do?" Joaquin asked defensively. "I didn't anticipate this delay." He paused then to make certain Eduardo had not followed them before he lowered his voice and continued, "I'm certain you must have noticed that Lopez tends to exaggerate his own importance. If one of his sources doesn't produce the information we need soon, then we'll all pack up and go home. He can send me a wire when he discovers the whereabouts of El Lobo's camp and then Rafael, Domingo, and I can come back to finish our business with that lying bandit. Can't you be patient just a while longer?"

"How much longer?" Alicia wanted to know, for each day she spent in the same house with Rafael Ramirez would seem like an eternity.

Joaquin chuckled at her efforts to pin him down. "Another week or two, no more. We all have good reasons to return home, and since I'll not allow Domingo to go chasing Villalobos alone, I'll insist he come with us."

Alicia sighed unhappily. "I have tried to be patient, but I never should have come on this trip. It was a dreadful mistake."

That admission made her seem so fragile, so vulnerable, and Joaquin gathered her into his arms and brushed the glossy curls nestled atop her head with a tender kiss. "I'm not going to plead Rafael's cause, since he is far more eloquent than I, but I wish you would be more patient with him, too."

Shocked by such an impossible request, Alicia slipped out of her brother's embrace, her expression as bitter as her words. "No, I'll not be any man's second choice, and it's plain his ideals are far more important to him than I will ever be."

She had always been independent, but Joaquin saw something far more serious than wounded pride in her pain-filled gaze. Dropping his hands to his sides, he asked bluntly, "Just how far has this gone between you?" The burst of crimson that flooded her cheeks gave him his answer immediately and he began to swear. "By God, I will not allow him to turn his back on you, Alicia. If you want him for your husband, then I'll—"

"Stay out of this!" Alicia interrupted in a frantic whisper. "I do not want him, can't you understand that? I will never want him!" She broke away from him before he could stop her, but as she left the parlor she collided painfully with Domingo, who had been waiting for her in the hall. He reached out to grab her around the waist to keep her from falling.

"Miss Caldwell!" he cried out in surprise. "Are you all right?"

"No! I've never been worse!" Alicia revealed breathlessly. She shoved him away and continued down the hall but turned to go out the front door rather than onto the patio with the others. It was not until she had gone some distance from the house that she heard footsteps behind her and realized Domingo had followed her. "You needn't come with me." She tossed her words over her left shoulder without breaking her stride.

"I do not think you should be alone," the young man explained shyly.

The injured tone of his voice pained her greatly, and knowing he was not the one who deserved her anger, Alicia apologized as best she could. "Oh, Domingo, I'm sorry, but I'm not fit company for anyone, it seems. I just want to go home!"

"You're homesick?" the handsome youth asked in dismay.

"No, not at all." Alicia continued down the path that led toward the sea, and when he moved up to walk by her side, she did not complain. They walked a long way, neither of them speaking, and when the path grew rocky, he reached for her hand to make certain she did not stumble. That gesture was so sweet she left her hand in his when the way again became smooth. When they came to the bluff overlooking the water, she quickly realized her mistake when he pulled her around in front of him and tried to kiss her. "Please don't." She turned her head away to block his move, but he was surprisingly persistent. She was a long way from the house with a young man who had frightened her badly the last time he had held her in his arms, and recalling that incident, she began to struggle more violently. "Domingo, let me go!"

Disappointed she had suddenly turned so cool, Domingo reluctantly released her and stepped back.

"What is it? Do you hate me because my father is a thief?"

His question struck Alicia as absurd, since he certainly could not be held accountable for his father's lack of character. "No, of course not. I don't hate you at all." Unable to make any sense of his question, she turned back toward the sea, hoping the timeless rhythm of the water would prove as soothing at night as it usually did during the day. There were lights on board *La Reina* and she wondered what the crew might be doing to pass the time. "I envy the men on board *La Reina,* Domingo, for a sailor's life is wonderfully free of care."

Reining in his anger, Domingo took several paces away, then too furious to keep quiet, he turned back to give her a radically different opinion of life at sea. "How can you think that, when it's nothing but backbreaking toil? I have blisters on my hands that will never heal and you think a sailor's life is easy!" He was tempted to justify his thoughts in far more graphic terms but caught himself at the last instant and swallowed the obscenities that were about to erupt from his lips.

Since it had obviously been a serious mistake to stray so far from the house with such a volatile companion, Alicia hurried back toward the path. "Forgive me. I was thinking of the romance of sea travel, not the toil of the crew. I'm sorry. I seem to be doing nothing but apologizing to you this evening, but I warned you my company would be worthless." Just as she had begun her walk, she started back without looking to see if Domingo was following, but he quickly caught up with her.

"Life is not always like your books, all romance and adventure without any work or pain."

"I know that, believe me I do." Yet as she strode briskly toward the house, she began to wonder if what he had said weren't true. What did she really know of the harsh realities of life, when since birth she had been protected and pampered as the precious daughters of wealthy parents always were? She had known very little about life when their trip to Mexico had begun, and now she feared she understood even less.

Joaquin waited until they had taken Domingo out for target practice the next morning before he confronted Rafael. They may have been friends for more than twenty years, but that fact only increased his rage. "We'll keep working on marksmanship," he began with deceptive calm, "but I'd like you to be able to hold you own in a fist fight too, Domingo. Let's see if Rafael and I can't provide a few pointers for you. First of all, if we find ourselves slugging it out hand to hand with El Lobo's men, our situation will be desperate and there will be no point in dancing around trying to avoid blows. Just dig in and do the most damage you can before you get hurt. If you can break a man's nose with your first punch, you'll usually put him out of the fight right there." Joaquin was very quick for a man his size, and as if to demonstrate his point, he grabbed Rafael's shoulder with his left hand and swung him into range. He then put enough power behind his blow to drive jagged shards of his friend's nose clear up into his brain but took careful aim and instead went for his jaw. Caught completely off guard, Rafael went down like he had been shot, but before he hit the dirt he knew why.

There was no point in trying to reason with Joaquin when clearly he intended to give him a beating, so Rafael scrambled to his feet and, dodging another fearsome blow, launched a series of jarring combination punches that did considerable damage to Joaquin's midsection before he could stagger out of range. They had fought too many times as children not to know each other's style as well as their own and each used that knowledge well. They might have been able to control their emotions with other opponents, but when they fought each other neither held anything back. Joaquin was a few inches taller and had a slight weight advantage, but Rafael more than made up for those deficiencies in cunning alone. He had the wiry toughness of a tightly coiled whip and he unleashed it on his old friend time and again until neither could see for the blood streaming into his eyes.

Domingo had been astonished to see the two friends attack each other with such a vicious fury. He tried only to stay out of their way as they moved around the small clearing. They were kicking up so much dust that all three were choking, but the two combatants continued to exchange bone-crushing blows that made Domingo wince with each impact of fist upon flesh. Then he began to believe they might actually kill each other, and fearing somehow he would get the blame for their deaths, he jumped between them, desperately trying to hold them apart, but he succeeded only in taking a savage beating himself for his trouble. Crumpled over in pain, he provided an obstacle around which Rafael and Joaquin had to maneuver, but neither was ready to concede that the other had beaten him.

Alicia spent the morning riding with Flame and Eduardo. She had attempted to clear her mind and simply enjoy the sunshine, but time and again her thoughts grew dark. When her companions were ready to return to the house for the midday meal, they were discussing the merits of the mares Flame had selected, and knowing they could do without any comments from her, Alicia trailed far behind them. As they neared the ranch house, she was the first to see the three battered men approaching, but she needed no more than one glance at their postures to know something was dreadfully wrong, for none had the proud bearing he usually displayed astride a horse. They were slumped forward as though they were desperately tired, but since they had only been gone a few hours, she could not imagine what they possibly could have done to become so haggard. Flame and Eduardo saw them then and reined their mounts to a halt, but when the men were close enough for their faces to be seen clearly, the horrified redhead leapt from her horse and ran to her husband's side.

In the confusion that followed, Alicia was able to understand only one thing: Joaquin had started a fight with Rafael and Domingo had been crazy enough to try to stop it. While their faces were bruised and bloody, they insisted none was badly hurt, but Flame's tears of fright continued to roll down her cheeks as she slipped her arms around her husband's waist to lead him into the house. Eduardo left to call stable boys to attend to their mounts, Domingo limped off to care for his own wounds, but Rafael simply stared coldly at the distraught blonde.

"Just exactly what did you tell Joaquin?" he finally asked accusingly.

Alicia feared she was going to be sick as the sight of his cut and bruised face twisted her stomach into painful knots. "I told him nothing!" she explained as she rushed toward him. "Oh please don't start an argument with me now. Let's just go inside and get you cleaned up." Before he could offer any verbal objection, she had locked her arms around his waist to lead him toward the house. Nothing mattered to her but the fact that he was hurt, badly hurt, and he believed it was her fault. When she loved him so dearly, how could he even imagine she would wish him such pain? "I'd never tell him about us, never! Do you think I wanted him to do this to you?"

Rafael found it difficult to believe that the tears now spilling over her lashes had anything to do with him, but he was too sore to argue. He had to use his full powers of concentration just to put one foot in front of the other to make his way to his room. While he did not want to, by the time they reached his door he was leaning heavily upon his slender companion. "I'm all right," he mumbled through swollen lips.

Alicia pushed open the door, and as Veronica went running by with a bucket of hot water for Joaquin, she called out to her requesting another tub and hot water as soon as it could be brought. "I am praying when we wash off the blood and dirt you're not as badly hurt as you look."

Rafael staggered over to the bed and collapsed upon it, leaving his left leg dangling precariously over the side. "What do you mean 'we'?" he asked hoarsely.

Alicia yanked off his left boot and when he moaned slightly in response she was far more careful about the way she removed his right. "In the shape you're in you'd probably drown, so don't bother to ask me to leave you alone because I just won't do it."

"For some reason I thought you'd be glad to see me drown." Rafael's eyes were closed, making him look more than half dead already.

"I am in no mood for your jokes, Rafael. Joaquin had no right to do this to you, no right at all!"

"Didn't you get a good look at him?"

Alicia had begun a restless pacing beside the bed but stopped in mid-stride. "Not really. I just saw you."

"Well, he got the worst of it," Rafael announced with a lopsided grin, obviously very proud of himself. "I know I cracked a couple of his ribs and he didn't get any of mine."

"Oh, my God," Alicia whispered faintly, certain her brother would never speak to her again. Veronica came to the door then with soap and towels, followed by a young man who brought in a good-sized copper bathtub, which he then fetched hot water to fill. The maid did no more than hover around the doorway, too curious to leave, but as soon as the tub was full Alicia sent her and her companion away and locked the door. She turned back to Rafael then, certain he would need help getting out of his clothes. "I'd better help you out of your clothes and into the tub. You'll probably want to sleep all afternoon."

Rafael opened his eyes slowly, then struggled to sit up. When he had trouble unbuttoning his shirt, Alicia moved forward to help him. Two of the buttons had been torn off in the fight, but the three remaining were clearly too much for him. His knuckles were torn and bloody, rendering his grip too feeble even for as slight a task as slipping a button through its hole. Her tears fell on his hands and he looked up, shocked to find she was so concerned about him. "I don't feel as bad as I look, which I know must be awful, so I can manage alone. You needn't stay with me."

Alicia leaned down to kiss his bruised cheek. "I want to stay."

Rafael frowned slightly, then deciding he had nothing to lose if she chose to remain, he did not question her motives. He rose shakily to his feet and without further protest allowed her to undress him. Her touch was gentle as she peeled away the layers, her manner not at all like it had been when passion's heat had inspired each of them to nearly rip the clothes from

294

the other. They had been in this very room, he recalled with a slow grin, made love in this very bed.

"What are you grinning about?" Alicia asked curiously, surprised he still had the strength left to smile.

Rafael reached out to touch the tendrils of golden hair that had escaped the knot atop her head as she had been riding. His fingertips brushed her throat and he felt her shiver before he drew his hand away. His pride had almost cost him her love. No, he reminded himself, it was her pride he couldn't abide. Even in the state he was in, he knew this made no sense at all. She helped him out of the last of his clothes and made certain he did not slip as he stepped into the tub. The warm water was so comforting he slid down into it, sighed contentedly, and again closed his eyes.

Alicia stood back for a moment, then deciding he would simply enjoy soaking for awhile, she sauntered over to the window and looked out. "I didn't tell Joaquin about us. He drew his own conclusion, which unfortunately was correct, but I told him to stay out of it. I thought he would, but obviously he didn't. Even if he decided to make some kind of demand that you marry me, you needn't worry. I'd never consent to such a marriage."

Rafael found turning his head to look in her direction surprisingly difficult and feared all his muscles would be stiff by morning. He scooped up a handful of water and gingerly washed the blood from his face. Slowly the water in the bright copper tub took on a pink tinge. Soaking in his own bloodstained water was so gruesome a prospect he wanted the bath over, but as he reached for the soap it slipped from his hand and went skittering across the floor. "Would you get that for me, please?"

"Of course." Alicia scooped it up without breaking

her stride and brought it back to him. "You'd better let me do this. You'll just drop the soap again and again with your hands so badly bruised."

Rafael tried to recall the last time a woman had bathed him, then realized it had been midway through an extremely pleasurable evening. He had not thought he would ever have an opportunity to share that same kind of enjoyment with Alicia and welcomed the chance. "Would you please?" he asked without giving away his delight. He leaned forward slightly so she could begin with his back, and just as he knew it would be, the feel of her soft, soapy hands as they moved over his shoulders was absolutely delicious. Her touch was delicate, yet sure, and after washing his back she worked to clean all the grime from his hair without letting the soapy water drip in his eyes. Then she knelt down beside and began to rub the bar of soap over the dark curls that covered his chest. He leaned back to get more comfortable, hoping she would not become bored with her task before the water cooled, since he never would. As if she could read his mind, her fingertips strayed down his chest to the hard muscles of his stomach, but after a slight hesitation, rather than moving lower, her hand skipped over to his thigh to make a long sweep to his knee. "You can do better than that," he teased in an enticing whisper.

"I offered to help you bathe, Rafael, nothing more." Yet she had been affected as deeply as he by the renewed sense of closeness the intimacy of bathing him had created. Since he could transport her to the heights of rapture with his touch alone, she wondered if she could do the same for him. Laying aside the bar of soap, she watched the faint trace of a taunting smile play across his lips as she let her fingertips again slide down his stomach. Moving lower still, she was surprised to find him fully aroused, a fact the soap bubbles that floated atop the water had completely concealed. She traced lazy circles around the smooth, blunt tip of his manhood before wrapping her hand tightly around the rigid hardness of the shaft. Rafael's fingers covered hers then, silently teaching her the vigorous rhythm that would make the pleasure she gave him extremely sweet. Alicia thought it remarkable that no matter what excuse had brought them together, they were again making love. How could Joaquin have beaten him for being her lover when she found him impossible to resist? Without the slightest trace of shyness, she watched in rapt fascination as his whole body responded with quivering excitement to her tantalizing touch. When he could bear no more of that exquisite torture, he surrendered to the blessed oblivion of a shattering climax, leaving himself far closer to drowning in the tub than he had feared he would be.

Alicia felt only a slight twinge of the fiery warmth that flooded Rafael's battered frame, but she felt wonderfully content all the same. She waited quietly by his side, her fingertips making lazy trails through his hair, until he finally opened his eyes and smiled widely before he recalled such carelessness would cause his lips considerable pain. As he winced, she reached for a towel and rose to her feet. "You needn't say anything. Just let me help you up and into bed."

"It would be rude of me not to say thank you," Rafael offered as he struggled to stand.

"All right then, you're welcome." Alicia thought such polite formality ridiculous and could not help but giggle. She dried him off with light pats to keep from hurting the scrapes and bruises that covered his shoulders and arms as well as his face, then led him over to the bed. She pulled back the covers, waited until he had made himself comfortable, and then tucked him in. Without thinking, she leaned down to kiss him lightly upon the lips before she turned away.

"Alicia?" Rafael called out sleepily.

"What?" she replied from the doorway.

"I mean it. Thank you for everything."

What did he mean? she wondered. Had he thanked her for the few moments of intense pleasure, or for the love that had motivated her to give it? Sorry she did not know, she again whispered, "You're welcome," and left him to rest alone.

Chapter XV

Eduardo Lopez returned from the stables in time to see Alicia disappearing into his house with her arms wrapped snugly around Rafael. When in response to his questions Veronica informed him that the pretty blonde had stayed in the man's room to help him bathe, he was forced to come to grips with the painful truth. No matter how charming he had been, he had failed to win the lovely young woman's affection because even if she would not admit it, she was in love with the attorney. That made no sense at all to the silver-haired rancher, for while Rafael Ramirez was undeniably handsome, he was also brutally sarcastic and gave no indication whatsoever that he returned the sweetness of Alicia's affection, or indeed, that he was even capable of it. If the couple were in love, wouldn't they have declared that fact openly and announced their engagement? Surely Joaquin would not object to such a match, so the only possible reason they were not betrothed had to be the attorney's unwillingness to marry, while apparently Alicia would not consider marrying anyone else. That so delightful a creature would be pining away for an arrogant man who cared nothing for her caused Eduardo a great deal of stress.

It did not take him long, however, to realize he had the means to end that relationship before it destroyed any chance he would ever have of wining Alicia for his bride. When he had spread the word he would pay handsomely for information concerning El Lobo's whereabouts, he had been confident he would soon have some valuable tips, but what he needed were accurate clues immediately. As he sifted through his options time and again, his mind came to rest upon Veronica's uncle. Her family was large, but close, and many of their number worked for him. He knew the girl would not betray her renegade relative unless she had no choice, but once she had, she would undoubtedly see that the man received a warning of what was to come. Terrible accidents might easily befall men who went searching for bandits through rugged mountain terrain and the odds were very good that none of Joaquin's hunting party would live to return. Eduardo chuckled at that thought, since he was certain he had figured out an extremely clever way to get rid of Rafael Ramirez without ever having to lift a hand. It was all up to El Lobo, for once that lying bandit knew he was being hunted, the arrogant wolf would come down out of the mountains to turn hunter himself.

To his amazement, Joaquin, Rafael, and Domingo appeared at dinner. Their faces and hands bore deep purple bruises as well as an assortment of gruesome cuts and scrapes as evidence of their fistfight, but they seemed to bear each other no ill will and the conversation at the table was surprisingly relaxed. It was really a far more pleasant evening than many they had shared, but as soon as his guests had retired for the evening, he made his way to the servants' quarters located in the rear of the main house and rapped lightly upon Veronica's door. She was dressed in a thin cotton nightgown with a frayed hem, but thinking her visitor would be one of the other maids, she did not hesitate to answer her door.

"Señor Lopez!" she exclaimed in surprise, blushing deeply that her attire was so inappropriate to receive such an important guest.

Eduardo smiled warmly to put her at ease, then explained his terms: she would provide the information he needed about El Lobo, or at sunrise he would fire her along with every last one of her relatives. "The choice is yours, little one. Tell me where my friends may find El Lobo, or your entire family will have to find work elsewhere."

Veronica backed away into her room. Her quarters were small, providing space for little more than a narrow cot and a small trunk to hold her possessions, so when Eduardo followed her inside and closed the door, she felt trapped and panicked.

As she tried to dash past him, Eduardo caught the girl's arm and pulled her close. "There is no reason for you to be afraid, Veronica. You heard Señor Villarreal's assurance your uncle will come to no harm. He's after Villalobos, not his men. It is a private score he wishes to settle."

Tears flooded the petite brunette's eyes as she attempted unsuccessfully to pull free. "No! He might kill them all!" she protested sharply in Spanish.

Eduardo scoffed at her worries. "Or Joaquin and his men might be killed. That's a possibility too. I'm not concerned with what might happen; that is for God to decide. All I want from you is the location of El Lobo's camp and I know you know it." That much was clear in the fear that shone so brightly in her large brown eyes. Gripping both her hands in one of his, he began to explore her slender figure with a taunting caress. When she tried to avoid the touch of his wandering fingers, he merely gripped her more tightly. "I have always been very nice to you. Now it is your turn to do something nice for me." He had no intention of raping the child but drew up the thin fabric of her gown slowly, as though that were exactly what he had in mind. He then ran his hand over her exposed hip and when she began to squirm with revulsion, he knew he had selected the right strategy. While she was a flirtatious tease, he was certain she had had little real experience with men and was most likely still a virgin. "Tell me where I can find El Lobo, Veronica, or I will stay here all night." She was powerless to escape him and he was certain her own fear that she would have to submit to him was far more terrifying than any verbal threat he could make. He just let his fingertips trail lightly over her bare skin as he smiled down at her. "Tell me what I want to know, or I will spend the night with you and still fire you and all your family in the morning. Why should you sacrifice yourself and your whole family to protect El Lobo?"

"But he'll kill me if I tell!" Veronica wailed pitifully, her terror of the bandit chieftain far worse than her fear of her usually kindly employer.

"Of course not," Eduardo assured her, but his hand was now cupped firmly over the small swell of her right breast in a grasp he was certain could not possibly be pleasant, for she was trembling with fright. "He'll never learn how Joaquin found him. He won't live to. Your uncle will never suspect you either. No one will ever know. In the morning I will tell Joaquin that a stranger appeared in the night with the information he needs. The others will all hear me say that and no one will suspect you had anything to do with it."

Veronica bit her lower lip until she tasted blood. Her family owned no land; if they did not work for Lopez they would starve. She had never been forced to make such an agonizing choice, but she was far more worried that her parents would beat her if they all lost their jobs than she was that El Lobo would come after her. Besides, she was certain one of her cousins could reach El Lobo's camp to warn him before the men from California arrived. Clinging to that hope, she reluctantly revealed what she knew in broken sobs. "El Lobo has many camps; I know of only one. It is on the far side of the mountains. You must follow the river, then bear to the left at the fork. It is above Ciudad Altamirano."

Eduardo considered her words thoughtfully, then released her hands. "Thank you. If El Lobo is there, I'll see you're given a nice reward. If he isn't, well then you'll have to tell me the location of his other camps."

"But I do not know where the others are!" Veronica protested weakly.

"Well, I'm sure you can find out, little one. Good night." Eduardo slipped out of her room as quietly as he had entered. He did not return to the main house, however, but waited in the shadows by the kitchen where he had a clear view of Veronica's door. In less than five minutes she left her room and ran to the small adobe house her parents occupied. In a few minutes her father appeared and he walked swiftly to the bunkhouse where several of his nephews lived. He was inside a long while, but when he left to return to his home, one of the young men with whom he had just finished talking saddled his horse and rode away. Satisfied his plan had been set in motion, Eduardo went to his room to prepare for bed.

When their host gave them the news at breakfast, Joaquin could scarcely believe their luck. "You'd not seen this man before?" he asked incredulously.

Eduardo shook his head. "No, never. I heard him at

303

the door just as I was on my way to bed. He did not even want to step into the house, so I did not get a good look at his face, but his voice was not familiar. He had heard I had a friend who wished to speak with El Lobo. He was a shabbily dressed peasant, so it was undoubtedly the promise of a reward that loosened his tongue."

Joaquin turned to Rafael. "What do you think? Should we go now, or wait a while longer and see if this same information comes from another source?"

Rafael had no reason to trust Eduardo's judgment, but thought better of saying so to his face. "We made such fools of ourselves yesterday we're in no condition to ride. Why don't we give this report a few days' consideration. If no one else provides any other information, then we'll have to follow it as it will be our only lead."

Eduardo nodded in agreement. "A wise choice." He smiled widely at Flame and Alicia, doing his best to cover his disappointment, since he had hoped the men would be inspired to leave that very day. That evening as they lounged about the patio listening to his musicians strum lively melodies on their guitars, he could barely contain his excitement. If any survived the ambush he was certain El Lobo would prepare, it would be Joaquin, for his men would protect his life with their own. Rafael had no such loyal following though, so surely he would be killed and a grieving Alicia Caldwell would turn to him for comfort. He would pretend to be as stricken as she that her brother's mission had ended in disaster. He'd offer warm sympathy, and surely at such a troubled time Alicia would mistake her gratitude for love. It was a beautiful plan, and one he spent the next three days praying would work.

*　　　*　　　*

Alicia had no explanation for the difference in her mood, but since the morning of the ridiculous fight, she had found it impossible to become angry with Rafael. Seeing him so badly beaten, she had realized instantly that loving him was far more important than clinging to foolish pride. She still didn't want him to risk his life pursuing El Lobo, but since she knew he knew that as well as she, she kept still about it. Their difference of opinion could not be resolved without shattering the precious bond between them, so she simply pretended no disagreement existed. The men were now smart enough never to mention El Lobo's name when she and Flame were present but waited instead to plot their strategy when they were alone with Domingo. That courtesy was misleading, however, for when Joaquin announced at dinner that they would be leaving at dawn, Alicia was again overwhelmed with despair. Not talking about what they intended to do had merely been calling a truce, but now the war had resumed in earnest and the graceful blonde could not pretend she didn't care. When merely glancing in Rafael's direction brought indescribable pain, she excused herself immediately after dinner and went to her room. They had not been alone together since she had helped him bathe. She had promised herself she would not go begging at his door hoping for one last night of bliss, but now that that moment had arrived, she doubted she would have the strength to stay away. Still fully clothed, she sat on her bed, her posture rigid as she wept bitter tears for the man she loved. Between racking sobs, she prayed that when he returned they might finally reach a lasting accord . . . if he returned. When she heard a light knock at her door, she rose wearily and went to open it, thinking it would be Veronica come to wish her good night.

"May I come in?" Rafael asked in a conspiratorial whisper. "I had no chance to tell you good-bye and we're leaving too early for me to see you in the morning."

Embarrassed that he had found her crying, Alicia turned from him as she frantically brushed away her tears. He closed the door and quickly turned the key in the lock.

"I don't want us to be disturbed while we're talking," he explained, his manner unusually serious. "I've made a great many mistakes with you, but that's only because I care so much about you. Maybe we'll never agree on anything; maybe that doesn't even matter," he offered with a shrug. "Perhaps all that's really important is, well, simply this." He reached out to catch her hand and, drawing her into his arms, gave her a lingering kiss so tender, the awkwardness between them was quickly shattered into a thousand meaningless bits. "I can't promise you anything until I get back. You'll simply have to have faith that I'll be able to set everything right then."

As he spoke, Alicia calmly regarded his expression through eyes half closed with dreams of love. He was so deeply tanned his bruises were not apparent at first glance, but while fading, they were still there. She knew exactly how he usually moved, with a masculine grace that made his sleek body all the more handsome, but since the fight his motions had been stiff, silently revealing the jarring pain he thought none could see. When his best friend could hurt him so badly, she dared not imagine what El Lobo would do. She knew then she would not have been able to remain in her room much longer. She would have gone to him that night rather than squander the last hours they might ever have to share. She raised her arms to encircle his neck, the eagerness of her kiss a more than eloquent reply.

Rafael tightened his embrace as he welcomed her affection. Only a few days earlier his choices had seemed so clear. He would never walk away from his obligation to his best friend, but now honoring that pledge was becoming the most difficult thing he had ever had to do. Tearing his lips from hers, he finally gave voice to the torrent of emotions that overflowed his heart. "I love you, Alicia. God, how I love you! I think I've loved you from the very first moment I saw you. I was on board *La Reina* and you blew me a kiss from the cliffs. Do you remember that?"

"Oh, Rafael, was that you?" Alicia was so amused by the memory of that day she could not help but laugh. "I was dreaming of love and adventure. When you waved, I wished I could be on board *La Reina* too."

"Since that wish came true, would you like to make another?" Rafael asked with a teasing grin.

"The only wish I have is that you'll come back to me, and I know you will try."

"I will do far better than merely try," Rafael promised again and this time he did not end his kiss until he realized that when he had told her he loved her, she had said nothing of her feelings for him. "Isn't there something you want to say to me?" he prompted hopefully.

Puzzled, Alicia shook her head. "What is it you wish me to say?"

Disappointed, Rafael sighed deeply. "For some reason I thought you loved me too."

"Well, of course I do!" Alicia assured him with another enthusiastic kiss. "Didn't I just say that?"

"No, you did not."

Alicia threw herself back into his arms. "I love you, I love you, I love you. Are you satisfied now?"

Rafael's reply was a devilish chuckle from deep within his throat. He swept her up into his arms and carried her the short distance to her bed. "No, I am not nearly satisfied, but I soon will be." He placed her gently upon the high feather bed, then stepped back. "I was certain I'd given you enough time to slip into your nightgown. Did you plan to stay up all night?"

"You seemed so very serious when you came in. I thought you meant to tell me good-bye. Now you're admitting this was what you were after all along?"

Rafael had already removed his coat and vest and looked up as he unbuttoned his shirt. "I am not after anything but you, and I'll readily admit it. I want you very much and I'm sure I always will."

Alicia reached for the hooks on her bodice, now in as great a hurry as he to disrobe. "I cannot imagine ever tiring of your company either." She slid off the bed so she could place her gown in the wardrobe rather than leave it lying upon the foot of the bed, but she was not nearly as careful with her lingerie and let it lie where it fell. When she returned to the large bed, he was waiting for her to join him. As always, the warmth of his smile dissolved any hint of shyness she might have had. "Do you remember the first time we made love?"

"Of course. It was a totally unexpected pleasure, but one I'll never forget."

While she knew he must have had many women, Alicia was pleased his memories of her were so very sweet. She wanted him always to think of her with love. Always. As she leaned down to kiss him, he reached up to release her bright curls and their softness brushed against his chest with a teasing promise of the delights to come. "I love you," she whispered as her lips traced a light path from his mouth to his ear, then down his throat. His thumbs were circling the tips of her breasts, coaxing them into flushed peaks. The warmth of his touch spread in a delicious curl to fill her loins with longing. Curious as to his reaction, she lowered her mouth to his right nipple and carressed it playfully with her tongue. "Does that feel good to you?" she asked softly.

"Dear God, everything you do feels good to me," Rafael whispered hoarsely.

Alicia's touch was filled with love as her fingertips moved over his chest and down his stomach. His muscles were taut, his body perfect, inviting a teasing exploration with hands and lips. She wanted the same privilege of savoring his flesh that he had taken with hers, but as her lips brushed the blunt tip of his swollen manhood, he moaned so deeply she drew away. "Do you want me to stop?" she asked in a throaty purr, certain that would be the very last thing he would ever want her to do.

"No!" Rafael gasped, his breathing now ragged. As her lips returned to torment him anew, he wound his fingers in her golden curls to press her closer still. He had never met a woman who gave love in such lavish abundance and he had to struggle mightily against the overwhelming impulse to scream as the splendor of her deep kisses drew him to the brink of madness, then held him suspended on that delicate edge for what seemed like an eternity before she at last allowed the glorious tide of ecstasy to sweep away the last shred of his reason. Instantly his soul took flight, soaring ever higher until it touched the heavens before drifting slowly back to earth in a languid spiral that ended in the thick, warm sea of contentment. When he could again draw an even breath, he found Alicia snuggled in his arms, her head resting lightly upon his left shoulder, and unable to contain his enthusiastic praise, he gave her a boisterous hug. "You are the most incredibly loving woman ever born and I don't care if you refuse me a thousand times, I will never stop asking you to marry me."

"Is that a proposal?" Alicia asked sweetly.

"Isn't every other word I speak to you a proposal?" The lively blonde rose up on her elbow to look down at him. "I would have said yes the first time you asked me if only you'd said then that you loved me. That's all I've ever wanted to hear from you."

At first the shadow of confusion filled his expression at her delightful confession, then Rafael's mouth burst into a wide grin. "I thought it was much too soon for you to have fallen in love with me."

"Why did you think I made love with you?" Alicia asked pointedly. "Do women usually fall into your bed as easily as I did? Is that it—are you simply so spoiled by the ease of your conquests you do not recognize real love when you find it?"

Rafael thought her question remarkably perceptive but was far too wise to tell her so. "Women usually like me, that is true, but you are so totally unique I've never compared you to any others."

"I hope you never do." Alicia leaned down to kiss him, a long, slow kiss that he continued as he shifted his position so he could better provide the deep pleasure to her that she had given him. He loved the smooth, soft swells of her lithe body and caressed them tenderly with his hands and lips until she lay trembling beneath his touch, her surrender as complete as his, and he could abandon himself to the endless pleasures of her embrace. Their bodies entwined in rapture, they were so lost in love that the hours vanished like mere seconds, and all too swiftly it came time to part.

"Please don't get up," Rafael requested wisely. "I couldn't bear to tell you good-bye in front of the others."

He was all dressed, while Alicia still lay nude amid a tangle of bedclothes. "I understand. I couldn't bear it either. I don't want to ever tell you good-bye, not even here in private."

Rafael leaned down to brush her cheek with a light kiss. "Then I'll say no more than I love you, and I always will."

"I love you too." Alicia's vision was blurred by a mist of tears as he moved silently through her door, leaving her with no more than a promise of love and memories so sweet they would never fade. She buried her face in her pillow, and clinging to it as tightly as she had clung to him, she wept for the man she loved and feared she might never see again.

When Alicia again awakened it was nearly noon. Knowing she had missed the ride with Eduardo, she made her way out to the patio where she found Flame and Veronica practicing the steps of an intricate dance. "Oh, there you are!" the petite redhead cried in welcome. "Come and try this with me. Veronica knows many pretty dances that I've never seen. If we learn a couple this morning, tonight we can ask the musicians to play the tunes for us and try them with the music."

Dancing was the last thing Alicia felt like doing, but Flame's enthusiasm was so infectious she soon found herself joining in. The fact that Rafael could dance so well was an inspiration too. She knew all the dances popular in San Francisco society but none of the traditional dances of Mexico with which he had been raised. When Eduardo came to find them for lunch, she was in so lightheaded a mood her smile was the most dazzling he had seen.

Taken aback by the delight in her glance, the rancher failed to notice how quickly Veronica slipped away. "I didn't expect to find you dancing. Will you dance with me tonight?"

The confidence Rafael's assurance of love had given

her made that an easy request to grant. "Yes, I'd like that very much."

"Good." Eduardo beamed with pleasure. He escorted the two pretty young women into the dining room and did his best to keep them amused while they ate. He found them both so charming and attractive he hoped it would take a long time for the news of their men's fates to reach them. When they parted company to return to their rooms for a *siesta,* he was eagerly looking forward to the coming night, when the merriment of dancing would provide the perfect excuse to hold Alicia in his arms.

Flame covered a wide yawn as she reached her room. "Come in for a minute. I want to talk with you alone." She kicked off her slippers, then stretched out on the large bed she had shared with Joaquin and patted the place at her side to invite Alicia to make herself comfortable too. "I couldn't go back to sleep this morning after the men left. Joaquin told me you'll be marrying Rafael when they return, and I was so excited by that news I couldn't seem to close my eyes. I can understand why you want your engagement kept a secret while we're here, since it's certain to depress Eduardo terribly, but I'm anxious to talk to you about it."

Alicia drew up her skirts and sat down on the edge of the bed. Surprised Flame knew that she and Rafael planned to marry since they had only just decided upon it that very day, she needed a moment to reply. "I'm amazed Rafael had an opportunity to tell Joaquin about it before they left this morning, since we haven't had the time to make any plans at all."

Flame sat up and, folding her legs to sit comfortably, began to pull the combs from her hair. "What do you mean? He and Joaquin discussed your marriage several days ago. Didn't he tell you that's what prompted that awful fight between them? Joaquin was furious with him, and before Rafael could explain he planned to marry you the instant *La Reina* put out to sea, they were both black and blue, to say nothing of what happened to Domingo."

"You mean Rafael told Joaquin we were to be married then? He told him that right after the fight?" Alicia asked suspiciously, not at all pleased by Flame's remarks.

"Of course! Didn't you realize that's what they were fighting about?" Flame couldn't help but laugh then. "I must say you two have been wonderfully discreet. I kept hoping you would fall in love, but I had no idea you already had."

Alicia did not know which was worse, that Flame seemed to know she and Rafael were lovers, or that Rafael had told Joaquin they would soon be married before she had agreed to become his wife! She was hurt, angry, and horribly embarrassed all at the same time.

Flame thought Alicia's bright blush very charming and reached out to lift her chin. "I think being in love is marvelous. You've no reason to be ashamed."

"I'm not ashamed," Alicia denied proudly. "I'm just confused. Rafael told me he'd won that beastly fight, but what's the truth? Is Joaquin forcing him to marry me?"

"Of course not!" Flame insisted quickly. "How could you even think such a dreadful thing?"

"Rafael has asked me to marry him several times, but I thought it was only because he regarded it as something he had to do, a matter of honor. I turned him down each time, until last night when he said he loved me."

"You only just agreed to marry him last night?"

313

Flame gasped incredulously, her green eyes wide with dismay.

Alicia nodded. "He came to my room around midnight and didn't leave until dawn."

Flame considered Alicia's version of her engagement thoughtfully, since it failed to coincide with the story Rafael had told her husband. If there was one thing her marriage had taught her, it was to be diplomatic, and she attempted to be extremely so now. "Do you love him?" she asked first.

"Desperately," Alicia admitted readily. "Although we argue constantly, I can't imagine myself ever falling in love with another man after knowing him."

"All right then, you say Rafael has asked you to marry him several times and apparently he was convinced eventually you'd agree to become his bride. Since you finally have, it obviously wasn't simply wishful thinking on his part. Please don't let this misunderstanding upset you. It's not worth it. You love the man and he loves you. That's all that truly matters."

"Is it?" Alicia asked with a shy smile, grasping for the hope that her sister-in-law's words were true.

"Yes! There is nothing more important than love, Alicia, and you mustn't allow yourself to forget that important fact for an instant." Flame reached out to hug the pretty blonde, certain what she said was true. "Now I'm very sorry if what I said upset you, but let's just assume Rafael loves you so dearly he'd not have taken no for an answer from you much longer and that was why he told Joaquin you two would be married so soon. You do want to marry him soon, don't you?"

Alicia giggled with impish delight at her question. "Oh yes, very, very soon."

"Good, now let's start making plans for the wedding right now so we'll be all ready." Flame liked nothing better than planning wonderful parties and insisted she and Joaquin would host a reception California would never forget as soon as they returned to their ranch. That delicious excitement made the afternoon pass quickly and both of them hoped the days until the men they loved returned would fly by with the very same astonishing haste.

The next morning Eduardo again took his two lovely house guests riding. He was relaxed and carefree. If possible, his compliments were even more effusive than they had been in the first days of their visit, but the two young women simply exchanged knowing glances and pretended to be flattered rather than merely amused by his ceaseless efforts to charm them. After they had rested in the afternoon and changed into evening clothes for dinner, Flame again asked Veronica to teach them a new dance. The pretty, dark-eyed maid had never served as a tutor for anyone, but she found Flame and Alicia such appreciative students she was happy to give them lessons. They were graceful, bright, and learned the steps she showed them after no more than a few minutes' practice. Although they could not speak Spanish well enough to hold much of a conversation with her, she could not help but like them. They treated her with courtesy, as though she were a friend rather than the lowly servant most of Eduardo's guests considered her. That they were so sweet to her proved excrutiatingly painful. She was certain El Lobo would kill their men, and knowing she was responsible for betraying them, her guilt grew increasingly difficult to bear. On the third evening the women had been alone there, she went into Flame's room to help her prepare for bed, and when the petite redhead gave her a beautiful tortoiseshell comb for her hair, she burst into tears.

"Veronica?" Flame could not imagine why the maid would have such an astonishing reaction to her gift. She tried as best she could to encourage the girl to explain the reason for her tears, but Veronica was so miserable she could do no more than sob a brief word of thanks before running from the room. When Flame described the incident to Alicia the next morning, she was equally perplexed.

"I thought she enjoyed giving us lessons. Maybe she doesn't," Alicia replied with a shrug. "Could she just regard it as more work?"

"Possibly, but I thought she was having as much fun as we were." Flame did not know what to think, but that afternoon when she and Alicia went out to sit on the patio before supper, Veronica again came out to meet them. Since the girl still looked wretchedly unhappy, Flame slipped several gold coins into her hand and told her they would not need any more dancing lessons. Veronica seemed relieved to be dismissed and hurried away, but later than night she again appeared at Flame's door. Flame thanked her for helping to put away her clothes, but when the girl seemed reluctant to leave, she encouraged her to stay and talk for awhile. Her burden of guilt suddenly too heavy to bear, Veronica tearfully explained that she had been the one to supply Eduardo Lopez with the location of one of El Lobo's camps and that one of her cousins had gone to warn her uncle that Joaquin was on the way.

"Dear God in Heaven!" Flame exclaimed. She could barely catch her breath she was so terrified by that startling confession. She grabbed Veronica's hand and ran quickly to Alicia's room, where she encouraged the distraught maid to repeat her story in words the blonde could readily grasp. Since Alicia could understand far more of the Spanish language than she could speak, she

316

soon became as frightened as Flame.

"El Lobo was warned? Is that what she's telling us?"

"Yes!" Flame replied hoarsely. "If only she had told us this sooner we might have overtaken the men, but now they'll be walking right into a trap and there's not a damn thing we can do about it!"

"Of course there is!" Alicia argued, then realizing it would be a grave mistake to say anything more in front of Veronica, she quickly ushered her out the door. Putting her finger to her lips, she waited a moment and then opened her door to be certain the maid had gone. Finding the hallway empty, she closed and locked her door. "Look, isn't it possible El Lobo is not even in that camp since he supposedly has several?"

Flame nodded. "Yes, Mexico is an enormous country and he could be anywhere," she said more in an effort to reassure herself than Alicia.

"The camp might be deserted. In that case Joaquin and Rafael will already be on their way back here. Even if El Lobo is there, they're far too clever to ride right into his camp as though they were old friends. He might have tried to ambush them, but I doubt he's half as clever as they are."

"He can't be," Flame agreed, but she was still horrified by their dire situation. "I think we should go after them, right now, tonight. Joaquin told me they planned to follow the river. Either we'll meet them on their way back here, or—"

Alicia interrupted before Flame could describe the danger in any of the other far more terrifying possibilities. "Eduardo said a peasant told him the location of the camp. We know that's a lie now so we dare not trust him."

"Frankly, I never have." Flame forced away the tears that threatened to overwhelm her and walked quickly to the door. "If we tell the men left on board *La Reina* what's happened, they'd leave immediately, but they'd just make us stay behind so we have no choice but to go alone."

"I'm sure you're right." Alicia tried to think what they would need to succeed on their own. "Change into your riding clothes and come back to my room as soon as you're finished. We'll take what we can from the kitchen. There must be weapons in the house we can steal. We can saddle the mares we've been riding and be gone within the hour if we hurry."

"Don't worry," Flame replied with a shudder. "I won't waste a minute of our time."

When she had gone, Alicia closed her door and leaned back against it, praying that since she had no idea how to shoot a rifle, Flame did.

Chapter XVI

Domingo wiped the sweat from his brow on his shirt sleeve, then replaced his broad-brimmed hat atop his head and tilted it low to shade his eyes. There were twelve of them, and since he had been treated as an equal from the moment they had left the Lopez ranch, it was easy for him to forget how few skills he had brought to the mission. The smooth walnut handle of the Colt revolver nestled in his worn holster no longer felt strange when his hand brushed over it, but he had not forgotten their intended target for an instant. Joaquin had told him time and again that he had no intention of starting a wild shooting melee. Instead he planned to lure Julio Villalobos out into the open where the man would have to face him alone. It was a coolly logical plan, but he lacked Joaquin's desire to hear his father's explanation of what he had done. All he wanted was a clear shot at the bastard, but he had not argued with Joaquin. He had followed his directions to the letter. He had cared for the horses, fished in the stream to catch their supper, and taken turns at watch while the others slept. He had eagerly done more than his share whenever there was work to do, but his lust for revenge was so strong he regarded none of the tasks he was assigned demeaning. He considered each moment a rare privilege because it brought him closer to the man he despised. They were within hours of meeting him now and he could not wipe the wicked grin from his face.

Rafael turned in his saddle to look back over his shoulder and make certain their line had not become dangerously long. The old Indian trail they were following along the edge of the Balsas was not only rutted and narrow but also overhung with thick branches, making any sort of disciplined march impossible. "I don't like this," he announced ominously. "We should reach the fork in the river tomorrow if Eduardo's maps are accurate. I'll wager El Lobo's stronghold won't be far from the water and we don't want to simply wander into it like drunken fools."

"No, indeed," Joaquin agreed with a deep chuckle. "It's too late for you to go on ahead this afternoon though. Wait until dawn and then I'll send you out to scout for us. Domingo will probably insist upon going wtih you. Do you want to take him along?"

Rafael gave his best friend a skeptical glance. "No, of course not, but I will. He wouldn't be content to be left behind and I don't want him sneaking off in hopes he might be able to kill El Lobo before we can reach his camp."

"Neither do I. I plan to settle my score with that black-hearted bandit before I hand him over to Domingo for execution."

The late afternoon sun filtered through the leaves, casting a menacing shadow across Rafael's face. "What's going to become of that young man once he's killed his father? Do you think that's something he can forget?"

"Would you?" Joaquin asked skeptically.

"Never, but I'm afraid not killing the man would be far worse for him."

"It's an impossible choice then. Let's cease worrying over it and make camp here for the night."

Rafael raised his hand in a jaunty salute. "Aye, aye, Captain. I'll pass the word."

While they had overtaken a peasant or two that day, they had seen little evidence of traffic along the dusty trail, but nevertheless guards were again posted to ensure their security. The horses were tethered where they could graze upon the thick, sweet grass that grew close to the riverbank, while the men dined on pan-fried fish and *tortillas*. Sailors rather than cavalry troops, they had adapted with remarkble ease to life upon the trail once they knew the importance of their mission. When the last flickering flames of the cooking fire had become no more than smoldering coals, the men lay down upon the rocky ground and, making themselves as comfortable as they could possibly be in their bedrolls, fell sound asleep. It was not until dawn, when they were rudely awakened by angry shouts, that they discovered that sometime during the night they had been completely surrounded by a silent swarm of heavily armed men.

Joaquin was on his feet at once, cursing himself for not being more alert. The Mexican countryside was plagued by roving gangs of bandits, but he had been certain the precautions he had taken would be enough to protect them. When he could not recall who had had the last shift of guard duty, he searched the strained faces of those near him and was relieved to see Domingo and Rafael had not been slain as the two sentries surely had. Most likely a knife in the back had prevented them from sounding an alarm, but Joaquin was by no means defeated. If this was El Lobo's gang, he would give them one story; if it was another man's, then he would simply enlist his aid in fighting The Wolf. When he saw the bandits' leader approaching, he was elated to find he would not have to waste his time doing either.

Julio Villalobos was very pleased with himself for he had gained the upper hand without firing a single shot. He entered his prisoners' camp astride a palomino stallion, rode straight up to Joaquin, and spoke with a sarcastic sneer. "I was so deeply honored when I heard you wished to pay me a call I decided to provide you with an escort."

"That won't be necessary," Joaquin responded confidently. "We need travel no further than this."

Domingo's heart leapt to his throat as he realized the man talking with Joaquin was his father. He would have recognized him anywhere, for their finely chiseled features were identical. He had been shocked that he bore so little resemblance to Joaquin until he had been forced to accept the fact that there was absolutely no reason why he should. It was plain the years had been extremely kind to Julio Villalobos, for his hair was still a glossy black, his handsome face unlined, and his muscular physique that of a vigorous young man. Yet what fascinated Domingo most was the evil light that shone in his father's eyes. He had left his holster slung over his saddle horn during the night and he knew he would have to drop to the ground, grab the Colt, and fire before any of the men training rifles upon them had a chance to shoot. He had expected to risk death, however, and began to inch toward his holster, but the burst of gunfire aimed at his feet stopped him cold.

El Lobo tore his gaze from Joaquin's to see who had been so stupid as to go for a weapon. He recognized Domingo instantly and after giving a booming laugh, he ordered sharply, "Come here. I want to have a look at you."

"Do as he says, for now," Rafael whispered under his breath. He was as furious as the rest of them that they could have been surrounded while they slept. That El Lobo had chosen to address them openly rather than merely shooting them all dead from ambush had to mean only one thing: the man knew exactly why they had come and that his son was in their party. How could he have known that? Rafael wondered angrily, certain they had been betrayed and anxious to find out by whom so that such treachery could be severely punished.

Domingo stepped up to Joaquin's side, his posture proud and his expression filled with fury. "Your curiosity is long overdue. You're a dead man now."

That threat was met by loud jeers from the surly group of bandits who clearly had great faith in their leader. Amused rather than insulted, Julio laughed again. "I see you are as great a fool as your mother."

Joaquin grabbed Domingo by the scruff of the neck before the headstrong boy could reach his father. He had not brought him so far to have him shot in the back by one of El Lobo's men and kept a firm hold on him. "His mother was a virtuous woman whom you abused cruelly. Fortunately he shares her fine character rather than yours."

"Was? Is the little slut dead?" the bandit chieftain asked disdainfully.

Before Domingo could let fly with his usual string of scathing insults, Joaquin answered for him. "Carmela is dead and I've come to demand satisfaction not only for myself but for her as well. I'll not allow any man, and most assuredly not an arrogant coward like you, to use my name as though it were his own or to treat a fine woman as though she were a whore!"

Unimpressed by his strongly worded challenge, El

Lobo arched a brow cynically. "You are in no position to demand anything. You have five minutes to saddle your horses." He then wheeled his mount around in a tight circle, and calling to his men to remove their prisoners' weapons, he prepared to lead the way to his mountain hideout.

When Villalobos was out of earshot, Joaquin released Domingo and whispered, "Just be patient. You'll have your chance at him. I promise you that."

Furious, Domingo opened his mouth to protest, but he saw instantly that Joaquin had never been more serious. His dark eyes burned with a fierce determination that readily convinced the young man to obey. He had learned from experience that Joaquin Villarreal was a man of his word, a man who could be trusted, and he did no more than nod. Hot tears of frustration burned his eyes, but he forced them away. "How dare he call my mother a slut?" he asked hoarsely.

"He is misnamed," Joaquin told him as he pulled on his boots. "He should be called El Ratón, not El Lobo, for that is how he behaves."

"The Rat?" Domingo agreed. "Yes, only a creature who thrives on garbage would call her that."

Joaquin gave him an encouraging wink before turning away to roll up his bedroll. They would have no trouble being on the trail in five minutes, for the bandits' camp was precisely where they had planned to go.

As they mounted their horses, Rafael drew up alongside Domingo. "Sailors are very fond of knives," he whispered softly. "These stupid thieves didn't get half of them either. You were right. Villalobos is a dead man, along with his entire gang."

Domingo's eyes widened in surprise, but he was too clever to ask questions. If just one of them still had a knife they would be able to get away, and if what

Rafael said was true, then their worries were truly few. He took a deep breath and swung himself up into the saddle. He knew without a moment's deliberation that Rafael's assurance was indeed true. It was going to be a long ride, but he knew he had never been in better company and that thought filled him with courage. "I think I am very lucky," he said optimistically, "that you and I are fighting on the same side."

"Damn lucky," Rafael agreed as he allowed Domingo's horse to cut in front of his. In spite of their initial disagreements, he had grown fond of the young man and would do his best to protect him from the dangers that lay ahead.

By ten o'clock Flame and Alicia were so tired they could barely see, but they did not stop to rest until noon. Alicia had cast frequent furtive glances back down the trail, expecting to see Eduardo Lopez pursuing them at a furious pace, but there was no sign they were being followed. "We've often slept late. If Veronica doesn't check our rooms until noon, we'll have nearly a twelve-hour advantage. Does that seem like enough time to keep Eduardo from overtaking us?"

Flame lay sprawled on her back in a thick patch of grass, her right arm thrown over her eyes to provide shade from the sun's burning rays. "No, but right now I'm far too worried about Joaquin to give a damn about him."

Alicia stretched out at the river's edge, scooped up several handfuls of the icy water, and splashed it on her face. "Well, I'd rather worry about him than what might have happened to the men we love. I can't bear to think of them being in such grave danger."

"It's El Lobo who is in danger," Flame insisted with

stubborn determination. They had rested for perhaps half an hour, and thinking the horses had had ample time to graze, she forced herself to sit up. "Let's get going. With luck we'll be able to tell where the men made camp the first night. Let's try to go beyond that point. If we can ride further each day than they did, eventually we'll be able to overtake them."

Alicia covered a wide yawn as she sat up, then began to massage her lower back. "I've never ridden for so long at one stretch, but you're right; we have no time to waste pampering ourselves."

"Pampering ourselves?" That was such a ludicrous description of their brief rest that Flame couldn't help but laugh. "We are terribly spoiled, aren't we? We've only gone riding for pleasure, never for a reason as serious as tracking two-legged game." She rose to her feet, then offered Alicia a hand. "Come. If the horses can make it, let's ride until sundown."

The lithe blonde did not argue, for she was as determined as her petite sister-in-law to keep going. The sun had already begun to set before they again called a halt, but while they had seen plenty of hoofprints and broken branches to indicate a large group had passed that way, they had found no evidence to indicate where their menfolk had camped along the trail. "Do you suppose they didn't bother to build fires at night, or could they have pushed the ashes into the river and swept their camp clean each morning?"

"That's undoubtedly what they did, so let's do it too. In fact, let's go quite a ways from the river to make our camp. Then if Eduardo does come after us, he won't find us asleep at the side of the trail."

Alicia was so grateful to stop, she would have agreed to sleep in a tree. "Frankly, I'm too tired to build a fire. Let's just eat our food cold and go to sleep."

"We're bound to feel better tomorrow, don't you

think?" Flame asked optimistically. "Surely we'll get used to riding all day before too much longer."

Alicia gave the redhead a wistful glance. "I certainly hope you're right. I've never thought of myself as weak, but I guess that's just because I've never attempted anything in the least bit physically demanding."

"Wait until you have a child," Flame teased playfully. "Nothing can ever be more physically challenging than that."

Startled by such an unexpected confidence, Alicia dared not consider just how soon that might be. "I'm sure you're right," she agreed and fell silent.

Determined to hide their camp, they led their mounts off the trail and through a dense stand of trees to a secluded spot where they could not be seen by passing travelers. Flame quickly unfastened her mare's cinch and swung the heavy, tooled-leather saddle to the ground before turning to face her companion. "I haven't given any thought to turning back, but I hope you don't consider what we're trying to do so foolish we shouldn't go on."

"No, of course not! It's not a bit foolish!" Alicia insisted. "No one would tell a grown man not to take a ride of several days' duration, so why shouldn't we be up to that task?"

Flame looked away for a long moment, then smiled with an impish grin. "Please don't think I want to go back, but I thought maybe we'd rushed out of the house so quickly last night you hadn't really had time to fully consider what it is we're trying to do."

"Oh, believe me, I know Joaquin and Rafael will be furious with us for coming after them. Maybe we'll be of no help at all to them, but how could we have stayed at Eduardo's ranch once we knew El Lobo had been warned they were after him?"

"We couldn't," Flame agreed. "Besides, I think

they'll be so glad to see us they won't question why we followed them."

The young women were far too exhausted for a more serious debate of the merits of their undertaking. They saw to their mounts' comfort, ate no more than a few bites of the beans and *tortillas* they had taken from Eduardo's kitchen, and, still dressed in their riding clothes, went to sleep. When they awakened the next morning, neither felt refreshed, but a bath in the chill water of the Balsas gave them energy to press on with their quest. The second day on the trail passed in a merciful blur, while the third found their apprehension growing to near suffocating proportions. Had the men accomplished their mission, they would have been on the way back by now. When they made camp for the night, their mood was deadly serious. The tracks left in the dust of the trail were numerous, but they had not seen any camp sites, so they did not know if they had been able to equal the men's progress each day or not.

"We heard little of their plans, but I'm certain Eduardo mentioned that the bandits' camp was just beyond the fork in the river, above Cuidad Altamirano."

Alicia nodded. "There's obviously no point in going into the town then. We'll skirt it, and do our best to find the bandits' hideout on our own."

"We'll find it," Flame promised confidently. "It can't be that difficult to find so large a group of men. There has to be smoke from cooking fires if nothing else. Farmers cultivate land in the valleys, but thieves will be hiding out in a mountain pass."

"Yes." Alicia sighed softly, the bitterness of her thoughts needing no further expression. They sat silently staring into the small fire they had built to ward off the evening's chill. They had had only fruit left to eat, but neither was hungry. They stayed up late that night, quietly plotting how best to approach the

328

bandits' den, their hearts filled with equal parts of love and dread.

Shortly before noon the next day they rode into what had clearly been a hastily abandoned camp. Excited to have found evidence that their men had spent a night there, they dismounted to search the area for further clues.

A blackened circle of stones, which had been used to contain a fire, had been left in place. "They couldn't possibly have come this far in just one day, so they must have been carefully erasing all traces of their presence just as we've been doing each morning. Why would they have stopped taking such precautions?" Flame picked up one of the smaller stones and turned it over in her hand. "Do you suppose they had no choice?"

Alicia walked down the trail for several yards, taking her time as she tried to imagine what could have happened there. Finally, she strolled slowly back to Flame's side. "I've absolutely no skills as a scout, as you well know, but there are hoofprints everywhere, far more than we've seen before now."

Flame rose to her feet and brushed the dust of the trail from her once attractive riding skirt. She scarcely noticed the stains she had gotten along the trail as her tiny hands moved over the soft suede. "More men then? But whom could they have met?"

"We've no way of knowing," Alicia replied regretfully. She continued to explore the camp, silently cursing the fact that she knew so little about reading the clues that would be plainly visible to the trained eye. Something struck her as clearly wrong, yet she could not quite decide what it was. There was nothing tangible to account for her uncomfortble sense of foreboding, but that bit of logic did nothing to dispel it.

"Have you noticed anything strange about this place, Flame? An evil presence perhaps? I know it sounds foolish, but something just isn't right here." She hugged her arms across her chest, chilled despite the heat of the sun.

Just as uneasy, Flame nodded. "Yes, I do. Maybe we'd better search a bit further. I'll take the river." She walked along the water's edge until she found a fishing line still secured to the trunk of a small tree. The fish caught for someone's breakfast had long been dead, but she bent down to free the hook and wrapped the line around her hand. "I've found a fishing line, so maybe we'll have a good supper after all."

"I doubt I'll be hungry." Alicia walked away from the water, tracing a broad semicircle until a disagreeable odor assailed her senses. It was almost painfully pungent compared to the fresh scents of the natural setting, so, while apprehensive, she thought it worth investigating. When she suddenly came upon a man's horribly mutilated body, she was too terrified to scream. He had been dead several days and his body so badly mauled by animals she could not even recognize him from what was left of his face. It was not until she heard Flame calling her name with increasing urgency the she found the strength to turn away from the grisly sight and run back toward the river.

Flame needed no more than a brief glance at Alicia's ghostly pallor to know something was dreadfully wrong. "What is it? What did you find?"

Alicia ran to the water and took several thirsty gulps to settle the queasiness in her stomach. "I think it's one of the sailors. He's very dead."

"Dead?" Flame shrieked in disbelief. "Where is he?"

"Do you really want to see?" the shaken blonde gasped as she took in deep gulps of fresh air to keep herself from falling into a faint.

"No, but he should be buried and there's no one else here to do it but you and me."

Alicia shuddered uncontrollably. "We've no shovel, but we can at least cover the body with stones from the river."

"Let's just get it over with quickly." Flame started off in the direction from which she had seen Alicia come, and lured by the horrible stench of rotting flesh, she found the dead man easily. His throat had been slit from ear to ear, or at least what she assumed had been his ears. She looked around for a sharp stone or a fallen branch, anything that could be used as a makeshift tool for digging. By the time Alicia reached her, she had scooped out only a slight indentation in the rocky soil, and giving up that effort as futile, she tossed away the pointed stick she had found. "I know Joaquin would never have left this man unburied, so something must be dreadfully wrong."

Rather than comment upon the obvious truth of her statement, Alicia kept still. She could not bear to look at the corpse but helped Flame gather a sufficient number of stones to cover him. Although not certain of his name, they said a brief prayer for the repose of his soul, then returned to the river where the bubbling water and sparking sunshine gave no hint of their grim work. They washed their hands several times, but there was no way to remove the memory of what they had seen from their minds as easily as they had washed the dirt of the crude burial from their fingers.

After they had rested a few minutes, Flame rose to her feet. "You stay here and rest. I want to look around a bit more. There might be another body and—"

"You can't mean it!" Instantly Alicia was on her feet.

"I certainly hope there isn't, but it's worth taking a few minutes to look."

Alicia swallowed hard, sorely afraid she was going to become deathly ill. "I'll come with you then," she quickly volunteered. "That's not something I want you to face alone."

They started at the opposite end of the camp this time, first moving slowly through the underbrush, then climbing over the rocky terrain. They found nothing in the first ten minutes, then a wretchedly familiar odor led them around behind a large outcropping of boulders. This man had suffered the same fate as the first, and this time, overwhelmed with revulsion, they were both too sick to their stomachs to remain in control. A long while passed before they found the strength to gather stones, but they again managed to provide a respectful burial. After a thorough search of the area revealed no more gruesome discoveries, they mounted their horses and pressed on, certain their men were in desperate trouble and eager to do whatever they could to help them.

That night as they dined upon freshly caught fish, the two young women began to put together a workable plan. "First we'll have to find El Lobo's camp," Alicia began.

"And then see if he's holding our men," Flame continued.

"The two of us can scarcely surround the place, but we could create some sort of diversion that would allow the men to gain the upper hand."

"A diversion?" Flame mused aloud. "Yes, that might be exactly what they need, simply a diversion. We can provide one easily enough."

"We can?" Alicia asked in surprise. "Do you already have a plan?"

Flame gave her lips a tantalizing lick with the tip of her tongue. "If these men are bandits who spend their time either robbing wealthy travelers or hiding in the

332

mountains, they'll surely have a store of liquor and be eager for a night's entertainment. We can certainly provide that."

"You're not serious!" Alicia protested sharply.

Flame waved that objection aside. "Of course not, but if two extremely attractive young women came riding into his camp, do you honestly think El Lobo would send them away?"

"Not until he and every other man there had had a chance to rape them. How do you propose we avoid that sort of barbaric reception?"

"We'll strap our knives to our thighs for starters, but just who do you think would go first?"

"El Lobo," Alicia responded with a satisfied grin. "He'd want to be the first.

"Precisely. So no matter whom he chooses, we'll simply see he get no further than the tip of our blades."

While Alicia knew they had the courage to make such a plan work, she could not help but anticipate problems. "We're obviously not Mexican women. Don't you think El Lobo will be suspicious of our motives the instant we appear?"

"Another day out in this sun and I'll be as deeply tanned as Joaquin. We'll have to stop in Cuidad Altamirano for dresses, some flashy jewelry, and scarves to cover our hair. If we arrive at sundown and flirt outrageously, I doubt the bandits will notice our eyes aren't brown."

"I knew I'd be sorry my Spanish isn't any better than it is."

"Alicia!" Flame exclaimed with a giggle. "Those men don't want to spend their time talking with us, don't you realize that?"

The pretty blonde licked the last tasty bite of fish from her fingertips and nodded. "Yes, I understand. We'll just ride into El Lobo's camp, flirt a bit, get the liquor flowing freely, and then insist upon sleeping with him first. Without their leader, that gang can't amount to much."

"Maybe we should take a couple of bottles of whiskey with us, just in case they run short," Flame suggested helpfully.

"Yes, that's a good idea. We'll do whatever we can to El Lobo, then start a drunken brawl. We'll have our men free in no time."

"Provided they are being held by El Lobo," Flame pointed out logically. "We can't be certain of that until we locate his camp and have a chance to observe it."

"Well, wherever they are, their hosts can't possibly be friendly, so I think we should follow the very same plan regardless of where they're being held."

"Yes, we should. It's a damn good plan," Flame insisted with a toss of her golden red curls. "I'm sure it will work."

They sat lazily watching the flames of their camp fire flicker and die until Alicia spoke her worries aloud. "What if everything goes wrong, Flame? What if we try our best to seduce El Lobo and he simply tosses us to his gang? What if we are raped?"

At that question, Flame's expression filled with fierce determination. "The villain who calls himself El Lobo despises my husband. If he has Joaquin, he'll kill him in the most horribly cruel manner possible. Now do you honestly believe I am going to sit here and worry about whether or not I might be raped when Joaquin could already be dead?"

"I didn't mean it that way at all!" Alicia protested tearfully.

Flame reached out and grabbed the blonde's shoulders and gave her a good shake. "If what you are really asking is if my husband would still love me if I were raped by one bandit or fifty, the answer is yes!

Have you no such faith in Rafael?"

Alicia shook her head sadly. "I know he is a man of honor and he'd say what he thought I needed to hear regardless of the feelings in his heart, but that really doesn't matter. If I were able to save his life, I'd be content no matter what price I'd had to pay. Even if he despised me, I'd love him still."

Flame's features softened at her heartbreaking response. "I think you've been out in the sun too long today, sweetheart," she cautioned sympathetically. "Rafael is too fine a man to despise you for any cause. Now let's go to sleep so we can leave at first light. We can't have much further to go now."

Alicia gave Flame a sweet kiss upon the cheek, then got up to find a comfortable spot to rest, wishing with all her heart she could be as confident of Rafael's love as Flame was of her brother's.

Chapter XVII

Rafael leaned over to peer through an opening between the warped boards of the crudely built hut's east wall. With his hands tightly bound behind his back and his ankles tied together, his freedom of movement was severely limited, so it took all of his considerable agility to strike a pose that allowed him a clear view of the shack El Lobo used as his headquarters. "There's still no sign of him," he reported to his eight companions.

"Where the hell could the bastard have gone?" Joaquin growled hoarsely. As soon as they had arrived in the bandit's camp, Domingo had been told to stand aside while they had been taken into an old, dust-filled cabin, tied up, and then been largely ignored. Their guards were a foul-mouthed lot who had treated them rudely, but at least they had been allowed to eat their own rations and were given a few minutes to exercise each morning and afternoon. While apparently passively resigned to their captivity, they were in fact merely biding their time to lull an unsuspecting Julio Villalobos and his band of cutthroats into a stupor of careless complacency. Since El Lobo had refused to speak with them again, Joaquin had decided to seize the initiative and bring about a face-to-face confrontation. That the bandit had suddenly left the camp before he could implement that plan frustrated him completely.

"Into town?" Rafael suggested absently. He continued to squint through the splintered slats, surveying the ramshackle buildings opposite the one that had served as their prison for three seemingly interminable days. "He went alone; perhaps he has a woman there."

"Surely not only one!" Tomás exclaimed with wry amusement.

Rafael chuckled, grateful for the attempt at humor. That the men were not too tired to joke amongst themselves proved they had the confidence to escape the minute Joaquin gave the order. Since they were badly outnumbered, such a high degree of self-confidence was imperative. "That probably depends upon how many really good-looking women there are in Cuidad Altamirano," he responded with a ready grin.

"There's still no sign of Domingo?" Joaquin asked anxiously, ignoring the high spirits of those who surrounded him.

"There are two men asleep on the porch of Villalobos's house and another three standing out by the corral. The rest must still be in the bunkhouse, but I haven't seen Domingo since he was taken into El Lobo's house yesterday morning." It had been the fact that Domingo had been separated from them when they had first arrived that had forced them to play a waiting game. At first he had been held in another of the half-dozen shacks that circled the dusty courtyard, and while their captors had missed no opportunity to abuse them, they hoped he had not been made to suffer too greatly.

"Villalobos is the most arrogant man ever born.

Unless I miss my guess, he's been trying to turn Domingo against us. In fact, I'm certain of it." Joaquin shook his head to discourage a particularly persistent fly, which seemed determined to meander through the week's growth of beard that adorned his cheeks and chin like a dark shadow.

"The man is a fool," Rafael snorted derisively. He leaned back against the uneven wall to rest a moment, but his keen mind continued to analyze what they knew of the bandits' leader. "When he finally accepts the fact that all Domingo will ever do for him is slit his throat, I think he'll take out his frustration on us. How much longer do you want to pretend we're helpless?"

His mind already made up, Joaquin answered immediately. "I don't see any point in wasting another minute. Villalobos's thinking is so twisted he might keep us here until our beards reach our knees before he decides to make a move. We could take over the camp right now and provide him with a rousing welcome when he returns, or we can wait until nightfall to do it. It's Saturday; maybe he won't be back before dawn. If these brigands get as drunk as they did the last two nights, it will be no challenge to wipe up the camp wtih them."

"None at all," Rafael readily agreed. They had found the bandits' routine to be amazingly predictable and remarkably dull. Few rose before noon, at which time they began to drink heavily. By nightfall they were staggering around their cooking fires, so drunk they were in danger of setting themselves aflame. "Let's do it now. It will be more dangerous in daylight, but we'll have the advantage of being certain of our targets. We don't want Domingo or any of the rest of us to die due to a case of mistaken identity."

Joaquin cast a quizzical glance toward the others, silently assessing their opinions, and to a man they

339

nodded their approval. They were all too restless to wait until nightfall to attack and were as eager as he to mount an assault. The knife hidden in a secret pocket in his right boot had escaped detection, and Joaquin had just begun to turn himself around so Rafael could withdraw it when the heard the sound of approaching hoofbeats. "Is that Villalobos?" he asked with a bloodthirsty grin, his patience with the villain at an end.

"Yes, and he's got a couple of women with him." Their hair was covered with brightly colored silk scarves, and despite their full, ruffled skirts and deeply cut peasant blouses, which gave a voluptuous grace to their slender figures, Rafael recognized them at first glance. *"Sangre de Cristo!"* he gasped sharply.

"Qué pasó?" the seven sailors asked in a whispered chorus.

Ignoring his companions' curiosity for the moment, Rafael stared in rapt silence as he watched the lovely young women dismount and walk with unhurried steps toward El Lobo's house. Their sudden appearance had aroused the men on the porch from their slumbers and while he still could not see their faces, he could tell from the delight of the bandits' expressions that the women were extremely pretty and he was certain they were the two he loved most in the world. Turning back to face Joaquin, he made a futile attempt to fight back the fury of his anger as he described the camp's astonishing visitors. "I know this will sound ridiculous, but El Lobo just rode in with two young women who look suspiciously like Flame and Alicia. In fact, I'm sure that's exactly who they are."

Dumbstruck, Joaquin simply stared wide-eyed at his friend until he finally grasped the enormity of his announcement, then he began to swear with the foulest vocabulary a life at sea could provide. Several minutes passed before he gained sufficient control of his temper to speak. "It has to be them! Only those two would dare to ride into a bandits' stronghold and they've undoubtedly come here meaning to rescue us!"

"We don't need to be rescued, *amigo,* but now they certainly do!" Rafael was as worried as Joaquin, for he did not want to see either Alicia or Flame come to any harm. "We've got to make our move right now before Villalobos realizes he's got three hostages rather than one. We might have been able to let Domingo tough it out for a few days as part of our plan, but I'll be damned if I'll let our women spend the night in that bastard's house."

"Get the knife out of my right boot," Joaquin commanded sharply as he scooted around behind his friend so he could extract the hidden stiletto. "Blast it all! We haven't a moment to lose. Unless we beat them to it, they'll try to kill Villalobos themselves!"

"You can't possibly believe that!"

Joaquin knew he had shocked Rafael, but he had no time to explain why he believed a woman as petite and pretty as Flame to be fully capable of murder. "Trust me. Those two will do whatever they must to help us. Now let's see to it it's damn little!"

"Just give me a minute." His fingers numbed by the cords that had been wrapped far too tightly around his wrists, Rafael needed several tries before he got a firm grip on the handle of the slender knife. Once he had withdrawn it from its concealed sheath, he worked quickly to cut himself free, but twice he dropped the dagger and had to squirm this way and that to retrieve it. It took more than ten minutes, but at last he was able to slice through the rope and free his hands. He then cut the others loose and those who also still had weapons took them out. Rafael had had the opportunity to use the knife hidden in his own boot on more than one

341

occasion. The handle was narrow and the blade razor sharp. The weapon was so superbly balanced it could be thrown with deadly accuracy. He tested the tip and was delighted to find it had not been dulled since he had last used it.

Stiff from sitting in such a cramped position, Joaquin rubbed his arms vigorously while he plotted aloud. "They should be here soon to escort us outside for our afternoon walk. "Lie down, Tomás. When the guards come in I'll say you've fallen ill and when they come close to look at you, we'll all go for them."

Tomás had a wicked-looking blade in his right hand, and after hiding it cleverly in the folds of his shirt sleeve, he stretched out in what at first glance resembled a dead faint. "Like this?" he asked agreeably.

"Perfect," Joaquin assured him. "We saw them take our guns into the bunkhouse, but I think we can do enough damage with our knives not to need them just yet."

Now on his feet, Rafael paced restlessly around the hut, checking the view from a variety of angles, but no more of the bandits had moved into sight. It was getting late, but the time could not pass swiftly enough for him. "Why in God's name would Flame and Alicia get such a crazy idea as to come after us, Joaquin?"

Joaquin flexed his fingers, then made two savage fists. "Because they love us, of course. Why else?"

"But it was so damn stupid! I don't know what I'm going to do with Alicia for this, but believe me, she'll know better than to interfere in my life ever again!"

The sailors turned away to hide their smiles, each too envious of his good fortune in having such a beautiful and loyal woman to agree with Rafael's complaints.

"This is hardly the type of work you do every day," Joaquin reminded him crossly. "Besides, we'll soon be rescuing them and Alicia will probably be so grateful, she'll see that you're in no mood to think of punishment."

"Impossible!" Rafael vowed emphatically, certain he would have to teach Alicia a lesson now or she would continue to create the same endless turmoil she had brought to his life since the day they had met.

Alicia felt as though she had been catapulted into the vortex of a hurricane, for the whole world seemed to be spinning rapidly around her and she had no way to step back into the serenity of the warm summer day she and Flame had left back on the trail to Ciudad Altamirano. They had bathed in the river, then entered the sleepy little town and used what little money they had to purchase the gaudiest new garments the single dry goods establishment stocked. The store attempted to provide everything a farmer and his wife could possibly require along with a few extravagances Flame and Alicia quickly selected. They dressed hurriedly in the rear of the shop but refused to satisfy the proprietor's curiosity about their business in his city. They simply giggled as they put on their new clothes and appeared to be two young women without a brain between them as they twisted silk scarves into pretty turbans to hide their bright curls and filled their arms with a dozen silver bracelets. They had decided to search for El Lobo's camp in their outlandish garb so that if they should be discovered by the bandits they would simply appear to be two ambitious whores eager to ply their trade. What they had not counted upon was meeting Julio Villalobos himself as they left the store ready to begin their ruse. He had blocked their way, an incredulous grin lifting his lips in a leering slant as his dark eyes raked hungrily over their seductively attired figures. His hands on his hips, the ruby ring he still wore proclaimed his identity several seconds before he introduced himself proudly, using his own name. Alicia and Flame had had time to exchange no more than a frantic glance before they had accepted his invitation to accompany him home to his ranch in exchange for a sum of money that was surprisingly generous. They had doubted he owned a ranch and were not surprised when he led them to an encampment comprised of no more than a few scattered shacks, but they kept right on smiling, as though his charming promises of a profitable and amusing evening were all that mattered to them. Truly, they were so frightened they couldn't have strung together two coherent thoughts if they had tried and were grateful that, just as Flame had predicted, he did not seem to expect them to be able to carry on a lengthy conversation.

While there had been no sign of their men, Alicia took note of those carrying rifles on El Lobo's doorstep and wondered if he always took such security measures. Before they entered his door, the man paused a moment and she tried to give him a bewitching smile and prayed he could not hear the frantic knocking of her knees. Her right hand rested lightly upon her skirt where she could feel the knife strapped to her thigh, and that gave her a renewed burst of courage. She had never flirted with a man, but she vowed she would be irresistibly charming that day. Like a dedicated actress playing a role, she was determined to do her best, even though her audience consisted of no more than one extremely dangerous man.

"I went into town today to look for a woman. To have found two such pretty creatures strolling about was a remarkable bit of good fortune, but then I have always been a lucky man."

"And also a very handsome one," Flame purred coquettishly, her Spanish accent nearly flawless.

"Thank you, but I asked you here to entertain my son. Let me introduce him to you now. You'll have to forgive his manners, but he is so handsome I am sure you will."

The house was dark, and for an instant Alicia thought the front room was unoccupied. Then she saw a movement in the corner and realized Domingo was sprawled across the bed. "We are not nurses!" she teased playfully. "Is he ill?"

"No, not at all," the man known as El Lobo replied with a deep laugh, greatly amused by this mistaken notion. "He is not used to hard liquor, but he'll soon acquire a taste for it, along with an enjoyment of pretty women. Although he will not admit it, he is probably still a virgin, so forgive him if he is clumsy the first time."

Flame rushed to the small table and quickly lit the lantern before the man could offer a protest. Placing her hands on her hips, she looked first at Domingo, who did not appear to be able to raise his head from his pillow, and then turned back to Julio. "I do not find virgins amusing, do you?" she asked with a saucy shake of her shoulders, sending the ruffles at the neckline of her blouse rippling suggestively.

El Lobo reached out to encircle her waist and drew her into his arms. "No, I like women who know how to please a man."

"In a hundred different ways?" Flame whispered invitingly as she rubbed her hips against his.

"You know that many?" the bandit asked appreciatively.

"Perhaps even more, but I would like a drink first, even if your son does not."

While Flame continued to entice the thief with promises Alicia knew she had no intention of keeping, she walked over to the rumpled bed and sat down

345

beside Domingo. She had to give his shoulder several frantic shakes before he opened his eyes, then she quickly dropped her hand to cover his mouth before he shouted her name. He nodded then, and certain he would keep their secret, she raised her hand to caress his cheek. "Your father says you are a virgin, but a young man as handsome as you must have had many women."

Astonished his situation had taken such a sudden turn for the better, Domingo pushed his hair out of his eyes as he scrambled to sit up. "The man lies about everything," he warned, and to emphasize his point he grabbed Alicia in a boisterous hug and gave her a long and savagely bruising kiss. He then whispered an apology in her ear before drawing away.

"Your son is no virgin!" Alicia announced with another of her nearly continuous nervous giggles.

Julio drew his revolver and leveled it at the pretty blonde. "Can the son of a liar be expected to speak the truth? Remove your clothes and get into bed with him. I want to see what he can do."

Horrified by his shameless demand, Flame had no intention of allowing Alicia and Domingo to be forced into putting on such a humiliating spectacle. "Can you do no more than watch?" she asked with a petulant frown. He had just handed her a glass of whiskey and without tasting it she slammed it down upon the table and turned away. "I came here because you promised it would be amusing. I think I would rather go back into town."

Julio caught her arm before she could reach the door. "Wait! We have all night and I'll pay you as well as I promised. I merely wish to give my son a little present, then you and I will see to our own pleasure." He held her pressed tightly against his side as he pulled a chair out from the table. With an ease born of many years of practice, he sat down and pulled her across his lap. Gesturing with the revolver, he gave his order a second time. "Well, get on with it. Take off your clothes and get into that bed."

Alicia looked over at Flame. El Lobo's luck was obviously holding, for the redhead was being held far too tightly for her to be able to reach her knife. They had made a very simple pact. Whoever had the first chance to kill the man would do it. Alicia rose to her feet and began to move with a seductive sway. Starting with her bracelets, she tossed them one at a time upon the table. While she pretended to give Domingo all her attention, in reality she was studying El Lobo from the corner of her eye. He was clearly a predator but a darkly handsome one, and the charm he had displayed while inviting them to accompany him back to his ranch had been considerable. It was no wonder he had such tremendous success with women, but he had no way of knowing they would have accepted even if he had been rude. Now that he had shown his true colors and drawn a gun on them, Alicia knew there would be no time for second thoughts. She would have to get close enough to stab him in the heart before he realized they posed a threat and shot one of them. "I'd like a drink too," she demanded abruptly. She had no intention of drinking the whiskey, but at least it gave her an exucse to approach the table.

Julio waved her away with his weapon. "Later. First I want to see you with my son. Are you as good as your friend?"

"No," Alicia replied with exaggerated sweetness, "I am better." When that brought a laugh to the man, she breathed a sigh of relief that what little Spanish she knew was at least correct. She tried to think of other equally amusing comments, hoping they would distract him and make him careless. Domingo was watching her closely, but she dared not whisper her plans to him for fear Julio would become suspicious. She placed her foot on the side of his bed and leaned forward, her pose utterly abandoned. "Your father is in a great hurry. Are you?"

"Yes!" Domingo answered with a lunge that caught her completely off guard. He pulled her down beside him and as he crushed her body against his own, he whispered a frantic question. "What in God's name are you doing?"

While Julio began to shout words of encouragement in a bitterly sarcastic tone, Alicia wrapped her arms around Domingo. She was trembling all over and the fact that he was exploring the lush contours of her figure with both hands was no help at all. When his wandering fingertips reached the handle of her knife, she felt him stiffen for an instant, but he did not give away her secret. Instead he shifted his position slightly so his actions could not be observed as he slipped his hand under her skirt.

"Stop wiggling!" he whispered between kisses, and in another few seconds he finally managed to pull the knife free. After slipping it beneath the pillow, he suddenly sat up and pushed her away. "I'd rather have the other one. This girl's too skinny."

Hoping she understood what he wanted her to do, Alicia leapt to her feet and pretended an anger she hoped would be convincing. "Burro!" she snapped. She rushed toward the table and made a grab for the bottle of whiskey as though she meant to break it over Domingo's head. At the same moment Flame began to struggle so violently that Julio had to release her. What followed had the beauty of a deadly dance, but the young woman's swirling skirts blocked the bandit's vision for the few seconds Domingo needed to cover the short distance between them. Before the villian had time to comprehend the urgent need to defend himself, the young man's shoulder had slammed into his chest, toppling him over backward and reducing his chair to a pile of kindling. As he leapt to his feet, Domingo crashed into him again, slamming him into the wall as he made ready to use Alicia's knife with deadly force. Many years of war, as well as peacetime thievery, had given Julio skills at hand-to-hand combat Domingo could not begin to approach, but the young man fought with a vengeance born of a hatred so deep, they were nearly equals. As their struggle grew increasingly brutal, Julio's revolver discharged, but the bullet smashed harmlessly into the rafters above Domingo's head and before he could fire again, the weapon was knocked from his hand. Flame and Alicia were doing their best simply to stay out of the men's way and since Alicia was closest, she grabbed up the gun and stood ready to shoot the first man who dared to step through the door. When a few minutes later it proved to be Rafael, she was so shocked she might actually have fired on him had Flame not quickly grabbed her wrist to prevent such a terrible tragedy.

Rafael was grateful to see Flame still had her wits about her even if Alicia did not, but he had no time to scold her, for despite being armed, Domingo appeared to be getting the worst of it from El Lobo. Recalling his conversation with Joaquin, he knew it was in his power to prevent the young man from having to live with the fact that he had killed his own father. In the next instant the bandit's back was turned toward him, and seizing that opportunity to spare Domingo what might well be an impossible burden of guilt, Rafael threw his knife with enough force to embed it between the man's shoulder blades all the way up to the hilt.

Astonished by the incredible burst of pain, El Lobo turned around slowly, his eyes filling with wonder as he gazed upon the face of the man who had dealt him that deadly blow. His knees buckled then and he pitched forward, collapsed across the remnants of the broken chair, and after an agonized moan of disbelief, lay still.

His face bloody and bruised, Domingo stared at the fallen man, outraged that he had been cheated out of the privilege of killing El Lobo himself, but before he could offer any protest, gunfire erupted outside and he knew it was no time to begin such an argument. From the sounds of it, a full-blown battle was in progress and he had no intention of standing idly by while the others fought for his freedom. When Rafael wrenched the revolver from Alicia's hands and tossed it to him, Domingo murmured a hasty word of thanks and followed him out the door.

Left on their own, Alicia and Flame quickly searched the small house for additional weapons but found none. "What do they expect us to do, hide in here with our hands over our ears until they come back for us?" Alicia wondered aloud.

Flame fought back the waves of nausea threatening to overwhelm her and nodded emphatically. "Yes. Otherwise I think we'd only be in the way." She took Alicia's hand and pulled her into the corner. "We'd better keep down. It will be safer."

While Alicia was certain this was true, she did not like sitting on the floor, since that put them far too close to El Lobo's body. "How did the men escape so quickly, Flame? We had meant to create a diversion so they could break free, but how did they manage to do it without our help?"

"Believe me, I'm sure we'll hear all about it." Flame was content to stay huddled in the corner for the time being, but when Joaquin appeared at the door, she sprang to her feet and rushed into his arms with a gleeful shout of joy.

350

He gave her no more than a quick hug before issuing a terse command. "Domingo has your horses right by the door. Ride out of here as fast as you can and don't look back!"

As they left the house, the two young women were enveloped in a suffocating cloud of smoke billowing from the roof of the bunkhouse, which was engulfed in flames. While gunfire was still coming from all around them, they bravely ran to their horses and swung themselves up into their saddles. Joaquin slapped Flame's mount on the rump and yelled, "Now get going!" But before they had covered ten yards, a bullet grazed Alicia's mare and she had to leap from her back or risk being thrown as the animal shuddered wildly with pain. Joaquin ran to his sister and quickly lifted her up behind Flame since her horse could easily carry two, but as he stepped back, he was hit from behind. The bullet passed cleanly through his shoulder, leaving the front of his shirt awash with blood. As the two young women looked on in horror, Domingo ran to grab Joaquin before he fell in the dirt and, shielding his body with his own, laid down a blanket of fire to protect him from further harm.

Rafael burst through the wall of smoke astride El Lobo's palomino and with Domingo's help pulled Joaquin up in front of him. With an angry shout for Flame to follow him, he led the way out of the bandits' camp at a furious gallop and did not slacken his fearsome pace until he reached Ciudad Altamirano, where to his horror, he found there was no doctor in residence. The golden stallion was well known even if he was not, and fearing he was one of El Lobo's men, the owner of the cantina rushed forward to invite him to bring his wounded comrade inside.

When Flame and Alicia arrived a few minutes later, they found the palomino tied to the hitching post outside the cantina. That his silvery mane was matted with blood frightened them all the more. Bursting through the crowd of onlookers at the front doors, they had only to follow the trail of bright red stains that made a grisly trail across the floor and up the stairs. The bedrooms on the second floor faced west and were filled with the last traces of the late afternoon sun, which dramatically silhouetted the action taking place on the bed. Rafael had stripped away Joaquin's shirt, and since no physician was available to provide emergency treatment, he was doing his damnedest to stem the flow of blood from his best friend's right shoulder with all the pressure he could exert. The owner of the cantina had torn several sheets into large pieces. Each time the cloth became soaked with blood, Rafael tossed it aside and grabbed another. He did not realize the women had arrived until Flame took Joaquin's left hand and called his name.

"He'll be all right. He's just fainted," Rafael assured her calmly. "The bleeding has almost stopped. I know this looks awful, but that's just because the bullet went clear through. I'm sure he was hit with a .45 caliber revolver rather than a rifle. It seems to have missed the bone, which is another piece of good luck."

"I understand," Flame replied softly, her voice choked with tears.

Seeing a small basket in the corner, Alicia quickly gathered up the blood-soaked rags scattered about the floor, then placed it at Rafael's feet. Her brother was a big man, tall and strong, but she did not see how any man, regardless of his size, could lose so much blood and survive. Rafael had seemed so confident when he had spoken to Flame, but when he glanced down at her she saw the fear in his eyes and knew he was as badly frightened as they were. She grabbed the next piece of muslin from the cantina's owner and folded it into a thick rectangle, then quickly made another. "Place this one on his back, and this on the front, and this time don't let up the pressure until you absolutely have to. If you're getting tired, I can take a turn."

Rafael was both surprised and relieved to see she was serious in her offer. "Thank you, but no, I've almost got the bleeding under control now. Really, I have."

Alicia glanced over at Flame, but her eyes had not left her husband's face. "We wanted to help you," she offered by way of explanation.

"We'll discuss that later," Rafael warned sternly. "You can count on it."

Alicia remained at his side. While he was making little effort to hide his anger, she was certain they had not been wrong in wanting to help, and she prayed that that desire had not cost her brother his life. The next time she had to hand Rafael clean bandages, she stepped in front of him. "You rest a minute. You're right. The bleeding has almost stopped and I can take over now."

Rafael opened his mouth to argue, then thought better of it since the muscles in his arms and shoulders were aching from the strain. He was so tired he knew he would not be able to continue unless he took a short break. Moving away from the bed, he quickly washed the blood from his hands and arms and took a long drink from the bottle of whiskey the owner had provided. "I'm sorry, what is your name?" he asked the man politely.

"Rosales, Guillermo Rosales," the stocky man replied with a broad smile. "Is there anything else I can provide? I would not want El Lobo to think I'd turned away his friends."

"That would be a dangerous move, wouldn't it, Guillermo?" Rafael knew he must look more like a bandit than a respectable attorney at the moment and forgave the man his mistake. "You need have no worries that El Lobo will be displeased."

The innkeeper gratefully accepted that promise. "You will need food. I will see it is prepared."

"Thank you, but there will be several others coming along shortly. They will need supper and lodgings too."

"They will have them." Seeing no further need for his services, Guillermo rushed from the room, eager to see that his guests would be pleased with what he had to offer.

Rafael walked around to Flame's side of the bed and gave her a comforting hug. He then slid his hand beneath hers to feel her husband's pulse. Finding it weak but steady, he prayed Joaquin had not lost more blood than his body could successfully replace. That he might lose the best friend he had ever had or could ever hope to have was a prospect he would never accept. "We'll get him home safely, Flame, I promise you that."

Flame tried to smile, but she knew he would say anything in an attempt to reassure her. He would want to believe his own words of hope too. "Yes, I know you will." She lifted her chin proudly. "We've been through a lot together, haven't we, and I'm certain this won't be the last of our adventures."

"No, I'm certain it won't be either." Rafael leaned down to give her a kiss, then returned to Alicia's side to see if she needed help. Blood was still seeping through the layers of muslin, but he was certain the flow had slowed considerably since she had taken over. Logic told him that it might simply be because Joaquin had little blood left to lose, but he refused to voice that fear aloud. As he began to fold more muslin, Tomás entered the room, followed by the other six sailors. Not a one seemed to have escaped injury, but none was as seriously hurt as Joaquin. "This town has no doctor.

You'll just have to sit down on the floor and I'll do what I can to make you comfortable. Where's Domingo? Didn't he come with you?"

When Tomás glanced at the others before responding, Alicia cried out in despair. "Dear God, he wasn't killed, was he?"

"No, señorita." Tomás leaned against the wall, so tired he could no longer stand without support. "We tried to get him out, but there were too many of them."

"Then we'll have to go back for him!" Alicia insisted emphatically. "We can't leave him there now that—"

Rafael clamped his hand over her mouth. "Hush. The less the people of this town know of our plans, the better. Do you understand me?"

Alicia glared angrily at him but nodded in agreement. When he dropped his hand, she remained silent, and as he went about tending the sailors' wounds, she did not argue, but she was determined not to allow him to leave her behind ever again. She poured all her defiant energy into caring for Joaquin. Before nightfall, the bleeding had stopped and he was resting so comfortably they prayed his life had been spared.

Chapter XVIII

It was after midnight when Rafael reentered Joaquin's room. Alicia was seated in a chair, resting her arms upon the side of her brother's bed to provide a comfortable cradle for her head while she slept. When Rafael touched her arm, she sat up quickly, embarrassed to have been caught napping. "Yes, what is it?" she asked anxiously as she looked first at Joaquin, then up at his friend. Flame was still sound asleep, curled up at her husband's side, and Alicia was greatly relieved to find he had not taken a sudden turn for the worse.

Rafael reached out to touch the injured man's forehead and finding it cool gave Alicia a reassuring smile. "He's doing fine. Come with me." He took her hand before she could offer a protest and led her into the room next door where a copper bathtub filled with steaming hot water and a bed with fresh linens were waiting. "It will take Joaquin a long while to recover his strength. Flame won't be able to care for him all alone, but you won't be able to help her if you fall ill from exhaustion."

He had taken the time to bathe and dress in clean clothes, but he had not shaved off his beard. While Alicia thought it fit the more rakish side of his nature quite well, she was nonetheless curious about his plans. "Doesn't that same precaution apply to you as well?"

Rafael pulled her close, and reaching for the waistband of her full skirt, he quickly released the hooks and let it slip to the floor. "Get into the tub. It took me a long while to lug all that hot water up here and I don't want it going to waste."

"You prepared the bath for me yourself?" Deeply flattered, Alicia responded with a delighted smile. "Thank you."

Rafael nodded impassively as he continued to help her undress, not about to reveal his true purpose. He waited patiently as she cast off the last of her undergarments, climbed into the tub, and washed her hair. When she finally closed her eyes and leaned back to soak in the soothingly warm water, he drew up a chair and sat down by her side. He had rehearsed this conversation a dozen times and hoped he had released enough of his own anger so that he would not arouse hers. "Tell me how you and Flame came to be with El Lobo," he asked with what appeared to be simply keen interest rather than the outrage it truly was.

The lantern that provided the cozy room's sole light was turned down low, surrounding them with a romantic glow, but Alicia was still surprised she felt so little in the way of embarrassment. Here she was bathing quite wantonly while the man she adored sat by asking questions for which she could scarcely recall the answers. She covered a wide yawn and then began at the beginning with what they had learned from Veronica.

"You mean it was not a peasant who supplied Eduardo Lopez with the whereabouts of El Lobo's camp?" Astonished by this news, Rafael sat forward and leaned his elbows across his knees, eager to hear more.

"That's right, he made up that story. The problem was, one of the girl's cousins came up here to warn their uncle you were coming."

"So that's how he knew Domingo was with us!" Rafael was amazed to find that his lovely blonde had the answer to such a perplexing question and encouraged her to continue her tale. "So you came to warn us?"

Alicia shook her head apologetically. "Well, no, we thought we'd be too late to do that. We really hoped to meet you on the way back, but when we found the dead sailors—"

"Dear God! You found their bodies?" Rafael listened with rapt attention as Alicia explained how she and Flame had first buried the two unfortunate sentries and had then hatched the plot to pose as whores to gain entrance to El Lobo's camp. Her expression was so disarmingly innocent, he now found it difficult to become angry with her, but he never wanted her to risk her life to save his ever again. Rising to his feet, he swung his chair aside and began to pace with a carefully measured stride. "While I'm naturally quite proud of you for having so much courage, we were never in any real danger, Alicia. We had the means to escape at any time. In fact, we'd already begun to do just that when you and Flame arrived. Julio Villalobos wouldn't have lived out the afternoon even if you'd stayed at Eduardo's ranch."

Alicia was appalled that he would dismiss their efforts to help them so lightly. "If it would have been so easy for you, then why didn't you just escape at once?" she asked accusingly, her temper rising dangerously near the boiling point.

"If you'll remember, we had expected to take El Lobo by surprise. When instead he surrounded us, we were too greatly outnumbered to make a stand. By not trying to escape instantly, we'd lulled the bandits into thinking we weren't going to try. Since El Lobo was away, we had decided to seize that opportunity to gain the upper hand, but when he suddenly reappeared with you and Flame, we had no choice but to drastically alter our plans." Despite his intention to remain calm, the sharpness of Rafael's tone clearly conveyed his hostility.

Since he was obviously annoyed with her, Alicia felt ridiculous remaining in the bathtub, but he had lain the towel on the foot of the bed where it was unfortunately out of her reach. She asked first that he hand it to her, and when he did, she rose gracefully to her feet and covered herself as modestly as possible before stepping out of the tub. She then told him exactly how absurd she thought his version of what had happened that afternoon truly was. "So what you're really saying is that we interfered as much with your plans as you did with ours!"

"Did you two actually have a plan?" Rafael scoffed sarcastically, giving up all hope of ending their conversation as pleasantly as it had begun.

Alicia glanced around the sparsely furnished room wondering what he had expected her to wear to bed, then realizing with a deep blush that he had probably thought she would be sleeping in the nude, she decided not to ask. "It's pointless to argue over what we might have done when the important thing is how we're going to rescue Domingo. I'm not at all sleepy. Do you want to go back up to the camp now? Surely they won't expect us to come back tonight, and this time we really can catch them by surprise."

"You can't possibly expect me to allow you to come with us!" It was such a preposterous idea that Rafael would have laughed out loud had he not been concerned about waking those sleeping nearby. "You'll stay right here where you belong and I will see to it that Domingo comes to no harm."

Alicia tucked the end of the towel more firmly above her breasts, then pointed out the error in his thinking. "You can't go alone, and I didn't see one of those sailors who looked like he could sit a horse again tomorrow. None of their wounds are serious, thank God, but each has suffered too much to be of any help to you in the next few days. You simply have no choice but to take me with you."

"No choice!" Rafael shouted, this time completely forgetting the inn's other guests. "I have a choice. Believe me, I have a choice, and you're staying right here!"

Now that he had completely lost his temper, Alicia felt an unexpectedly pleasant sense of calm knowing she had gained the upper hand. She waited a moment, then tried once again to make him see reason. "It's far too dangerous for you to go back into that camp alone. I can understand why you think I'd be too frightened to be of any help to you, but you're wrong. Had Domingo not been so eager to help us, Flame and I would have killed El Lobo ourselves. Domingo's life is too precious to risk just because of your pride. You can trust me to do whatever you ask as promptly as the men would."

Rafael continued to frown deeply, certain he would be an ever greater fool than she was if he took her along. He simply would not do it, and that was that. While she was probably right about the sailors, he was confident one man could slip into what was left of the bandits' stronghold and safely emerge with Domingo in tow. Just as he had boasted, he definitely had a choice.

It was very late and Alicia was impossibly lovely, even with her glossy curls clinging damply to the creamy smooth skin of her throat before sending a stream of warm droplets sliding down the elegant curve of her shoulder. Why should he waste another minute in debate when he would not change his mind about excluding her from his plans to free Domingo? She was too luscious a young woman to risk needlessly when clearly she had been born for a life filled with the glory of love rather than a reckless pursuit of adventure. "I'm far too tired to argue the merits of any plan tonight. I'm going to bed," he countered emphatically. He yanked his shirttail from his pants, then pulled the soft muslin garment over his head.

"Well, surely you don't plan to sleep here in my room!" Alicia protested as dramatically as her half-clothed state would allow.

"You're mistaken. This room is mine." Rafael tossed his shirt over the back of the chair and then sat down on the edge of the bed to remove his boots. "You're welcome to stay, of course," he offered with a rakish grin. "The bed is surprisingly comfortable and I can promise you'll enjoy the company."

The blue of Alicia's eyes began to glow with a defiant purple light as she approached the bed. "I know you told Joaquin we were to be married before I had accepted your proposal, but do you honestly think you can flaunt our relationship as openly as this and not infuriate him as well as me!"

Rafael yanked off his boots, then stood to unfasten his belt buckle and unbutton his pants. "It's not a matter of propriety, my love. It's purely a matter of logistics. This cantina has but three rooms available. Your brother and Flame have one, those poor, injured sailors you're so concerned about have the other, and that leaves this one for us. Now I fully intend to make myself at home and I suggest you do the same." With that suggestion, he cast off the last of his clothes, and after hesitating long enough to be certain she had had ample opportunity to fully appreciate the effect she always had upon him, he climbed into bed.

Ignoring the boldness of his words and blatant arrogance of his actions, Alicia refused to back down. "Am I to share no more of your life than your bed? Won't you ever trust me to do anything important?" She was furious with him and also with herself for missing a wonderful chance to kick him right where it would have done him the most good.

Intrigued by her questions, Rafael considered them well worth a reply, but first he propped himself up on his elbow to get comfortable. "I believe a wife should share her husband's life and he hers, but that doesn't mean every last second of it. This isn't a matter of trust, Alicia. Of course I trust you, but what I need now is someone who can back me up in a fight, someone who isn't afraid to slit a throat or two. I'll not turn you into a bloodthirsty killer. Don't ask that of me."

"Is that what you are, a bloodthirsty killer?" Alicia asked incredulously, but she had to admit that at that moment he certainly looked the part. It wasn't only the newly grown beard that gave him such a sinister appearance, but also the total fearlessness of his icy gaze. She had seen drawings of the Grim Reaper with more benign expressions than he now wore.

Rafael extended his hand. "I have been where it was necessary, like today, but that's the furthest thing from my mind right now. Please come to bed." He spoke in an enticing whisper, but he issued a politely worded command, not an invitation.

Alicia hung back, certain there must be something she could say to convince him she would be an asset rather than a burden, but at that moment she couldn't think what it might be. "You must take me with you, you simply must," she argued when logic failed her.

"I'll be back before you know I've been gone," Rafael

promised sincerely. "Now come to bed."

Torn by the raging emotions she felt powerless to fight, Alicia turned her back toward him and, using her towel, spent several minutes silently drying her long, tawny curls. When that delay provided her agile mind with nothing new in the way of persuasive arguments, she ceased to battle with her conscience and surrendered to the aching need in her heart. She tossed the wet towel aside and turned back to join him in the high bed. Snuggling against his side, she reached up to caress his cheek softly with the back of her fingers. "I simply couldn't bear to lose you."

She was overwhelmed with the horrible sorrow of that possibility and her expression was so downcast that Rafael gathered her up into his arms and pulled her so close that not an inch of their flesh was not joined. He realized then that his own anger had been quite selfishly motivated by the very same fear that fate would somehow tear them apart without ever giving them the chance to build a lifetime of happiness together. Pressing her lithe body closer still, he drank in the deliciously sweet fragrance of her bare skin as he spread a generous trail of light kissess down her throat. He combed his fingers through her damp curls and tried to imagine herself as his partner in any life and death pursuit. "I have no intention of losing you either, *querida,*" he vowed hoarsely. He used his fingertips, then his lips, to trace her delicate features, all the while murmuring such tender promises of love her initial reluctance to spend the night in his bed was swiftly forgotten.

Still resting upon his left side, Rafael drew Alicia's left knee over his right hip to provide each of them with a more comfortable pose. He was in an unusually patient mood, so he entered her only partially and then slowly retreated. He then began to tease the exquisitely sensitive softness of her flesh with the shameless hardness of his own. Time and again he made their two bodies one, gently brushing the very brink of rapture, only to withdraw once again. Finally the smoldering desire he had created with this deeply erotic game burst into flames too hot for Alicia to endure. When he again entered her with an agonizing stealth, she moved to capture him in her embrace with a passion so fierce he had no way to escape the tight bond of her need. She clung to him, her mouth devouring his as she pressed his hips hard against her own, forcing him down into the very depths of her being where the tremors of ecstasy that rocked her soul jolted clear through him with the blinding splendor of a fiery bolt of lightning. In teasing her, he had also teased himself, and in doing so had created a shared pleasure of stunning beauty. At her compelling insistence, he now abandoned all further effort at restraint and gave himself up to the vibrant waves of throbbing sensation that washed through his powerful body with a heat so intense it left them both bathed in the glory of its enduring warmth. Her beauty and passion were uniquely her own and making love to her satisifed him more deeply than any other woman ever had or ever would. Quite simply, he loved her, her fiery defiance as well as her sweet surrender, and he held her locked tightly in his embrace until the slow, easy rhythm of her breathing lured him into the enchanted world of her dreams.

As the first cock crowed to greet the dawn, Alicia felt Rafael's lips brush her cheek with a sweet good-bye kiss, and while that gesture was deeply touching, she nevertheless lay still, pretending to be sound asleep. She had been awake ever since he had left their bed to dress, but seeing no point in reviewing their argument, she had feigned sleep. When she heard the door close, she knew he would not depart before making certain Joaquin was well enough for him to leave. There was no point in dogging his footsteps when she knew exactly where he planned to go. She had paid close attention when El Lobo had taken them to his hideout and she was confident she could find it again. She could now hear the low murmur of conversation coming from Joaquin's room, as well as the sounds of the sailors moving about on the opposite side of the other wall. They all appeared to be early risers, but she continued to wait patiently in the bed, the memory of the night's lovemaking still too precious for such a show of ambition.

When she heard a door close, she held her breath, praying Rafael might come back into their room to speak with her, but he did not return. Since the barn had to be in the rear, she was sufficiently intrigued to push the tangled covers aside and leave the comfortable bed. Disregarding her nudity, she went to the window, hoping to catch sight of him. To her dismay, he soon appeared with not one horse but two: the chestnut gelding Eduardo had lent him as well as El Lobo's golden yellow palomino. Hoping the fact that he had saddled two mounts meant he intended to take her with him, Alicia was so excited she nearly called out to him, but in the next instant he swung himself up onto the palomino's back, and leading the gelding on a rope, he started off down the road leading toward the mountains.

"Damn the man!" she shrieked in a fit of angry frustration. "Why couldn't he have been reasonable just this once!" With no time to lose, she washed hurriedly and donned the only outfit she had. Since the ruffled blouse and full skirt were not practical for riding, she rushed downstairs to find Guillermo

Rosales and sent him over to the dry goods store to purchase the simple white cotton trousers and shirt the peasants favored, for she knew that to be the best they had to offer.

While she had gotten only a few hours sleep, she was far too determined to notice the fatigue that gnawed at her muscles. That Joaquin had been so badly hurt had upset her dreadfully, and that Rafael might meet with the very same fate, or worse, terrified her. Since this was scarcely what her brother and his wife would want to hear, however, she knocked politely at their door and tried to compose her thoughts into a suitably encouraging theme.

Flame had taken great care to bathe and dress prettily that morning, not about to allow her appearance to betray her fears, but as she drew Alicia into their room, she was quite honest in her greeting. "Joaquin's still sleeping," she whispered anxiously, "but Rafael doesn't think that's any cause for alarm. I know he'll be very tired and the rest will be good for him, but—"

"But you're still very worried about him, aren't you?" As she crossed to the bed, Alicia finished her sister-in-law's sentence for her. That Joaquin still looked so pale frightened her too, for she had not expected that, but she turned back and smiled sympathetically at Flame. "I think he's doing fine considering how much blood he lost. I'm sure Tomás and the others will be happy to help you care for him. He'll need lots of nourishing food, but Rosales seems very eager to be of service."

"He's too eager, in my opinion," Flame replied with a frown. "I don't trust him."

Surprised by her comment, Alicia licked her lips thoughtfully before replying. "I'm sure you needn't worry about him. Rafael will pay him well for his trouble and that will ensure all the loyalty we'll need."

"Just like Eduardo Lopez?" the petite redhead asked with a defiant flip of her curls. "I am personally going to see he gets what he's got coming to him."

Before Alicia could offer to help her carry out that threat, Joaquin moaned softly and their attention was immediately focused upon him. His eyes were dulled by pain as they fluttered open, but as he looked up at them, he tried to smile. Flame was at his side in an instant and took his hand.

"How do you feel?" the lively redhead asked anxiously.

"Half dead," Joaquin admitted with a lopsided grin. The pain in his right shoulder was an agonizing throb, but he tried to be brave for her sake. He drank the glass of water she offered and then another, but he didn't think he could eat anything without becoming ill and he didn't want to risk that possibility since he felt wretched enough already. "Where's Rafael?"

Flame gave Alicia an apprehensive glance, but when the blonde nodded encouragingly, she explained where he had gone. "In all the confusion yesterday, Domingo was left behind. He's gone to get him."

"What happened to the others?" Joaquin's usually deep voice was no more than a hoarse rasp that morning as he struggled to find the breath to speak.

"They are all safe," Flame stated simply, not wanting to depress him by enumerating their injuries when she could see how agitated he was becoming. "You've got to rest, my darling. Rafael can handle everything until you're better."

When Joaquin closed his eyes, the women thought he had fallen asleep, but in a moment he again looked up at them and tried to smile. "Did he take the men with him?"

When Flame could think of no tactful way to explain that Rafael intended to storm the bandits' stronghold

368

single-handedly, Alicia quickly stepped forward. "He went alone, but you needn't worry. I plan to follow him to be certain he brings Domingo out safely."

Joaquin had never felt more helpless, and when he reached out his left hand to take his sister's, he found he lacked the strength to give her fingers more than a gentle clasp. "I'd be wasting my breath to forbid you to do that, wouldn't I?"

"Yes." Alicia leaned down to kiss his cheek and her voice was filled with affection as she continued. "Please don't ask that of me. I love you, Joaquin, but this is something I simply have to do."

Her determination glowed so brightly in her pretty blue eyes that he did not doubt the sincerity of her words. "And the men? What do they plan to do while you and Rafael go off chasing bandits?"

"Unfortunately they got cut up pretty badly yesterday," Alicia explained regretfully. "Please don't worry though; they're all going to be fine. All you need do is concentrate on getting well. The rest of us can take care of ourselves."

She made it sound as though he had some sort of choice, when Joaquin knew damn well he didn't. The simple act of breathing filled his shoulder with a thousand needles of pain, and this time when he closed his eyes he fell into an exhausted sleep.

Still frightened, Flame leaned down to kiss his lips sweetly, then gently smoothed his hair away from his forehead. "I'm going to send for the nearest doctor. Joaquin seems to be resting comfortably, but I don't want to take any chances with his life."

That seemed like a wise plan and Alicia promptly agreed with Flame's decision. "Whether or not you like Guillermo Rosales doesn't really matter. He knows everyone in town and we don't. I'll have him send someone reliable for a physician. He can get you

369

something new to wear and provide everyone with good meals too. I'll tell Tomás to look in on you frequently, and if Joaquin's prediction proves to be accurate, we'll be back with Domingo before supper time."

"You know I'm not fond of Domingo, but I don't want to see him come to any harm." Flame sighed unhappily. "I'd like to reward him for risking his own life to save Joaquin's."

"That's very generous of you and I'm sure he'll appreciate whatever you wish to give him." Alicia gave her sister-in-law an enthusiastic hug, but as she started to leave, she noticed Joaquin's holster hanging from a peg on the back of the door and knew she would need it. If there was any trouble, she was confident she could fire his Colt well enough to be of some real help to Rafael. Flame's back was turned as she stood at her husband's bedside, so without bothering her to make such a request, Alicia quickly grabbed the holster and carried it into the room she had shared with Rafael. She laid the weapon on the bed beside the new clothes Rosales had provided, then went next door to tell Tomás that Flame would need his assistance.

"But of course I will help her," the man agreed readily, but his face was almost as pale and drawn as Joaquin's. "We will all help with whatever we can."

"I'm going to send for a doctor and I'll want him to see all of you," Alicia insisted emphatically, blocking an argument before he could make one. "I'll have Rosales send up some breakfast too."

"You are too kind, *señorita*." Tomás thought it truly remarkable that such a wealthy and beautiful young woman would be so sympathetic to simple merchant seamen, and her kindness was greatly appreciated.

"Nonsense, you would do the same for me. I'll see you later." With that noncommittal farewell she

370

hurried down the stairs to give Guillermo Rosales the numerous instructions she wanted swiftly carried out, but she did not reveal her own plans. She then returned to her room and hastily donned the white clothes of a Mexican peasant. She covered her hair with a bright red bandanna, then added a small straw sombrero. She had her own boots to wear, and while she knew she would not fool anyone at close range, from afar she hoped she would be mistaken for a man. She felt ridiculous wearing her brother's gun belt, but she reminded herself that what was left of El Lobo's ragtag band of desperados would be heavily armed. It was a shame the mare she had ridden all week had been injured, but Flame's horse had survived the previous day unscathed and she had her saddled in a matter of minutes. She had every confidence in Rafael but was positive her help would prove vital if only he would not be too proud to allow her to give it.

She rode for nearly an hour on the winding trail that angled up into the foothills above Ciudad Altamirano before sighting the entrance to the narrow path that led to El Lobo's camp. She stopped there a moment to consider what Rafael might have done. Would he have followed that well-worn path or approached the camp from another direction? Certain the latter would surely have been his choice, she dismounted and scanned the soft dirt for fresh tracks. Just as she had thought, there was a break in the underbrush a short distance down the trail and she was certain this was the way he had gone. Following his tracks, she paid close attention as she led her horse along slowly.

The bandits' camp had a perfect location, for it was on a rise commanding a clear view of the valley below, but Rafael was approaching it from the side where the chances he would be observed were remote. The mare balked, disliking the rocky terrain, but Alicia patiently

371

coaxed her along. They had traveled a long way up the mountainside before they suddenly came upon the palomino and chestnut horses after making a sharp turn. Following Rafael's example, Alicia left her mare tethered nearby.

The going was far more difficult here. The old trees had dropped many a broken branch, forcing her to crawl over them, and the thorny plants of the underbrush clawed at the coarsely woven fabric of her trousers, badly hindering her progress, while the sharp stones underfoot made each step excruciatingly painful. The smell of smoke still filled the air, so she knew she was close and crept forward stealthily until she was finally able to part the last barrier of tangled vines, which grew in wild profusion around the camp's perimeter. She was behind the small house El Lobo had called his own and could not help but shudder as she recalled the gruesome sight of his body. She wondered if he were still lying exactly where he had fallen. She tiptoed along the side of the house, thinking the scene unnaturally quiet, but when she peeked around the corner, she was shocked to find that none of the other structures were still standing. The blaze that had consumed the barn had apparently spread to the other buildings, leaving the camp in ruins.

Holding her breath, she listened closely, straining to hear any sound that would reveal the presence of someone nearby. The birds in the trees were squawking noisily, and when she got used to their chatter she could make out another sound in the distance. It was an unusual rhythmic scraping, which puzzled her for a moment until she recognized it as the sound of someone digging a hole. The blade of the shovel would scrape through the sandy soil, then the sound would cease as the dirt was tossed aside, then the scraping noise would come again. Surely the only hole anyone there would feel obligated to dig was a grave. She peered around the corner of the ramshackle house and, seeing no one about, quickly ran to the window. There was no one inside, nor, as she had feared, was El Lobo's body still lying upon the floor. She ran across the porch, then stopped to peek around the corner before moving out into the courtyard. At the far end a lone man was working. The brilliance of the morning sun obscured his features, but judging by his height, trim build, and the easy grace with which he moved, she was certain it was Rafael and jumped down off the porch. As she began to walk toward him, he threw down the shovel and, dropping to a crouch, drew his Colt. She was astonished by his speed and promptly raised her hands as she called out, "Unless you want to kill your own fiancée, don't shoot."

Rafael rose slowly to his feet, thrust his revolver back into his holster, and remained silent until she was within arm's reach. Then with an economy of motion a rattler would have envied, he grabbed her arm, sank to his right knee in the dirt, and after balancing her gorgeous figure over his left knee, he finally gave her the spanking he had thought for a long time she deserved.

Chapter XIX

When Rafael finally released her and stood her up on her feet, Alicia shied away from him, the expression on her face one of furious revulsion. "God help me, you warned me and I didn't even listen. You said Miguel Villarreal was like a second father to you. Is he the one who taught you that men ought to beat their wives!"

Her accusation was so unfounded it took Rafael several seconds to realize he had just made the most foolish mistake of his life. When he had lost his temper and spanked her, he had obviously lost every last bit of respect she had ever had for him. "No! Of course not. If he ever struck your mother, I never knew of it. He never recommended such brutality and neither would I," he argued in a vain attempt to make her see reason.

Alicia brushed the dust off her trousers, so furious with him it was difficult for her to speak. "My mother didn't know what sort of man Miguel was when she married him, but fortunately I now know all I need to know about you. I'll never take you for my husband, but if you think you can discourage me from going after Domingo you'll have to do a lot better than that." She lifted her chin proudly, daring him to strike her again.

"Damn it all, Alicia!" Rafael shouted in frustrated rage. "I could have shot you! Can't you understand that simple fact? I came within a hair's breadth of killing you just now! It was that peasant's outfit that made me hesitate. Had you borrowed some of my clothes you'd be dead!"

Alicia eyed him coldly. She was so certain he never fired without being sure of his target that she doubted she had been in any real danger. "That doesn't excuse what you did. I am not some little child you can spank for being naughty." Looking past him, she nodded toward the open grave. "Whom are you burying?"

Rafael was in no mood to discuss that grim task but bent down to grab the shovel and started digging once again. "They either took El Lobo's body with them or buried him some distance from here. They left two others behind and I'd bury any man rather than let the buzzards feast on his flesh. Didn't you notice them circling overhead?"

Alicia glanced up only long enough to make certain the evil birds were indeed in the sky, and they were. "If they lost only three men, how many bandits are left?"

"I can't be sure since I don't know whether they remained together or scattered in all directions. I won't know how many there are until I catch up with them."

Since he seemed to know as little as she, Alicia saw no point in pursuing that line of questioning and promptly dropped it. "If there's another shovel, I'll help you. We've already given them too much of a lead. We should have come up here last night as I suggested."

Rafael shoved his hat farther back on his head and leaned against the shovel to rest as he replied, "They were undoubtedly already gone by then and we wouldn't have been able to track them in the dark. You mustn't regard last night as wasted. I certainly don't."

Alicia ignored his suggestive reminder of the

intimacy they had shared, since that memory was far too painful to relive. "Is there another shovel?" she asked again, returning to a far safer subject.

Disappointed in her hostile aloofness, Rafael replied with equal disdain, "I found this one where someone had dropped it. If they had others, they must have been lost in the fire."

"I'll go get the horses then." As Alicia turned away, Rafael called her name. "Yes, what is it?" she snapped angrily.

"Does Joaquin know you have his Colt?"

Alicia shook her head. "No, but he'll have no use for it in the next few days and I will."

Not impressed by her show of bravado, Rafael issued a stern warning. "This is no game of hide and seek, Alicia. Several have died and there are bound to be others, but I don't want them to be you or I. Since you're so damned determined to come with me, I won't try to stop you, but you'll have to agree that I'm the one giving the orders. Is that a promise?"

"Or what? You'll hit me again?" Alicia taunted him proudly.

"I did not hit you!" Rafael insisted sharply. "I spanked you because you were behaving like a spoiled brat and that behavior will not only get us both killed but probably Domingo as well! Is that what you want?"

"No, of course not!" the fiesty blonde shouted right back at him.

"Then I want your word right now that you'll do exactly as I say without a single word of argument! Not even one!" Rafael held his breath, praying she would come with him on his terms, for that would be the first step in easing the tension that seemed to flare up endlessly between them.

Alicia's stare was still bitterly cold as she considered her options. She would become lost before noon if she

377

tried to track the bandits through the mountains by herself, so that certainly was not a viable choice. She couldn't stand being left behind again either. As distasteful as the prospect was, she knew she would have to agree to his demand. "I won't disappoint you," she finally promised grudgingly.

Rafael replied with a sly chuckle, "If that's the only promise you can make, I'll accept it." Indeed, Alicia was a continual challenge, but she had never once disappointed him. "Look in El Lobo's house and see if they left behind anything we might find useful: blankets, a canteen, food they might have forgotten. I don't want to have to waste any time going back into town for supplies."

His expression was still stern, his voice crisp, as though he were barking orders to a platoon of men rather than a lone woman. His arrogance grated harshly upon her ravaged nerves, but she would not allow his overbearing attitude to get the better of her. "I'll see what I can find." As Alicia strode away, she was proud of herself for not breaking down in tears, but she had meant what she had said: she would not marry a man who would take such delight in giving her a beating. He might regard what he had done as no more than a spanking, but as far as she was concerned it was an extremely poor expression of love, the worst she had ever seen, and for the first time she understood why her mother had divorced Joaquin's father. He might have been handsome and charming, but the flaw in his character had been a mile wide.

By the time she had finished searching El Lobo's house, Rafael had completed the burial detail. He met her on the porch and surveyed the small cache with an appreciative glance. "They must have lit out of here at a dead run or they'd not have left that food behind."

While it was scarcely gourmet fare, Alicia knew the

side of bacon would last a long time on the trail. There was a sack of the finely ground cornmeal used to make corn *tortillas,* but she had no idea how they were made. "Can you cook?" she asked hopefully.

Rafael swallowed the insult that filled his mind before it reached his lips and forced himself to reply in a civil tone. "I've been looking out for myself for a good long time."

That she had never been on her own was his clear implication, but Alicia let it pass. There was no point in arguing the point since he was correct. She had been raised as the pampered daughter of an extremely wealthy man, but that did not mean she lacked the courage to keep up with him. She stuffed the bacon, the sack of fine cornmeal, and the small bag of coffee she had found into an old flour sack that seemed clean enough to serve as a knapsack. She tossed in a frying pan, battered coffeepot, two tin plates, and two dented cups. The utensils she had found were not much good, but she preferred using them to eating with her fingers. There had been a threadbare blanket on the bed where they had found Domingo and she had rolled that up so it would fit behind her saddle. "I'll go get the horses," she offered without a trace of a smile.

"You followed my trail?"

"It wasn't difficult," Alicia replied matter-of-factly.

Rafael thought that unlikely but did not challenge her opinion. "Maybe you do have some talent after all. Have you ever fired a forty-five?"

"No, but I'm sure I can."

"Enthusiasm is one thing, Alicia, experience quite another."

"Then teach me if you think I'm so damn ignorant!" Alicia dared him brazenly.

Rafael treated her outburst as though it had been a sweetly worded reply, since the approach he had used to stop her from behaving like a brat had met with such disastrous results. "We've no time to spare for lessons now and if we're lucky they won't be necessary later. Come on, bring that stuff and we'll load it on the horse I brought for Domingo. Even if you can't shoot, I hope you can track half as well as you think you can." He started off around the corner of the house expecting her to yell at him for not helping her carry the things she had gathered. She surprised him, however, by just slinging the sack over her shoulder, scooping up the blanket in her other hand, and following him without complaint. He had to admit she looked rather cute in a peasant's casual attire, but that he had come so close to shooting her unnerved him still. "Can you whistle?" he called over his shoulder.

"Not well. Why?"

"I don't want you sneaking up on me again. If you can whistle well enough to send a signal, then we can avoid another near tragedy."

"You mean we should have some sort of code like the Indians do?" Alicia was intrigued by that thought, but truly she doubted she could whistle well enough to send any sort of recognizable signal.

When they reached their mounts, Rafael quickly took the bundle she had been carrying and secured it firmly behind the gelding's saddle. "Yes, Indians imitate bird calls. Can you do that?"

Alicia blushed as she shook her head. "I've never really tried, but I don't think so."

"Well, you'll have plenty of time to practice while we ride. Let's go." He waited for her to tie the blanket behind her saddle, then swung herself up on the palomino. "What do you suppose El Lobo called this beast?"

Alicia wondered why Rafael had suddenly become so charming, but her own mood had not improved. She was furious with him still, but they might have a long distance to travel together and she saw no reason to ride the whole way in angry silence. "He's a handsome animal. Maybe his name is Nugget, or something like that, since he's such a pretty golden color."

"Nugget he is then," Rafael agreed with a wink. "Let's go back the way we came and follow the main trail into camp. I think I know which trail they took but I want to be certain."

"Lead the way." Alicia waited for Rafael and the gelding to move past her, then turned the mare around to follow them. When they again entered the desolate camp, she could not help but shiver at the memory of the fierce battle they had raged there, even though little remained to remind her of it. "For so notorious a bandit, this wasn't much of a home," she remarked absently.

"He supposedly had more than one. Which way would you have run, north or south?" He turned in his saddle to make that query, but his expression was serious, not teasing.

"I'd follow the Balsas farther into the valley rather than cross the mountains and move closer to Mexico City. Wouldn't that be the far safer course?"

"Yes," Rafael agreed, but he dismounted and walked slowly around the perimeter of the camp to be certain the bandits had not headed deeper into the mountains as they had fled. "All the tracks lead back the way we've come, but I didn't hear them riding through town so they must have given it a wide berth. Come one, let's see if we can overtake them before nightfall."

Alicia thought surely he must be joking, but he took off at a gallop, clearly intending to make up for lost time. They alternated their pace to keep from tiring their mounts, hoping the thieves wouldn't be nearly as clever. They found that the bandits' trail made a wide loop around Ciudad Altamirano before veering back toward the Balsas, but by late afternoon they had not caught sight of them. When Rafael finally called a halt, Alicia was more than ready to stop. "They must have left their camp before nightfall yesterday to have gotten so far ahead."

Rafael nodded. "Probably, but we still couldn't have tracked them after dark." He unsaddled the stallion and the gelding, then took great care to tether them where they would have plenty of grass to eat but could not wander away. Alicia followed his example, but when he began to gather dry wood for a fire she grew worried. "Do you think it's safe to build a fire?"

"What did you have to eat before you came after me this morning?"

"Nothing," Alicia admitted reluctantly, for she did not want him to criticize her for failing to be well prepared. "I was in too great a hurry."

"Then neither of us has had anything to eat today and we can't help Domingo if we're faint from hunger. We can eat the fish from the river raw, but since I doubt you'd enjoy that, I'm willing to risk a fire." He turned away to hide his smile, for he had no desire to eat uncooked fish either.

Alicia swallowed nervously. She was hungry, but the mere thought of eating raw fish turned her stomach and she knew she would not be able to swallow a single bite. "We won't need a large fire to fry a few fish, and even if the bandits do see the smoke they might think it's coming from a house nearby."

"That's true," Rafael agreed. In a few minutes he had a fire started and stepped back to admire it. "If they follow their usual habits, they'll be too drunk tonight to notice each other, let alone a wisp of smoke." He still had a fishing line in his saddlebags and soon had his hook baited with a fat worm and had tossed it into the water. "This might take some time. Can you at least brew a pot of coffee?"

"I'll try." Drawing water from the swiftly flowing river, Alicia added a handful of coffee to the pot and after kicking two rocks into position to support it set it over the flames. She felt so hot and sticky she gazed longingly at the water but decided to wait until after dark to bathe. "If only we'd known they'd left the camp, we could have come a lot better prepared."

Rafael cast her a quizzical glance. "We have all we need to get by for a few days. Neither of us should suffer too greatly."

Alicia did not contradict him, but she was tired and sore, and not simply from riding either. He had done his best to inflict as much pain as he possibly could, but she was proud of herself for not letting him see how well he had succeeded. She was certain she had large purple bruises on her bottom that would exactly match the shape of his hand. She would not forgive him for treating her in such a humiliating fashion either.

When Rafael glanced over at his lovely companion, he was shocked by the fierceness of her expression. She was kneeling down beside the fire, apparently doing no more than watching the coffee boil, but it was easy to see that her thoughts were murderous. "Try to make some *tortillas;* it isn't difficult," he shouted above the roar of the river.

Eager for any task to occupy her mind, Alicia scooped out two cups of the fine cornmeal into the frying pan, then slowly added water until she had a mixture the consistency of bread dough. Pulling off a fist-sized ball, she tried patting it out flat between her palms, but without grease to keep it from sticking, she soon had so much dough stuck to her hands she had to use a spoon to scrape it off. Finally remembering that the bacon would work to grease her hands just as well as lard or butter, she cut off a slice and managed to do a far better job in patting out the next wad of dough. Since she had used the frying pan as a bowl, however, she had no place to fry it. When she glanced up at Rafael, she was certain he had turned away so she would not see him laughing at her, but undaunted, she draped the circle of dough over a smooth stone at the edge of the fire and made another. When she had finally succeeded in using all the dough, she washed out the pan, cut off several slices of bacon, and after cooking them began to fry up her *tortillas* in the hot grease. They looked nothing like the thin, flavorful pancakes she had eaten at Eduardo Lopez's ranch but instead resembled misshapen biscuits. She had completely forgotten the coffee but was certain it must have had time to brew and she set it off to the side, embarrassed she had made more of a mess than an appetizing supper.

Rafael pretended not to notice the difficulty Alicia had with the simple task of making *tortillas*. When she had finished frying the dozen globs of dough he was certain would be every bit as tasty as boulders, he had caught and cleaned two good-sized fish and tossed them into the waiting pan. While he watched them fry, he poured himself a cup of coffee. It was at least hot, but so thick he nearly gagged trying to swallow it. "If you don't mind, I'll add just a little more water to the coffee," he offered with a strained smile.

Alicia was grateful he had not spit it out, but until that morning he had always displayed very fine manners. "I should have moved the pot away from the fire sooner," she mumbled by way of apology.

"It's fine," Rafael insisted, "just a little bit strong." He smiled as best he could and was delighted when his second cup wasn't half bad. When the fish were done, he had no excuse not to try one of the gruesome little lumps she had fried up in an attempt to make *tortillas,* but they were not nearly as unpalatable as he had feared they would be. It was unusual to find bread dough so chewy, but the bacon grease that had absorbed while frying made them slide right down his throat. The freshly caught fish were tasty enough, but all in all he could not recall ever eating a worse meal. "As I said, we won't be gone so long we'll suffer much."

"Thank God," Alicia replied solemnly, for she had found the whole meal nearly inedible. Despite growing up on the Pacific Coast, she had never been fond of fish. These looked like trout to her and she knew many people liked them, but she took only a few bites and decided she had had enough. She forced down one of the lumps of fried dough, then looked up longingly at the trees. "I don't suppose we'll be able to find any fruit this late in the summer."

"Probably not." Rafael sighed regretfully, as he would have paid a princely sum for a succulent peach or tangy orange. "You're right. We've come shockingly unprepared for this trek so we'll have to complete it swiftly."

"How do you propose to do that?" Alicia asked skeptically.

Rafael poured himself more coffee, but when he offered to refill her cup she shook her head. "We'll stay right on their trail as we did today. They've obviously got a destination in mind, but with luck we'll catch up to them before they reach it. I'll wait until dark, sneak into their camp, and untie Domingo. Then the three of us will have to get as far away from there as we can before sunrise and they find that Domingo's escaped."

Alicia considered that plan a good one except for the fact that he had given her no part. "I don't want to be left with the horses, Rafael. At least let me go with you to cover your back."

"Even though you've never fired a gun?" Rafael shook his head, greatly amused by her offer. "No thanks. I'll take my chances on one of El Lobo's men shooting me in the back rather than you."

Since she had no intention of allowing him to ridicule her, Alicia got up and made her way back downstream. When she came to a suitable secluded spot, she turned around to be certain he had not followed her, then quickly yanked off the cotton shirt and trousers. Her own lacy undergarments were none too clean and she stripped them off too. She washed them out at the river's edge, left them draped over a boulder to dry, then wandered out into the chill waters of the Balsas. They had been traveling against the brisk current, but at the river's edge she was in no danger of being swept away. Unsure of how long her privacy would last, she bathed hurriedly, then washed her hair. She was so cold by the time she got out of the water her teeth were chattering, but to her dismay she found one of Rafael's shirts lying across the peasant outfit. It seemed he had followed her, after all, and he had undoubtedly seen all there was to see before he had gone back to their camp.

"Blast the man!" she muttered angrily, but since she had nothing else to sleep in she grabbed up the worn plaid shirt and quickly put it on. Then gathering up the damp lingerie and other garments, she walked back to their camp. Rafael had washed their dishes before he had also taken advantage of the proximity of the river to bathe. He was seated by the fire dressed only in his black riding pants. "Thank you for the shirt," Alicia offered through clenched teeth, sorely tempted to say much more.

"You're welcome." Rafael smiled slyly as he watched her hang her silk underwear over a low limb, his appreciative glance longingly caressing her long, shapely legs. "I have a couple of extra shirts and since you've no other clothes, I don't mind sharing them."

"How very generous of you!" Alicia replied sharply. She surveyed the rocky ground and wondered how she and Flame had been able to find comfortable spots to rest when they had followed the lower portion of the Balsas. Perhaps they had only been too tired to feel the uneven ground beneath them. "Where are you going to sleep?" she asked suspiciously.

Having given that question no thought, Rafael merely shrugged. "Since there are just the two of us, we'll have to take turns. Do you want the first watch or the second?"

"Do you actually expect them to come back looking for us?"

Rafael rose to his feet and came toward her. "We didn't expect trouble on our way to El Lobo's camp, but we posted guards anyway. I'm sure you haven't forgotten burying the two men who were slain. I know you'd probably just toss my carcass into the river if you found me dead in the morning, but believe me, there wouldn't be enough of you left for me to bury."

She had always regarded him as strikingly handsome. There was not an ounce of fat to mar the perfection of his lean, muscular build and she had a great deal of difficulty lifting her eyes from the damp curls that covered his broad chest to his taunting gaze. "You're not telling me anything I don't already know. Flame and I knew exactly what we were risking when we rode into El Lobo's camp yesterday, but we were willing to take that chance anyway," she responded with an icy calm that belied her wildly beating heart, for she could not help but recall exactly what had happened every time they had ever been alone together and feared this night would be no exception. The attraction that existed between them was as strong as ever, a physical force she might fiercely deny, but she could feel its incredible power still.

While he sincerely doubted they had given the risks any thought before they had begun their ridiculous masquerade, Rafael did not dispute her word. "Good, I'm glad to hear you're actually capable of formulating a plan, even if I've seen no evidence of it. Sleep near the fire and I'll wake you when it's your turn to keep watch." He turned away then and returned to his spot on the opposite side of the fire. He had been using his saddle for a back rest and appeared perfectly comfortable.

Alicia spread her blanket near the fire and sat down, taking great care to see that the high-cut sides of his shirttail did not provide a better view than she wanted him to have. "I'm not tired," she announced firmly.

Rafael crossed his arms over his bare chest and returned her obstinate glare. "You will be," he assured her.

It was growing dark, the high temperature of the day falling rapidly, and there by the river the fine spray suppressed the heat even more. She had nothing to look forward to but a long, chilly night with the most irresistible of companions, and she knew she would never be able to fall asleep before it was time for her to be up anyway. "I doubt it," she responded confidently.

The tension that filled her pose swiftly called to mind a mountain cat gathering its strength to spring. She was the predator and he the prey, but Rafael had no intention of allowing her to unleash the fury of her temper on him twice in one day. "Then I'll go to sleep first," he offered graciously, and without further comment, he stretched out on his saddle blanket, cradled his cheek upon his outstretched arms, and promptly went to sleep.

388

Alicia sat staring at the muscular contours of the handsome man's back, wondering where he had mastered the ability to relax so completely. She hugged her knees and tried to decide just what it was she was supposed to be doing. The constant hum as the waters of the Balsas tumbled over its rocky bed would mask the sound of approaching footsteps, whether human or animal, so she knew she would have no warning until danger was upon them. To avoid being caught defenseless, she got up to get Joaquin's holster, and carrying his revolver firmly clutched in her hand, she went to check the horses, who were still lazily munching the tall grass at the river's edge. She rubbed her arms and paced up and down by the fire for a long while before again sitting down. She had no idea how long a turn she was supposed to take but knew it had to be several hours. Since she had no watch, she wondered why Rafael had not given her his. That had probably been a deliberate oversight, she decided with a petulant frown. From time to time she got up to add wood to the fire, walked down the trail to check on the horses, and got an occasional drink from the river, but the hours passed with a maddeningly slow pace. The stars were very bright, but she had never been able to make out the mythological creatures ancient astronomers had made of their patterns. They were pretty, but other than the North Star and the Big and Little Dipper, she could not name any. A full moon bathed their camp in a soft, liquid glow, but her mood was scarcely romantic. Her depression deepening by the minute, she decided love was an impossible delusion kept alive by poets and musicians so they would not starve. The harsh truth of reality was that men and women were fortunate to be civil to one another; love was no more than an ideal state that few, if any, ever enjoyed for more than a few blissful hours at a time. That the intensity of her feelings for Rafael was undimmed by his beastly behavior only made her agony all the more deep.

When Rafael awakened, he glanced over to where he had last seen Alicia sitting, then leapt to his feet when he realized she was gone. He had been a damn fool to leave her on watch when she must have been easily overpowered. Taking a firm grip on his knife, he backed away from the fire into the shadows, waiting for the first telltale sign of movement that would give away the intruder's position. When Alicia suddenly stepped into the circle of light thrown by the fire and called his name, he nearly whooped with joy. "Where have you been?" he asked as he slipped his knife back into its sheath at his belt and joined her in front of the fire.

"Checking on the horses," the lively blonde replied flippantly. "Isn't that part of my duties?"

"Of course." Rafael had to admit she had been conscientious. Checking his watch, he was surprised to find it was nearly two o'clock. "Why didn't you wake me at midnight?"

Alicia gave him a weary glance. "I have no idea what time it is. Is it past midnight already?"

Rafael felt like a fool then. Why he had expected her to carry a pocket watch he didn't know. "I'm sorry. You lie down and get some rest. I'm wide awake now and I'll let you sleep until dawn."

Alicia did not feel a bit tired, just deeply melancholy, but when she lay down upon the old blanket Rafael quickly leaned down to wrap it snugly around her shoulders and she murmured no more than a brief word of thanks before she was asleep.

It was now Rafael's turn to contemplate the vast difference in the last two nights they had spent together. Just looking at Alicia's tangled curls made him ache with longing. He wanted to hold her in his arms and convince her most tenderly that he would never abuse her, and in his own mind he was certain he never had. She was simply far too independent for her own good when she had so few skills necessary for survival. A slow smile curved across his lips then as he recalled she had supplied the answer to that dilemma herself. She had dared him to teach her what she would need to know and he was positive that while she lacked Domingo's wiry strength, she would need little practice to outshoot him. The problem was that he had no time to tutor her now, so he prayed she would not need to know how to defend herself in the next few days.

As the sun rose high in the sky the next morning, Alicia found it increasingly difficult to stay alert. Rafael had had breakfast ready when he had awakened her, but the coffee she had consumed had kept her wide awake for no more than an hour or two. With only a few hours' sleep and half a dozen strips of bacon for breakfast, her reserves of energy were running dangerously low. She yawned repeatedly and kept reminding herself that her life, as well as his, might depend upon her being able to remain alert. She blamed herself when they missed the spot where the bandits had left the trail alongside the river. Rafael did not complain when they had to retrace their steps, but she knew that the mistake had cost them precious time they didn't have to lose. The new path was treacherous, narrow, and deeply worn. It left the riverbank and climbed gradually up the mountainside in a steep, winding route that left her dizzy whenever she dared look down. When they reached a spot wide enough for him to dismount, Rafael walked back to her.

"I'm going to go on ahead a little ways on foot. This

391

trail is too narrow to turn around, so we can't risk suddenly coming upon their camp. Wait here a few minutes and I'll come right back."

Alicia had again wound the bandanna around her curls and wore the sombrero to shade her eyes. She was a remarkably pretty peasant, and a very feisty one too. "Be careful," she warned earnestly. "I don't want to have to drag Domingo out of the bandits' camp all by myself."

"I intend to see you avoid that too," Rafael replied with a rakish grin as he turned away.

The rocky path was difficult to traverse, more suited to the talents of burros than horses and men, but he proceeded with care, glancing up frequently to be certain no one had a rifle trained on him from the rocks above. When the sandy soil beneath his feet suddenly gave way in a rumbling avalanche, he had no time to leap to safety and went sailing off the mountainside flinging his arms wildly as he clutched at the scrawny underbrush in a frantic attempt to break his fall.

When Alicia heard what had to be a scream, she leapt off her mare. She then had to inch carefully by the gelding and palomino to reach the open trail, where she did her best to run up the steep incline. What had happened was soon obvious. Centuries of melting snow had weakened the structure of the mountain's face and where there had recently been a path two feet wide, there was now a three-foot gap and no sign of Rafael. Terrified he had plunged to his death, Alicia dropped to her knees, then leaned out to look over the dangerously unstable cliff. Rafael's fall had been broken by a rocky ledge perhaps fifteen feet below the trail. He was on his hands and knees, shaking his head as if to clear it, while at his side an enormous rattlesnake, furious at having its sunny perch invaded, began to coil in preparation for a deadly strike.

Rafael's vision was blurred by blood dripping from a cut above his right eye, but as he looked up in response to Alicia's frantic screams, he saw her pointing Joaquin's Colt at him, and with his last ounce of strength he tried to dive out of the way as she fired. The sky spun crazily above him as he scrambled to keep from sliding off the narrow ledge, but being shot seemed to be the lesser of two evils at the moment. He had known she was mad at him, but he had never even considered the fact that she might wish him dead. Choking on the dust flying all around him, he looked back over his shoulder and found she had not been firing at him after all. Only a few inches away the rattlesnake lay twitching feebly as it died, a neat hole drilled cleanly through its wedge-shaped skull. He looked up at Alicia then, his admiration plain. "Nice shot!" he managed to call, then fainted facedown in the dust.

Chapter XX

"Rafael!" Alicia shrieked his name repeatedly, but there was no response. Had the snake already bitten him before she had reached the cliff? Was he dead? She studied the rocky surface of the mountainside, but it was far too steep a grade for her even to consider attempting to climb down to the ledge where he lay. That he had landed upon a jutting slab of solid rock that would surely support their combined weight should she be able to reach him was encouraging, but the trick would be to reach it safely. She could not simply leave him there and pray he was not too badly injured to climb up when he regained consciousness, if he ever did. No, Alicia knew she would have to do something to help him, and fast. Dashing back to the palomino, she grabbed the coiled rope looped over the saddle horn. She then took a firm hold upon the golden stallion's bridle, determined to lead him up the trail. He tossed his head, whipping her cheek as his blond mane went flying. He objected violently to progressing any farther up the narrow incline, but Alicia refused to allow him to balk and, berating him for his cowardice, yanked him right on up the path behind her. She stopped several feet back from the gaping hole, secured one end of the rope to the palomino's saddle horn, then tossed the other end over the precipice. It reached to within two feet of where Rafael lay, and grasping it tightly with both hands, she lowered herself down the face of the mountain. The coarse fibers of the sisal rope cut into her palms and tore the tender flesh of her fingers, but she hung on until she could safely drop down to the ledge. With a swift kick she sent the dead snake flying off into the canyon far below, then bent down beside Rafael. Overjoyed to find him breathing, she quickly unbuttoned his shirt and ran her fingertips over his skin, but there was no sign of a snakebite on his side or chest and she doubted the viper's fangs could have pentrated the tough weave of his riding pants or the leather of his boots. Grateful there was no sign he had been bitten, she sat down and cradled his head in her lap. She had lost her hat while descending the cliff but still had the bandanna. She tore it off and tied it tightly around his head to bandage the deep gash in his forehead. Her fingers moved over his face, softly caressing his cheeks and beard as she continued to call his name between deep, racking sobs. She hugged him tightly, terrified the thieves had heard the gunshot and would be upon them in a matter of minutes, though she knew she had had little choice about shooting the rattler. They were in such horrible trouble she did not see how they would ever get out, and to add to her despair, it seemed an eternity before Rafael began to stir.

Battered and bruised from the force of his fall, Rafael opened one eye tentatively before opening the other. Finding his face snuggled so comfortably between Alicia's ample breasts was an extremely pleasant sensation and he let her think he was still unconscious for another full minute before struggling to sit up. "Where's the snake?" he asked as he raised his hand to his painfully throbbing forehead.

"I shoved it off into the canyon," Alicia replied with a shudder of disgust. "Did you want to see it?"

"No, I wanted to fry it for supper," he explained with obvious disappointment. "They're very tasty."

Alicia knew she was going to be sick and it took every last ounce of willpower she had not to vomit all over him. "Please," she whispered hoarsely.

"No, really, rattlesnake is good to eat. The meat is white and tender so it's a lot like chicken."

Alicia shut her eyes tightly, took a deep breath, and held it. It took an enormous amount of concentration, but she was finally able to control her stomach and make it be still. Then she made no effort to conquer her anger. "Our most pressing problem is how we're going to get off this damn ledge. We can worry about what we'll cook for supper later!"

"That's undoubtedly true," Rafael agreed with a shaky grin, shocked he had again upset her. Glancing up toward the trail, he spotted the rope and then took her bloody hands in his. "Look what you've done to yourself," he murmured regretfully.

"It's nothing." Alicia yanked her hands away and wiped them on the sides of her trousers. "Nugget's too frightened to move. He's strong enough to bear your weight. Do you feel well enough to try going up the rope? I don't want the bandits to find us sitting here chatting."

Her tears had made salty trails down her cheeks and Rafael knew she was still badly frightened, yet he could do nothing to offer comfort there. "Hell, that fall damn near killed me! Going up that rope will be no challenge at all." He had landed on his hat, but after dusting it off, he managed to crimp the crown back into its original shape and jammed it back on his head. He then rose to his feet, took a moment to be certain he would not grow dizzy, and then gave her a hand to help her rise. It was then he noticed his shirt was unbuttoned and he gave her a quizzical glance.

"I was afraid you'd been bitten by the snake," she replied hesitantly, thinking that excuse sounded rather feeble, though surely he would know she had not undressed him simply for the fun of it.

"What would you have done if I had been bitten?" Rafael asked curiously.

Alicia shook her head. "I've no idea. I'd probably have fainted too."

"I did not faint!" Rafael denied hotly, appalled by her accusation.

"Oh, of course not," the feisty blonde replied sarcastically. "How could I have imagined such a thing? You had a bad fall, cut your head, and passed out. Is that a better description of what happened?"

Rafael was certain there had to be a difference between fainting and passing out, but at the moment he could not describe what it was since the resulting unconsciousness was exactly the same. He was certain, however, that grown men didn't faint, or at least they shouldn't. Feeling very foolish, he apologized. "I'm sorry. You saved my life by shooting that rattler and then risked your own to come down here after me. I didn't mean to sound so ungrateful."

While she was pleased he had decided to become more reasonable, Alicia was in a great hurry to reach safety. "You can thank me after we get off this blasted ledge. I think it's too soon for me to take any credit for saving your life."

Her modesty was highly amusing considering the fix they were in, but just smiling made his already severe headache worse and he did not dare laugh. "I'll go up first, then you can just tie the rope around your waist and I'll pull you up."

"Do you honestly feel well enough to do that?" Alicia asked skeptically.

"No, but I'm going to do it anyway," Rafael replied with grim determination. While she seemed to have a great deal of confidence in Nugget, he had no such faith. He doubted the horse had been well trained, but with luck he hoped he would make it up the rope before the animal grew skittish and plunged them both to their deaths. Since he had no intention of leaving Alicia stranded on the ledge, he gave the rope a good yank, and when Nugget did no more than glance down at him with an evil stare, he prayed the horse would not bolt while he climbed up the trail. He turned to look down at Alicia then, a slight smile teasing the corner of his mouth. "I love you. You haven't forgotten that, have you?"

The disheveled blonde shook her head, fearing she would again burst into tears if she tried to reply in words.

Rafael leaned over to give her a light kiss, and when she did not pull away he hoped that meant she might soon forgive him for spanking her. Since it was neither the time nor the place for a more generous expression of affection or to discuss their future, he gave her a comforting wink and, after taking a deep breath, scaled the mountain in a matter of seconds.

Alicia sighed with relief when Rafael waved to her from the path, but her hands hurt so badly it took her a long while to secure the rope around her waist. When she was finally ready, she called up to him, "Are you sure you feel up to this?"

"What's the alternative?" Rafael replied with a teasing chuckle, making light of their predicament. He ached all over, and he doubted his headache would go away in less than a week, but he would not leave the woman he loved dangling in midair on the end of a rope, and with the precision he had seen on board *La Reina,* he used a hand-over-hand motion to pull her up the face of the cliff. It was not until he had set her on her feet and untied the rope that he realized they were still in a great deal of trouble. "I think we're going to have to convince the horses to move backward down the trail until we can reach a wide enough spot for them to turn around. There's no way they can get up the speed to leap that break in the trail, so we'll just have to go back and hope we can find another route through the mountains."

Alicia turned around and studied the gap for a long moment with an intense gaze. "You and I could jump that, don't you think?"

"Madre de Dios!" Rafael gasped incredulously. "No, I do not think we could, and even if we could, then what? The bandits' camp might be several days' ride from here. It would be ridiculous to start off on foot now knowing how far we'll have to travel. We can't set Domingo free and then tell him he'll have to make a run for it on foot either!"

While she had to admit his objections to her suggestion were sound, Alicia hated to say so out loud. "I guess you're right. We will have to go back," she finally agreed grudgingly.

"You're damn right I'm right!" Rafael was grateful she had agreed with him for once, as he was anxious to be on their way. He had already untied the rope from around her waist and now re-coiled it and slung it back over the saddle horn. "This is going to be damn near impossible, but I think your little mare will back up if you talk to her real nice. Nugget here is going to do as I say simply because I say it, but that leaves the gelding in the middle and on his own. If he tries to turn around here, we'll lose him, so I think I'd better take the pack off him now."

"No!" Alicia argued immediately. "I'll take the mare down a few yards at a time, then I'll come back for the gelding. We might need him later for Domingo, so it would be foolish to resign ourselves to losing him now."

Rafael shrugged. "Give it a try." He watched her wiggle her way past Nugget, then the gelding, and hoped she would not find what she had set out to do impossible. Then recalling the dismal dinner they had shared, he realized losing their food would be a slight loss. Turning to Nugget, he began to explain exactly what they were going to do in a soft, soothing tone. Since Alicia couldn't overhear, he described the lovely blonde in terms he thought the stallion would appreciate. Whether the horse understood his words or not did not really matter, but the animal grew sufficiently calm to back his way down the treacherous trail that had nearly claimed his handsome new master's life.

After handling two nervous horses, Alicia was exhausted by the time they reached the bottom of the trail. She walked straight to the river and scooped up several mouthfuls of water. Once her thirst was satisfied, she lay down on her stomach and splashed water over her face and hair until she felt well enough to flop over on her back to rest. Rafael stood gazing down at her, but she raised her arm to cover her eyes and block out the sight of his disapproving stare. "Don't say a word. Just let me rest a minute and then I'll be ready to go on."

"You'll be going by yourself then, because I'm calling it a day." He strode off, leaving the horses to drink their fill.

Alicia nearly dozed off, glad he was too tired to continue too, but when he returned a short while later with the snake in his hand, she sat up abruptly. "Where did you find that?" she cried hoarsely.

As he spoke, Rafael turned to point up the mountainside. "The trail we followed has so many turns we're almost directly beneath that ledge right here. Knowing you, I figured you kicked this poor snake hard enough to send him all the way down here and I was right. This is your snake, all right. I'd recognize that hole in his head anywhere."

"Are you sure we can eat that?" Alicia asked suspiciouly. The idea of eating rattlesnake meat was still revolting, but she was getting too hungry to be concerned about their choice of *entrée*.

"Positive. I've eaten them many times." Rafael laid the snake several yards away, then stretched out by her side. He closed his eyes and sighed wearily. "Tomorrow we'll find another pass through the mountains."

"Fine," Alicia murmured softly. The low, gurgling sounds of the Balsas soon lulled them to sleep, and when she awakened it was nearly sunset. Whether she had been the one to move, or he, she could not tell, but she found herself snugly cradled in Rafael's arms. While that provided a reassuring degree of comfort, she moved away quickly, afraid he would awaken and think she had cuddled up close to him to encourage the affection she no longer dared accept. She got up, brushed the grass from her rumpled white trousers and shirt, then went to check on the horses. All three animals were grazing peacefully, totally unaware of their masters' predicament. She apologized for not unsaddling them sooner, but they seemed none the worse for that small bit of neglect. There was plenty of dry wood for a fire, but while she unpacked their meager rations, she hesitated to begin cooking. The *tortillas* had been a failure she would not repeat, but she was certain she could do better with the coffee. When Rafael opened his eyes, she knew she had

402

disturbed him.

"I'm sorry. I didn't mean to make so much noise I'd awaken you."

"I didn't hear anything." Rafael felt sick to his stomach, but whether that was because he was hungry or because his headache was growing worse he did not know.

He looked much too pale, even in the fading light, and Alicia quickly went to his side and dropped to her knees. "We ought to head back for Ciudad Altamirano right now, Rafael. You're simply not well enough to go on. You know you're not."

While he thought she might be right, he could not bring himself to admit it. "No, I'll be fine in the morning. I'll build the fire."

"No! You just sit still. I can do it." When he did not utter a single word of protest, Alicia grew even more worried. There were matches in his saddlebags and she soon had a fire laid and burning. She kept her eye on the coffee to make certain it did not boil too long and when she took him a cup he actually paid her a compliment.

"You learn fast." He gave her a weak grin, then asked for a second cup, which he sipped more slowly. He still felt rotten but got up to skin the snake so she would not have to do that herself. "I'll fix our dinner. I can do that much at least."

"Are you sure?" Alicia asked apprehensively.

"Yes, I'm sure." He cut a portion of the meat into two nice fillets, dusted them with flour, and, after frying a thick slice of bacon to make some grease, dropped them into the pan. "They'll cook in just a few minutes." He sat down beside her and rested his arms over his knees. "All we'll have to do is keep an eye on them."

The sizzling fillets bore no resemblance to their

source, but Alicia was still surprised to find that the aroma wafting from the frying pan was actually tantalizing. "I wish we had some wine," she remarked with genuine regret.

"I think I'm better off without it," Rafael conceded. He had to chuckle then. "This is sure to be one of those times we're going to remember for the rest of our lives."

"A story we'll tell our grandchildren, you mean?" Alicia asked without realizing the implications of her comment.

"Whether or not we have any grandchildren is entirely up to you, my love." Rafael saw her cheeks fill with a bright blush and thought better of pursuing that particular topic of conversation. "Try the meat; it should be done," he suggested instead.

Eager to change the subject to a far less personal one, Alicia removed a fillet from the pan and placed it on one of the tin plates. After cutting off a bite-sized piece, she handed him a fork. "You try it. I don't know what it's supposed to taste like, remember?"

"All right." Rafael popped the bite into his mouth and chewed slowly, his appreciation soon clear. "Superb. This is the best damn snake I've ever eaten. Go ahead, try some yourself." He watched her face closely, for her features were marvelously expressive. She took a tiny bite, gave it a few tentative chews, then broke into a delighted grin.

"Why yes, this is very good, isn't it?"

"Delicious." Rafael took the other fillet for himself and they sat by the fire quietly enjoying their meal until neither of them could eat another bite.

Rafael felt far better now and leaned back on his elbows, the comforting warmth in his stomach lending a momentary euphoria to his mood. "You were absolutely right. This venture would not be the success it is without your being here. I'm glad you came along with me."

Since Alicia doubted their enterprise could be regarded as a success on any level, she grew wary. "Is that another of your jokes? Are you just teasing me again?"

"No, that was meant as a sincere compliment," Rafael insisted with a widening grin. "I'm glad you're here. As I said before, you saved my life twice today and I'm extremely grateful to you for that."

There was still a taunting fire in the handsome man's dark eyes, which made her uneasy, but Alicia was in no mood for verbal sparring. "Thank you then," she replied simply. She gathered up their dishes and carried them over to the river to wash. Since they would need them for breakfast, she then stacked them by the fire rather than packing them away. "I'm going to bathe. I kept your shirt so I won't need another," she stated firmly, hoping he understood exactly what she thought of him for following her the previous evening. She unrolled her blanket, removed the plaid shirt, and walked back downstream.

It had been a far too long and frustrating day. They had come no closer to rescuing Domingo, and Rafael had nearly been killed. At least she knew she could shoot when she had to! That was scant consolation, however, when she considered how truly severe their problems still were. She was amazed that the fact Rafael had come so close to dying had done nothing to dampen the cockiness of his attitude. He was undoubtedly the most difficult man ever born and everything she did made only a momentary impression on him. Just as it had been that evening, his smile was more often taunting than loving. How could he again mention love when their relationship continued to be so stormy? Shouldn't lovers find the bliss of contentment in each other's arms as well as the thrill of passion?

She had not wandered far but took her time undressing, then again rinsed out her lingerie before entering the chill waters of the Balsas. The water numbed her body, but not her mind, and she continued to wonder if her fate truly lay with Rafael or whether their love was tempestuous because it had never been meant to be.

Rafael remained by the fire, but when Alicia did not soon return, he grew bored with his own company. He untied the bandanna, but the cloth had become saturated with his blood and was now stuck fast to the deep wound. Rather than merely rip it off, he cast off his clothes and went to the river to soak it loose. Once that feat was accomplished, he tossed the square of brightly printed fabric on the grass and swam with long, powerful strokes out into the river. The bright light of the moon was reflected all around him, shimmering with a romantic glimmer he longed to share. Since Alicia still had not returned to their camp, he moved on down the river, silently seeking the bathing spot she had chosen.

In a few minutes he came upon her. She was standing in a ray of golden light, shaking the last droplets of moisture from her long curls. He swam up behind her, then came to the surface and wrapped her in a fond embrace. His hands slid over the fullness of her breasts, cupping them gently as he lowered his mouth to the silken smoothness of her shoulder. "Do you think I am merely teasing when I say I love you?" he whispered hoarsely, his hunger for her undisguised.

The river swirled about her waist, but as she relaxed against Rafael's broad chest, Alicia scarcely felt its chill. Enveloped in his fiery warmth, she knew she wanted far more than a hasty encounter more suited to love-struck fish than two passionate humans. She longed to spend the whole night in his arms. Taking his hands firmly in hers, she stepped out of his confining embrace and turned to face him. "Come with me," she invited seductively, and with a series of light running steps she led him up on the riverbank. "We're too far away from the fire here," she advised softly, and after gathering up her clothes, she reached up to kiss him, then darted away through the trees, her laughter ringing as prettily as the last chorus of a love song.

Rafael flipped his hair out of his eyes and followed her, certain they were quite alone. His head still hurt, but he disregarded the annoying pain in his eagerness to satisfy his craving for her. Like a forest nymph, she skipped ahead of him, the moonlight bathing her pale skin with a sparkling sheen. Like a porcelain ballerina, she seemed to glide through the rustling leaves, glancing back over her shoulder to make certain he was not far behind. He overtook her as she reached her blanket, and while he felt like gathering her into his arms and tossing her up into the air, he was far more cautious and instead lowered her gently to the mossy ground. "You'll never know how much I wanted you last night," he confessed in a rush of emotion. "When I saw that snake ready to strike, my only thought was that I'd wasted the last night of my life by not spending it with you, but I'll never waste another."

As she pulled him down into her arms, Alicia knew she had spent the night alone because she had been outraged by his behavior, but she could not remember why. It had been something important too—she recalled that clearly—but what it had been eluded her now. "I love you," she told him again and again as she covered his face with teasing kisses, knowing she could not possibly have gone on living if she had lost him.

Responding readily to her generous affection, he moved to cradle her in his arms, his tongue savoring the dampness of her flesh as his mouth covered the pale pink tip of her breast. She was so wonderfully fair, her taste always sweet, and his hunger for her had grown with each new day. His fingertips slid over her ribs to the soft swell of her stomach before straying through the feathery blond curls that veiled the entrancing secrets of her femininity. He had the whole night to explore the delights of her slender body, and his lips slowly followed the warm trail created by his hands. His teasing nibbles became deep, searching kisses as he parted her thighs. He lavished upon her the most exquisite pleasure until the tremors of rapture that swept through her loins beckoned to him with an irresistible call. His lips sought hers then, his tongue filling her mouth as he brought their hips together, joining their bodies with a smooth, swift thrust. He rode the wave of her cresting passion, controlling the urgency of his own desires until the fires of her inner heat made the effort to continue such self-discipline insanity. With a deep growl of triumph, he buried his face in the glorious tangle of her silken curls, overwhelmed once again by the beauty of her love.

Alicia lay with Rafael snugly wrapped in her arms, a blissful smile lighting her whole face with happiness. She ran her fingers up his spine, then tousled his hair. "I'll bet you've been with thousands of women, haven't you?"

Rafael rose up on his elbows, certain some devious purpose had inspired her question. "Thousands, Alicia? Do you think I have the appetites of a satyr?"

"No, of course not, but you're an extremely attractive man."

"I'm also a very busy one too. Have you forgotten that? It used to be the source of all our arguments." Rafael leaned down to kiss her eyelids lightly before playfully nuzzling her throat.

"That seems so long ago," Alicia replied with a wistful sigh. "A lifetime at the very least."

"It's been no time at all," Rafael contradicted persuasively.

"It only seems that way to you because the changes in your life have been slight compared to the upheaval in mine."

Rafael shook his head. "No, you're completely wrong." He had lost track of how many times he had proposed to her, half a dozen perhaps, but only yesterday morning she had sworn most emphatically that he would never be her husband. The possibility she might one day be another man's wife was unthinkable, however. "You've turned my life upside down, lady, and still I love you desperately."

Alicia gave him a joyful hug. "I love you too, but why can't we ever be happy for more than one night at a time? Why does the magic always disappear the moment I leave your arms?"

Rafael smiled down at her, certain she knew the answer to that question herself if only she would admit it. "You must learn to trust me, for I will always do my best to see that you are as happy at dawn as you are right now. If you'll make the same promise to me, then I think this time we'll be able to make our happiness last."

"Forever?" Alicia whispered breathlessly.

"We'll both have to try, my pet. I can't do it alone." He lowered his mouth to hers before she could reply, his kiss so full of love their bodies again melted into one, that fusion slow and sweet, as graceful as the moonlight that bathed them in its radiant glow.

Alicia surrendered not only her lithe body but offered up her very soul to the man she adored as the last tiny remnant of her uncertainty was dissolved by the magnificence of his affection. She knew he was right. She would have to trust him completely, to believe in him and think of them as one being in all things, not merely when they made love. He filled the night with the magical splendor she craved and their spirits as well as their bodies entwined in a perfect union. Their words were few but incredibly loving, and as the first light of dawn broke over them, each had found the strength to trust completely in the other.

Rafael came awake suddenly. Startled, he sat up and strained to listen, certain he had heard a noise that was totally out of place at the river's edge. When it did not come again, he took a deep breath, hoping it had been no more than the call of some strange bird. Alicia was snuggled against him, her expression sweet as she slept. As his eyes traveled down the tantalizing curve of her hip, he was jolted by the deep purple bruises he had been unable to see during the night. She had not shed a single tear when he had spanked her and discovering now how badly he had hurt her pained him greatly. Although it seemed far too late to apologize now, he would most certainly do it. He pushed her tawny curls away from her ear and leaned down to give her throat a playful nibble. "Wake up, love, it's time for us to get up."

Alicia's long lashes fluttered slightly, then lay still as she continued to enjoy her dreams. He bent down again and this time spread teasing kisses from her cheek to her lips. "Wake up, Alicia. We've too much to do for us to spend today as I'd like to."

The lovely blonde yawned sleepily, then rolled over, clutching the worn blanket to her breasts so it covered her shapely form completely as she continued to ignore him.

Rafael laughed as he rose to his feet. "All right, since you insist, I'll start breakfast." He grabbed his pants and swiftly yanked them on. His head no longer pained him as much, but he knew the present dull ache would last a day or two more. He reached up to touch his forehead gingerly, then wished he had not been so foolhardy when a fresh burst of pain nearly dropped him to his knees. Still reeling from that wretched surprise, he again heard the sound that had awakened him and dove for his holster, only to find his Colt gone. He dropped to a crouch, not about to provide the hunter stalking him with a good target. He had heard the crisp snap of a dry twig as it had broken beneath a careless footstep. He had been so drunk with pleasure the thought of standing guard had slipped his mind and now he cursed himself heatedly for being so foolish. He waited, every muscle of his powerful body tensed as he listened for the man's next move to reveal his location. Alicia was still so sound asleep she had heard nothing, but as he glanced down at her, he saw that Joaquin's holster lay beneath her pile of clothes. Was his Colt still nestled inside? If he moved closer to Alicia, a careless shot could easily end her life and there was no way he would risk inciting such a tragedy. Raising his hands into the air, he straightened up slowly and called out in Spanish, "I wish you no harm. Come out where I can see you."

Nearly a minute passed before an elderly man in the tattered white garb of a peasant emerged from the stand of trees at Rafael's right. While his grip was shaky, he had a firm enough hold upon his pearl-handed revolver to shoot with deadly aim. "You have seen your last sunrise, El Lobo," he called out in a menacing shout.

Rafael broke into a wide grin. "I hate to disappoint you, but I killed El Lobo myself three days ago."

"You are El Lobo," the old man insisted. "I would know his stallion anywhere."

"Yes, that was his horse. I took him after I'd killed

the murdering swine. You should be thanking me for saving you the trouble of killing him, not threatening me!" Rafael could not tell how clear the old man's mind was, but he was standing too far away to risk making a sudden lunge to retrieve his Colt.

"You have his horse and one of his whores. You are El Lobo," the peasant argued logically. "You are a dead man."

"No one calls my wife a whore!" Rafael shouted defiantly. "You apologize to me immediately for that insult!"

Shocked that his prisoner would demand an apology, the peasant did not see Alicia's hand inching toward her brother's holster. He knew El Lobo to be an arrogant bastard, but he had never heard the man was married. "El Lobo has no wife!" he finally replied. "I owe you no apology."

In one fluid motion Alicia sat up and fired. She had no wish to kill the old man, but she would not allow him to shoot Rafael either. She thought she had aimed several inches above his head, but the bullet tore through the crown of his sombrero, sending it sailing off into the river. "You'll drop that gun and apologize to me right now!" she commanded sharply. "I am no whore of El Lobo's, but this man's wife!"

Alfonso Lujan was so terrified that the blond beauty's next shot would pierce his heart and leave his dear wife a widow, he dropped Rafael's pearl-handled Colt instantly and began to plead for his life. "I beg you, *señora.*"

"Save it." Rafael walked over to pick up his revolver and extended his hand. "I am Rafael Ramirez from California and this is my charming bride, Alicia. Won't you join us for breakfast?"

Alfonso bobbed his head up and down nervously. "My pleasure, *señor.*"

412

As Rafael turned around, he winked slyly at Alicia. "That's three times you've saved my life in only two days. If you could only whistle, you'd be perfect."

As always, he was making jokes, but this time Alicia finally saw the humor in the situation and laughed happily as she rose to her feet. She wrapped the rumpled blanket around herself, replaced Joaquin's Colt in his holster, then started toward the river. "Do you by any chance have some food with you, *señor?*"

"Lujan, Alfonso Lujan," the peasant stuttered nervously. "I have only a few *tamales* and some figs."

Alicia stopped to give him an enthusiastic hug. "Wonderful! We'll have a feast!"

The old man watched in fascinated silence as Alicia moved toward the water. He had never seen such a pretty young woman, but he was more impressed by how well she could shoot. Turning back to Rafael, he asked curiously, "She is really your wife?"

Rafael grinned with a rakish grin. "Yes, she's mine." Since he hoped their wedding was only a few days off, he felt justified in claiming her as his own.

"If my wife could shoot as well as that, I would be a very good husband," Alfonso remarked seriously.

"Oh, you can be certain I am!" Rafael agreed with a hearty laugh. He quickly filled the coffeepot with water, tossed in a handful of coffee, and then lit a fire to brew it. "I mean to wipe out all of El Lobo's gang, Señor Lujan, and I think you are just the man to help me do it."

Alfonso sat down quickly, fearful he might faint. The morning had taken so strange a turn he could not wait to hear what this handsome stranger would say next, but to be invited at his age to chase bandits was a thrilling prospect indeed. The hope that he would be paid for his trouble was even more inspiring.

Chapter XXI

Alfonso pursed his lips thoughtfully as Rafael explained in the most logical manner possible why they intended to rescue a young man he openly admitted was El Lobo's son. "With such an evil father, how can he possibly be a good man?" the peasant finally asked suspiciously.

"He takes after his mother," Rafael insisted firmly, in no mood to debate the quality of Domingo's character, since he was determined to resuce him without further delay. "As I told you, the route the bandits took is now impassable. Do you know another place where we might cross the mountains?"

After a long pause during which he was clearly considering his options very seriously, the old man replied, "I have lived in this valley all my life, Señor Ramirez. I know more than a dozen places were a man on horseback might make his way"—he glanced over at Alicia then—"but not a woman."

When he finished his sentence with that unfounded opinion, Rafael spoke immediately to defend the woman he would not leave behind. "My wife goes wherever I go, Lujan. Now which is the pass closest to the one just above us here. If I can traverse it safely, then there's no reason why Alicia can't do it too."

That he would speak with such conviction on her behalf pleased the pretty blonde immensely, for it made the fact that they were an extremely devoted couple more than plain. "I've ridden horses all my life, Señor Lujan. I'm not afraid of traveling over steep mountain trails." She hid her hands in her lap, for they were still tender and she did not want to give him an additional reason to worry about either her abilities or her stamina.

The old man sighed wearily, certain no well-mannered young woman should take such foolish risks, but if her husband was so eager to permit such recklessness, he would not waste his breath in arguing against it. "I learned many of the paths from my grandfather. They are old Indian trails and must be regarded as sacred."

"I understand." Rafael nodded in agreement, having no real idea how he was expected to behave on sacred ground but in too great a hurry to leave to worry that they would not show the proper respect. "Will you come with us, or would you prefer to just show us where the trail begins?"

"I am no longer young, that is true, but there is too great a danger you will become lost if I don't accompany you," Alfonso insisted with a fatherly grin.

Rafael had to smile, certain their safety was not the man's only concern. "We appreciate your help. You'll be well paid when we return to Ciudad Altamirano. I promise you that."

"It is only fitting that one traveler help another," the peasant replied modestly, as though money were not always a pressing need in his household.

Curious about what they might find, Alicia leaned forward slightly. "Señor Lujan, the bandits are obviously following a route they know well. Have you

416

ever heard of a hideout hidden in these mountains?"

"Mexico is full of bandits, *señora,* but it is not wise too know too much about them if you wish to live in peace."

"That's true of bandits everywhere, my friend." Rafael rose, then reached down to give Alicia a hand. "We'll clean up our camp and be ready to leave in a few minutes. Do you need to stop by your home to tell your family you'll be away several days?"

Not wanting them to believe he was a man who needed his wife's permission for such an endeavor, Alfonso shook his head. "I was on my way to town and then meant to visit my brother. I will not be missed for a week. Will we be gone longer than that?"

"Let's hope not," Rafael prayed aloud. "Your *tamales* won't last us nearly that long." They had again eaten rattlesnake fillets for breakfast and had saved his meager supply of food for later. "Have you a mount?"

"A donkey of little worth," Alfonso admitted reluctantly, "but they are good for the mountain trails."

"That they are." Anxious to leave, Rafael soon had his small party ready to ride, but had Alfonso not been serving as their guide, he was certain they never would have discovered the entrance to the winding path he chose to follow up the mountainside. It had been obscured by fallen branches, apparently unused for decades, but it was a far easier trail to traverse than the one they had followed the previous day. The genial peasant went first, swinging his machete to clear the trail, and by noon they had reached the crest of the mountain and dismounted to study the surrounding terrain.

Alfonso found a firm perch upon a flat rock and raised his hand to shade his eyes since his sombrero had been swept away by the Balsas. "There are many small

417

valleys. I can only make a guess as to which one El Lobo might have chosen."

"If his other camp was any indication of his preferences, then he likes an area he can easily defend. Perhaps one with only one entrance," Alicia mused aloud.

Rafael readily agreed. "Yes, a high plateau that provided a good view of anyone approaching would be ideal. Dangerous for us, of course, but perfect for the bandits." He was as hot and tired as the rest of them and sank down where he had a large boulder to serve as a backrest. He passed around his canteen, then took a long drink himself. "That other trail wasn't too far from this one. We might already be close."

"Oh, do you really think so?" Alicia wished they had had a pair of binoculars to bring, since she was afraid they might be practically on top of the bandits' camp without knowing it.

"A plateau?" Alfonso wondered aloud, his expression growing dark.

"You know of one?" Rafael prompted eagerly, certain that he did.

The weary peasant nodded slightly. "I know of one, but it is an evil place."

"Evil?" Alicia sat down beside Rafael and took his hand. "How can a place be evil?"

The old man laughed at her question, for he considered the answer obvious. "Restless spirits wander the world. In the places where they gather, the living are not welcome."

"The plateau is haunted?" the curious blonde gasped in disbelief.

Alfonso's many wrinkles deepened as he frowned. "My grandfather warned me it belonged to ghosts and not to go there. I will show you how to reach it, but you will have to go alone."

Rafael glanced over at Alicia. Her eyes were sparkling with mischief and he knew she didn't believe in ghosts any more than he did, but he phrased his reply so as not to insult the elderly gentleman's beliefs. "I'd like to get close enough to see if it's occupied, that's all. I'd rather not disturb either ghosts or bandits until I'm ready to go in for Domingo."

Alfonso rose to his feet and gave a vigorous stretch. "I will take you as close as I can and wait for you there. You will have to creep up the sheer side of the cliff if you want to take them by surprise."

"That's precisely what I don't want to do," Rafael confided as he stood up. "The two of us can't take on two-dozen bandits. We'll simply have to sneak into the camp late at night, release Domingo, and escape with him. With luck, he won't be heavily guarded. We can accomplish our mission in a matter of minutes and he won't be missed until dawn."

The superstitious peasant shrugged. "I thought you wished to wipe out El Lobo's whole gang."

Rafael broke into a cocky grin. "When they realize Domingo's been set free right under their noses, they'll think twice about moving on as a group. I think they'll scatter then and that will be the last anyone ever hears of El Lobo or his men."

"Perhaps," Alfonso commented skeptically.

"A leaderless gang is like a snake with no body," Rafael pointed out logically. "It can't go far."

"Please, not another mention of snakes," Alicia pleaded with a shudder. She went back to her mare and got ready to continue their ride. She was excited and more than a little frightened, but Rafael was so certain they could rescue Domingo she did not doubt that they could and that they would do it soon.

Alfonso followed first one overgrown trail and then another until there was scant underbrush to impede their progress. When the narrow path they had been following ended at the summit of the ridge, he turned back to face them. "You must go on foot from here," he announced firmly.

"How did the bandits manage to go all the way on horseback?" Alicia asked curiously as she swung down from the mare's back.

"They were on another trail, remember?" Rafael reminded her before Alfonso could point out her error.

"Of course. I'm sorry, I'd forgotten that," the blonde offered by way of apology to their guide.

"Women are not expected to know such things," Alfonso responded matter-of-factly, excusing her mistake as an unfortunate feminine trait. "I will wait here with the horses. The plateau is clearly visible when you round the next bend. If the bandits are there, you will be able to see them, but be careful because they will also be able to spot you watching them."

Worried by that prospect, Alicia glanced up at Rafael. The gash in his forehead would leave a horrible scar and while she knew it was a silly thing to worry about now, she could not help it. He was so impossibly handsome, the mere sight of him always set her heart aflutter. She blushed then, afraid he would read her mind and be shocked at how inappropriate her thoughts truly were. Forcing herself to concentrate on their immediate problem, she smiled invitingly. "Let's go and have a look. If no one's there, then there will be plenty of time to look elsewhere before nightfall."

"Let's just hope they are there." Rafael took her hand and led her cautiously around the curve in the trail. Just as Alfonso had promised, opposite them there rose another of the mountain range's many peaks, but this one had the rounded top of a cathedral dome. For some reason it struck him immediately as resembling a skull far too closely for his liking. There were a half dozen scraggly trees growing feebly from crevices in the rock, but even if the bandits had used the plateau for a camp, he saw no evidence of them still being in residence. "It looks deserted," he announced with obvious disappointment.

Crouching down behind a boulder, Alicia raised her hand. "Just a minute. Maybe they're out hunting. That's possible, isn't it?"

"Yes, but highly unlikely. I've seen no sight of game." Nevertheless, her suggestion merited consideration and he knelt by her side. "What does that peak look like to you?" he asked softly.

"A skull. It's no wonder it's thought to be the home of evil spirits." Her gaze swept over the smooth surface of the rocky dome before traveling slowly down the mountainside. "Rafael, look!" she cried out excitedly. "About halfway down, what do you see?"

Rafael put his arm around her shoulders so he could follow her line of vision. He was chagrined to find she had seen something he had missed, but she had discovered a camp of some sort, that much was unmistakable. There were several wooden cabins hugging the cliffs. They were partially hidden by the trees, but since no one would build a ranch in such a precarious location, he knew it had to be another of El Lobo's mountain retreats. His, or another of his fellow thieves. The local residents would not approach that mountain because of the legends of ghosts and no strangers traveling by would stray that far from the river. "Yes, it's a perfect spot for a hideaway. Now all we need do is figure out how to get over there." Yet as he looked into the sapphire blue of her eyes, that was the last place he wanted to go. His hand still rested upon her shoulder and he turned her gently toward him to give her a slow, seductive kiss that left them both slightly breathless.

There was danger aplenty and yet Alicia could discern only the promise of pleasure as Rafael's tongue continued to tease hers with a provocative curl. They would soon risk their lives for a young man who might never show his gratitude, but that sorry fact mattered not at all to either of them. Domingo had risked his life to save Joaquin's and they would repay that favor as swiftly as they could. For the moment, however, the heat of the afternoon sun warmed their bodies and lit their blood with the unquenchable flame of desire. As Rafael's hands slipped beneath her shirt to caress her breasts, she unbuttoned his shirt and ran her fingers through the dark curls covering his chest. The warmth of his sleek, well-muscled body felt so good to her touch. His strength was now focused solely upon bestowing pleasure and she did not bother to remind him that Alfonso was resting only a few yards away. The old man was apparently so frightened of the skull-like plateau he would not venture close, but she would not have cared even if he did. All she wanted was to be as close to Rafael as she could possibly be. Her hands moved down the flat planes of his stomach to free his belt from the silver buckle, then wantonly peeled away his riding pants as she encouraged the intensity of his affection to ever greater heights.

Rafael's only conscious thought was that Alicia continually wore far too many clothes. He deepened his kiss as he lifted her slightly to yank off her white cotton trousers. He then fumbled so long with her lace-trimmed pantaloons she finally tore them off herself. He pulled her down across his lap then, gently guiding her parted thighs until they enveloped his throbbing manhood and with a savage upward thrust he impaled her upon that swollen shaft. He wound his fingers in her long curls, holding her mouth captive beneath his own. His searing kiss ravaged her mouth as he buried himself even more deeply in her velvet-soft center. He held her imprisoned in his arms, lost in her wondrous loving as he fought to hold back the tidal wave of ecstasy that threatened to inundate his loins with a liquid fire. He allowed that glorious pulsating pleasure to swell until it could no longer be contained and burst forth in wave after wave of blinding rapture. He clung to her, feeling her joy building within the same shattering climax that shook every inch of his powerful frame. That stunning splendor again left his heart overflowing with the beauty of perfect peace and the wonder of her love.

Alicia lay snuggled in Rafael's arms, her flushed cheek resting against his bare shoulder. "I think this is the single most depraved thing we've ever done together."

"Or separately," Rafael conceded with a deep chuckle. "But it isn't depraved to make love. I love you, and I don't care if an eagle or two knows about it either."

The lovely blonde sat up then and looked him straight in the eye. "This is not going to be the last night of your life, so if that passion-filled escapade was meant as a spectacular good-bye, then—"

Rafael leaned forward to kiss her then, and not merely to silence her but to again enjoy the delights of her sweet taste. "That was no tender farewell, my pet. How could you mistake it for such?"

"I don't ever want to tell you good-bye, not tenderly or any other way," Alicia murmured softly. She moved away from him then and picked up her badly wrinkled pantaloons, but as she turned away, Rafael groaned, and thinking somehow he had hurt himself, she turned back quickly to face him. "What's the matter?"

"I meant to leave my image on your heart, not my handprint on your bottom. Can you ever forgive me for doing that?"

His expression was so sincere Alicia glanced over her shoulder and was shocked to find the bruises she had suffered the day he had spanked her still clearly visible. "It's only that I am very fair, but you shouldn't have hit me. You really shouldn't have."

"I know it. I won't ever do it again either," Rafael promised quite earnestly.

"Not even if you mistakenly believe I deserve it?" Alicia asked in a teasing whisper as she straightened the waistband on her lingerie. She reached down to pick up her trousers and quickly pulled them on.

"Of course you'll never do anything to deserve it, will you?" Rafael asked slyly. He got to his feet and rearranged his clothing so he was again properly dressed.

"Oh, I'll probably upset you quite often, but you're not to hit me again and that's all there is to it," Alicia insisted proudly.

Rafael responded by pulling her into his arms and kissing her lightly upon both cheeks before he released her. "I gave you my word, Alicia, and you can be certain it's always good."

His hair hung down over his forehead, concealing the deep gash, while his dark beard made his smile all the more rakish. He looked far more like a bandit than El Lobo had and she wasn't surprised Alfonso Lujan had mistaken him for the man. "You are a handsome devil, Rafael Ramirez, and when I see you like this, so at home in the mountains, I can't imagine how you can enjoy working in a stuffy old courtroom."

Rafael raked his fingers through his hair before replacing his hat upon his head. "It's possible for a man to enjoy many things."

"And a woman too," Alicia replied with a saucy toss of her tangled curls. "Now let's see if Alfonso has fallen asleep while waiting for us."

The peasant had not fallen asleep, but he had grown very suspicious of the attractive young couple's long absence. He needed only one glance at the sparkle in Alicia's eyes and pretty blush in her cheeks to know what they had been doing and he was shocked to think they could be so easily distracted from the task at hand. "Well, what did you see?" he asked gruffly.

Rafael crouched down beside him to get comfortable as he explained. "There's nothing on the plateau, but there are several houses about midway up the mountain. How can we get over there?"

"You are certain you wish to go?" the old man asked skeptically.

"Yes. If Domingo's there, then we have no choice about it. We have to go and get him." When Rafael glanced up at Alicia, she nodded in agreement. "Can you tell us how to go about it?"

Alfonso spread his hands helplessly. "I have tried to warn you, but if you will not listen, there is nothing more I can do."

"This is not a matter of choice," Rafael insisted emphatically. "It is something we must do."

The peasant shrugged, apparently resigned to giving what help he could. "Keep following this trail over the hill and down into the valley below. When you reach the bottom, take the path to the left. It will lead you up toward the plateau."

"Will you wait here with the horses?" Alicia asked hopefully.

"Yes, I would like to meet El Lobo's son."

"You'd be wise not to mention that relationship to him," Rafael warned. "It is a mere accident of birth, not something for which Domingo is responsible."

"I will not say a word then. I will only look," the curious peasant promised. "It will be a long night. Shall we share the *tamales* before you go?"

Rafael looked up at Alicia's delighted smile and nodded. "Yes, it's always better to tackle a challenge on a full stomach. Let's have supper now and then we'll be on our way."

Rafael and Alicia traveled down the mountain and as far as they dared through the narrow valley before sunset. He led the way, tightly grasping his knife. He found it useful for slicing away tangled vines and he also wanted the advantage of having a blade in his hand if they should meet one of the bandits out for a late afternoon stroll working up an appetite for supper. When they had left the deserted camp above Ciudad Altamirano, he had had no idea how indispensable his lovely companion would become, but he fully intended to protect her from harm and turned back frequently to give her a reassuring smile. "We're near the bottom of the trail and they should have a sentry posted. If they do, I'll take care of him. We mustn't make any noise to alert them that their hideout's been discovered."

Alicia nodded nervously, her mouth so dry she did not trust herself to speak. They crept stealthily through the underbrush, but when they reached the trail that led up to the plateau and found no sign of a guard, her heart beat no less wildly in her breast. She had had no time to consider the dangers when Rafael had fallen to the ledge or when Alfonso Lujan had gotten the drop on him. She had simply done what she had had to do without a moment's thought or hesitation. Now Rafael was counting on her to display the same fierce courage and she was so terrified she would fail him when he needed her most she was trembling all over. Even though the main trail appeared unguarded, they veered away from it, threading their way slowly up the mountainside. As the gloom of night descended, they circled around the bandits' camp and approached it from the far side, where intruders would be least expected.

Rafael took Alicia's hand and pulled her close to his side so he could whisper in her ear without fear of being overhead. "I want you to follow me as closely as you have been. When we reach a good spot to observe the camp, we'll stop and watch for Domingo. Count each man you see so we'll have a better idea of how many there are."

"I understand," the fearful young woman whispered hoarsely. They hoped to rescue Domingo that very night, but if they could not, they at least wanted to learn all they could about the hideout. They had only the moon to light their way now and a thin layer of mist encircled their feet, engulfing their steps in an eerie fog. Whether or not the skull-shaped plateau was haunted Alicia didn't know, but if it wasn't, she thought it certainly should be. They could hear the bandits' voices now and raucous laughter. Despite the gloom of the night, the men seemed to be in high spirits, and knowing that would be a great help to them, she took heart. The more distracted the thieves were, the more easily they could free Domingo. She inched along behind Rafael, marveling at how silently he moved over the unfamiliar terrain. She took care to place her feet where he had stepped to avoid making any noise as they drew close to the stronghold. When it became obvious there were no guards anywhere about, Rafael led her so close they could feel the heat of the campfire. They knelt down behind the shrubbery just outside the ring of light created by the blaze and huddled closely together while they watched the gang of cutthroats preparing their evening meal. A boisterous group, they drank heavily and none seemed inclined to watch the large iron kettle of meat and beans simmering over the open fire. Although largely ignored, it bubbled merrily and sent up a tantalizing aroma that made Alicia's half-empty stomach gurgle noisily. Forcing her thoughts away from food, she searched the faces outlined by the flames for the one she knew. In the same instant she spotted Domingo Rafael sighted him too and gave her shoulder an enthusiastic squeeze.

The young man was seated on the far side of the fire. He was staring into the flames, oblivious to those milling about him playfully exchanging mock blows and swilling whiskey as though it were water. His expression was subdued, his mood clearly morose, but most surprising of all was the Colt revolver he wore in his holster. Alicia turned to look up at Rafael, her unspoken question nearly deafening upon the rapidly cooling night air.

Rafael sat back on his heels, certain the situation could not possibly be as dire as it appeared to be at first glance. When he had taken a badly wounded Joaquin from Domingo's arms, the young man had been left to defend himself as best he could. Had he survived that day by simply becoming a turncoat and joining his father's gang? That would have been a cowardly choice and he had thought far better of the young man, but he could not deny that was what had apparently happened. He leaned close to speak to Alicia. "Whether or not he wants to go, Domingo is coming with us."

The astonished blonde shrugged helplessly, totally confused even though she understood his reasoning. When she tried to smile, he gave her a comforting hug. Their original plan had been to wait until the bandits went to sleep; then they had meant to help Domingo escape. She could not believe what they would actually be doing was kidnapping him. Astounded by this bizarre turn of events, she watched in rapt fascination as the bandits continued to amuse themselves while Domingo sat silently observing the flames.

One day had blurred mercifully into the next with the ease of butter melting in the sun, but Domingo felt only a bitter contempt for the men who surrounded him and he had made no effort to learn their names. They were ruffians all, mean-tempered men with little more intelligence than God gave mules, but they had welcomed him into their ranks as though he had inherited the ability to be their leader. They had brought him along to bury his father. A disagreeable task under any circumstances, it had proved an impossible burden here. Julio Villalobos was dead and surely Joaquin Villarreal was as well. The two men who could not have been more different merged in his mind into one being: the laughing scoundrel who had never wanted him for a son. He was of less value as a person than the dirt upon which he sat, but at least now his direction was clear. He would follow in El Lobo's footsteps and become a bandit chieftain with far more cunning than that villain had ever shown. He would steal every last coin Mexico minted until his name was known in every city as the prince of the thieves. All his life he had longed to be a son who would make his father proud and now fame was within his grasp. The flames licked at tendrils of the strange mist that hung over the camp like a damp shroud, but as he looked into the fire he saw only the joy of demons dancing around the throne of Satan and was perfectly content.

The laughing and drinking went on for several hours, and while Alicia's and Rafael's limbs grew stiff from their cramped poses, they continued to spy on the rowdy camp. Some men fell asleep on the fringes of the fire, while others stumbled off toward the crudely built cabins that were perched awkwardly against the mountain's rocky face. Gradually the numbers near the fire were reduced to a few men slumbering in drunken stupors and Domingo, who had shared their supper but not their passion for strong drink. That it had grown very late had escaped his notice, and after getting up momentarily to add more wood to the fire, he returned to the spot he had occupied all evening and continued his solitary study of the path of the leaping flames.

When Rafael took her arm, Alicia rose to her feet and stretched to dispel the chill of the night air, which had seeped through her cotton clothing to dampen her skin. "Stay here. I'll go and get him." She started toward Domingo, but Rafael grabbed her arm and pulled her back.

"No! In those white clothes you'll be too easily seen by any man still sober enough to focus his eyes. I'll go get him."

Since his explanation did make sense, Alicia did not argue but stepped aside to let him pass. "I love you," she whispered softly.

"I love you too!" Rafael replied and he hesitated long enough to give her a sweet kiss. "Don't move. I don't want to have to go looking for you."

"I'll be right here," Alicia promised. She watched him step out of the shadows and move toward the fire with a confident stride, as though he belonged there in the bandits' camp. He sat down beside Domingo and placed his hand upon the young man's arm as he spoke in a compelling whisper she strained to overhear.

"Domingo! It's Rafael. Stand up and come with me. We've horses waiting near the bottom of the hill."

Annoyed that he had been disturbed, Domingo

turned slowly, then his eyes widened in dismay as he recognized the man at his side. He opened his mouth to cry out, but Rafael caught him with a right hook that went flying into his jaw, snapping his head back and leaving him too dazed to give the alarm. He was yanked to his feet then, and when his knees buckled, Rafael simply tossed him over his left shoulder and strode off into the woods that grew up around the hideout.

The new wood Domingo had added to the fire increased its heat, and uncomfortably warm, one of the bandits stirred from his slumber. As he sat up, he saw Domingo being carried away and began to mumble incoherently to his still-sleeping companions. Desperate for some way to save their mission before the man awakened everyone, Alicia looked down at her cotton outfit. Surely Mexican ghosts were clothed in white, and with a wicked hiss, she leapt from the shadows and danced toward the man. She curved her hands into claws and as she reached out she gave a high-pitched wail, her moan that of a banshee.

Terrified of the fearsome yellow-haired apparition coming toward him through the mist, the bandit scrambled to his feet and tore off in the opposite direction, leaving the camp veiled in deep silence once again. Alicia froze, praying she would need to frighten no one else, and when the only sound she heard was the rumbling of a far-off snore, she darted back into the bushes, but to her horror there was no sign of Rafael.

She dared not call out to him as she fled down the mountainside. The coarse underbrush tore at her trousers, leaving long scratches on her legs, but she had no one to break the trail for her now. Her only hope was to reach the bottom of the godforsaken plateau so she could find the trail back over the adjacent ridge at the first light of dawn. As she ran down the steep embankment, she suddenly stepped upon a patch of loose gravel and, losing her footing, went tumbling head over heels. Unable to regain her balance and stop her fall, she continued to plummet down the jagged face of the cursed mountain until her badly bruised body slammed into a tree stump. Certain she had broken every bone in her back, she lay too dazed even to whimper in pain.

Chapter XXII

It was not until Rafael stopped to rest that he realized Alicia wasn't just a few steps behind him. He looked back over his shoulder searching for a glimmer of white in the moonlight, but the darkness that surrounded him was complete. He lowered Domingo to the ground and gave him a savage shake to rouse him. "Wake up!" he growled fiercely.

Domingo came to swinging. He grabbed Rafael around the waist in a clumsy bear hug, trying to wrestle him, but he swiftly got the worst of it and found himself pinned to the ground flat on his back.

Rafael straddled the angry young man, holding him down as he forced him to see reason. "I don't care if you've turned bandit. You can rejoin your father's gang after you've talked with Joaquin, but—"

Determined to sit up, Domingo continued to struggle, but Rafael simply slammed his shoulders back into the dirt to knock the breath out of him. "Joaquin is alive?" the beleaguered young man finally managed to gasp hoarsely.

Puzzled by his question, Rafael eased up sightly on his hold. "Of course. You saved his life and he'll want to thank you for it, but right now we've got to find Alicia."

"Well, where is she?" Domingo asked crossly, now as badly confused as Rafael.

"You damn fool, I don't know where she is! That's why you've got to help me find her!" Sensing at last he had Domingo's full attention, he released him, rose to his feet, then reached down to yank him upright. "She was right behind me when I carried you away from the fire, but somehow she's gotten lost."

Domingo brushed himself off and straightened his clothes. "How could you have brought her here?" he asked incredulously.

"Domingo," Rafael snarled contemptuously, "my reasons really don't matter. The only important thing is that she should be right here with us and she isn't! Now we've got to find her before your pals sober up and start looking for you."

Domingo shook his head, his thinking still badly muddled. "I thought Joaquin was dead. His blood was all over me and—"

Unwilling to waste his time in meaningless conversation, Rafael gripped the young man's shoulders with viselike strength, suppressing the temptation to give him another vigorous shaking. "Joaquin is fine! It will take a lot more than that to kill him, no matter how bad his gunshot wound looked to you. Now we've got to stop wasting precious time and find Alicia before she comes to any harm!" If she hasn't already, he didn't dare whisper even to himself. "She must have stumbled and lost sight of me. If we go back up the mountain the way we came, we should be able to find her. The longer we wait, the more time she'll have to get lost."

Domingo stepped back quickly to put more space between them when Rafael released him. He had learned the hard way that it never paid to be standing too close to the attorney when he was angry and in the mood to start throwing punches. Certain he had had a

434

hat, he began to look around for it. "Where's my hat?" he mumbled peevishly.

"Hell man, you don't need a hat at night!" Rafael knew Domingo had not been nearly such a fool when he had last seen him. "What have they been doing to you the last few days?"

Determined to find it, Domingo got down on his hands and knees and crawled around searching for the missing hat. Much to his delighted relief, he found it lying not three feet away. He slammed it on the back of his head and stood up. "We came here to bury El Lobo. It was some kind of ghastly joke, but I didn't understand it. They haven't harmed me."

Rafael doubted that, since Domingo seemed so unlike himself. "Let's go." He gave the young man an encouraging nudge to propel him along. "Stay close. If you hear or see anything, speak up."

"I will." Domingo still could not understand why Alicia had come on such a dangerous errand. "They'll rape her," he warned apprehensively.

"Not if we find her first! Now let's go!" Rafael led the distracted young man along, stopping every few feet to listen for the sounds of someone else traveling the steep mountainside, but other than the occasional hoot of an owl or the mournful howl of a distant coyote, he heard nothing.

Alicia grew so cold she began to shiver uncontrollably. She knew she had to get up and continue down the mountain, but the severity of her fall had left her so weak she could barely move, let alone stand. Dazed, she strained to listen, hoping to hear the comforting sound of Rafael's voice calling to her, but as she gradually became aware she was no longer alone, her fears compounded tenfold. She recoiled at the unmistakable rasp of heavy breathing, then had to fight the compulsion to scream as that frightening sound was interspersed with low, menacing growls. The beast was circling her slowly, sniffing the chill breeze, and she knew his tiny brain was undoubtedly analyzing her scent before he came in for the kill.

Alicia was lying atop her holster, wedged against the stump so tightly she had not even noticed the pain inflicted by the cold steel of the Colt pressing against her hip bone. She had never felt so utterly alone, but even as helpless as she was, she had no intention of being a tasty meal for any mangy coyote. As the animal tightened his circle, she closed her mind to the pain that racked every inch of her slender body and struggled to draw her knife. If the cursed creature made a flying leap at her, all she would have to do would be hold the knife steady and she could use the force of his own momentum to disembowel him. Intellectually that was an appealing plan, practically, however, she doubted she could grip the knife that firmly. The beast would probably knock it from her hand as he went for her throat, leaving her defenseless. No, she would have to do better than that if she wanted to survive, and she most certainly wanted to live. Inching over slowly, she rolled to her left to free her holster. Her fingers encircled the handle of the Colt with a loving caress as she began to withdraw it.

Sensing a change in his quarry's mood, the coyote raised his muzzle to again sniff the breeze. The night air was heavy with a variety of intriguing scents ranging from that of the small rodents that were not worth his trouble to kill to that of his worst enemy: man. Puzzled, he dropped his belly to the dirt and crawled forward to get a better look at his prey.

Terrified though she was, when he drew near enough to be seen, Alicia found herself as curious as the coyote.

436

He was so close she could smell him, but while that pungent aroma chilled her blood, she continued to stare in rapt fascination, for she feared the instant she looked away he would sense her fear and spring. He was the largest of his kind she had ever seen and his rippling gray fur was so thick it had an astonishing beauty. His forehead was wide, but his close-set yellow eyes glared with a menacing light as he appeared to be debating whether or not she was capable of putting up any resistance. He uttered a louder and more challenging growl but came no closer.

Since the coyote showed no fear, neither did Alicia. She returned his growl with a fierce snarl of her own, distracting the beast as she leveled Joaquin's Colt at his head. "Come on, you bastard. Just try to take a bite out of me and I'll blow your brains to hell!"

Confused by the hostile tone of the feminine voice, the coyote rose and resumed his restless circling. He did not like this creature's attitude. It was not frightened although it appeared to be wounded. He growled once more, mocking his prey, but he again felt only defiance in the response, not a bit of the paralyzing fear his presence usually brought. He sat down and licked his slender muzzle hungrily. The night was long and he could wait.

Domingo grabbed for Rafael's sleeve. "Did you hear that?"

"What?" Rafael continued to gaze into the darkness, alert for any sign of the beautiful young woman he loved.

"A growl, I think. Maybe it's only a coyote, but it sounded very close."

Rafael strained to listen and this time heard the suspicious sound too. Afraid one such animal would soon bring a pack of four-legged hunters swarming over the mountain, he urged Domingo to hurry. "That's coming from over to the right. Stay behind me." Drawing his gun, he moved silently through the underbrush. "Alicia?" he called insistently, hoping she would still be able to answer him. When he heard a faint cry, he gave up all attempts at being quiet and lunged toward the sound. He saw the massive coyote and the injured blonde in the same instant yet hesitated to fire a shot and awaken the whole gang of thieves. He bent down, scooped up a handful of dirt, and threw it in the beast's eyes. *"Ve tú!"* he yelled as he dashed forward, praying he would be able to scare the animal into running off. Domingo hurled a fistful of small stones to back him up, and seeing he was outnumbered, the disappointed coyote turned tail and trotted off in search of easier game.

Alicia looked up at Rafael, so overjoyed to see him she didn't know where to begin. "Do you really think that coyote understands Spanish?"

Dropping down by her side, Rafael could not help but laugh at her question. "Of course he does. This is Mexico, isn't it? What else would he speak?"

"That makes sense," Alicia admitted with a bewitching grin. "He did run off when you told him to go."

"Damn right he did," Rafael agreed, but while he longed to hug her, he knew she would not be lying there unless she was badly hurt. Not wanting to add to her pain, he did no more than caress her hair lightly. "Can you get up?"

Alicia replaced the Colt in her holster, and while she tried her best to rise, she had no success. "I'm afraid not," she admitted apologetically.

Fighting valiantly to keep the panic out of his voice, Rafael forced himself to appear calm. "Can you wiggle your toes, move your legs?"

"Yes, I can move. It just hurts terribly to do it, that's all." She had not meant to ignore Domingo and gave him a faint smile as she included him in their conversation. "Are you all right?"

How she could be concerned about him when she couldn't even stand, the young man didn't know. Embarrassed by her interest, he nodded sheepishly. "I'm fine. I only wish you were too."

"We can spend our time exchanging pleasantries tomorrow," Rafael interrupted sharply. "We can't wait until morning to move you, though. I'm going to lift you; if I hurt you too much, just say so and I'll stop."

"I will." Alicia held her breath, expecting the worst, but Rafael was so very gentle she found herself almost floating in his arms and did not suffer unduly.

"Well?" he asked hopefully, "how are you doing so far?"

"I'll make it, but do you think you can carry me all the way back to the horses?"

"We can take turns," Domingo offered, eager to be of help.

Rafael doubted the young man could manage the task but didn't insult him by saying so. "I'll let you know when I'm tired."

But as Rafael turned to lead the way down the mountain, an immense shadow suddenly crossed his path and a booming voice called out a challenge. In the darkness Rafael could make out little more than the man's enormous size and the shotgun in his hand. The bandit presented an unexpected obstacle he found himself unable to overcome with Alicia nestled so snugly in his arms. Why an armed sentry had to appear now of all times he didn't know, but he silently cursed the rotten turn of luck, knowing they would have to depend upon Domingo to have all his wits about him to keep them from being taken prisoner.

As if speaking on cue, Domingo leapt forward. "It is Domingo," the young man called out confidently. "My sweetheart and her brother followed our trail hoping to join us but became lost in the darkness. She is badly hurt and you'll have to help us carry her up to the camp." He spoke without a trace of shyness, the lies rolling off his tongue with the skill of a man long practiced not only in deceit but also in giving orders.

"Your sweetheart?" the startled felon inquired incredulously.

"What can I say? I inherited my father's luck with women, and wanting to be with me, my beloved forced her brother to bring her here." Domingo laughed as though the situation were highly amusing. "She is so lovely I cannot be angry with her, but as I said, we'll need your help to carry her to the camp."

Rafael kept his head tilted low, and the brim of his hat shielded not only his own face but Alicia's as well so there would be no chance that either of them would be recognized. "She has little sense," he snorted derisively, "but I should have had more."

"Let me see this woman." As the curious thief stepped forward, Domingo grinned and moved out of his way, but as soon as the heavyset man had lumbered by, he drew his knife and with a strength born of desperation he buried it in the side of the villain's massive neck. The wounded man staggered slightly, horrified not only by the piercing pain in his throat but also by the sudden gush of blood that sprayed out over his chest and hands. He tried to wheel around to face Domingo, his motions agonizingly slow, but before he could make a quarter turn, Rafael thrust out his left boot and tripped him.

Alicia stared on in terrified silence as the bandit fell with a resounding crash, which seemed to shake the very earth beneath Rafael's feet. The sounds he made

440

were pitiful as he tried to call for help only to find his words garbled into an unintelligible whimper as he choked on a bubbling fountain of dark red blood. He was a dead man and obviously knew it, but that did not stop him from trying to take Domingo to hell with him. He rolled over on his back as he raised the shotgun to fire, but before he could pull the trigger Domingo lunged out of the way and then darted in close. With a savage kick, he knocked the gun from the bandit's trembling hands. Grabbing the weapon, he turned to Rafael.

"Get her out of here!" he ordered emphatically.

As Rafael turned away, Alicia heard a sickening thud and was certain Domingo had used the stock of the shotgun as a club. Thoroughly sickened by the gruesome sight she had just witnessed, she shut her eyes tightly, and although Rafael moved with bone-jarring speed down the mountainside, she was so frightened by their brush with disaster she did not feel a single twinge of pain.

Rafael could hear Domingo running along behind them and did not stop for a breath until they finally reached the level ground of the small valley that separated the plateau from the ridge where Alfonso Lujan sat waiting with the horses. He found a grassy spot for Alicia to rest and lowered her gently to the ground. Kneeling down beside her, he needed a moment to catch his breath before he looked up at Domingo. "That certainly wasn't the prettiest killing I've ever seen, but it was definitely the most timely. I owe you one now too. Between you and Alicia, I'm beginning to feel like a cat who's running through his nine lives."

"Alicia has saved your life?" Domingo asked in dismay."

"More than once," Rafael admitted with a sly grin,

"but I'll have to tell you about our adventures later. I doubt anyone will miss that man until dawn. We'll rest a minute and then make our way back up to the horses. It's a pity we had to leave them so far away."

Finding it difficult to believe he had actually killed a man in such brutal fashion, Domingo collapsed in the grass and cradled his head in his hands. "You owe me nothing, Rafael. Had you not come to tell me Joaquin is alive, I'd have been a worse criminal than my father ever was. He only used people, but he didn't hate them the way I did."

Alicia knew without asking for an explanation that Domingo had once been so consumed with hatred for the father he had never known that he had been unable to utter a civil word. She felt light-headed, sick to her stomach, and ached all over, but she felt a warm sense of accomplishment too. "You are too fine a young man to have ridden with a band of outlaws and you know it, Domingo. You have your whole life ahead of you and you'd not have wasted it so recklessly."

"What makes you say that?" Domingo asked sarcastically. "You know who my father was."

"El Lobo was never a father to you," Alicia was quick to argue. "You are nothing like that cowardly villain or you'd not have gone to Joaquin's rescue so swiftly or to ours just now. Had you not come forward to protect him, I'm sure my brother would have been shot several times and undoubtedly would have died. You really did save his life and ours as well, and we're grateful to you for that. Lord only knows what dreadful things would have happened to us had we fallen into the hands of that brutal gang." She shivered then as several gruesome possibilities flooded her mind in sickening detail.

Rafael was emphatic as he rose to his feet. "While they are most certainly deserved, this is no time for testimonials, my pet. We've got to keep moving. We can't afford to be sitting here chatting when the sun rises in a few hours. Now this time let's see if I can carry you on my back. That will be much easier since we'll be going uphill and I'll need to see the way clearly." He got down on one knee and waited for her to wrap her arms around his neck. Then, grabbing her knees, he stood up to carry her piggyback. "Is that comfortable for you?"

Alicia was so tired she was beginning to feel numb. This position hurt no worse than the other and she snuggled close. "This is fine, as long as I'm not too heavy for you."

"Do you even weigh one hundred pounds?" Rafael waited for Domingo to rise before he turned toward the trail.

"Yes, and a few pounds more, or at least I did," Alicia revealed sleepily.

"Well, it can't be many more now," Rafael insisted, for she seemed no heavier than a child.

"No, probably not." Alicia yawned widely, then rested her cheek against his shoulder and, secure in his comforting presence, fell sound asleep. She did not wake up until they had reached the horses, and taking one look at her, Alfonso began to shriek in alarm.

"What's the matter?" the disheveled blonde peered over Rafael's shoulder to ask in a dejected moan. "Do I look as awful as that?"

"Oh no, Señora Ramirez, forgive me. It is only that I feared you had been badly injured."

"Señora Ramirez?" Domingo whispered under his breath.

As Rafael bent down to allow Alicia to slip from his back, he sent the young man a glance so threatening he hoped Domingo would make no further remarks about how the elderly man addressed the willowy blonde. He turned then to ease her into a comfortable position to rest. "Is there any reason for you to even attempt to ride?" he inquired thoughtfully.

Alicia feared she had cracked, if not shattered, several ribs when she had careened into the stump, for she was still in considerable pain. Taking a deep breath was agonizing and she knew it would be the height of foolishness to pretend she was well enough to ride when he would soon see she wasn't. "No, but what can we do?" She knew he would never agree to leaving her behind to save himself, so she did not even suggest that frightening alternative.

"I'll simply carry you in my arms. After I mount Nugget, Domingo can help me lift you across the middle. The stallion can easily carry us both." Turning then to Alfonso, he made another suggestion. "Why don't you ride Alicia's mare? Your donkey will follow you of his own accord."

Eager to be gone before the dawn arrived, the old man swiftly agreed. "As you wish, *señor.*" He turned then to study Domingo closely and, finding his dark stare disconcerting, decided against making any effort to get to know El Lobo's son. "I will lead the way again so there is no danger of our becoming lost."

When their guide was out of earshot, Rafael fetched his canteen to give Alicia a drink, then drew Domingo aside. "Alicia is my wife in every way that matters. Do not insult either of us by questioning that fact ever again."

The young man stepped back, but he did not back down. "I am as worried about her as you are," he hissed angrily. "But I am not the one who has insulted her!"

Infuriated by that belligerent response, Rafael cursed the fact he could not spare the time to reply with a well-placed punch. "You'll be quiet about us or I'll rip your tongue right out of your head! I hope you remember I never waste my breath making idle threats

444

either!" He stormed off then to get Nugget, for Alicia was far too precious to him to allow her to suffer a moment longer than necessary while he reminded Domingo of his manners. *"Sangre de Cristo!"* he muttered to himself. It seemed as though he had spent half his life trying to convince Alicia to marry him and he would not allow anyone to mock him just because he had yet to accomplish that goal.

With the distracting blonde cuddled so close, Rafael soon found that his argument with Domingo had slipped from his mind. Her eyes were closed, her pose a relaxed one, and he hoped the fact that she was again sleeping so peacefully meant she would feel better when she awoke. He kissed her fair curls tenderly, his affection plain in his every gesture, but he did not draw a relaxed breath until they had crossed the mountain and had the river in sight. "Is your home near here?" he called to Alfonso.

"Yes, but I will go with you into town," the helpful man replied. "That is where I was bound when we met."

Any sort of dwelling would offer more in the way of comfort than again camping at the river's edge, so Rafael quickly suggested another plan. "I'd like Alicia to rest and have a good meal before we return to Ciudad Altamirano. I would pay you most generously for your hospitality if you'd allow us to spend the night at your home."

Alfonso shrugged his shoulders, stalling for time as he considered the possibility that such an invitation might well cost him and the members of his family their lives if the bandits should give pursuit and track Domingo to his humble farmhouse. He hated to seem ungracious but could not agree to Rafael's request. "I think it would be far better if we continued into town, since my house is so tiny it cannot accommodate us all comfortably."

445

They were still two days' ride from Ciudad Alta-mirano, but readily understanding the elderly gentle-man's reluctance to entertain them, Rafael did not embarrass him any further by pressing the issue. "We'll stop for a brief rest when we reach the river, then go as far as we can before sundown." He turned to relay that message to Domingo, who was at the rear of their column, and began to plan as best he could how they might spend a restful night under the stars. At least there would be three of them to stand guard, but he was far more worried about Alicia's health than any retaliation El Lobo's gang might attempt.

As he had throughout the day, that evening Rafael lavished so much tender attention upon her that Alicia began to feel very guilty for causing him such deep concern. Alfonso and Domingo had caught fish for their supper, and now lulled into warm contentment by a full stomach, she wanted only to bathe and go to sleep. She had tried without success to decline Rafael's offer to help, but he had insisted upon coming down to the river with her. After a full day's rest, she had been able to take a few steps on her own and was certain a little exercise would be beneficial rather than over-tiring.

"What if you faint in the water?" Rafael pointed out logically. "You'd be unable to call for help and I'd never forgive myself for allowing you to drown."

His expression was so charming, more teasing than stricken, that after a moment's consideration Alicia knew he was right. She still felt far from well and it would be foolish to risk drowning when he was so willing to guard her life with his own. She looked down at her dirt-smeared trousers and shuddered in disgust. "I must look a fright."

"I will admit there have been times you've worn more fashionable dress, that is true." Not bothering to muffle a hearty laugh, Rafael scooped her up into his arms before she could offer another protest about his company. "I'll lend you that plaid shirt again to sleep in and I'll wash your clothes while you're in the water."

While she was flattered that he was being so considerate, she did not enjoy the role of an invalid and had to protest. "I can wash my own clothes, Rafael. You needn't do it."

"I want to do it," the determined man explained with a dark glance that let her know instantly he considered the matter closed.

Giving up her argument as futile when he wore such an implacable expression, Alicia allowed herself to be carried to the water's edge, where she was so delighted by the sight of an Ipomoea tree in full bloom she swiftly forgot her objections to his help. The magnificent tree was close to twenty feet in height, adorned with large clusters of white flowers with shockingly bright red throats, and she could not recall ever seeing so splendid a tree. "Oh, please, put me down right here!" She squeezed his shoulders excitedly as she made her request. "Aren't these flowers gorgeous!"

Rafael took great care to put her down upon her feet gently as he agreed. "Yes, they are very pretty. They remind me of you."

Amused, Alicia laughed as she reached out to touch one of the colorful blossoms. "In what way?"

Rafael slid his hands around her waist and pulled her back against his chest where she could rest in his arms. "You're very fair, but you have a spirit of fire, just like these white flowers that seem to have been touched by flames."

Alicia laid her hands over his, too content to move. She was dreadfully tired, still ached all over from more

447

bruises than she could count, and wore filthy clothes that had been designed for a man rather than for the curvaceous figure of a beautiful young woman, and yet her fatigue, injuries, and sorry apparel seemed slight concerns now. She was with the man she loved in a spot of such perfect beauty she longed to remain there forever, where the fragrant tree and sparkling river provided the most sensuous of settings. While she knew that pretty dream was impossible, she wanted very much to be with him always. "Will you marry me, Rafael?" she whispered hesitantly, as though she were truly uncertain of what his answer might be.

"What did you say?" the astonished man asked.

"You heard me," Alicia replied, lifting her chin proudly. "Is it yes or no?"

Rafael turned her around slowly to face him. "I have asked you at least a dozen times," he explained with a rakish grin. "Of course my answer is yes, but did you really think you needed to ask me?"

Alicia raised her arms to encircle his neck as a radiant smile spread over her lovely features. "I have been very rude to you, and as I recall, the last time I mentioned marriage it was to tell you I'd never take you for my husband."

"So now you're taking back that vow?" Rafael inquired with a satisfied chuckle.

"Yes," Alicia whispered softly as she lifted her lips to his. His kiss was very soft and sweet, so gentle and loving she could not bear to remember how often they had quarreled when it now seemed she had always loved him so dearly. She clung to him, her loving mood too enticing for him to resist, and he moaned softly as he deepened his kiss. That wistful sigh tore at her heart, for she could imagine no problems too great for them to overcome together. "I love you," she whispered again and again as she covered his face with tender kisses.

Rafael was tempted to tell her to try to keep that fact in mind for once, but he was enjoying her spontaneity too much to want to give her a lecture on how fickle she had been. He adored her and lowered her carefully to the soft blanket of deep green moss that grew beneath the spectacularly beautiful tree. The sunlight had only just begun to fade, and as he peeled away her soiled clothing he kissed the dark purple bruises that marred the creamy flesh of her side. "I'm so sorry you were hurt. I don't know how I failed to hear you fall."

Alicia licked her lips nervously, and, not wanting him to feel negligent, confessed how they had become separated. "One of the bandits saw you carrying Domingo away, so I remained behind a minute to convince him we were ghosts."

Astounded by her revelation, Rafael sat back on his heels. "You did what?"

Half nude, Alicia thought her pose far too erotic for a serious discussion, so she kept her answer brief. "The plateau was supposed to be haunted. I was certain El Lobo's gang would know that too, so I just enhanced what must have already been in the man's imagination."

Rafael could not believe his ears. "What in God's name did you do?" he asked hoarsely.

"I'll have to show you sometime when I'm not so stiff," Alicia promised with an enticing smile. She reached for the buttons on his shirt, distracting him quite easily from asking any more question.

Once he shed his own clothes and had helped Alicia remove the last of hers, Rafael carried her into the river. Its invigorating chill did little to cool their ardor and they shared a playfully loving bath. The fair beauty's damp curls fell about her shoulders, giving her the enchanting appearance of a mermaid, and when he could control his passion no longer, Rafael carried Alicia back to the inviting bed of moss and made love to her with a tantalizing sweetness. His caress was feather light as it slid slowly over the softness of her curves, his fingertips silently worshiping the smoothness of her flesh as he whispered adoring promises in her ears. The challenge of winning her love was the most exciting of his life and he enjoyed her shudders of pleasure as deeply as his own. The problems that had plagued them seemed insignificant now when their future was so very bright. He cradled her tenderly in his arms as they became one vibrant being so lost in pleasure nothing existed for either of them but the enchantment of loving the other.

Chapter XXIII

After resting all day, Alicia was wide awake as she lay nestled in Rafael's arms. Her fingertips moved in slow circles across his broad chest and down his side. Their adventure was nearing its end. They would soon be returning to California and she tried to imagine how she would introduce the man she adored to her parents. When they arrived in San Francisco, he would probably shave off his beard, dress in well-tailored suits, and again present the image of so proper a gentleman that no one would ever suspect how tempestuous their love affair had been. She would never forget it, however, nor would she ever allow the delicious excitement they had found to disappear from their relationship. Recalling the awkwardness of the first evening they had spent together in her brother's home, she began to giggle, then gasped as her ribs complained with a sharp burst of pain.

Rafael lay on his side with Alicia's head cradled upon his outstretched arm, and fearful he had accidentally caused her pain, he moved over slightly to give her more room. "Are you all right?" he whispered anxiously. He had been so careful as he had made love to her, since he knew her fall had made her delicate beauty all the more fragile.

Once she had caught her breath, Alicia pulled him close. "Yes, I'll just have to remember not to laugh. I was just thinking of the afternoon you arrived at Joaquin's ranch. You were so dashing and—"

"Dashing?" Rafael repeated that word with a sly chuckle, considering that description greatly amusing since he never thought of himself in such theatrical terms. He recalled his thoughts of her on that day with astonishing clarity too. It had been obvious she had been as taken with him as he had been with her, but he put a stop to his memories right there before he began to blame himself for the unfortunate twists their romance had continually taken.

"Yes, very dashing!" Alicia insisted brightly. "Renegade is a magnificent stallion and yet you rode him with such masterful ease. That was very exciting, but that night you walked into the parlor dressed so conservatively, as the successful attorney you are, I suppose. You were so aloof and formal in your manner then. I longed to turn back the clock to the afternoon when your rakish grin and adventuresome glance had been so much more appealing."

Not at all insulted by her candid comments, Rafael leaned down to brush her lips lightly before sampling the delights of her kiss more fully. "I can be many men, my pet. Can't you love them all equally well?"

Alicia pondered that question a long moment before replying with a query of her own. "Which man do you plan to portray when I introduce you to my parents? The teasing rake, or the proper gentleman?"

"Isn't the gentleman the one you'd prefer?" Rafael trailed teasing kisses along her brow, down her temple, and to her ear, where his playful tongue again made her giggle though she took care not to breath too deeply.

"No, I wish there were some way for them to see you

as I first did: mounted on Renegade, all dressed in black. You're so very handsome, they couldn't help but be impressed," Alicia revealed with a satisfied purr.

"That would impress them, all right, but probably not favorably. Domingo thought I was Joaquin's hired gun. Is that what you want your parents to think? That you've married some high-priced killer?" Rafael could not help but be amused by that thought, since it wasn't all that far from the truth. He was a predator, all right, but he preferred to use the law rather than bullets to get the results he was paid so highly to achieve.

"They are bound to be dreadfully shocked no matter how I introduce you," Alicia confessed. "I know they despaired I would never find a husband."

"Oh, now I see your plan," Rafael mused thoughtfully. "You think they'll be so delighted I've taken you off their hands they won't complain no matter how I look, so you want it to be very romantic. Is that it?"

"Well, you are very romantic. You know that, don't you?"

"I think that fact is better left our secret." Rafael's kiss proved the truth of his words as he enfolded her in a gentle embrace. "I don't want any questions about the brevity of our engagement or the haste of our marriage."

Their moods at last in perfect harmony, Alicia raised her fingertips to caress his cheek. "I think our love will be so very plain, no one will have any question as to the reason for our marriage."

Rafael drew back slightly to enjoy the soft glow the moonlight cast upon her lovely smile as he pointed out something she had obviously forgotten. "I already know your parents, *querida*. Your mother knew me as a child and your father and I have been on opposing sides in lawsuits several times. No matter how I choose to look when we arrive at your home, they will know exactly who and what I am, but I want you to believe your own heart no matter what they might have to say about me."

Greatly intrigued, Alicia made no effort to stifle the curiosity he had just aroused. "What is it you think they'll try to tell me? Are you an even bigger rascal than I've found you out to be?"

"Oh, I'm definitely a rascal!" Rafael admitted with a boisterous laugh. "I'm a rascal and then some, but I'll not borrow trouble by outlining your parents' objections to me if they aren't already clear to you. No matter what they say, however, you must promise to let me give you my version of the truth."

While he had not satisfied her curiosity, Alicia saw no reason not to give him the assurance for which he had asked. "I couldn't love a man I didn't trust. You needn't worry I'd believe some fanciful tale about you."

"By the time a man reaches his thirties he's usually made enemies as well as friends, and the tales you hear might not be all that fanciful, Alicia," Rafael warned with a disarming smile.

Alicia didn't care what he said, for surely he had behaved no differently in the time she had known him than he ever had. She knew him to be a man of great courage. He was fiercely loyal to her brother, honest, and so incredibly loving it broke her heart to think how often she had jeopardized their love with her foolishness. "I trust you. I'm only sorry I didn't trust you completely from the very beginning. That would have saved each of us so much pain."

"We've both made mistakes, but there's one thing I certainly wouldn't change."

"And what is that?" Alicia asked in surprise, wondering what he meant.

"This." Rafael's honey-smooth kisses swiftly grew from a loving warmth to a bright heat of passion, enveloping her in a love so lavish she was nearly smothered in affection. He was, as always, more concerned with providing her with pleasure than with taking his own and was the most considerate of lovers. He felt her silken skin warm to his touch as his fingertips moved over her breasts with teasing circles that coaxed the pale pink crests to flushed peaks. He loved the sweetness of her kiss and his lips returned to hers each time they strayed to sample the rich pleasures of her lush curves. The flesh of her smooth, flat stomach was delicious and he tarried there a long while before spreading teasing nibbles up the inside of her slender thighs. Not one to tease when he sensed she wanted far more, his deep kisses soon invaded the last of her wonderfully alluring figure's most fascinating secrets. The caress of his tongue was feather soft as he filled her graceful body with a rapture so intense it swelled his own heart to nearly bursting. With Alicia, he shared a closeness he had never even hoped to find with a woman, and that she would be his wife forever was the most incredible of dreams come true. When she called his name in an enticing whisper, inviting him to now lose himself in the pleasures she was so anxious to bestow, he moved to cradle her in a protective embrace so his weight would not cause her the slightest twinge of pain. He longed to show her how deep his devotion to her truly was, and with both skill and imagination, he turned the night into an endless celebration of their love. While he had not slept a single wink, he took the last turn at watch and greeted the dawn remarkably refreshed.

When the small group reached Cuidad Altamirano late in the afternoon of the following day, Rafael not only tipped Alfonso Lujan generously for his help, but in addition provided the man with a large measure of credit at the dry goods store so he might take home presents for his family. He also bought a new shirt for Domingo and sent him off to the room in the cantina that Tomás and the other men shared to make himself presentable. He then purchased another ruffled blouse and a bright-red tiered skirt trimmed with bands of lace for Alicia. Once the detail of suitable clothing had been taken care of, he carried her up the back stairs of the cantina to the room he considered theirs. Tired from their journey, they bathed each other with a playful rather than erotic tenderness, then dressed in clean clothing and went next door to see how Joaquin and Flame had fared in their absence.

The petite redhead was so relieved to see that Alicia and Rafael had returned safely, she included Domingo in her enthusiastic hugs when he followed the two lovers to her door. "Oh, please come in, all of you. Joaquin is dreadfully tired of my company and so anxious to go home I can hardly keep him in bed." With her usual grace, she swept out of their way so they could greet her husband.

Joaquin was sitting up in bed, propped against three feather pillows so he would be comfortable. "You know I'd never grow bored with Flame's company. It is my own that is driving me to distraction," he explained with a ready grin. "The blasted doctor she found is so conscientious he sewed me up like a damn quilt and forbade me to leave this bed for a week for fear I'd ruin his handiwork!"

While Rafael and Alicia laughed with Joaquin as he recounted his efforts to circumvent the physician's orders, Domingo found it difficult to believe the vital man in the bed was the same one he had thought had expired in his arms. No longer pale, Joaquin's deeply tanned skin was flushed with embarrassment as he continued to describe the enforced confinement he had been made to suffer. He blamed neither the doctor nor Flame for being so cautious, however, but could not forgive himself for having been so stupid as to have been shot in the first place.

As the young man watched the two couples, the happiness that lit their eyes and the tenderness of their gestures as they constantly touched made him feel like a complete outsider in their midst. After having had the opportunity to closely observe Rafael's consideration for Alicia for two days, Domingo no longer had any doubts that the man would not only soon marry the pretty blonde but would make an exceptionally devoted husband as well. He had no quarrel with him when clearly he meant to provide the best of lives for Alicia. He was still horribly embarrassed about the way he had treated Joaquin, since the man had deserved none of the abuse that had rightfully belonged to his true father, Julio Villalobos. It was soon painfully obvious to Domingo that he had no business at all being in that room and he began to back slowly toward the door. He had nowhere to go, but clearly he had no reason to remain where he knew he was neither needed nor wanted.

Joaquin brought his wife's hand to his lips for a kiss, then noticing Domingo edging self-consciously toward the door, he called out to him. "Can't you stay with us a while longer? I promise not to bore you with any more of my troubles."

"I am not bored," Domingo contradicted sharply, then realizing he had been too brusque, he fingered the brim of his hat nervously, uncertain what was expected of him. "I am glad to see you are nearly well."

"I have you to thank for that," Joaquin assured him with a broad smile. "Come over here. I want to talk to you about something."

Domingo feared the subject would be money, and he was undecided how he should respond. He could not deny that he desperately needed funds, since he had none, but surely it would be wrong to accept any when Joaquin had been hurt trying to rescue him. It would appear that he was most ungrateful if he were to take money from him, and that was not the case. "You've already thanked me. You needn't say more," he responded shyly.

"Come here," Joaquin insisted in a more emphatic tone. He waited until Domingo had finally taken a step forward, then motioned for him to take still another before he began. "I have given a great deal of thought to your name."

Puzzled by his totally unexpected remark, Domingo could do no more than gape. "What's the matter with my name?" he asked suspiciously.

Seeing he had unintentionally confused the young man, Joaquin was more careful in his choice of words. "Well, I believe there is some confusion about what it is. Since you've called yourself Villarreal all your life, I'd like you to continue to use my name. Do you have any objection to that?"

Domingo was so startled his hat slipped from his grasp and he had to bend down to pick it up before he replied. While he was absolutely astonished by it, he knew Joaquin's request was an extremely generous one. He glanced over at Flame and saw by her pretty smile that she obviously had no objection to her husband's offer. "You are not afraid that I will disgrace you?"

"Oh, hell," Joaquin denied with a deep chuckle, "I've already done that several times myself. Nothing you can ever do will harm our name and I'd be proud for you to have it."

Domingo looked down as his eyes filled with tears.

He had not given the question of his name a moment's thought, but he knew he did not want to be known as the son of Julio Villalobos, even if that was who he was. Joaquin's offer overwhelmed him though. "No, this is too much. When I saw you were hit, I wanted to help you. I don't need to be paid like this. You would have done the same for me and expected nothing in return."

"Yes, that's true, but since I have something valuable to give, I'd like you to have it." Joaquin then continued in a more thoughtful tone. "Do you think I'm just trying to reward you for saving my life?"

Domingo shuffled his feet nervously, making his discomfort plain. When he looked up, he lifted his chin proudly in an all too familiar gesture of defiance. "I don't need to be paid for helping you after all the grief I've caused you and your family."

"I won't argue that you haven't done that, but it was understandable. You thought I was your father and you had every right to demand I acknowledge that fact. We've solved the puzzle of your parentage and I'm glad we did, but that still doesn't change the fact that I'd like you to be part of our family. Perhaps it is my own vanity, but I simply feel too young to call you my son. I always wanted to have a kid brother though. Would you object to that?"

Domingo searched Joaquin's expression, astonished to find it sincere. "Do you really mean that?"

"Of course. Come home with us. We'll find something you'd like to do, whether it's ranching, or sailing, or perhaps you have some talent for business and would like to learn about my commercial interests. Or maybe you'd like to go to school. We could use a doctor or another good attorney in the family."

When she realized Domingo was nearly in tears, Flame reached out for his hand and gave it a comforting squeeze. "You needn't decide anything today, but I hope you won't keep us waiting too long for your answer."

The warmth of her smile made Domingo's decision easy. He had gone to California to find a father he despised and had found instead a man he could not only admire, but also love as one brother loves another. "Yes," he replied with a lopsided grin. "I'll be your brother, Joaquin, and I swear I'll make you proud of me."

Joaquin shook his head. "You already have, Domingo. You already have." Delighted the young man had been so reasonable, he shook his hand enthusiastically, then moved on to the next subject on his mind. "I know I'd be a fool to try riding back to *La Reina,* but there's got to be someone in town with a boat we can hire to get us back down the river. "Do you think you can handle that?"

"Consider it done," Domingo agreed immediately. "Do you want to leave at dawn?"

"Yes, the sooner we get home the better." Joaquin could not help but laugh as the young man rushed from the room. "I think you'd better pack up what little we have, Flame. If I know Domingo, he will have secured a boat before nightfall."

Alicia leaned down to give her brother's cheek a sweet kiss. "That's the nicest thing I've ever seen anyone do."

"Well, thank you, but I meant it. That lad is so determined, I don't want him working for anyone but himself, or me. Now does anyone else have any good news to share?" he asked with a quizzical glance that swept over Alicia before coming to rest upon Rafael.

Rafael's hand rested upon Alicia's waist and he drew her close as he replied. "As soon as *La Reina* is at sea we'd like you to marry us. Is that the news you wanted to hear?"

"Precisely," Joaquin confessed with a sly grin.

Flame raised her hand to stifle a giggle, then gave up the pretense of being surprised by Rafael's announcement. "You can see we've been very busy while you've been gone. You've already heard our plans for Domingo, but there's something else that concerns the two of you."

"I can just imagine," Rafael replied with a teasing wink. "Well, out with it. What is it?"

Flame laced her fingers in Joaquin's as her expression grew more thoughtful. "I know you prefer to live in San Francisco, and you'll undoubtedly make your home there, but I want you to have the house you and I built together on my father's ranch."

Dumbfounded by her generosity, Rafael began to argue the second he caught his breath. "Oh Flame, no, I couldn't take your house."

"Nonsense!" the feisty redhead exclaimed. "It is my wedding present to you. I want you to have not only the house but all the land I inherited. I know you once had far more, and I've never felt comfortable knowing that land was rightfully yours. Please say you'll accept it. You needn't live there permanently but it would be a wonderful place to bring your children each summer and the four of us could have such fun together."

Rafael now knew exactly how Domingo had felt when confronted with such overwhelming generosity as Joaquin and Flame displayed, and he was nearly moved to tears himself. "I don't know what to say," he finally mumbled hoarsely.

Flame moved to his side to give him a kiss as she took Alicia's hand. "Please just say thank you; that's all that's necessary. Nothing would please me more than to return to you what is rightfully yours. That we were clever enough to build a lovely house for you is all the better."

Her smile was so enchanting, Rafael knew her gift was motivated by love rather than guilt and to refuse it would be impossible. He turned to Alicia then, and when she nodded her encouragement, he grabbed Flame in an enthusiastic hug and nearly tossed her into the air. "Thank you!" he shouted happily. "That is a marvelous wedding present and I'll thank you for it every time I see you."

When he placed her upon her feet, Flame returned to her husband's side. "Your happiness will be all the thanks I'll need. Now let's have a party. Since Joaquin can't leave his bed, will you join us for supper here in our room? Rosales, the innkeeper, has been preparing our meals himself and they really are quite good."

Alicia's mouth began to water at the mere mention of food. "I am so hungry I do not care what he serves; I will eat every last bite."

"Then you'll stay with us?" Flame asked hopefully. "I can't wait to hear all about how you freed Domingo."

"We'll stay," Rafael promptly agreed, "but I think we'd better wait until we've finished supper to tell you how we've spent the last few days."

Joaquin frowned in disgust. "Damn it all. Here I am stuck in this wretched bed while you two were out chasing bandits. I should have been with you."

"We managed quite well on our own, Joaquin," Alicia assured him, determined to make her fall seem quite minor. She could hardly wait to get Rafael alone, for she was very curious about Flame's remark about her house. They had ridden by it several times, and while she had always admired the beautifully decorated Victorian home, she had had no idea Rafael had had anything to do with its construction.

It was quite late when they returned to their own room, but she stretched out across their bed fully clothed and propped her head on her hand. "I want to know all about you and Flame, every last detail. How did you happen to build her house? Are you an architect in addition to being an attorney?"

Rafael sat down to remove his boots, then slowly pulled his belt through his belt loops, stalling for time while he tried frantically to discover a way to describe his relationship with his best friend's wife without sending Alicia into a jealous rage. "It would take hours to relate 'every last detail,' *querida*. It's an old story, really. I met Flame first, but once she had met Joaquin, she forgot I existed. I helped her rebuild her late father's home while he was in Mexico. She was expecting Marissa and needed something to occupy her time." As he looked up, he gave the lovely blonde a smile so dazzling he hoped she would be sufficiently distracted to forget she had ever asked him about Flame.

Alicia, however, was not in the least bit distracted. She sat up slowly, a worried frown creasing her brow. "You were in love with her, weren't you?"

Rafael stood up as he began to unbutton his shirt. There were several possible answers he could give, but suddenly he realized he owed Alicia the truth. "Yes, but she didn't love me. You needn't feel sorry for me, though, as I got over it without suffering too greatly."

Knowing how serious an individual he was, Alicia could not believe he hadn't been heartbroken. "Surely that's not true. If you loved her, it must have hurt terribly to have lost her to Joaquin."

Rejecting her sympathy, Rafael sighed impatiently as he tossed his shirt aside. "It was a long time ago, Alicia. There's no reason for you to dwell on it now."

"It can't have been all that long ago," Alicia insisted softly as she moved off the high bed and went to him. Laying her head upon his bare chest, she wrapped her

463

arms snugly around his waist and gave him a comforting hug. "I love you so much, Rafael. Is it very wicked of me to be glad Flame married Joaquin instead of you?"

With the luscious blonde snuggled so close, Rafael could not imagine her ever being wicked. He had been afraid she would be jealous if he admitted his love for Flame, but instead she had thought only of his feelings and how sad he must have been to have lost the woman he loved to his best friend. "You are an amazing woman, Alicia, truly amazing. Someday I'll tell you all about Flame, but you need know nothing more tonight than the fact I love you ever so much more than I ever loved her."

Alicia looked up at him, the long sweep of her dark lashes lending an enticing air of mystery to her glance. "Really?" she asked with unabashed delight.

"Really," Rafael promised as his mouth covered hers for the first of a long series of deep kisses, which led to another night so filled with pleasure the lithe blonde did not awaken until noon.

Finding herself alone in their bed, she bathed and dressed quickly, then went next door to learn how their plans to leave Ciudad Altamirano were progressing. "I thought we were going to leave this morning," she began in a breathless rush. "I hope I've not kept everyone waiting."

"No, not at all. That's why there was no reason to wake you." Joaquin reached out his arms to draw his pretty sister into a brotherly hug. "Domingo found a boat, but it needed repair. Tomás and the others are handling that task while Rafael and Domingo went on ahead with the horses." While he was still resting in bed, he obviously had the situation well in hand. "If all goes well, we'll be leaving here tomorrow or the next morning at the latest."

"Rafael is gone?" Alicia had heard nothing after Joaquin had said that. She simply could not believe he would leave without telling her good-bye. "Why didn't he wake me before he left?" she asked anxiously.

"He said you needed your rest," Flame replied with an impish smile, but she then reached into the pocket of her skirt and withdrew a folded sheet of paper. "He left this for you."

Alicia grabbed the note and hungrily devoured its brief message before looking up at her brother and sister-in-law. The note was brief, but so filled with love she forgave Rafael instantly for not waking her. "He says he'll miss me and that I'm to be ready for the wedding so I'll not keep him waiting when he reaches *La Reina*."

"I've never had occasion to perform a wedding ceremony, but I'm certainly looking forward to this one," Joaquin remarked with a ready grin. "I hope there will be time for me to practice once or twice."

"You'll do a magnificent job, I'm certain of it," Flame assured her husband with several of the light kisses she was so fond of giving.

As Alicia watched her brother pull his charming wife into his arms, she could not imagine a more perfect couple. Surely Flame's fate was entwined with Joaquin's, just as her destiny was to love Rafael. "Life is amazingly complex, isn't it?" she asked suddenly.

Startled by that question, Flame and Joaquin first looked at each other before turning toward Alicia. "Just exactly what do you mean?" he asked apprehensively.

"I mean everything is working out beautifully. You're getting well so rapidly. Domingo finally has a family. Rafael and I will soon be married. We've even found a boat to take us back down the river." It was not until she had taken two steps toward the door that

465

Alicia remembered Eduardo Lopez. She wheeled around then, her expression frozen into a mask of horror. "Oh, dear God. Rafael's taking the horses back to Eduardo's, isn't he? He'll tell the man exactly what he thinks of him too for allowing one of his hands to warn El Lobo you were coming after him. Does he intend to kill him? Is that what he plans to do?"

Joaquin's gaze grew dark in reaction to his sister's hysterical outburst. "Had Villalobos not been warned, I wouldn't be lying here in this bed and two of my men wouldn't be dead. Think about that for a minute and then tell me if Lopez deserves to die."

Alicia did not bother to reply before she tore out of the room and rushed outside to the stables. The mare she had been riding was gone, along with Nugget and all their other mounts. Rafael's note was still clutched in her hand and in a blind fury she ripped it to shreds and tossed it to the wind. So much for his declarations of love, she thought with bitter disgust. He had shut her out as forcefully as he had when they had first met. Clearly none of the many dangers they had faced and conquered together to rescue Domingo had meant a thing to him. If the adventures they had shared meant so little to him, what possible value could he place on their love? He had clearly thought her presence would be a liability rather than an asset when he confronted Eduardo so he had made it impossible for her to join him. After all they had been through, he had shut her out of the final drama and that was an insult she would never forgive.

Whenever Rafael turned and found Domingo by his side rather than Alicia, he was overwhelmed with a chill wave of disappointment. The earnest young man's manner was now so obliging he was very good company, but he was not, however, the companion Rafael longed to have. He could not in good conscience have subjected the lovely blonde to several days' ride when he knew how swiftly a boat would reach the sea. He knew she would soon be resting comfortably on board *La Reina,* but he had not dreamed how miserable he would be without her. He had not wanted any tearful farewells when the tears had been so likely to be his own, but now he was sorry he had not told Alicia good-bye in person as it would have been another opportunity to tell her how dearly she was loved. He and Domingo had strayed slightly from the path along the riverbank to make better time with the horses so they had not seen the boat when it had gone by. In many ways he considered that a blessing, but as they drew near the Lopez ranch, Rafael focused his thoughts on revenge rather than love.

"I have some unfinished business with Eduardo Lopez. Would you like to be there when I take care of it?" Rafael's expression was too serious to give Domingo the impression he would be making no more than a social call.

"I met Veronica's uncle. I know what happened," the young man responded eagerly. "Lopez is no friend of mine either and I will be happy to tell him so to his face."

"Good, but let's not accuse him of anything at first. We already know he betrayed us, but I want to know why."

"Don't you already know why?" Domingo asked skeptically. "Because of Alicia, that's why. He was jealous of you and made no effort to hide it. He merely wanted to rid himself of any competition for her hand."

Rafael regarded the tall youth with an admiring glance, pleased he had drawn precisely the same conclusion he had. "I think you're right, and while we

467

all suffered because of his betrayal, his fight will be with me, not you. Are you sure you still want to come along?"

"I wouldn't miss it!" Domingo exclaimed enthusiastically. "Just tell me what it is you wish me to do."

Rafael clapped the young man soundly on the back. "Finally. If you've at last learned how to follow my orders on this trip, I will consider it a resounding success."

Domingo blushed deeply as he denied he deserved such teasing. "It is not so surprising I did not trust you in the beginning."

"No, but since you do now, let's make certain we agree on our plan." As they rode the final leg of their journey, Rafael refined his strategy, choosing to portray a disarming innocence rather than confront Eduardo immediately with his treachery. They rode through the gates of his ranch and led their string of borrowed horses around to the front of the barn. When a stable boy came running to greet them, Rafael sent him to alert Eduardo of their arrival, and in a few seconds the man came sprinting from his house.

Eduardo's dark complexion paled to a ghostly pallor as he saw that Rafael and Domingo were alone. "Where is everyone?" he asked in a strangled cry.

Rafael appeared surprised by his question but replied calmly, "Joaquin and his men have gone to his ship. Domingo and I have come to return your horses and pick up the mares Flame wished to buy. If you'll tell her and Alicia we're here, I'm sure they can soon be ready to return to *La Reina* and we'll provide an escort."

Astonished by his request, the silver-haired rancher stared first at Rafael and then at his young companion, but he could read nothing in their expressions that was not in the attorney's words. "I don't understand what's happened, but Alicia and Flame aren't here. When they rode off to follow you, I returned all of your belongings to *La Reina!*"

"What?" Rafael asked with exaggerated dismay. "How could you have allowed such a thing? Two such beautiful young women shouldn't be out wandering the Mexican countryside all alone. Why didn't you go after them and bring them back?"

"Well, I did try to find them, but—" The man cringed visibly as he tried to justify his actions without revealing his own guilt.

"But you did not?" Rafael rested his hands on his hips, clearly incensed by the man's failure to safeguard the women they had left in his care.

"They left in the middle of the night!" Eduardo explained in a rush. "I did send men out after them, but they weren't anywhere to be found."

"You did not think such an important errand worthy of your own attention?" Rafael asked accusingly.

Eduardo straightened his shoulders proudly, attempting to gain control of what was clearly a disastrous situation and swiftly growing worse. "When they were not found within a few hours, I assumed they had joined you."

Rafael's dark eyes narrowed to menacing slits as he regarded the man with a piercing glance that traveled slowly from the part in his neatly trimmed hair to the tips of his highly polished boots. "Isn't it closer to the truth to say you assumed they had fallen into El Lobo's hands? Isn't that what you had hoped had happened to us all?"

Eduardo's throat had grown so dry he could barely pry his tongue loose from the roof of his mouth to speak. "Why should I have thought that?" he asked in a breathless rasp.

Had Rafael had any doubts about the man's

motives, they would have been swiftly resolved as he watched the rancher try to squirm out of taking the blame for the ambush. He had given the man a chance to provide a plausible explanation for his deeds, or simply to fall on his knees and beg for mercy, but Eduardo had not been clever enough to do either. "Let's keep to the truth. You wanted Alicia and thought with me out of the way you'd succeed in making her your wife. Rather than having the courage to challenge me yourself, however, you tried to tip the odds in your favor by giving El Lobo the chance to kill me." He shook his head then. "You're a stupid fool, Lopez. I killed El Lobo and now I've come to settle the score with you."

Knowing that stern tone of voice all too well, Domingo swiftly moved out of Rafael's way. Lopez was unarmed, but he thought Rafael had reason enough to shoot him without pausing to consider so minor a detail. His right hand brushed the handle of his Colt as he wished there were some way for him to join in the fight.

Rafael was not nearly as cold-blooded as Domingo thought, as his next words revealed. "You needn't look so terrified, Lopez. I enjoy a fair fight. I'll even allow you to select the weapons. Which would you prefer? I shoot very well, but I don't mind knives if you prefer to use one," Rafael offered graciously.

Eduardo Lopez had despised Rafael from the moment they had met, and his hatred showed clearly now. The attorney was tall and lean, very quick, and undoubtedly strong, but the rancher had been through more than his share of fights and thought the odds good he could survive another. "I don't need any weapon. I can kill you with my bare hands," he boasted proudly.

Rafael unbuckled his holster and handed it to

Domingo. "I insist you have a second since I have one."
He waited patiently while Eduardo called to the stable
boy to fetch another hand. When that man arrived, he
withdrew his knife and placed it in Domingo's care.
Tossing his hat aside, he favored his opponent with a
wicked grin. "Send the boy now for the mares, so I
won't be kept waiting when I finish with you."

Incensed by that taunt, Eduardo went for Rafael
with a flying lunge the wily man easily avoided. He
stepped aside at the last possible instant, and caught off
balance, the rancher stumbled. Rafael quickly capi-
talized on the man's forward momentum, kicked him
squarely in the seat, and sent him sprawling in the dirt.
"It's no wonder you had to rely on El Lobo to kill me.
You've no skill at all with your fists."

Outraged to have been made to look like a fool,
Eduardo scrambled to his feet and wheeled around to
face Rafael. "And you're a dandy who'll faint at the
sight of his own blood!"

Greatly amused, Rafael laughed out loud at that
insult. "Who knows? I've seldom seen it." Despite the
hilarious tone of his response, he was on his guard, and
when Eduardo made the mistake of straying too close,
he stunned him with a savage right and left combination that found their marks with bone-crushing
intensity.

As might have been expected, a crowd of curious
onlookers swiftly gathered around, and knowing they
were greatly outnumbered, Domingo slowly withdrew
his gun from his holster. They had had little choice
about challenging Lopez on his own ground, but he
wanted to make certain they had no trouble walking
away once the fight was over. He watched Rafael with
growing admiration, for the man had the speed to
avoid the majority of Eduardo's blows while he had no
difficult landing brutal punches of his own. It took the

young man only a short while to realize that Rafael was simply toying with the rancher. With a deadly grace he was giving the man so fierce a beating the contest was pitifully one-sided. None of the ranch hands took a step to interfere, but Domingo kept his finger on his trigger to make certain they maintained their neutral stance.

Eduardo Lopez gasped for breath as he tried to remember what he had done to deserve the shameful punishment he was taking. He could only dimly recall a beautiful woman had been the cause of his pain, but now he could no longer even remember what she looked like. It seemed ridiculous to die for such an elusive beauty, and when on his next futile attempt to land one of his blows he slipped and fell, he remained where he had fallen, too exhausted to rise.

An embarrassed silence filled the air as the ranch hands one by one turned away. They had no idea what had provoked such a spectacle, but clearly their boss had lost the fight and they had no reason to stay. They had all thought their employer had more courage than he had displayed and feared they might lose their jobs for witnessing his shame. The household servants pressed close, then, their curiosity satisfied, they drifted back into the house until finally only Veronica and the two young stable boys remained.

Rafael bent down and grabbed a handful of Eduardo's silver hair to force his befuddled gaze up to his own. "I gave you a fair chance to kill me. That's far more sporting than the underhanded trick you played on us. I ought to put a bullet right through your thick skull, but it would probably miss your brain. Now I'm taking those mares. After what you've done to us, I know you'll be far too embarrassed to ask for payment so I'll consider them a gift." Rising to his feet, he called to the taller of the two stable boys. "Do you remember which mares Señora Villarreal chose?" When the boy

472

nodded nervously, he gave him a sharply worded command. "Well run and get them. I'm in a great hurry to leave." He walked over to the watering trough and washed the blood off his hands, but it was all Eduardo's rather than his own. He replaced his knife in its sheath, then reached for his gun belt. "Well, Lopez, at least we discovered the sight of your blood doesn't make me faint, but we still have no idea of the effect of my own."

Eduardo tried to rise, but the effort was too great for him. He was certain from the intensity of the pain that filled his head that his nose was shattered in at least a thousand pieces, but he considered himself lucky to have suffered no more serious injuries than that. Rafael Ramirez had not only the strength of the devil himself but the speed of lightning, and he wanted only to see him gone.

Veronica's sweat-soaked hands wrinkled the sides of her ruffled skirt as she studied the men. Eduardo Lopez had simply used her, and having lost that gamble, she doubted that the reminder she would constantly present would make her welcome in his home. Seizing an opportunity she knew would never come her way again, she rushed to Domingo's side. "Please take me with you. Your women like me and I would be happy to be their maid."

Domingo turned his back on her. "No thanks. No one needs a servant with the heart of a viper."

"Oh, please take me with you, please!" Veronica begged in a frantic cry.

Domingo replied with a taunting sneer, "Have you forgotten so swiftly that the blood of El Lobo flows in my veins? The last time I was here you would not even give me the courtesy of a smile. Now go away and leave us alone!"

A new surge of energy raced within Eduardo's veins as he watched the scene being played before him. The pretty maid had distracted both men momentarily, and gathering all his strength for a final assault, the rancher leapt to his feet and with a running dive rammed his shoulder into Rafael's stomach with a force that sent him skidding backward into the side of the watering trough. Eduardo then made a grab for the Colt in Rafael's holster while the attorney fought valiantly to shove him aside. Furious at having been caught off guard, Domingo drew his gun, but when he could not get a clear shot at the rancher, he fired into the air, an action that brought absolutely no results.

Seeing her only chance for a future in grave jeopardy, Veronica did not wait for Domingo to take further action but instead leapt upon Eduardo's back. The little spitfire wrapped her arms so tightly around the man's neck he had to struggle for breath, and in an instant Rafael had pulled free of his grasp. Thoroughly disgusted by the man's unsportsmanlike display, Rafael drew his Colt and leveled it at Eduardo's heart.

"You've made a fatal mistake, Lopez. I do not enjoy killing vermin, but I will make an exception in your case. Get out of the way, Veronica."

Seeing the face of his own doom, as the maid released him Eduardo made a grab for her wrist and swung her around in front of him to shield himself. "Go ahead and shoot, but you'll have to kill the little bitch too!" he dared with a hysterical laugh.

Since Rafael had no way to fire without hitting Veronica, Domingo took careful aim. He was at an angle and debated a moment before lowering his sights from the rancher's temple to his left knee. When he fired, Eduardo released Veronica with a terrified shriek as he collapsed in the dirt, blood gushing from his shattered knee.

Rafael stared at the injured man for a long momnet, but the terror that filled Eduardo's eyes sickened him so greatly he returned his Colt to his holster rather than merely execute him. He beckoned to Veronica then. "I'm no more happy to have you with us than Domingo is, but you've earned your passage to California. Now let's go."

His tears flowing into the blood dripping from his broken nose, Eduardo sat screaming for someone to come help him. Ignoring the pathetic man's plight, Rafael mounted Nugget and pulled Veronica up in front of him. When the stable boy returned with the mares, Domingo leapt upon the back of the first, and leading the other two, he followed Rafael back to *La Reina* so proud of the way he had handled himself he could not stop smiling.

Chapter XXIV

When he looked out toward *La Reina* and saw Alicia leaning against the rail, Rafael gave her an enthusiastic wave, but the tall blonde merely turned away with cool disdain and disappeared from sight. Shocked by that unexpected and in his opinion totally undeserved snub, he lowered Veronica to her feet and turned back to make certain Domingo had control of the mares before he swung himself down from the saddle. "It won't be easy getting the horses on board, but I'll wager Joaquin will know how to do it."

Domingo's dark brown eyes glowed with awe as he gazed out at the China clipper that lay at anchor at the mouth of the small natural harbor. He was so eager to begin the return voyage to California he was not in the least bit concerned about how the horses would travel. Then he saw that the long boat swiftly approaching shore carried Arturo Duran in addition to half a dozen men and he feared he would again be made to do the major portion of the work. "Am I to be part of the crew again?" he asked apprehensively.

"You'll have to take that up with Joaquin." Rafael had no idea what his friend had planned for his new brother, but he doubted this voyage would be half so

477

strenuous as his first. "Don't worry about it. I was the one who talked him into letting you work to keep you too busy to cause any mischief on the way down here."

"You did that to me?" the young man inquired with a weary moan. "I should have known."

"You don't know how lucky you were to have been given a choice." Rafael regarded Domingo's woebegone expression with a deep chuckle. "Joaquin would have preferred to confine you in the brig and I think from the taste you got of that punishment you'd be grateful you were allowed to work no matter how demeaning the labor. Your situation will be entirely different now since you're one of the family."

"I certainly hope so," Domingo declared with obvious relief.

Arturo was the first one out of the boat and he greeted Rafael and Domingo with a welcoming shout. "I am glad to see you two looking so fit. Do you feel up to a bit of work?"

"What sort of work?" Rafael asked impatiently, while Domingo did no more than wince. The attorney was anxious to straighten out what he feared was another unfortunate misunderstanding with Alicia, while he knew his young friend was dreading more backbreaking toil.

Arturo planted his feet firmly in the sand and folded his arms across his chest as he explained his problem to his reluctant volunteers. "Horses are not my favorite beasts, but I understand Señora Villarreal expected to take three mares home and I've had stalls built for them. Is that big yellow horse going with us too?"

"Of course!" Rafael replied emphatically. "He's mine and I'll not leave him behind."

Too excited to stand still, Veronica moved in and around the men with tiny, dancing steps. She was so delighted to be making the trip to California she was

478

ready to offer to sleep with the mares should there be no other place for her. "Will you have to build a dock to get them on board?" she asked with impish curiosity.

Arturo scoffed at that suggestion. "There's no time for major construction projects, my girl. The horses will have to swim out to the ship. Then we'll wrap a canvas sling around their bellies and pluck them out of the ocean with the winch."

Thinking that as good a plan as any, Rafael turned around to unsaddle Nugget. The stallion laid his ears flat against his head, apparently having understood Arturo's description of what lay in store and wishing to lodge a strong protest. While he had to laugh at that show of defiance, Rafael wasted little time in soothing the horse's fears. "If we don't hurry, it will be dark and I don't want to spend the night here on the beach like sitting ducks."

"Do you think Lopez will send someone after us?" With an anxious gaze, Veronica scanned the trail leading to the bluff overlooking the beach and was relieved to see it was empty. "You two should have killed him," she insisted with a haughty toss of her dark braids.

Insulted by her remark, Domingo quickly took exception to it. "The bastard wasn't worth killing." At least he had had no heart for such a drastic measure since Rafael had been satisfied to let him off with a beating. "If you are going to criticize everything we do, then you might as well go on back to the ranch," he suggested crossly.

The petite girl's dark eyes widened with fear as she refused to go. "Forgive me. I meant nothing. I'll do whatever you say."

"Just keep still!" Domingo ordered sharply. "Go sit in the boat and stay out of the way."

When the pretty maid did as she was told, Rafael

gave the young man some valuable advice. "Be careful with her. A pretty woman is often more trouble than she is worth."

"You are right about that one, but surely not all pretty women are the same," Domingo argued persuasively. "You would never say such a thing about Alicia."

Rafael glanced over his shoulder at *La Reina,* hoping the enchanting blonde might again be standing at the rail, but there was no sign of her and he cursed under his breath, knowing he was undoubtedly in for another bitter scene when he was in no mood to face it. "Alicia provides a uniquely rewarding type of trouble, that is true, but it's trouble all the same." Reluctant to reveal more about his problems with the volatile beauty, he pulled the heavy saddle off Nugget's back and thrust it into Domingo's hands. "Put that in the boat for me, please." Taking the stallion's reins in a firm grasp, he led him toward the sea. "Are your men ready for us, Arturo?"

"As ready as they'll ever be. We'll practice on the stallion, since he's the least likely to drown."

"That's a comforting thought, but have you no worries about me?" Rafael removed his gun belt, boots, and hat, and gave them to Domingo to place in the boat with his saddle. "I'll see you on board *La Reina.*" He started to go, then turned back with a sudden afterthought. "We'll have to be several miles out at sea before a marriage performed by Joaquin will be legal, but I'd like you to be my best man."

"You really want me?" Domingo asked with a deep blush of pride.

"Yes. I hope after all we've been through I can consider you a close friend, and since Joaquin will be performing the ceremony, he won't feel insulted. Now don't keep us waiting." Rafael had expected the waters

480

of the Pacific to be cold, but he was quite pleasantly surprised by the warmth that enveloped his legs as he entered the waves. "Come on, Nugget, don't let the mares think you a coward or you'll never hear the end of it." He coaxed the golden stallion out into the surf, determined to make him swim, and not knowing the worst still lay ahead, the horse followed his new master after offering no more than one derisive snort of complaint.

While the transfer of horses took place, Alicia sat alone upon her bunk. Her knees were drawn up to her chin and her arms wrapped firmly around them. Her expression was a petulant pout. She had not expected Rafael's sudden appearance to provide such a jolt to her emotions, and she had dashed to her cabin to seek the solitude in which to gather her thoughts. She was still furious with him, but she had missed him so terribly she feared she would not be able to stay angry with him for long enough to tell him what she thought of him for deserting her so casually in Ciudad Altamirano. It had been wrong of him to abandon her, but she could not seem to find the words to express her anguish in terms he would understand. She had rehearsed one speech after another only to find herself either totally incoherent or reduced to tears. What the man had been doing with Veronica she didn't even want to guess, and while more than an hour passed before she heard a knock at her door, she had still not thought of the best way to greet him.

When he heard no reply to his knock, Rafael opened the door slightly and peered inside. Wrapped in a blanket, his thick hair still dripping wet, he flashed his most charming grin as he waited for an invitation to come inside. When Alicia did not even look his way, he entered and closed the door. "I hope you will disregard my appearance. I do plan to change my clothes before our wedding, but for some reason I thought you'd be as anxious to see me as I am to see you. If that's a mistake, then I'll go, since you'll need time to dress too."

The proud aloofness of Alicia's expression did not soften as she replied, "I've no reason to change my clothes."

The pale blue dress she was wearing was attractive, but Rafael thought their marriage deserved one of her finest gowns. He opened his mouth to argue with her, then realized her choice of apparel was not really the issue. "It isn't really clothes you want to discuss is it?"

"It's pointless to discuss anything with you, since you'll tell me one thing and then do quite another behind my back," the distraught blonde responded in an accusing tone.

Disregarding his soggy attire, Rafael crossed the small cabin and sat down by her feet. He tried to keep in mind that while she had all the charms of the most sophisticated woman, Alicia was no more than eighteen and would proably continue to see his actions in an inappropriate light if he did not succeed in regaining her trust. "I've really missed you." He slipped his hand beneath her hem and began to slowly caress her trim ankle with his thumb. "Domingo is a clever boy, but he can neither brighten my days nor enhance my nights as you always do."

Startled by his flattery since it was so unlike him to give it, Alicia finally risked looking at him directly, a decision she instantly regretted, for the sincerity of his expression made her heart lurch painfully. His hair curled down over his forehead in damp waves, making him look all the more boyishly appealing, and she had to dig her nails into her palms to force herself to focus up on the subject at hand. "Do not tease me, Rafael.

Had you spent even one second thinking of the joys of my company, you would never have snuck off in the night without me."

Despite his vow of patience, Rafael could not allow her description of his actions to go unchallenged, since it was far from the truth. "It was long past dawn when I left the inn, *querida,* and that was after we had shared every last minute of the night in a most enjoyable fashion. How can you have forgotten the beauty of those hours so swiftly? I'm positive I never will."

The slow, tantalizing motion of his hand as his fingertips strayed up her calf kindled the flames of desire Alicia recognized as the first sign of her body's impending betrayal. With a hostile shove, she pushed him away and wrapped her skirt more tightly around her legs to prevent a repetition of his sensuous wanderings. "I was wrong when I said you were dashing. What you truly are is reckless! You didn't stop to think of me, of us, of the chance for happiness you might be destroying when you chose to go after Eduardo Lopez alone. Isn't that the truth of the matter? You were far more concerned about punishing him to satisfy your pride than you were about marrying me!"

Even having suffered the sting of her temper on more occasions than he cared to count, Rafael had not expected Alicia's outrage to take so violent a form. He still considered her anger totally unjustified, however. "Do you really think I'm as foolish as that?" he challenged caustically.

"Well, aren't you?" the feisty blonde demanded hotly.

Rafael rose with a surprising display of dignity for a man wrapped in a damp blanket. "You couldn't be more wrong, Alicia. I thought only of you and how difficult the trip on horseback would be for you. I meant to save you pain rather than cause it. I thought my note made it clear that I loved you and looked forward to our marriage with eager anticipation. As for Eduardo Lopez, it was scarcely a matter of pride that motivated me to confront the snake. The jealous fool nearly got us all killed, and I'd not let anyone get away with the treachery he displayed. Think about that aspect of my trip for a moment and you'll see why his ranch was the last place I'd ever take you. Now I plan to go and get dressed. I want you to meet me in Joaquin's cabin in an hour and we can either be married or say good-bye. You must know what I want to do, but I'm a gentleman despite your constant insults and I'll leave that choice entirely up to you."

Alicia's rapidly pounding heart drowned out the sound of her own voice as she called out to him. "Wait! What did you do to Lopez?"

Rafael sighed cynically as he paused to lean against her partially open door. "How you can call me selfish when you care so little about what might have happened to me is truly amazing. If you'd had the slightest regard for my welfare, you would have been in the boat when Arturo and the others came ashore." He slammed the door to emphasize his point, clearly demonstrating the hostility of his mood as he started for his cabin.

Alicia's lower lip trembled as she fought back what threatened to be an endless torrent of tears. Had Rafael's failure to include her in his plans been motivated solely by love? Was he wonderfully considerate and she the selfish one? Since Joaquin was still recovering from his injuries, who else could have dealt with Eduardo? Was that confrontation as he described it—a noble quest rather than a reckless adventure? "Oh, damn him!" she swore in an anguished cry. How could she have forgotten he was so fine an attorney? He

484

could undoubtedly make any tale he told wonderfully convincing. What kind of life would she have with such a man for a husband? Was he merely manipulating her feelings for his own gain or was he truly sincere? Would he be the loving partner with whom she longed to share her life, or a scoundrel she would be a fool to trust another minute? Agonizing questions continued to bombard her brain with splitting waves of pain and she cradled her head in her hands, praying for the answers that simply eluded her. Rafael had given her only an hour to make up her mind, and she hardly dared hope she could think clearly enough to make the right choice.

Excited by the prospect of being Rafael's best man, Domingo rushed to his cabin as soon as he arrived on board *La Reina,* hoping to borrow something suitable to wear. When he found the attorney stretched out on his bunk still in his wet clothes, he wondered if perhaps he had misunderstood him. "I thought I'd need dry clothes or I would not have bothered you. Have you and Alicia changed your plans?"

Rafael wore a savage frown as he glanced over at his young friend. "I haven't changed my plans, but apparently she has changed hers. I told you pretty women cause nothing but trouble, but a true beauty can create mayhem on a grand scale!"

"Then you aren't marrying her?" Domingo asked with a perplexed frown.

"Oh, I will marry her, all right. It may not be tonight, but I will marry her someday."

Domingo looked down at the puddle forming around his bare feet. "I have other clothes. I just thought for your wedding I should wear something special."

Rafael rolled off the bunk, and after quickly sorting through the apparel he had available, he tossed the young man a pair of grey wool pants and a white linen shirt. "I have no extra coat, so that will have to do. As soon as you are dressed, go to Joaquin's cabin. We will at least have supper together, even if there is no wedding."

Too confused to make sense of the attorney's remarks, Domingo thanked him for again sharing his wardrobe and left. When he passed by Alicia's door, he paused, and overhearing the unmistakable sounds of weeping, he did not bother to knock before peeking inside. "What is the matter with you two?" he asked accusingly. "Rafael is furious and you are in tears. I thought you loved each other."

"We do!" Alicia insisted dejectedly. "It's just that . . . oh, I don't even know what's wrong. All I know is that he's the most impossible man who ever lived!"

"I thought I was," Domingo offered with a good-natured grin.

"Oh, you certainly were when you first came to the ranch, but you aren't now. You've changed a great deal, and all for the better in the last few weeks," Alicia complimented him sincerely.

"Well, I'll admit I needed to change, but Rafael surely doesn't," the tall youth declared with obvious admiration for the man.

Alicia sat staring at the young man with a studious frown as she dried her eyes with an embarrassed haste. He was no longer so painfully thin and she was impressed not only by how handsome he had become but also by how intelligent he had proved to be. "It wasn't too long ago that you hated him."

Domingo shook his head sadly. "I was too lost in my own problems to see him for the man he is."

"And just what type of a man is that?" Alicia whispered anxiously.

Noticing he was still dripping water, Domingo turned back toward the door. "I've never met anyone quite like him and Joaquin. They're very strong, but wise enough to have compassion, even with someone really undeserving of it, like me."

He was gone before she could argue that he was a worthwhile person too, but to guard against any further interruptions Alicia slid off her bunk and quickly locked her door. Domingo was obviously in awe of Rafael, so his opinion was scarcely unbiased, but she knew very well what the others thought of him. Joaquin clearly trusted him with his life and treated him as a dearly loved brother rather than merely a valued friend. Flame had frequently voiced her praise for the handsome attorney, so she knew the redhead regarded him very highly too. Everyone she could name seemed to think Rafael the best of men, so why were she and he constantly at each other's throats? She began to pace with a preoccupied step as she probed the secret longings of her own heart, totally unaware that the minutes of her allotted hour were swiftly drawing to a close.

When Rafael reached Joaquin's cabin, he was deeply disappointed to find that Alicia had not arrived before him. The fact she was so reluctant to join them had to mean only one thing. While he tried to hide his despair, he knew he would never fool his two good friends. "I hope you haven't spent too much time rehearsing. I invited Domingo to join us for dinner, but I'm afraid there's not going to be any wedding."

"And why not?" Flame inquired with her usual dramatic flare.

Rafael shrugged. "I'll not offer any excuses, but you

487

can see for yourself that Alicia isn't here."

"Well, then go and get her!" The petite beauty placed her palms upon his chest to give him the encouragement she sensed he needed. "You can hardly expect her to arrive at her own wedding without an escort."

Alicia's cabin was the last place he wanted to go, but as he caught Joaquin's eye, Rafael saw his emphatic stare, and he realized instantly that whether or not she knew it, the pretty blonde truly had no choice about marrying him. Her brother was far too strict a man to send her back to her parents when he knew she was no longer a virgin. The resulting scandal if she were to find herself pregnant was simply too great a disgrace to risk. Since marriage had always been his goal, Rafael knew he had given the highly likely consequence of pregnancy no thought, but now he realized it should have been his foremost concern. Rather than regard their wedding as a joyous occasion, he suddenly felt as though he had stumbled into the hellish jaws of a steel trap. He had discovered Alicia to be a remarkably rebellious young lady, but was she rebelling against his demands or Joaquin's? Did she feel as though she were caught in a trap too? That was a question he had to have answered, and he knew he had not a second to lose. "I'll go and get her right now, Flame. I'm usually not so lacking in manners."

"I will forgive you, since you obviously have so many more appealing thoughts on your mind," the green-eyed beauty responded coquettishly.

Rafael tried to smile at her jest as he left their quarters, but he doubted his forced expression had fooled her. He felt like a complete idiot confronting Alicia, since he already knew what her decision about their marriage must have been, but the reasons behind that decision were too important to ignore. Just as he raised his fist to knock smartly on her door, it swung open and he had to step back so as not to block her way. The graceful blonde's glossy curls were arranged in a flattering crown, while the soft rose of her satin gown was a perfect match for the delicate blush that filled her cheeks. She was so heartbreakingly lovely, the sight of her took his breath away, and for several seconds he could not remember what it was he had wanted to say.

Rafael had shaved off his beard and while she had liked the dark highlight it had given his classic features, she found him equally handsome without it. A deep burgundy waistcoat brightened the somber tones of his well-tailored suit, but his startled glance warned her that something was amiss. "I'm so sorry. Am I very late?" she asked breathlessly.

"Why no, you're not late at all," Rafael lied reassuringly, but as she slipped past him, he reached out to catch her arm. "Wait just a minute. I've never wanted anything so much as I want you to marry me, but if Joaquin is forcing you to become my wife against your will then—"

Shocked by his totally unfounded supposition, Alicia quickly drew him back into her cabin and bolted the door to ensure their privacy. "Joaquin said nothing of the kind to me, and if he threatened you in any way I'll put a stop to it right now!" she vowed hoarsely.

Rafael could not help but laugh at her eagerness to rush to his defense, since he would never allow a woman to fight his battles. He had to struggle to suppress his amusement in order to force into a coherent stream the frantic tangle of thoughts that threatened to overflow his mind. "What I'm trying to say is that I'm sorry I behaved like such an overbearing bully earlier this evening. If you have any doubts at all about marrying me, then we won't go through with it. Or if you think we should marry just to avoid any

489

possible scandal in a few months' time, then I'll marry you tonight and give you a quiet divorce with a generous settlement whether or not we have a child. Your happiness means everything to me. If you don't want to marry me, then we won't be married. It's as simple as that. If that decision outrages Joaquin, then I'm the one who will face the consequences, not you."

Alicia opened and closed her delicate ivory fan as she tried to give voice to what was truly in her heart. Her gestures were like the motions of a graceful dance, however, rather than flirtatious, as she responded, "Do you honestly believe I'd marry you simply because my brother insisted upon it?"

"I know you are extremely independent, but Joaquin can be very persuasive and he has every right to demand that we marry. Your mood was so sullen this afternoon. I thought perhaps you felt cornered, or that you had no choice. The truth is, you do have a choice. I want it to be a lifetime of love with me, but it has to be without the slightest twinge of doubt, for I have none about you."

A slow smile played across Alicia's lips as she confessed the truth. "You've just dissolved whatever lingering doubts I might have had about the wisdom of our marriage. I always want to be as important to you as you are to me. I love you so desperately I can't bear it when you shut me out of your life, but if my happiness truly does mean so much to you, then I think in time you will remember to include me in all you do. I don't expect to always be with you, but I'd at least like to know what you're doing when it's something that affects us both. If only you had told me good-bye in Ciudad Altamirano, I wouldn't have been so angry about your going after Eduardo alone."

Rafael stepped close and slipped his hands around her waist. She was so very slender his fingers met easily. "That's a damn lie and you know it. You would have insisted upon coming with me and you'd have ended up right in the thick of things when we reached his ranch."

Alicia knew better than to deny his accusations when he put it in such colorful terms. "Well, I really should have been there and—"

Rafael leaned down to kiss her then, and his lips were so wonderfully inviting he swiftly stilled all her objections. When he felt her relax in his arms, all resistance melted away by the warmth of his affection, Rafael leaned back for a moment to explain. "When I saw you sleeping so peacefully, your pose as carefree as a child's, I simply couldn't bear to wake you and say good-bye. I don't ever want to have to say those words to you, *querida,* not ever." He again enfolded her in his embrace, the sweetness of his tender kisses convincing her quite easily of the truth of his words. When a furious pounding upon her door suddenly interrupted them, he was as startled as she but moved aside to allow her to open it.

Joaquin glared angrily at the attractive pair of lovers. "I'll not be kept waiting any longer! Alicia is my sister, not my daughter, but by God, even if I've only got one good arm, I'll—"

The lively blonde rose up on tiptoes to interrupt his demanding tirade with a teasing kiss. "You are a marvelous brother, if not a patient one, and I love you dearly, but you needn't threaten Rafael with a beating when he is so eager to become my husband. Now, if everyone is ready, so are we."

Rafael gave his best friend a sly wink as they moved through the door. "I hope you and I have settled our last argument with our fists, Joaquin, and tonight promises far more pleasant things. What could be more romantic than a wedding at sea?"

Alicia turned back to give the man she adored a sparkling smile. "I think you already know the answer to your own question, my love, but if you've forgotten, remind me to show you later."

"Oh, I most certainly will," Rafael promised as he gave her fingers a playful squeeze.

When they reached the captain's cabin, they found Domingo talking with Flame, and she quickly included them all in their conversation. "Domingo had completely forgotten you have two very pretty younger sisters. Don't you think they'll like him?"

"Oh, they most certainly will," Alicia agreed enthusiastically. "You'll be wonderfully popular, Domingo. A handsome bachelor from a fine family is welcome everywhere. Didn't you find that to be true, Rafael?"

"Oh, yes, it is, but I've already warned him to be cautious of pretty women, for the temptations they present are especially dangerous. If your sisters are anything like you, then they'll be no exception."

His admiring glance mirroring the depth of his affection, Domingo laughed with them, knowing Rafael was teasing him as well as Alicia. He remembered the first time he had met his four charming companions. He had regarded them all with bitter contempt, but how mistaken he had been in his opinions! They had become the best friends he had ever had and now had welcomed him warmly into their family even though he would no longer make any claims about being related. He was so happy his heart was nearly bursting with gratitude, and better yet, he considered Flame's comments most intriguing. She had seen the wistful look in his eyes as they had spoken about Alicia and she had teasingly reminded him that the blond beauty had two lovely younger sisters. That delightful prospect was so tantalizing a thought, he hoped the voyage home would be swift.

The playful banter concerning the remarkable popularity of eligible bachelors continued as they began to take their places for the wedding. As Rafael favored his stunning fiancée with an encouraging smile, he was suddenly overwhelmed with curiosity. Knowing there was one more question he simply had to ask, he begged the others to excuse them for a moment and took Alicia's hands in his to draw her aside. "You must tell me the truth. You were on your way here when I went to your cabin. What had you planned to tell me? Was it yes, or good-bye?"

Alicia was amazed to find her answer was still in doubt. "I thought you were the most clever of attorneys. How can you be so blind to the evidence?"

"What evidence?" Rafael asked with a befuddled frown.

"Do you think I'd have gone to the trouble of dressing so attractively if I'd intended to refuse to become your bride? You told me yourself to change my gown, so why should you wonder at the reason why I did?"

Delighted by this news, Rafael threw her a rakish grin. "Then you had already decided to marry me before I spoke to you? You'd come to that decision entirely on your own?"

Alicia tapped her fan impatiently upon his chest. "Must I ask my brother to put a stop to your incessant questions? This is supposed to be a wedding, not a trial!" she insisted with a provocative flutter of her long, upswept lashes.

Rafael raised his hands in a gesture of surrender. "All right, I know enough to quit when I'm ahead. Since you are so anxious to become Señora Ramirez, I will not keep you waiting another minute." Taking her arm to draw her close to his side, he turned back toward Joaquin. "If you're finally ready, Captain, I'd

493

like to make this charming young woman my wife."

"If I'm finally ready!" Joaquin exploded in a hearty burst of laughter, his spirits now as high as Rafael's. "I've waited years for you to take a bride. That she's my darling sister, Alicia, makes this occasion all the more sweet." With a sly wink for his own dear wife, Joaquin gathered everyone close. He opened his small book containing the many ceremonies conducted on board *La Reina* and his voice filled with pride as he began the poetic introduction to the exchange of vows he knew Rafael and Alicia would honor for a lifetime.

Surrounded by love so intense it was nearly tangible, Alicia looked up at Rafael, her bright blue eyes brimming with joy. Someday when they had more time she would explain why she had chosen to marry him. In the hours she had spent alone with her own thoughts, the answer had become crystal clear. She loved him so deeply she was convinced it was their destiny to share their lives as man and wife. She savored that word in her mind. Yes, to love and be loved by Rafael was her destiny, and it was a proud destiny indeed.

THE ECSTASY SERIES
by Janelle Taylor

SAVAGE ECSTASY (Pub. date 8/1/81)   (0824, $3.50)

DEFIANT ECSTASY (Pub. date 2/1/82)   (0931, $3.50)

FORBIDDEN ECSTASY (Pub. date 7/1/82)   (1014, $3.50)

BRAZEN ECSTASY (Pub. date 3/1/83)   (1133, $3.50)

TENDER ECSTASY (Pub. date 6/1/83)   (1212, $3.75)

STOLEN ECSTASY (Pub. date 9/1/85)   (1621, $3.95)

Plus other bestsellers by Janelle:

GOLDEN TORMENT (Pub. date 2/1/84)   (1323, $3.75)

LOVE ME WITH FURY (Pub. date 9/1/83)   (1248, $3.75)

FIRST LOVE, WILD LOVE
Pub. date 10/1/84)   (1431, $3.75)

SAVAGE CONQUEST (Pub. date 2/1/85)   (1533, $3.75)

DESTINY'S TEMPTRESS
Pub. date 2/1/86)   (1761, $3.95)

SWEET SAVAGE HEART
Pub. date 10/1/86)   (1900, $3.95)

Available wherever paperbacks are sold, or order direct from the Publisher. Send cover price plus 50¢ per copy for mailing and handling to Zebra Books, Dept. 2134, 475 Park Avenue South, New York, N.Y. 10016. Residents of New York, New Jersey and Pennsylvania must include sales tax. DO NOT SEND CASH.

SEARING ROMANCE

REBEL PLEASURE (1672, $3.95)
Mary Martin
Union agent Jason Woods knew Christina was a brazen flirt. But his dangerous mission had no room for clinging vixen. Christina knew Jason for a womanizer and a cad, but that didn't stop the burning desire to share her sweet *Rebel Pleasure*.

CAPTIVE BRIDE (1984, $3.95)
by Carol Finch
Feisty Rozalyn DuBois had to pretend affection for roguish Dominic Baudelair; her only wish was to trick him into falling in love and then drop him cold. But Dominic has his own plans: To become the richest trapper in the territory by making Rozalyn his *Captive Bride*.

GOLDEN ECSTASY (1688, $3.95)
Wanda Owen
Andrea was furious when Gil had seen her tumble from her horse. But nothing could match her rage when he thoroughly kissed her full trembling lips, urging her into his arms and filling her with a passion that could be satisfied only one way!

LAWLESS LOVE (1690, $3.95)
F. Rosanne Bittner
Amanda's eyes kept straying to the buckskin-clad stranger opposite her on the train. She vowed that he would be the one to tame her savage desire with his wild *Lawless Love*.

Available wherever paperbacks are sold, or order direct from the Publisher. Send cover price plus 50¢ per copy for mailing and handling to Zebra Books, Dept. 2134, 475 Park Avenue South, New York, N.Y. 10016. Residents of New York, New Jersey and Pennsylvania must include sales tax. DO NOT SEND CASH.